THE START OF SOMETHING WONDERFUL

ESCAPE TO THE LAKES BOOK 1

JESSICA REDLAND

Boldwood

First published in Great Britain in 2023 by Boldwood Books Ltd.

Cover Design by Lizzie Gardiner

Cover Photography: Shutterstock

A CIP catalogue record for this book is available from the British Library.

Paperback ISBN 978-1-80162-475-6

Large Print ISBN 978-1-80162-474-9

Hardback ISBN 978-1-80162-473-2

Ebook ISBN 978-1-80162-476-3

Kindle ISBN 978-1-80162-477-0

Audio CD ISBN 978-1-80162-468-8

MP3 CD ISBN 978-1-80162-469-5

Digital audio download ISBN 978-1-80162-472-5

Boldwood Books Ltd
23 Bowerdean Street
London SW6 3TN
www.boldwoodbooks.com

To my amazing husband, Mark, who held my hand as he calmly guided me down Blencathra when I was afraid of falling and encouraged me to keep going round Derwent Water when my legs didn't want to work anymore. All my love, always and forever xx

The Lake District is our happy place and it's such a privilege to write a series set in this beautiful part of the UK which is loved by so many. I therefore also dedicate the start of the Escape to the Lakes series to those who were born here, live here, work here or who have visited and fallen in love with this wonderful place, just like us xx

AUTHOR'S NOTE

The Willowdale series is set around Derwent Water in the Lake District National Park – an area I know and love from many wonderful holidays since childhood – but I had one burning question. Is it Derwent Water or Derwentwater? As it happens, there's no definitive agreement, with the versions being used interchangeably. I have chosen to consistently use the two-word spelling of Derwent Water because both Ordnance Survey and the National Trust use this. Neither version is incorrect.

There are also variations in spellings of fells and other places (e.g. Cat Bells and Friar's Crag), in which case I have also gone with the Ordnance Survey's spelling.

1

The glass door to my manager Madeline's office was wide open, as always. Her elbows were resting on her desk, with her fingers pressed against her temples, as she stared at something on her computer screen. Whatever she was looking at, it wasn't good, stirring nervous butterflies in my stomach. Could there be restructure news already? We'd been warned there'd be changes in the New Year, but I'd assumed we'd have a couple of weeks to settle back in before any announcements were made. Only one way to find out! I straightened my shoulders, took a calming breath, and knocked on the glass.

Madeline raised her head and her face lit up instantly with a warm smile. 'Autumn! Happy New Year!'

I slipped into the chair on the other side of her desk. 'And to you. Have you had a good break?'

Madeline nearly always had a Christmas dinner disaster story to share, usually featuring either a burnt or raw turkey. This year had seemingly been the worst yet after a misunderstanding between her and her husband meant nobody actually collected the turkey from the butcher.

'The pigs in blankets were coming from the butcher too,' she said, shaking her head. 'On a positive note, the roasties were a triumph, thanks to your grandma's method. Thanks for sharing it.'

I smiled, thinking of Grandma's amazing roast potatoes – light and fluffy on the inside and crunchy on the outside. Cooking had been one of her two greatest passions – the other being painting – and she'd always been happy to share her recipes and tips. I loved the thought of her legacy living on in recipes passed down through other families.

'How was your Christmas?' Madeline tilted her head to one side and looked at me with sad eyes. 'How's your granddad?'

'He's still with us,' I said, my voice catching in my throat as the words *for now* floated round my mind. 'It was good to see Maman and Papa.'

'Have they gone back to Paris now?'

'Yes, they were only here for a week. They always go to the New Year's Eve show and fireworks on the Champs-Elysées and Granddad was adamant they mustn't change their plans to be with him. He said he'd refuse to see them if they stayed any longer, so they left on the 30th.'

I'm half English, half French. My parents – Claudette and Darius – met and fell in love when Papa was undertaking a year out in Paris as part of his French and Politics degree. After graduating, he secured a job in the British Embassy in Paris, where he's worked ever since. Maman's passion is art and she has an amazing job as a senior curator for Le Musée du Louvre.

I was born in France and completed my primary education there, but my parents wanted me to go to senior school in the UK. I therefore spent school terms from the age of eleven living with Papa's parents in Sutton – South London or Surrey depending on who you spoke to – and most of the holidays with my parents. I continued my further and higher education in the UK and the original plan had been to return to Paris after I graduated from university, but Grandma passed away at the start of my penultimate term there. I'd found it hard enough worrying about Granddad facing life without his beloved wife when I was only forty-five miles away from him in Brighton, so there was no way I could consider leaving him to return to France. Settling in the UK also meant there was no danger of seeing the man back in France who'd broken my heart, which was definitely a good thing because, if our paths ever did cross, I doubted I'd have the strength to resist him and would likely end up with my heart broken all over again.

'Paris at New Year must be wonderful,' Madeline said, a dreamy expression in her eyes. 'Back to work, though, and I hate to start the New Year with bad news, but the restructuring plans have been confirmed and it's as we suspected – there will be a headcount reduction.'

My stomach sank. 'By how much?'

'Twenty-five per cent,' she said, with an apologetic shrug. 'Across all levels.'

'So we're both at risk?'

'I'm afraid so.'

I was a junior illustrator for the UK's leading designer and manufacturer of greetings cards, Thoughtful Cards, where my specialism was woodland animals. Madeline had been my mentor when I secured the job ten years ago. She'd been promoted to head of department four years later and I… well, I hadn't changed role in all that time. It wasn't that I didn't want to progress, but the past six years had been tough with Granddad getting sick too. Sometimes there were more important things than climbing the career ladder and I was glad I'd spent as much time with Granddad as I could.

'What happens next?' I asked.

'We're offering voluntary redundancy and early retirement but will have to make compulsory redundancies if there aren't enough takers. Those who want to stay will be interviewed next week with Ross and me and asked to pitch one design for a brand-new range of greetings cards.'

I slumped back in the chair, shaking my head slowly, my stomach in knots. 'A *new* design? I can't. Not with everything... I just can't.'

'Autumn Laine!' she cried, raising her eyebrows at me. 'Don't you *dare* take yourself out of the game like that!'

'But—'

'But nothing! I know the last few years have been tough and I know how hard it is to be creative with cute and cuddly woodland animals when your world is falling apart, but you're still the most talented illustrator I've ever worked with and I know you can pull it out of the bag.'

Madeline was an amazing manager and had been so understanding with me that I'd have loved to reassure her and make her proud, but I couldn't. My mind was blank.

'I'm sorry,' she said, her voice softening. 'It's not the welcome back I wanted to give you.'

I pushed the chair back. 'I guess I'd better get back to the drawing board.' I somehow managed to inject some positivity into my voice, even though I didn't feel it.

'I believe in you. You just need to believe in yourself,' she said, as though reading my mind. 'Dig deep and I know you'll get your mojo back.'

I nodded and left the office. Dig deep? Even if I had a pneumatic drill, I wasn't sure I could dig deep enough to retrieve my lost mojo. I'd been going through the motions over the past year, managing to add to my existing, familiar ranges – the animals I could draw with my eyes closed – but any attempts at creating something new had ended in failure. I had nothing. My creative well was empty. Madeline had gone above and beyond with her patience, but her empathy and belief in me weren't going to count for anything when I stood in front of her and the Creative Director next week with nothing to show except a blank screen. I shuddered at the thought of it. I couldn't do that to her or to me. I'd dig as deep as I possibly could and I'd find something. At least if I didn't retain my job, I'd leave knowing I'd tried.

2

'It's freezing out there,' I said when I arrived at Juniper Gardens after work – the hospice where Granddad had been staying since early November.

'They're predicting snow next week,' the receptionist said, grimacing.

I shuddered at the thought of it and rubbed my cold hands together before picking up the pen and signing the visitors' register.

Granddad's room was on the first floor. I knocked softly but there was no answer, so I gently pushed the door open. A small table lamp cast a warm glow across the bed, catching the steady rise and fall of Granddad's chest as he slept.

The curtains were still open so I slipped my coat off, unwound my scarf, and went over to the window. Granddad liked to watch the birds attracted to various feeders spread around the garden and gaze upon the enormous cherry blossom tree in the middle, but there was nothing to see in the darkness except a few lights in rooms across the quad, so I closed the curtains and settled into the armchair beside his bed.

Granddad's eyes flickered then opened.

'Hi, Granddad,' I said, smiling at him.

He slowly turned his head on the stack of pillows so he could see me.

'Hello.' The word was low, husky and brought on a coughing fit.

I poured a fresh glass of water from the covered jug beside his bed and held it to his cracked lips so he could take a few sips.

'So I've survived the first day back at work,' I said, trying to sound enthusiastic. 'A shock to the system, but lovely to see everyone.'

'Busy day?'

'Always. Madeline's asked me to come up with a design for a new range of cards to pitch to her and Ross Lyndon next week.' My tone and accompanying smile conveyed excitement rather than fear. Granddad didn't need to be burdened with the full picture.

'So proud,' he whispered.

'I know you are, and it means the world to me. Good genes, you see. I've got you and Grandma to thank for that.'

Although neither of them had attempted to make a career from it, my grandparents had both been talented artists but with very different styles. Grandma loved watercolours and had been drawn to nature, spending hours in the garden with an easel or in local parks with her sketchpad. It broke her heart when her hands became so riddled with arthritis that holding a paintbrush was impossible. Granddad favoured pencil or charcoal and was drawn to industrial settings and people in a style reminiscent of the northern artist L. S. Lowry.

I took his hand in mine. It felt cold and the skin was so thin and pale that it was almost translucent.

'Peggy would have loved your drawings,' Granddad said. 'She loved nature.'

'When I'm drawing, I sometimes imagine her peering over my shoulder, giving me advice. She had such a great eye for detail.'

There wasn't a day that went by when I didn't think about Grandma and wish she was still around. At home, she smiled at me from the many framed photos scattered round the rooms, and I was reminded of her talent in the watercolours hanging everywhere. Every time I looked in the mirror, I could see her gazing back at me. Around my birthday each year, she'd find a photo of herself at the same age and we'd joke that we were twins born two generations apart – same dark blonde hair, warm brown almond-shaped eyes, wide smile and square jaw.

Right now, I could really use her advice. I swear I'd learned more from her than any of my art tutors. She'd know how to put the sparkle back into my work, although, if she'd still been around, I wouldn't have lost it.

Feeling the melancholy taking hold, I changed the subject. 'I haven't seen any of the nurses yet. How've you been today?'

'Sleepy.'

His eyes were flickering already and I knew I wouldn't have his attention for much longer.

'I'm not sure what I'm going to make for dinner yet,' I said. 'I stocked the fridge yesterday but I don't feel like cooking. I might pick up a crusty loaf on the way home and just have some soup. What do you think?'

He'd already drifted off. I lowered my head and closed my eyes, my fingers curling more tightly round his. Today had been a bad day and I wanted it to be over, but every moment I still had Granddad was so precious, so there was the contrasting desire to cling on and hope the day would never end.

Half an hour or so passed and the door opened. Adele, one of the senior nurses, smiled at me. 'You were looking for an update?'

I released Granddad's hand and tucked his arm under the covers, nodding my head towards the corridor to speak to her outside.

'I can guess what you're going to ask me,' she said.

'I didn't want to ask over Christmas, but I know it can't be long.'

'He's sleeping most of the time and we're managing the pain. I'd say a couple of weeks at the most, but things can suddenly change. It's impossible to say for definite. I'm sorry.'

'Do my parents know?'

'Yes.'

I thanked Adele and returned to Granddad's bedside. Maman and Papa had stayed with me over Christmas, although we'd spent more time here than we had at home. Papa had told me he didn't want to have the *how long* conversation but he was a planner and a pragmatist so there was no way he hadn't asked the question. When the cancer in Granddad's throat returned for a third time along with the diagnosis that it was now stage four, having spread to his lungs, he'd refused further treatment. At that point, I knew we were travelling the end-of-life road. I'd wanted to beg Granddad to reconsider but it was obvious he was too weak for another round of treatment. I had to prepare to let go and count my blessings that I'd had him in my life for so long. Ninety-five was a grand age.

I removed my iPad from my bag and started drawing, but my eyes were soon burning from fatigue and I had to accept defeat. I studied what I'd drawn and tutted. The woodland animals were carbon copies of everything else I'd created. Why was I finding it so hard to think differently?

'Why the frown?'

I hadn't noticed Granddad opening his eyes, so his voice startled me.

'I'm not happy with my drawings.'

'Show me.'

I put his glasses on for him and held up the iPad so he could see.

'They're good.'

'Thank you, but I need to create something different, and this isn't it.' Realising I was in danger of unburdening, I flicked the cover over the iPad and placed it down on the bed with a smile. 'Fresh start tomorrow, I think.'

Granddad opened his mouth to speak, but coughed instead, so I helped him with his water once more.

'That thing,' Granddad said, pointing a gnarly finger towards my iPad as he settled back onto his pillows.

'I know you hate it, but the app I use is amazing and it's not like I have much choice. Everyone at work uses it.'

Granddad had engaged me in several discussions over the years about whether drawing on an app really was drawing. He was immensely supportive of my work and full of praise every time I showed him one of my designs in its final form as a greetings card, but I was never going to convince him that anything other than a drawing on a piece of paper or a canvas was 'real'.

'Watercolours,' he whispered, his eyelids heavy.

'I can create watercolours on the app.' Not that I used the watercolour tools because my remit at Thoughtful Cards was to use 'bright colours that pop'.

'Real ones.' He'd closed his eyes and I could only just make out those two words.

It was my cue to leave. 'You sleep well, Granddad,' I said, slipping my iPad back into my bag. 'I'll see you after work tomorrow.'

'Like Peggy's,' he whispered.

* * *

At home a little later, with my hands wrapped round a mug of tea, I stood in the lounge studying the large watercolour canvas above the fireplace. Grandma had painted it of me, aged six, on the long-gone wooden swing in the back garden when we'd visited during the summer holidays. She'd added glitter to the paints and thickened some to give more texture. The colours danced in a painting full of movement which instantly transported me back to childhood.

I thought about what Granddad had said. What if the design for my pitch used watercolours? That didn't have to mean pastels. Watercolours could also be vibrant as one of my heroines, Beatrix Potter, had proved long ago with the bright blue of Peter Rabbit's jacket.

I placed my mug on the mantelpiece and was about to go into the dining room to dig out my Beatrix Potter collection and anything else that might inspire me when the doorbell rang. It was nearly 9 p.m. so it was late for someone to be calling.

I approached the front door tentatively, then relaxed at the familiar sight of our next-door neighbour, Mrs Slade, peeking through the glass side panel.

'I'm sorry to call round so late, dear,' she said when I opened the door. 'The postman delivered this letter to me by mistake.'

She handed me a small cream envelope and I smiled as I recognised the handwriting.

'Is it from Rosie?' she asked.

'Yes. Thanks for dropping it round.'

'I know I could have pushed it through your letterbox, but I wanted to ask if there's any news about your granddad.'

'He's as well as can be. When I see him tomorrow, I'll tell him you were asking after him.' I waved the letter at her. 'Thanks for dropping this round. I'd invite you in, but I'm on a deadline and I need to work.'

'I understand. I need to get back to my programmes anyway. Give Arthur my love.'

'I will.'

I adored Mrs Slade but I'd learned long ago that inviting her inside wasn't a good idea unless I had several hours to spare to listen to the latest scandal about a bunch of people I didn't know. It was best to visit her instead so I could catch up on how she was but leave when she started discussing the neighbours.

After deadlocking the door and pulling the chain across, I took the letter into the lounge, retrieved my part-drunk tea, and curled up on the sofa to read Rosie's news. Rosie Jacobs and I had been penpals since my first year at senior school in the UK, aged eleven. My English teacher, Mrs Traske, had invited our class to participate in a penpal exchange with a class in Cumbria which her sister taught. Within a month, we'd sent initial letters and the first batch of replies had arrived.

As soon as I read Rosie's first letter, I felt like I'd found a special friend. She was an only child like me, liked or hated most of the same subjects at school, and was into the same music and TV programmes, so we had plenty of common ground to write about. There were differences too. Rosie was heavily into horse riding and helped out at the riding stables her mother – who she called 'Mam' – managed, whereas horses scared me. I loved art and, by her own admission, Rosie couldn't even draw a stickperson, but those differences made the letters even more interesting as we learned more about each other's passions.

By the end of that school year, all the penpal relationships had fizzled out except ours. Our friendship grew and Rosie had remained my one consistent friend throughout senior school. Unlike my classmates, with whom I struggled to maintain friendships because I was never around to socialise during the holidays, it made no difference to her that I disappeared to Paris at the end of each term. It was simply a different address on the envelope.

Even when we both had email addresses and mobile phones and could have moved our contact onto tech, we agreed that there was something special about writing and receiving physical letters. Rosie and I had spoken on the phone when we'd really needed a friend, but most of our contact had remained via the post.

I slit open Rosie's latest letter and began reading.

Dear Autumn

I'd normally have started this letter saying I hope you had a great Christmas and New Year but I know it'll have been a tough one for you. I was thinking of you and I hope having your parents over brought some comfort at a difficult time.

It was just Mam and me for Christmas dinner – just as we like it. Mam felt she should ask his Lordship if he wanted to join us – just a courtesy thing, mind. He only went and said yes! Thankfully he dipped out at the last minute in favour of a liquid lunch. Big relief all round although I wish he'd got his act together sooner so we could have had a roast chicken instead of getting in a turkey – so much nicer in my opinion!

Anyway, thank you for the gorgeous Christmas gift, especially when gift shopping must have been the last thing on your mind.

Fun fact for the start of the New Year: the last letter you sent me was your 400th. How amazing is that? 24 years of friendship and 400 letters. Not bad for two people who've never met!

Apologies this is such a short one but I just wanted to let you know you're in my thoughts and I don't expect you to rush to write back to me as I know you have more than enough on your plate right now. I'll write again in a week or so. If the worst has already happened or it happens soon and you feel you need to get away, you'll always be welcome here. The horses won't bite, although I can't make the same promise for his Lordship.

In the meantime, if you want to talk about it, you've got my number. Call me any time.

Hugs

Rosie xx

It might be short but a letter of any length from Rosie never failed to lift my spirits. The man who she referred to as 'his Lordship' was the owner of the riding stables where Rosie and her mam both worked, and where Rosie had taken over as manager several years back. The stables and Horseshoe Cottage where Rosie and her mam lived were in the grounds of an old manor house called Willowdale Hall on the shores of Derwent Water. I'd never been to the Lake District but Rosie sometimes sent me photographs and it looked beautiful.

During my university years, we'd discussed me visiting after I graduated but with Grandma dying and me wanting to be there for Granddad, it never happened. When the subject was raised again, Granddad had received his first cancer diagnosis and there'd never been a right time since.

I re-read the letter and glanced at my watch. Was it too late to FaceTime her? I really wanted to talk to someone about today's news, but Maman and Papa already had enough on their plates worrying about Granddad while living in another country.

'Hi, Autumn,' Rosie said, answering within three rings and smiling brightly.

'Hi. I've just been reading your letter and I know it's getting late, but you said to call you any time.'

'And I meant it,' she said softly. 'How's your granddad?'

'Not so good. They reckon he only has a couple of weeks left and, on top of that, I've just found out that I'm probably going to lose my job...'

As I knew she would, Rosie listened as I spilled it all out.

'I'm wondering if I should just tell Madeline to put me down for voluntary redundancy,' I said.

Rosie raised her eyebrows at me. 'Is that what you *really* want?'

'I don't know. It would be easier.'

'Probably, but that doesn't make it the best option. Have you got any ideas, even just a flicker of something?'

I shook my head. 'Complete blank.'

'You might feel differently after you've slept on it. Bear in mind, today was your first day back after a fortnight off. It might take a few days to get back into the swing of things.'

'True, but time's not on my side. The pitch is a week today and I don't know if it's worth the stress.'

'You've always said in your letters that you love your job,' Rosie said. 'Is that still true?'

'Yes.'

'Then it's worth fighting for.'

'But what if nothing comes? Or what if I present something and it's dire?'

'At least you'll have tried,' she said gently. 'Remember when we were sixteen and we were obsessed with *A Cinderella Story*?'

I nodded, wondering where this was heading. We'd both watched the film repeatedly – a modern-day take on the Cinderella fairy tale – relating strongly to the Hilary Duff character being the outsider at school and wondering whether we'd ever meet our prince.

'What's that Babe Ruth baseball quote on the diner wall?'

I smiled at her. She knew exactly what the quote was, but it would have more impact if I was the one who said the words.

'"Never let the fear of striking out keep you from playing the game",' I said, picturing the scene in the film. The words had been covered up by the main character's 'wicked stepmother' but were revealed at a key climax moment, giving her the strength to face a future on her own without her stepmother's financial support.

'So are you going to play the game?' Rosie asked.

'Okay. You've convinced me. I'll give it my best shot. I'll probably regret it if I didn't try.'

'There's no *probably* about it! You'd *definitely* regret it. And even though I can't draw, I'm here for you if you want to toss some ideas around.'

'Thank you. I'm so glad I called you.'

'I'm glad you did too. You've got this, Autumn. And if the outcome isn't positive, then that's because there's something different waiting round the corner for you.'

We chatted for a little longer before saying our goodbyes. I felt so much lighter and more positive for talking to Rosie, especially that point she'd made about something different waiting round the corner for me if it was the end of the line at Thoughtful Cards. I had no idea what that could be, but the thought of it made 'striking out' seem a little less scary.

3

A week later, judgement day arrived. I was 'playing the game' but I would definitely be 'striking out'.

I'd been through all my old designs – including those which hadn't progressed to cards – hoping to find inspiration, but none came. I'd even gone back to my university portfolio and a box of flipbooks I'd made which I found at the back of my wardrobe – a short book with an illustration at the bottom right corner of each page which changed as the user flicked through the book, giving the appearance of animation – but nothing popped.

Desperate not to let Madeline or myself down, I'd finally cobbled something together using vibrant watercolours. It was good, but it wasn't my best work. The only way to redeem it was to present the hell out of it, even though I knew impressive words and enthusiasm were not going to compensate for good rather than outstanding.

I ditched my usual work 'uniform' of jeans and a shirt in favour of a smart charcoal-grey shift dress, matching jacket and a pair of colourful Parisian designer stilettos – a gift from Maman which I never thought I'd find the occasion to wear. She swore the right clothes and a pair of good heels could give a woman inner strength and I was starting to believe her, although I'd had to parade round the house in them each evening, practising my presentation while trying to find my balance.

If they were handing out jobs on the basis of confidence and strength of pitch, I'd be safe. I almost believed what I was selling. But the reality was that they were looking for talent and innovation and I hadn't delivered.

Presentation complete, Madeline gave me an encouraging smile and they both thanked me, but I already knew it was over and it didn't matter what I said in the interview because my work had done the talking.

* * *

'Dare I ask?' my colleague Tim said, grimacing at my downcast expression as I returned to our office.

'The pitch went brilliantly, but my design was rubbish.'

'I don't believe that for one minute.'

'That's sweet of you, Tim, but I've lost my spark since Granddad's diagnosis. So maybe it wasn't rubbish, but it wasn't good enough. How did yours go?'

'Okay, I think. I hope.'

I gave him an encouraging smile and was about to return to my desk when my attention was drawn to something moving outside the window.

'It's snowing!' I exclaimed.

Tim and I watched the snowflakes and I could have stayed there for ages, but I needed to check my phone in case there was news from Juniper Gardens. I removed it from my handbag and my heart leapt into my mouth. Four missed called from the hospice, one from Maman and one from Papa. *Please don't say I'm too late.*

There were two voicemails, the first being from Juniper Gardens. 'Hi, Autumn, it's Adele. It's nearly time. If you can, you might want to make your way to the hospice.'

The second message was from Papa. 'We've just heard from the hospice. Maman and I are on our way to the airport. We'll catch the first flight out. I'll send you the details when I know them.'

'I've got to get to the hospice,' I said to Tim, grabbing my coat and bag and dashing for the door. 'Can you tell Madeline where I am?'

As I did my best to hurry to the station, skidding in the snow but miraculously managing to stay upright, I rang the hospice to make sure I wasn't too late. *Still with us. Hurry.*

I arranged for an Uber to collect me from Sutton train station then spent the rest of the train journey staring at my screen, challenging my phone not to ring with the news that Granddad had gone. Every minute ticked by agonisingly slowly.

In the Uber, I stared out of the side window, focusing on the large tumbling flakes. Granddad loved the snow. Even if we only had a sprinkling, he would drag me out into the garden to make a snowman. Across the weekend, he'd insisted on keeping his curtains open so he could watch it if it came, but the forecast kept shifting. *Snow expected tomorrow... the day after... the day after that.*

At Juniper Gardens, the receptionist waved me past, calling, 'I'll sign you in,' as I power walked down the corridor and ran up the stairs to Granddad's room, the lump in my throat restricting my breathing.

Adele must have been alerted to my arrival as the door opened.

'Do you want me to stay?' she asked.

'Is there anything you need to do?'

'No.'

'Then thanks, but no.'

'You know where I am if you need me.' She closed the door softly behind her.

The bedside lamp was on and the curtains were closed. I shrugged off my coat and strode to the window, pulling the curtains back.

'Hi, Granddad, it's me. That snow you wanted has finally appeared and it's so beautiful outside. Look!'

I gazed down at him, hope in my heart, even though I knew he wasn't about to open his eyes.

Moving round to the armchair, I sat down and took his hand in mine. It was cold and his fingers didn't wrap round mine like they usually did. I took a deep shaky breath and swallowed down the painful lump. I didn't want to spend our final moments together sobbing. I needed to talk to him.

'Remember that time when the snow was so heavy that we built an entire snow family? Maman, Papa, Grandma, you and me, and we even made a snow dog and cat because I'd always wanted pets. You joked I could keep them in the freezer.'

For the next hour or so, as the snow tumbled down, I talked non-stop. I started with wintery memories and moved on to anything that came to mind. Granddad's breathing became slower, shallower and every so often I held my breath when I thought he'd drawn his last, but there'd be a rattle on his chest and he'd breathe once more.

'I wish this wasn't goodbye,' I said, stroking his hand. 'I wish I could keep you forever but Grandma needs you now, doesn't she? She's been waiting for you so patiently, and it's time I let go so you can be together again.'

I drew his hand to my lips and gently kissed it. 'I've said it before and you've brushed it off, so I'm going to say it again. Thank you for everything you've done for me. I've learned so much from you and Grandma and I'm so grateful.'

I bit my lip, my stomach churning. I needed to say it while I still had the chance. 'And thank you for keeping my secret. You promised you would and you kept that promise and I'm so grateful. So I'm going to make a promise to you. Even though I'm going to miss you every second of every day, I *will* be fine. You don't need to worry about me anymore. There's some stuff going on at work and things are going to change, but change can be a good thing, right? So you can let go and go to Grandma knowing that your work here is done.'

The tears spilled down my cheeks and onto my hand clasped round Granddad's, my heart breaking as he took his final few slow breaths.

When I was certain he'd gone, I brushed his wispy white hair back and kissed his forehead. 'Goodnight, Granddad,' I whispered. 'I love you.'

I looked towards the window and imagined his soul floating among the delicate flakes, soaring ever higher. I pictured him and Grandma together, holding hands as they walked through the park, laughing as she held out a spoon for him to taste her pasta sauce but dabbing him on the nose with it before he could, gazing at each other lovingly as they waltzed round the lounge.

'Take care of him, Grandma,' I whispered. 'Thank you for letting me keep him for so long.'

I sat there for maybe twenty minutes or so, holding Granddad's hand but looking past him at the falling snow. I should probably let Adele know that he'd gone, but I didn't want to leave him alone. I picked up my phone to call reception, but it pinged with a text message.

FROM PAPA

We've landed at Gatwick. Waiting to get off plane. Be with you as soon as we can. Any news? x

It wasn't the sort of news I wanted to give over a text, but he'd want to hear it straight.

TO PAPA

I'm so sorry. He went peacefully about 20 mins ago xx

FROM PAPA

Had a horrible feeling we wouldn't make it in time. Are you OK? x

TO PAPA

Very sad but holding up. Be careful in that snow and see you soon xx

Papa must have told Maman as a text pinged through from her.

FROM MAMAN

Je suis tellement désolé, ma chérie. Envoyer des câlins xx

The virtual hugs were gratefully received and I looked forward to receiving one in person from each of them.

* * *

Despite the airport being a little over half an hour away, the snow had caused chaos on the roads and it took my parents over two hours to get to Juniper Gardens. We hugged and cried, and I told them about Granddad's final moments, then I left them to have some alone time with him while I went in search of a comforting hot chocolate.

The residents' lounge was deserted so I took my drink over to the floor-to-ceiling windows, looking out over the garden. Roughly three inches had fallen already and it was still tumbling down. Granddad would have loved building a snowman in it.

I felt so weary that I could have easily closed my eyes and drifted off, so I picked up my phone to keep myself occupied. There was a text from Madeline.

FROM MADELINE

Tim said you'd had to leave for the hospice. My thoughts are with you and your family

I didn't want to go into work tomorrow so I might as well check now that she was okay with that.

TO MADELINE

Thank you. Granddad passed away this afternoon. I made it in time so he wasn't alone, but my parents were still travelling. Am I okay to take tomorrow off?

FROM MADELINE

I'm so sorry. Yes, definitely take tomorrow off and let me know if you need longer

Clicking into my emails next, my heart sank as I spotted the subject line of one of the messages in my inbox. I knew what it was going to say and, even though I didn't want any more bad news today, I might as well get it over with. I couldn't feel worse than I already did.

To: Autumn Laine, Illustrator
From: Ross Lyndon, Creative Director
Subject: Outcome of interview
Thank you for attending the interview this morning and for presenting your new design.
It has been a difficult decision but we regret we are unable to offer you one of the positions. As you are aware, a company-wide restructure means your role is now redundant and you are therefore asked to attend a meeting with Madeline Hill at 9.30 a.m. tomorrow morning – Thursday 11 January – to discuss the next steps.

I looked at the time on the email – sent at 4.17 p.m. – and sighed. The last interview of the day had been scheduled to end at four, so they certainly hadn't wasted time making up their minds and delivering the news. It was strange that Madeline hadn't told me to ignore the meeting request in our text exchange. Unless she'd requested the email be put on hold and it had slipped through the net. I texted her again.

TO MADELINE

I've just seen the email about the interview outcome. Can I come in for the meeting and have the rest of the day off?

FROM MADELINE

You got the email? I'm so sorry. That's awful timing. Your email was meant to be on hold until we knew what had happened with your granddad. Yes, that's fine but we can postpone the meeting if you prefer

TO MADELINE

I appreciate you trying to put the news on hold. I'd rather start the ball rolling so see you at 9.30 tomorrow

Sighing, I switched my phone to silent and put it away in my bag. I'd lost my granddad today and now I'd lost my job. I just hoped that saying about things coming in threes wasn't about to come true.

4

I lay under the duvet in my bedroom at the back of my grandparents' 1930s-built semi, curtains open, staring into the darkness. It was 3 a.m. on Thursday morning and the snow had stopped falling steadily about an hour ago but, every so often, there was a little flurry as though it didn't want to say goodbye completely. Like me with Granddad.

I wondered if Maman and Papa, staying in the guest bedroom, had been able to sleep at all. It had been after 10 p.m. when we left Juniper Gardens. The funeral director had collected Granddad and we'd cleared his room of his few clothes and belongings. When we got home, I told them about the work situation.

'What a horrible way to start the New Year,' Maman said, giving me another hug. 'I'm so sorry.'

'Me too,' Papa said, shaking his head. 'Any thoughts on what you'll do next?'

'I'm not sure. If I wanted a job with one of our competitors, I'd have to pitch a design which will be tricky when the creative well's dry.'

They both looked at me sympathetically.

'No rush to make a decision,' Maman said. 'Take some time out. Stay in Paris for a while. Stay forever!'

I smiled at her gratefully. 'I appreciate the offer and I promise to think about it.'

And that was what was keeping me awake right now. I loved spending time with my parents, but had always felt more at home living here than in Paris. Would I still feel that way now that Granddad was gone? With no relatives, no close friends in the area, and no job, what was there to keep me here? Could I return to Paris with my parents and start over there?

So many potentially life-changing decisions lay ahead of me, but there was only one decision I needed to make for now and I'd already made it. I didn't want to work my notice. Hopefully they'd take my bereavement into consideration and I could clear my desk tomorrow and start gardening leave.

* * *

'I'm so sorry about your granddad and about the email arriving and…' Madeline shook her head, her expression sorrowful. 'I'm sorry about everything. Your design was good, Autumn. I loved the watercolours and so did Ross.'

'Thank you, but we both know it needed to be exceptional and it wasn't. I'm sorry I let you down.'

'You didn't. I've always been immensely proud of you, and you did well in difficult circumstances. I'm gutted I'm losing you from the team. Our loss will be a massive gain for someone else. You'll have a glowing reference from me.'

'I need my mojo to come back before I can think about applying anywhere else.'

'It will. I'm sure of it.' She gave me an encouraging smile.

'I have a favour to ask. I'm going to need some time off and, under the circumstances, any work I do isn't going to be value-adding, so is there any chance I can clear my desk and slip away quietly so I can spend some time with my parents?'

'They're staying for a while?'

I nodded. 'Until after the funeral.'

'I'm glad you've got some support. As for taking gardening leave, I figured you'd want that so I've already got Ross's approval. If you're sure about that, I can go to HR and get some paperwork together. I shouldn't be more than half an hour if you want to clear your desk and get yourself sorted.'

'I'm sure about it. Thanks for everything.'

* * *

An hour later, I took the lift down to the lobby with my personal possessions in a couple of tote bags. I handed in my security pass and looked round me for one last time. Over a decade working for the same company and now it was over.

I'd miss Madeline, Tim, and the rest of my colleagues, and I'd miss the job, but it might be for the best. I'd become too comfortable in the same job for ten years and it was time for a new challenge. Maybe.

With my phone playing a relaxing playlist through my EarPods, I caught the train back to Sutton, feeling surprisingly calm about leaving Thoughtful Cards without another job to walk into. It helped that money wasn't a worry. Granddad had signed the house over to me when I turned eighteen so that I'd always have a home in England, whatever happened to them. My redundancy pay would cover the bills for several months and, after that, there was always the option of selling up and downsizing to release some funds. But where would I set up my new life?

As the train drew closer to Sutton, my stomach tightened. Once I got back home and told Maman and Papa that I'd left Thoughtful Cards, Paris would be mentioned again. It was ridiculous for me to feel so anxious when Étienne wasn't even living there anymore. Or at least I assumed he wasn't. What if he'd moved back? What if I bumped into him? Fourteen years should have been more than enough time to get over Étienne Toussaint. But it wasn't. And how could I even begin to explain that anxiety to my parents who had no idea there'd been anything more than friendship between us?

5

TWO MONTHS LATER

I tutted at the mess of pencil lines on my sketchpad and placed it down beside me on the steps of the Sacré-Coeur basilica, shaking my head. This was the fifth location I'd visited already this morning and if I couldn't find any inspiration in Montmartre – *the* district in Paris for artists – there wasn't much hope for me.

The views across my birthplace were spectacular but something just didn't sit right with me here. Funnily enough, I felt the same in central London. I'd been on the London Eye and visited Parliament Hill and Greenwich Park, all of which afforded visitors magnificent views across the UK's capital, but none of those views made my heart sing. I could appreciate a cityscape and feel impressed by the architecture and detail, but it didn't inspire me as an artist. My fingers didn't twitch to pick up my pencil like Granddad's would have done.

I hadn't drawn a single animal since leaving Thoughtful Cards. I'd thought about it, but every time I picked up my pencil and started drawing, the face I created was angry instead of adorable, which was why I'd been trying to find fresh inspiration.

After Granddad's funeral, I'd finally accepted my parents'

invitation to join them in Paris for a while. Some subtle questioning had confirmed that Étienne's parents were still living in Bordeaux and renting out their apartment on the floor above my parents' place so there was no danger of bumping into them. Or him. I'd thought I'd be able to relax in that knowledge, but I'd felt on edge the whole time I'd been here, which wasn't helping me with my mission to find my missing mojo.

Missing Granddad wasn't helping either. I frequently found myself staring into space, lost in my memories of him and Grandma. Maman, Papa and I talked about him a lot. Papa felt guilty that he hadn't spent more time in Sutton, particularly after Grandma died, but I was able to reassure him that Granddad was immensely proud of him for the career and life he'd created in Paris. He strongly believed that children should find their own way in life and never feel tied to the same location as their parents – something Maman and Papa had also embraced through my UK education and never pressurising me to be with them in Paris.

Today, I felt particularly sad thinking about Granddad and could feel tears burning in my eyes. I didn't want to cry, especially not in public, so I hugged my knees to my chest and focused on the hubbub of activity around me. It was a Tuesday in mid-March but that didn't stop it being busy. Although the first day of spring hadn't officially arrived, the blue sky, warm sun and bursts of colour everywhere had firmly shoved winter aside. Couples, friends and families jostled for prime positions to take photos, selfies and videos. An excitable squeal drew my eyes to the left where presumably the man on bended knee had just proposed to his girlfriend. Suddenly there was a throng of people surrounding them, phones pointed in their direction, as they kissed.

As I wandered down the steps past them, I wondered about

the romance of popping the question surrounded by so many people, captured on film, posted on social media. Loads did it but I'd always thought that if the man of my dreams asked me to marry him, it would be somewhere meaningful to both of us, away from prying eyes. Man of my dreams? I didn't have one of those. Well, I did, but very definitely only in my dreams and not in reality anymore.

I had one more stop planned today – the Wall of Love, or *Mur des Je t'aime*, in a small public garden by Place des Abbesses. It was a forty square feet mural which had been erected at the turn of the century with the words 'I love you' written on it in 250 languages.

As soon as I stepped into the garden, I knew I'd made a mistake. There was a couple kissing and several others holding hands or embracing and I felt a pang of loneliness. It had been so long since I'd had someone special to hold and kiss me. Not feeling the love right now, I left the garden and returned to the apartment.

I checked the post locker in the lobby, hoping there'd be a letter from Rosie. I was just locking it up when the external door opened and a tall, slim woman around the same age as Maman stepped into the building. She looked effortlessly chic in a long camel-coloured coat, cream blouse, wide trousers and stilettos. As she removed her large sunglasses and looked my way, my stomach plummeted to the floor.

'Autumn Laine!'

'Madame Toussaint!'

She came closer and we exchanged the typical French greeting of *la bise* – cheeks together and making a kissing sound then repeating it on the other side.

'Let me practise my English,' she said, her French accent

strong. 'I have been too long in the country. You look *fantastique*. You are living again in France, yes?'

'Only temporarily. My granddad died and I lost my job so I'm taking some time out to decide what to do next.' I wasn't sure why I'd given her so much detail. Nerves probably.

'I am sorry you have two bad things at one time.'

'It's not ideal, but that's life sometimes. What are you doing here? Maman said you were still in Bordeaux.'

'Yes, we move for work but we only leased the apartment so we can come back if we miss Paris too much.' She gave me a doleful look and patted her heart. 'Jacques and I miss Paris too much, so we were to return next month and I was to let your mother know, but our tenants leave early and I am back sooner to make the apartment fresh for the big move. Surprise!'

My stomach lurched but I forced a smile. 'Maman and Papa will be pleased to see you again. I know they've missed you.'

'We have missed them too.' Her phone began to ring. 'I must answer but you and your parents can come for drinks on Friday evening, yes?'

'Sounds good. Thanks, Madame Toussaint.'

'Sylvie, please. See you at seven.'

With a wave, she connected her phone and stepped back outside to take the call. Heart thumping, I raced upstairs to my parents' second-floor apartment. Sylvie Toussaint could return at any moment and I didn't want to be around when she did because, if we spoke again, she was bound to mention Étienne and I wasn't ready for that. At least going for drinks on Friday would give me three days to psyche myself up. Not that three days was enough. Three months probably wasn't even enough. Why did she have to be back? This was the last thing I needed right now.

6

On Friday morning, I sat at the dining table picking chunks off an almond croissant and dipping them in my hot chocolate while Maman and Papa shuffled round each other in the kitchen, preparing for work.

'Why do you both keep looking at me like that?' I asked, catching another concerned glance from Maman.

'We're a little worried about you,' Papa said.

'Why?'

'You've been very quiet this week,' Maman said, approaching the table. 'You're normally full of tales of where you've been and what you've done, but you've barely said a word over the last few days.'

'I'm fine. There's no need to worry.'

'You're sure? Because we're here for you if you do have something on your mind.' Maman planted a kiss on my forehead.

'Everything's all right. I promise. Off to work, both of you.' I smiled brightly, hoping I looked and sounded convincing.

As soon as they'd gone, I slumped back in the chair. Here was me thinking I'd been behaving as normal. Clearly I'd need to ramp up the sunshine levels several notches tonight. Drinks with Étienne's parents had now become a meal and I was dreading it. Neither set of parents had any idea what had happened so they had no reason to avoid mentioning Étienne this evening. As far as they were concerned, we were old friends. What if there were photos of him in the apartment? Even worse, what if there were photos of him with a beautiful family? My stomach lurched at the thought and I pushed aside the part-eaten croissant, my appetite gone.

I needed to get out of the building or I'd spend the day fretting, but I wasn't sure what to do with myself. I'd already visited every museum, landmark and major gallery, some of them several times. I'd spent a ridiculous number of hours on benches, walls and in parks hoping to find inspiration, and none had come.

I settled on another boat trip along the Seine followed by a walking tour round Le Marais. The chic district was home to designer stores and boutiques – not something that interested me – but it also had some stunning old houses and churches. The amazing architecture and decorative features offered glimpses into Medieval Paris and kept my mind focused away from Étienne Toussaint. Almost.

* * *

Unlocking the post locker back at the apartment block later that afternoon, my mood lifted at the sight of a brown A4 envelope addressed to me in Rosie's handwriting. It was thick and heavy, as though it contained a brochure. Even though it was tempting to rip it open and dive straight in to find out, I liked to savour Rosie's words, so I took it upstairs unopened.

In the apartment, I made a coffee and stepped out onto the

balcony. Breathing in the fresh aroma of the coffee beans, I ripped the envelope open, revealing a handwritten letter and the item that felt like a brochure wrapped in brown paper. She'd written in capitals across it:

DO NOT OPEN ME UNTIL YOU'VE READ THE LETTER!

Intrigued, I placed the package down on the metal table and opened out the letter.

Dear Autumn

I'm sorry you're struggling to get your creative mojo back, but I'm not really surprised for two reasons.

Firstly, you've been through an emotional time with your granddad's illness and losing him. It's bound to take its toll on your creativity.

Secondly, it's Paris. I do think it's good that you're with your parents as you all need each other right now, but I can't help thinking that Paris isn't the place for you to get creative again. Buildings? The Eiffel Tower? The Seine? They're not you so no wonder you're struggling to draw. When was the last time you saw a red squirrel scrambling up the side of the Eiffel Tower or a roe deer roaming through Montmartre?

When was the last time I saw those creatures? This morning! The deer passed me on the way to the stables and the squirrel was perched on a fence. It waved at me and said, 'Do you know what your bestie, Autumn, should do? Come and stay in the Lake District and follow in the footsteps of her heroine Beatrix Potter while rediscovering her mojo.' I thought that was unusually enlightened for a squirrel. Usually all they do is ask me where I've hidden their nuts. Perhaps he was a descendent of Potter's Squirrel Nutkin.

Okay, so I'm being a bit flippant here but I'm worried about you. I knew you'd feel a little lost when you first went to Paris but you've been there for nearly 2 months. Even though you didn't directly say it in your last letter, I could read between the lines and could tell you feel even more lost and adrift than when you first arrived which isn't good. You're not you when you're not drawing. You've told me that so many times.

So how do you get to be you again? How do you get to draw again? By finding what inspires you and is there anyone who inspires you more than Beatrix Potter? She's the reason you started drawing animals in the first place! Fun facts for you about BP – I live in the grounds of the house where she holidayed for over 20 years. She settled in the area. She owned most of the area! And if you need further inspiration, you can now open the package.

Thinking of you, sending you creative vibes, and hoping this might be the solution for you. Mam and I would love to finally meet you.

Hugs, Rosie xx

I placed the letter aside and opened the package. Inside were two National Trust guide books – *Beatrix Potter's Lake District* and *Beatrix Potter's Hill Top*. I picked up the Hill Top one first, Hill Top being the first farmhouse of fifteen that Potter purchased in Cumbria. I smiled as I flicked through the pages of each guide book, studying the illustrations and photographs, and reading the occasional paragraph, before returning to Rosie's letter.

She was spot on with everything she'd written. Paris was only ever meant to be temporary to give me some thinking time, but almost two months of thinking time hadn't drawn any conclusions. I was no closer to a decision on what to do with my life than the day I'd arrived. As well as stifling my creativity, was being here stopping me thinking? I liked Paris but I didn't love it, and there was that constant fear of seeing Étienne again. It didn't matter that I knew he'd moved to Dijon. Every time I saw a blond-haired man of his build, my heart skipped a beat, and that tension had escalated since bumping into Sylvie.

Was it time to leave Paris? If I returned to Sutton, I couldn't imagine feeling any more creative than I felt here, but I'd be able to relax there and if I could relax, perhaps I'd be able to draw again. But I'd be alone. Where Rosie lived looked so beautiful. Would a complete change of scenery inspire me like it had inspired Beatrix Potter or would I feel worse than ever if I stayed there? Rosie had the riding stables to run so I'd be on my own for much of the time in an unfamiliar place. Might that be a little too overwhelming?

Shaking my head, I gathered everything together and took it into my bedroom, slipping it into one of my drawers. Paris might not ignite my creativity but it was familiar and, with so much change going on in my life right now, familiarity was good. Except the Toussaints were moving back into the building and that wasn't good. Maybe I would take Rosie up on her offer. It wasn't like it was going to be a permanent move. A week or two holidaying in the Lake District couldn't do any harm.

* * *

Jacques and Sylvie's apartment was on the third floor directly above Maman and Papa's. I wore a smart navy dress with my posh designer stilettos, and pulled my hair back into a loose chignon.

'You look lovely,' Maman said as we made our way upstairs. 'Stop fiddling.'

'I can't help it,' I said, adjusting my dress round my waist. 'I don't like getting dressed up. I never feel me.'

'It's only for a few hours.'

'It's definitely just going to be us?' I asked. 'We're not going to discover they've invited the whole building?'

'Just us as old friends,' she reassured me.

'Since when did a big group bother you?' Papa asked.

'It doesn't. I just like to know what to expect.' And I wanted reassurance that Étienne wasn't going to be a surprise guest.

Jacques greeted us at the door and, after kisses all round, welcomed us inside.

'Sylvie is convinced her English has slipped,' he said, 'so she would like to speak in English this evening.'

It didn't bother me either way. I'd been raised bilingual and conversations with my parents flitted between English and French, sometimes even in the same sentence.

Sylvie was in the kitchen and broke away from chopping tomatoes to greet us all while Jacques poured drinks. The apartment was sparse with basic furniture and none of the personal items that made it a home, which thankfully meant no photos of Étienne. I could relax. A bit.

'Our belongings arrive tomorrow,' Sylvie said, catching me looking around. 'It will look better with paintings and photos.'

'Does it feel good to be back?'

'Oh, yes. My heart, it is always in Paris. It's the same for Étienne.'

My heart started pounding at the mention of his name and I was grateful to Jacques for passing me a glass of wine. I hoped for a subject change, but Maman had questions.

'How is Étienne?' she asked. 'It's such a long time since we saw him.'

'He is not so good. His heart is broken, as is mine.'

'Oh! What's happened?'

Papa and Jacques were in the kitchen so Sylvie indicated that we should sit in the lounge. Her expression darkened. 'Étienne is getting divorced. His wife is with another man and she tells him to leave. Childhood boyfriend. Pah!'

I stared into my glass as Maman commiserated with Sylvie while she went off on one about how disappointed she was with her daughter-in-law and how distressing it was for their two girls. So he'd got the two children he'd always wanted. Just not with me.

I hated that my heart had leapt when she'd said Étienne was getting divorced. It shouldn't excite me that he was single again. I shouldn't care at all. He'd made his choice and it hadn't been me. She might have broken his heart, but he'd broken mine first.

'I got distracted, Autumn,' Sylvie said, bringing my attention back to her. 'I was telling you that my heart is always with Paris and so is Étienne's. He has a new job and will be moving back in with us until he finds his own place.'

'He's moving back?' I asked. My throat had gone very dry and it was an effort to force out the words. 'When?'

'Tonight, but he is catching a late train so you won't see him, but perhaps you two can catch up tomorrow or Sunday?'

There was no response to that, so I smiled politely and took another sip of my wine.

'So, Claudette,' Sylvie said, 'we both have our grown-up children back. They may fly, but they will always return.'

'It's lovely to have your child home,' Maman agreed, smiling across at me. 'It doesn't matter how old they are.'

Sylvie smiled at me too and I could see the cogs whirring. *Don't say it!* But she did.

'You are single, *n'est-ce pas*, Autumn?'

'Yes, but I don't think—'

I didn't get to tell her what I thought because Jacques shouted,

'*Mon Dieu!*' and strode purposefully towards the door, his arms outstretched towards his son.

My stomach did a backflip.

'*Bonsoir à tous. Je pensais arriver tôt et te surprendre...*' Étienne's eyes met mine, 'but it looks like I'm the one who's getting the surprise. Hello, Autumn. It's been a long time.'

My heart was pounding and I felt lightheaded as I stared at him. The years had been good to him and he was even more handsome than I remembered. His thick blond hair looked ready for a cut, but the extra length suited him. He still had a fringe framing those gorgeous grey eyes, and the unshaven look was alluring.

I gulped and tried my hardest to sound casual. 'Hi, Étienne.'

7

NINETEEN YEARS AGO

I'd seen Étienne Toussaint dozens of times – impossible not to when we lived in the same apartment building and our parents were friends – but I'd never paid much attention to him. He was three years older than me and, as a kid, had been painfully shy so I'd long given up trying to get any conversation out of him.

When I was sixteen, I returned to Paris for the summer after completing my GCSEs in the UK. My parents were at work and I'd been out for a walk with my sketchpad that first week back. As I approached the apartment building, the skies darkened and the heavens opened. I sprinted down the street, my feet squelching in my canvas shoes, burst through the door, and bowled straight into a tall blond man I didn't recognise.

Reeling back and apologising profusely, I was stunned when the man said my name.

I pushed my hair away from my face and looked up into a pair of grey eyes peeking at me from beneath a long blond fringe.

'Étienne? Oh, my God! You look so different.' The last time I'd seen him, he'd been a young boy who could barely look anyone in the eye but he'd transformed into an incredibly good-looking man with cheekbones, style and an air of confidence.

'So do you,' he said, smiling at me.

I felt the colour rush to my cheeks. Last time he'd seen me, I'd been a girl, but now I had curves.

'You look good,' I blurted out, immediately wincing inside.

'So do you,' he repeated. 'It seems growing up has been good for both of us. I'll see you around, Autumn Laine.'

He headed towards the door and I had an overwhelming urge to prolong the conversation, but I couldn't think of anything to say to somebody I'd spent the last decade not talking to.

'It's raining!' I declared and immediately kicked myself. No words would have been better.

He gave me a warm smile. 'And here was me thinking you'd been for a swim. *A bientôt.*'

And then he was gone, out into the rain, leaving me dripping water in the lobby and feeling a little breathless.

A whole week passed before I saw him again. This time he was coming down the stairs as I left the apartment and he immediately struck up a conversation with me, asking about my studies in England and whether I was back in Paris for good.

'Where are you going today?' he asked as we left the building together.

'No plans. Aimless wander.'

'I have no plans either. Would you like some company on your aimless wander?'

We walked miles around Paris that day, talking non-stop. I'd never have attributed the word 'interesting' to Étienne prior to that day, but I found myself not wanting the day to end.

He told me he had a girlfriend called Chantal who was spending the summer in Dijon with her family. He'd been invited to join them but he wouldn't see much of her as she'd be working, so they'd decided he'd be better staying in Paris where he had a part-time job in a bistro.

'I've enjoyed today,' he said as we returned to the apartment late that afternoon.

'Me too. I don't really have friends here anymore, so it was nice to have someone to talk to for a change.'

'You want to do this again?' he asked.

'I'd love to.'

So we exchanged phone numbers and made arrangements to meet a couple of days later, and a couple of days after that, and so it went on for the rest of the summer.

I loved Étienne's company. He talked a lot and, even though I joked that he was clearly making up for the lack of conversation as a child, I was happy to listen to him. He knew such a lot about so many different things – music, film, the arts, food, history – that I was a little in awe of him.

I was also more than a little attracted to him but, even if he'd been single, I needed to be realistic about my situation. I was returning to England at the end of August and I wanted to fully immerse myself in life at sixth-form college without pining for a boyfriend in France. Friends was for the best.

If only it had stayed that way.

8

PRESENT DAY

Sylvie launched herself at Étienne but, as they embraced, he kept his eyes fixed on mine. I couldn't read his expression. Was he pleading with me not to say anything? To act like we'd never been more than friends? To leave? I wanted nothing more than to escape but what could I say without arousing suspicion?

Jacques grabbed Étienne's suitcases and the three of them disappeared into Étienne's bedroom.

'Do you think we should leave them to have a family night?' I asked Maman.

'Sylvie wouldn't allow that. There'll be plenty of food for Étienne too.'

The volume of food was the last thing on my mind right now.

'It's a shame you two lost touch,' she continued. 'You spent so much time together in the holidays. I thought you'd have stayed friends.'

'I don't think we should be talking about him when they come back in the room,' I said, anxious to change the subject. 'How was work today, Papa?'

We were in the midst of our small talk about work when Sylvie and Jacques returned to the lounge.

'Étienne is taking a shower after his long journey,' Sylvie declared and my heart fluttered at the thought of him stripping off and stepping under the water jets. 'He'll join us when he is fresh. Who would like another drink?'

I held my glass out, more than ready for a top-up.

Étienne reappeared a little later, his hair damp at the ends from the shower, and joined us in the lounge. Every so often, I felt his eyes on me but, if I turned to look, he averted his gaze. Was he finding this as excruciating as me? Could he still feel my touch on his skin, my lips against his? Did he ever think about how and why it ended or was I the only one who couldn't move on? Probably. While he'd spent years playing happy families, he probably hadn't given me a second thought.

I must have been at primary school the last time I'd spent any significant time in Jacques and Sylvie's company and I'd completely forgotten how talkative they were. They barely paused for breath throughout dinner and I wondered if that's why Étienne has been so quiet as a kid – unable to get a word in edgeways. On the positive side right now, it meant there was no opportunity for awkward silences.

Midnight arrived and despite both sets of parents having already shifted an astonishing amount of wine between them, there looked like there'd be no let-up any time soon. My eyes were burning and my head was thumping from the effort of smiling and acting 'normal'. Thankfully Maman noticed.

'You look tired,' she said while Jacques was opening yet another bottle of wine and Sylvie was spooning olives and gherkins into ramekins.

'I've got a headache,' I admitted.

'Why don't you call it a night? Jacques and Sylvie won't be offended.'

Our hosts completely understood and, after a flurry of kisses, I closed the door behind me and hurried towards the stairs. I paused at the top, taking deep breaths. It was such a relief to get out of there and away from Étienne. I hadn't seen him for fourteen years but he still had the same effect on me, making my heart race and my palms sweat.

I'd almost made it to the second-floor landing when I heard running steps.

'Autumn!' Étienne called.

I stupidly looked up and caught his eye.

'You really have a headache?' he asked, catching up with me as I reached the landing.

'Yes. It's been a long day.'

'I hope you feel well soon. I thought you might be leaving early because of me.' His tone was playful and it angered me.

I planted my hands on my hips. 'If I was, I think it would be justified, don't you?' I snapped.

'Autumn,' he said, his voice soft. 'I'm sorry.'

He reached out his hand towards me but I backed away. Being in the same room as him had been hard enough. Being in such close proximity was even worse and there was no way I could let him touch me because, even after all this time, I wasn't convinced I'd be able to resist him.

I held his gaze but could already feel myself getting lost in his eyes, like I'd done many times before. So much hung unspoken between us, but it needed to stay that way.

'I can't do this,' I murmured.

He took a step closer. 'Do what?'

He reached out once more and I wasn't quick enough. His

fingers brushed across my cheekbone and the touch sent electrical pulses racing through me.

'I've missed you,' he whispered.

'Don't say that.'

His hand was against my cheek and I couldn't help closing my eyes for a moment as I melted into his touch.

'It's true,' he said, his voice low and soft. 'I made a mistake. If I could turn back the clock, I'd do it differently.'

'But you can't. What's done is done.'

He was right in front of me, his body almost touching mine. His breathing was rapid, like my heartbeat. The lighting timed out, leaving only the lights of the city illuminating the landing. Étienne looked so alluring in the semi-darkness.

He lightly placed his other hand on my neck, teasing the tendrils of hair that had broken free from my chignon and then he said the words I'd longed to hear again, deep and husky.

'I still love you, Autumn. I always have.'

I felt his warm breath on my face as he tilted my chin upwards.

'It was always you,' he whispered. 'Tell me you feel the same.'

Of course I did! Étienne was the only man I'd ever loved and those feelings had never left me.

'Why?' I asked. 'It made no difference when I said it fourteen years ago.'

'Is that a yes?'

'I can't.'

But my body disagreed. When Étienne's lips met mine, my arms wrapped round his neck and pulled him closer. His stubble scratched my skin as he kissed my mouth, my cheeks, my neck. There was an urgency that hadn't been there before and it sent a wave of desire through me as I lost myself in his kiss.

The light flicked on and laughter and chatter drifted up the stairs, pulling us apart. I looked at Étienne's dishevelled hair, the shirt untucked and partially unbuttoned and my brain finally caught up with my heart.

'I *can't* do this,' I said, my voice stronger this time. 'I won't. Goodnight, Étienne.'

Without waiting for a response, I powerwalked across the landing. *Do not look back! He's watching you, but you must not look back!*

Closing the door to my parents' apartment, I released a shaky breath. What would have happened if those people hadn't appeared? In that moment, I'd forgotten where I was and had been completely swept away in the dream of being back in Étienne's arms, where I'd always thought I belonged.

A little later, I lay on my back in my bed, staring at the ceiling. Étienne's parents' apartment was directly above ours. Étienne's bedroom was directly above mine. Was he lying in his bed right now, thinking of me?

I turned to my side, hugging my pillow, re-living that kiss in my mind. Amazing as it was, it should *not* have happened. I shouldn't have let it. I was vulnerable right now and so was he. In theory, he was available – going through a divorce – but he had to be on the rebound. Sylvie had said that his wife was with someone else, so the divorce was presumably instigated by her. Even if Étienne had been the one who'd called time, she'd been the unfaithful one, so his heart had to be broken.

I brushed my fingertips across my lips, my heart racing once more and I scrunched my eyes tight shut, cursing my behaviour tonight. I couldn't get involved with Étienne Toussaint again. We'd had our chance and he'd thrown it away. If I let him in, he'd hurt me again, and I wasn't sure I'd ever recover.

9

FOURTEEN YEARS AGO

Étienne and I fell into an easy pattern with each other. Whenever I was home for the college holidays, we met up. We'd rack up miles walking the streets of Paris or while away the hours lazing in the various parks. He still talked a lot, but he encouraged me to open up too and at the start of our second summer together – when I was halfway through sixth-form college – one conversation changed everything for me.

'I know everything about your life in England,' Étienne said as we lay top to tail on the grass in our favourite park – the Parc des Buttes-Chaumont – late one July afternoon. 'But I feel like I know nothing.'

'You've lost me,' I said, sitting up and frowning at him.

He put his hands behind his head and fixed his gaze on me. 'I know the names of your teachers and how well you're doing in lessons, but these are facts that you'd share with your parents. We've been friends for a year but you keep me at a distance. Why?'

'I don't! I...' But he was right. I kept everyone at a distance. I shrugged. 'What do you want to know?'

'How is it really? Are you happy in England?'

I didn't know how to answer that question. 'I love living with my grandparents,' I said after a pause.

He propped himself up on his elbow. 'That's not what I asked. Are you happy in England?'

'Yes and no.' I sighed. 'But it's the same answer for Paris.'

'Tell me more.'

'I don't feel like I have a home and it's not because I spend my time switching between Sutton and Paris – it's because I don't love either place and I can't put my finger on why.'

'You like one better?'

'Sutton, but I can't give you a reason for that either. It's not like I don't like living with my parents.'

Étienne sat up properly, his mouth downturned as he faced me. 'I've made you sad,' he said, gently. 'I'm sorry.'

'No, it's fine. It's just that…' I tailed off, shrugging, but he gave me an encouraging nod. His friendship was so important to me and, if I was going to hang onto it, I couldn't keep him at a distance any longer.

'It's just that sometimes I feel a bit lonely,' I admitted. 'I felt like an outcast at school and I had big hopes for that changing when I started college, but it hasn't. If anything, it's worse. But it's only for one more year.'

'And then what?'

'And then I have to hope that university's different.' My voice caught in my throat and tears blurred my eyes as I imagined university panning out the same as school and college – always on the outside, never quite fitting in but not understanding why, wondering if it was me that was the problem.

I hadn't noticed Étienne shuffling closer until his strong arms wrapped round me and pulled me close. I rested my head on his shoulder as tears trickled down my cheeks and he stroked my back.

'It'll be all right,' he whispered. 'I found myself when I started university. You will too.'

I hoped so, but at least I had my parents, my grandparents, and Rosie. And considering the tight hug, I had Étienne too.

The tears stilled, but he kept hold of me and I didn't want him to let go. I felt warm and safe and cared for. For that brief moment in time, it felt like we were the only two people in the world and we had each other's backs.

'Are you okay now?' he asked, releasing his hold.

'Yes. Thank you.'

That was the day I let Étienne in, but it was also the day I started to see him as more than a friend. My heart leapt each time he texted me and butterflies soared whenever we met, but he was still with Chantal, so I had to keep my feelings hidden.

I didn't understand why they were still together. I'd never met her but, from what he'd told me about her, they didn't seem like a good match. He was laid back and easy-going but she was moody and demanding, initiating stacks of arguments. I was tempted to point out what appeared obvious to me – that their relationship seemed to work best when she was in Dijon and he was in Paris, so why stay together? – but I didn't want to cause tension in our friendship, so I kept quiet.

It wasn't the only thing I kept quiet about. Each school holiday, I fell a little more deeply in love with Étienne and I never breathed a word about it to anyone except Rosie. The pair of us analysed looks and conversations by letter and over the phone. She was convinced he had feelings for me too but we agreed it would be wrong for me to say anything or make a move on him while he was with Chantal. That relationship had to end first. Except it never did. It was painful carrying the hope that one day he'd wake up and realise that I was the one he should be with and not Chantal.

Two years after our friendship started, Étienne graduated from university and secured a junior management position with RATP – the company responsible for running the public transport system in Paris. Chantal got a job back home in Dijon. Travelling by high-speed train, Étienne could go door to door in two hours, but I wasn't convinced that was sustainable in the long term and I wondered if it might finally spell the end for them. And perhaps the start of something for us?

Étienne and I sat on a bench in the Parc des Buttes-Chaumont late that summer, looking out over the lake.

'Are you excited for university in September?' he asked.

'I am, although it's going to be weird living away from my grandparents, especially with Grandma's health problems.'

I'd chosen the University of Brighton partly because of the degree, specialising in illustration, but mainly because of the close proximity to home, even though I'd assured Granddad that the former was key to my decision.

'Why do we not stay in touch when you're in England?' Étienne asked, plucking at a few blades of grass. He fixed his eyes on mine and there was such intensity in them that my heart thudded, especially when he added, 'I miss you when you're there.'

'I miss you too,' I said, my voice husky.

I swear there was a moment between us – something sizzling in the air – but when Étienne didn't say or do anything, I had to go and ruin it.

'You'd better not let Chantal hear you say that,' I said, wagging my finger at him. 'She'll be convinced she was right all along.'

My friendship with Étienne had been the subject of several

arguments between them over the years because Chantal didn't believe that heterosexual men and women could just be friends.

Étienne didn't respond, but he didn't avert his eyes. I battled the urge to shout, *She* was *right. I want more than friendship. Dump her and be with me instead!*

'You write to your friend, Rosie,' he said eventually. 'What is it you call her?'

'My penpal.'

'Perhaps you and I can become penpals?'

I raised my eyebrows at him, doubtfully. 'You want to write to me at university?'

'I do. Is that all right with you?'

'I'd love it, but I can't see you keeping it up.'

'I will. You watch me!'

I thought he'd manage one letter, maybe two, before the novelty wore off but Étienne surprised me by writing regularly. Keeping in touch all year round brought us even closer together, but I still shied away from the one thing I really wanted to say – how I felt about him. I continued in my little fantasy world that we would be together one day.

Then towards the end of my second year, I received a letter from Étienne which shattered that fantasy and broke me. Chantal had accepted that a distance relationship during the holidays had been possible but a full-time one was unsustainable. She'd secured a job in Paris, and they were moving in together. I spent three days in bed crying and eating junk food, distraught that I'd spent four years kidding myself that things between Chantal and Étienne would fizzle out.

Stopping writing letters to Étienne would have been the right thing to do but I couldn't seem to cut those ties. I kept thinking he'd stop – after all, with Chantal now living with him, it had to be harder to find the time and opportunity to write to me and surely it would make her jealous – but the letters kept on coming so I kept on replying.

Grandma's health continued to deteriorate and, during my final year, Maman and Papa came to Sutton for Christmas. It was the first time I hadn't spent the holidays in Paris since I was sixteen, but there was no question of me leaving Grandma. I hoped the space would help me get over Étienne.

In the New Year, I reluctantly returned to Brighton for my penultimate term, fearing I may have said my final goodbye to Grandma. Sure enough, a couple of weeks later, I received the phone call I'd been dreading. Feeling numb, I caught the train home, anxious to comfort Granddad and to seek his comfort in return.

I returned to Brighton two days after Grandma's funeral, reassured that Granddad had friends such as Mrs Slade next door who'd look out for him. There were a couple of letters waiting for me from Étienne. The first was fairly chatty, telling me how much he'd hated not seeing me over Christmas and sending his best wishes to Grandma. The second, sent a week later, begged me to get in touch. He hadn't heard from me since before Christmas and was worried. Chantal knew there was something on his mind and hated it when he'd told her he was worried about me, so they'd had a massive bust-up. Again. I tossed the letters on my bed, exhausted by their drama.

I wasn't much of a drinker but I went out with my housemates that night to celebrate Grandma's life. I celebrated a little too hard and, back in my bedroom, feeling melancholy, it seemed like a good idea to reply to Étienne and tell him the truth. The whole truth.

Dear Étienne

I'm sorry I haven't written since before Christmas but my

grandma died a fortnight ago and it was her funeral on Thursday. I'm devastated and so is Granddad. I wanted to stay home with him but he wouldn't let me so I'm back in Brighton and my heart is breaking thinking of him all alone without the love of his life. They were together for 60 years. Can you imagine that?

I long for what my grandparents had – to find that one special person who I love unconditionally and with whom I want to spend the rest of my life until death cruelly separates us. Thing is, I've already found him. He's my best friend, my confidante and my soul mate. But he's with someone else and, for the life of me, I can't fathom why. She doesn't understand him like I do. She doesn't make him happy. So my heart breaks for him too.

Yes, Étienne, of course I mean you! Probably (definitely) shouldn't be writing this to you but I've had a few drinks to toast Grandma and I'm in a reflective and honest mood. Besides, this is the last letter I'm going to write to you and I feel that, after nearly 5 years of valuable friendship, I owe you an explanation as to why I can't be your penpal or your holiday friend anymore. It hurts too much to be with you but not really with you.

I think it's time to say goodbye. I won't be coming to Paris for Easter as I want to stay with Granddad and I'll only have a brief visit over summer because I'll be working by then (I hope!) so our friendship has probably reached a natural ending anyway.

I'm going to miss you so much. I wish it wasn't the end for us but it needs to be. I've spent too long hoping our friendship could be something more and it's time to accept it never will and make that clean break.

When I was at home over Christmas, I think Grandma must

have known it was the last time we'd be together because she said something poignant to me that I'm going to pass on to you. Be courageous, be adventurous, but most of all be happy.
Autumn xx

I scribbled his address on the envelope, added a stamp, and ran to the postbox at the end of the street to send the letter before I changed my mind.

The following morning, I awoke with a thumping head and squinted across at my desk. Why was my writing paper out? With a gasp, I remembered writing furiously last night and clapped my hand to my forehead, crying out, 'No!' I'd only gone and drunk-written to Étienne telling him how I felt about him and posted the sodding letter. What an idiot!

Thank goodness his parents had rented their apartment out and moved to Bordeaux last year so it wasn't like I was going to bump into him or them in the building next time I visited my parents. There was no reason for me to ever see him again.

The thought of that made me gasp for breath and the tears came thick and fast. What had I done? I'd just lost Grandma. Could I bear to lose Étienne too?

When the tears finally subsided, I asked myself whether never seeing Étienne was worse than having him in my life knowing that his happy ever after was with Chantal. No. The drunk letter had been stupid, but it was for the best. I picked up my phone and blocked Étienne.

'Goodbye,' I whispered, as I deleted his contact details. I knew his address off by heart but I'd stay strong. I wouldn't write again, no matter how much I'd had to drink. So that was it. Over.

* * *

I arrived home from lectures on the Friday afternoon of that week. One of my housemates, Tizi, was already home.

'You've got a visitor,' she said, grinning at me. 'A very hot visitor with an accent to die for.'

I ran upstairs to my bedroom, my heart thumping. There was only one person I knew who matched that description, but it couldn't be. In all the years we'd known each other, he'd never once suggested visiting me.

I pushed open my door and there he was, the man I loved, peering at the photographs pinned around my noticeboard.

'What are you doing here?' I asked.

'I got your letter.' He took it out of the back pocket of his jeans and held it up. 'Did you mean what you said in here?' His voice was soft, his expression tender.

'Which part?'

'The part about being in love with me.'

My cheeks burned with embarrassment that I'd written that, but I somehow found the nerve to hold his gaze. 'Yes.'

'Why didn't you say anything before?'

'I'd have thought that was obvious. You were with Chantal.'

'Not all of the time. We had break-ups.'

I shook my head. 'Come on, Étienne. Even when it was off, it was only a matter of time before it would be on again. You couldn't seem to stay away from her. I couldn't compete with whatever hold she had over you, so I didn't try.'

'Do you know why I stayed with Chantal?'

'No! I've never understood it, but what do I know about relationships? I've never had one. I'm the idiot who hung on for five years hoping her best friend would fall in love with her.'

'What if your best friend *was* in love with you, but didn't think the feeling was mutual?'

He took a step closer and the air in the room suddenly felt alive, crackling with electricity.

'What if your best friend kept going back to his girlfriend because he thought it was never going to happen with you?'

I gulped. 'You stayed with Chantal because you thought I wasn't interested?'

'You never gave me any signs.'

'Because I didn't want to lose you as a friend. You never gave me any either.'

'Because I didn't want to lose you either.' He waved the letter again. 'But I've still lost you.'

'You can't have us both. I can't do it anymore.'

'I don't want you both. I only want you, Autumn.'

My heart leapt and I searched his eyes for the truth. Was he really saying my feelings were reciprocated?

'I'm sorry it took me so long to say it,' he said gently, taking another step closer. 'I don't want to say *goodbye* to you. I want to *be* with you.'

'What about Chantal?' I asked.

'It's over. She's gone back to Dijon to her family. She doesn't like Paris.' He rolled his eyes. 'She tells me she doesn't like me either.'

My heart raced even faster. 'When?' I whispered.

'Two weeks ago.' He slipped my letter back into his pocket. 'It really is over.'

'You say that, but it never is.'

'This time it's true because this time I know how *you* feel.'

We were so close now that I was sure he'd be able to hear my heart pounding.

'Can I kiss you?' he asked, his voice husky.

'It's *definitely* over with Chantal?'

'Definitely. It's always been you.' He ran his fingers down the side of my face. 'Since I was a young boy and too shy to speak to you, you were the one I wanted. I love you, Autumn.'

Tears pricked my eyes. 'I love you too.'

His eyes searched mine for a moment before he pulled me close and kissed me. Our first kiss was everything I'd ever dreamed of – gentle at first, then increasing in passion as he ran his hands through my hair and down my back. We tumbled down onto the bed, still kissing, but as his hand crept under my T-shirt and stroked my side, I tensed.

He pulled away, looking down on me with concern. 'Did I hurt you?'

'No. I'm sorry. I just...'

'This is too fast?' he asked when I tailed off.

'No. I want it. It's just... I've never... This would be...' I placed my hands over my face, cringing. Why was it so hard to say the words?

He gently eased my hands away and kissed them. 'It's your first time?'

I bit my lip as I nodded. 'I was waiting for you. I know that's silly.'

'Not silly. Romantic.' He lightly kissed me then rolled off the bed and reached for my hand. 'Let me take you out for dinner.' He pulled me to my feet and wrapped his arms around me. 'There's no rush for anything more. It is my turn to wait for you.'

Étienne was true to his word. He stayed in Brighton for the weekend and shared my bed, but there was no pressure to take the next step. It was Valentine's Day on the Saturday and he could have taken advantage of that, but he didn't try. Not that I doubted him when he told me he loved me, but him giving me time gave me the reassurance that he was in this for the long haul.

We talked about what the future might look like for us. His job was in Paris and I didn't have one yet so, in theory, I could hunt for a role there. Even though it was my dream to be with Étienne and I was willing to make compromises for that to happen, the one compromise I couldn't make was location. Moving to Paris would mean leaving Granddad alone and, while I knew he'd encourage me to follow my heart and not worry about him, I couldn't leave him. I didn't want to.

'We'll work something out,' Étienne promised. 'We're meant to be together.'

My heart ached for Étienne over the fortnight that followed. We spoke often, texted constantly, wrote long love letters to each other, but it wasn't enough for me. I wanted to kiss him, to touch him, to feel his body against mine. How did couples cope with long-distance relationships because this was killing me?

At the end of February, he visited me in Brighton again. As soon as his lips met mine, I knew I couldn't wait any longer. I'd been ready for this moment for years and there was no reason to hold back.

Étienne visited a fortnight later and a fortnight after that. I showed him around Brighton and we had several romantic walks along the pebbly beach, although we didn't cover much distance, constantly stopping to kiss. All those miles we'd walked round Paris together and I'd dreamed of this and now it was really happening. The only thing that stopped me being truly happy was the distance. It was the way it needed to be at the moment and, much as I missed him, the time apart meant I could focus on my degree. But what about when I graduated? Would the distance become too much of a strain?

On Étienne's fourth visit, we sat on the beach, watching a spectacular sun set behind the remains of the burnt-out pier.

'It's beautiful here,' Étienne said. 'You'll miss Brighton when you graduate?'

'I will. If I can find a job here, I'd rather stay here than work in

London. I'd still be close to Granddad and no further from the airport than if I moved back in with him.' I sighed. 'I wish we could be together properly. It's already so hard being in different countries. If it wasn't for Granddad...' My unfinished sentence drifted away with the light breeze that ruffled my hair.

Étienne tightened his arms around me, but he didn't say anything and I felt a stab of fear. What if he thought I was unreasonable not moving to France? He was, after all, the one with the job and the apartment and it made far more sense for me to fit into his life than for him to leave everything. Was I being unreasonable? If I wasn't moving back in with Granddad, did it really matter whether I was a flight away rather than a drive? Was I using Granddad as an excuse because my heart had never been in Paris?

'You once told me that you hadn't lived anywhere that felt like home,' Étienne said eventually. 'Does Brighton feel like home?'

I pondered on that before nodding. 'More than the other two. I like it here a lot. It has a happy vibe.'

'I agree. It's a good place to raise a family, I think.'

'It is. It's great for families.'

'Then I think I could live here with you and we could raise our family here.'

I gasped. 'You mean that?'

'I mean it all. I can see us being very happy together here with our family. Two children, I think. Would you like that?'

'I'd love it. Thank you.'

'My heart is where you are and you need to be with your granddad so this is where we should be. You said in your letter to be courageous, adventurous and happy. It would take courage to move to a new country, but it would be an adventure and I know it would make us both happy forever.'

He reached into the pocket of his jacket and my heart pounded as he removed a silver ring.

'This is a promise ring. It's my promise to always love you and that we will be together.'

'It's beautiful,' I said, studying the Celtic design. The twists of silver wrapped round a white stone looked like infinity symbols.

'It's white topaz,' he said. 'It's the stone of courage, which is fitting because courage brought us together.'

He took the ring back from me and slipped it onto the ring finger on my right hand where it fit perfectly then took my left hand and lightly kissed my bare ring finger. 'I will get you a ring for this one after you graduate, when we are settled.'

None of it felt too fast. We had, after all, secretly been in love with each other for years. As we kissed passionately, everything now felt perfect in my world. My heart still hurt from losing Grandma, but the pain wasn't quite so acute because I'd found the same sort of deep, lasting love she and Granddad had shared.

If only Chantal hadn't had other ideas.

10

PRESENT DAY

I had a restless night after dinner with the Toussaints, the memories of those weekends in Brighton swirling around my mind as vivid and as real as though they had only been this year.

Maman and Papa were going to Versailles and had invited me to join them at the start of the week. Having visited already, I'd passed on the trip but, as I showered, I weighed up the merits of changing my mind. A day away from the apartment would be a welcome physical escape from Étienne, but it wasn't going to stop him occupying my thoughts. My parents had already noticed that I was quiet and distracted after being invited to dinner with Jacques and Sylvie and that was when I wasn't expecting to see Étienne. They'd definitely notice something was up if I spent the full day with them, and it wouldn't need many sleuthing skills to trace it back to Étienne's appearance last night, which would lead to questions. I didn't want to tell them about our relationship because that would mean telling them *everything* and I didn't want to go there. I couldn't.

I prolonged getting dressed, only emerging from my bedroom ten minutes before the time I knew they planned to leave.

'Are you sure you don't want to join us?' Papa asked. 'Final chance.'

'I'm sure, but thank you. You two have a fabulous day.'

'What are your plans?' Maman asked.

I smiled ruefully. 'The continued search for my lost mojo.'

They wished me luck and left. As soon as the door closed, my gaze shifted to the ceiling. Was Étienne awake? Had he had a restless night too, thinking about that kiss? Thinking about what could have been if he hadn't broken his promises to me?

'This is ridiculous,' I muttered, shaking my head.

It was going to drive me mad staying here knowing he was right above me so I pulled on my jacket and grabbed my bag. As I walked away from the building, I had the strongest sensation of being watched. I glanced back to see Étienne in his bedroom with the doors to his Juliet balcony open. He raised a hand but I ignored him and quickened my pace. I couldn't give him any encouragement. Last night had been a huge mistake and I was so thankful to those people for arriving back when they did because it could easily have gone a lot further. I'd wanted it to.

I had no idea where I was going. Every single street, monument and park held memories of Étienne.

I needed to focus on my art. Rosie had commented on buildings not being me and she was right. It was time I stopped trying to find a new direction and follow my heart, even if that meant following my broken heart. Étienne and I had spent so much time in the Parc des Buttes-Chaumont that I'd avoided it since returning to Paris, but it was the best place for wildlife and for inspiration thanks to the grottos, waterfalls and a folly.

Sitting on the same bench where we'd often sat by the lake, I took my sketchpad out and looked around me for inspiration. I drew rough pencil sketches of the bridge and the folly – the Temple de la Sybille on top of the grotto – but sighed at my work. They were good likenesses but where was my sparkle? Where was the magic? Was Rosie right about Paris being the problem to the point where I couldn't even find inspiration in a park filled with nature and wildlife? Or was today's struggle more about Étienne's reappearance?

Frustrated, I slammed the pad onto the bench beside me and held my head in my hands. A few hours in his company and one kiss – albeit an incredible one – and I was broken again. My head was filled with memories of Étienne that I'd tried so hard to bury and, now that he was back and living in the same building as me, there was no way I could stay.

I took out my phone and searched for flights back to Gatwick. There was one this afternoon, but there was no way I could do that to my parents. Tomorrow was Mother's Day in the UK and, as we had no idea whether I'd be around for France's equivalent in June, I had plans to celebrate with Maman. But I could leave on Monday.

'Leaving already?'

I snapped my head up, my heart thumping. 'What are you doing here? Did you follow me?'

'No, but I was looking for you,' Étienne said softly. 'I hoped you might be in one of our places. Can we talk?'

I stuffed my phone, sketchpad and pencils into my backpack, shaking my head vigorously. 'You said all you needed to say fourteen years ago when you broke your promises to me and chose Chantal.'

'What did you expect me to do?'

I rolled my eyes at him, pulled my backpack on, and stormed off along the path. He ran after me.

'Autumn! I made a mistake and I've regretted it all these years.'

'That makes two of us,' I snapped, speeding up my pace. 'I

should have known it wasn't over between you two, that she still had some weird hold over you.'

'I didn't lie to you. It *was* over. I meant every word I said to you. I admit that I did love Chantal, but I loved you so much more. I wanted you. I chose you.'

I stopped and stared at him. 'But you didn't. You chose Chantal.'

'Only because I had no choice.'

'Yes, you did! There's always a choice. And yours was to be with Chantal.'

'A big mistake for all of us. Chantal and I could never be happy together because I still lo—'

'Stop!' I shouted, putting my palm out towards him to emphasise the word. 'Don't say it again! That's not fair.'

'Life isn't fair. And I *will* say it! I love you. I always have, I always will, and I'll do anything to make it up to you.'

My heart was thumping so rapidly, I felt lightheaded. I wanted to run, but I couldn't seem to make my feet move. How often had I longed to hear him say those words? I could have put last night's declaration down to a combination of drink, surprise and nostalgia, but what was today's excuse?

'Say something,' he urged.

'It's too late,' I managed eventually, hoping I sounded convincing.

'It's never too late and you know it. I felt it in your kiss. Like mine, your feelings haven't changed. We were meant to be together.'

'Yes, we were,' I said, the words catching in my throat. 'But you let me down and you broke my heart and there's no way I'm letting you do that again.'

'I wouldn't. I promise.'

I shook my head. 'Your promises don't mean anything. Goodbye, Étienne.'

'You're lying,' he said, desperation in his voice. 'You're still wearing my promise ring.'

It took all my strength to keep walking.

'I still love you,' he called after me, but I kept going, shoulders straight, tears streaming down my cheeks. As soon as I got back to the apartment, I was booking that flight and I would take Rosie up on her offer to visit her in the Lake District. I needed to be somewhere with no connections to Étienne.

11

'Wow!' I exclaimed for the umpteenth time as I travelled along the A66 towards Keswick late on Friday afternoon. I'd seen photographs but nothing quite prepared me for the majesty of the mountains and fells in the Lake District National Park which rose on either side of the road. No wonder Rosie loved it here.

Maman and Papa had understood my need to return to England and admitted they'd been surprised I'd stayed as long as I had because they could tell I hadn't settled. It had been a relief to hear that as it meant they were unlikely to connect my departure to Étienne's reappearance.

Rosie had been thrilled when I rang her to accept her offer of a place to stay and we'd agreed a fortnight starting today with the opportunity to stay longer if I wanted.

During my three days back in Sutton, I'd been into London to meet Tim for lunch and Madeline for dinner. Tim hadn't secured one of the positions either but had started a new job with a graphic design company and was loving it so far. Madeline surprised me with the news that she'd taken voluntary redundancy and had accepted a position with one of Thoughtful Cards' competitors. Glitter Box were fairly new but they'd made a positive impact and were rapidly expanding. They had a great reputation for fairness and innovation and I could see Madeline fitting in really well.

'Being on enforced gardening leave is a killer,' she told me. 'I'm so bored not working, but that's what happens when you move to a competitor. I'd have you on my team in a flash if a vacancy arrives. Do you think you'd be interested?'

'I'd love to work with you again, but I don't know if greetings cards is the way forward for me. In fact, I don't know if illustrating is. I haven't drawn anything that excites me in so long.'

We left it that she'd get in touch once she was settled at Glitter Box, but I wasn't convinced it was for me anymore. I couldn't shake the feeling that I was meant to go in a different direction. What that direction was, I hadn't a clue.

'Turn left at the next junction,' my satnav instructed.

I flicked on my indicator at the signpost for Willowdale and butterflies took flight. Nearly there! I was so excited about finally meeting Rosie but I was a little nervous too. I'd put my inability to maintain friendships down to circumstances – me flitting between France and England at school, feeling like an outsider at college, and my university friends being scattered all over the country after graduation – but what if it was what I'd feared and I was the problem? What if I was boring to be around or too intense and that's why my friendships had quickly fallen apart? Or what if the friendship aspect was fine but I wasn't inspired by the Lakes? What would I do next?

Feeling the nerves build, I wound down the window and let the fresh air kiss my cheeks. I needed to stop overthinking everything and make the most of where I was. What would be would be.

As I entered the village, there were cottages on either side of the road. Some were whitewashed and others were made from slate. There weren't any vehicles behind me so I slowed right down to get a better look.

There was a pub called The Hardy Herdwick on the main road and a village hall set back down a side road just before it. More cottages flanked the main road, the signs outside indicating that many of them were holiday rentals.

I slowed down even more, taking it all in. It was so quaint and pretty. A lone cyclist passed me in the opposite direction and gave me a curious look, so I accelerated, realising I probably looked a bit odd crawling through the village with my head sticking out my car window.

'In 100 metres, veer to the right,' the satnav told me.

It looked like I was in the centre of the village now. On the corner to my right was a village green with a beautiful giant willow tree, a bench, and a postbox. I wondered whether the village got its name from the tree or whether the tree had been planted because of the name.

On the left was a narrower road which passed a village shop on the corner, a gift shop, and more pretty white and slate houses. Opposite the gift shop was another pub called the Lakeside Inn and beyond that was the lake – Derwent Water.

As I veered to the right, I slowed down to let a group of walkers cross the road in front of me. They smiled and waved their thanks. It was no bother – gave me an excuse to pause and admire the lake. The calm water shimmered in the late afternoon sunshine and it was everything I'd imagined and so much more.

Continuing my journey, I passed a café on my right called The White Willow with wooden tables outside, most of which were occupied. I loved a coffee and a slice of cake, so I looked forward to visiting The White Willow soon.

I drove past cottages on either side of the road and a marina on my left, giving me further tantalising glimpses of Derwent Water. There were more properties beyond the marina, mainly large detached houses surrounded by trees. The road curved gently to the left, the right, and left again and, as I went round that final bend, I saw a large cream sign.

WILLOWDALE HALL
Riding Stables & Equestrian Centre

'You have reached your destination.'

'I have indeed,' I whispered, switching off the satnav with a smile.

Grand wrought-iron gates with an elaborate floral design on them opened inwards with a creak after I entered the four-digit number Rosie had given me into the keypad. After I'd driven through, they closed behind me with a satisfying 'thunk'.

Gravel crunched beneath my tyres as I drove past a cottage which had probably been the gatehouse when the estate was first built. It looked empty now and in need of some TLC, with plants hanging from the guttering and paint peeling off the window frames.

Some way ahead of me, I could see Willowdale Hall itself – a beautiful mansion in grey slate with sandy-coloured stone window frames and features.

Rosie had told me to turn left and follow the road, past the stables, where I'd find Horseshoe Cottage. Moments later, I spotted it and paused to take it in. The pretty one-storey cottage was built from slate, crawling with green and red ivy, and surrounded by trees. From Rosie's letters, I knew that her mam's bedroom was downstairs and the loft had been converted into a second bedroom for Rosie. I could see a couple of skylights behind one of the large chimneys. The teeniest of gardens behind a low stone wall wrapped round the front and side of the cottage.

I pulled onto the drive and parked round the back beside an old green Land Rover jeep. Exiting my car, I heard a dog barking and a beautiful reddish-gold cocker spaniel came bounding over to me.

'You must be Toffee,' I said, bending down to let her sniff my hand. 'You're even more beautiful in real life than in your photos.'

She gave me a lick then dropped onto her back, legs in the air, so I could rub her belly.

'And you're just as demanding as Rosie said you were.'

'Autumn! You're here!'

I stood up and smiled widely as Rosie rushed over, arms outstretched, and pulled me into a hug.

'It's amazing to finally meet you,' I said, holding her tightly.

'And you! I've been so excited all week. I can't believe it's taken us twenty-four years to meet.'

She stepped back and we both looked at each other. She was maybe four inches taller than my five foot five frame and slimmer too. I could imagine that the combination of riding and the physical work needed to run the stables kept her toned. Her long dark hair was tied back in a fishtail plait and she had brown eyes like me but hers were much darker.

'I'm so jealous of your dimples,' I said. 'Apparently I asked *Père Noël* for dimples when I was seven. My parents like to remind me of that.'

'That's so cute.' She pressed her fingers to her cheeks. 'I used to hate them when I was little, but I like them now. Let's get you inside and introduce you to Mam. We can get your bags after. You must be gasping for a cuppa after that journey, eh?'

'I am! I've never driven anywhere near this far on my own before.' It had taken me nearly seven hours to travel the 330-mile journey, stopping for lunch and a couple of breaks en route. 'I've actually never been further north than the Cotswolds so this is all new for me. It looks beautiful.'

'It is. I can't wait to show you round.'

'How is your mam?' I asked, lowering my voice. Rosie's mam had been the pedestrian in a hit and run accident when Rosie was a teenager and, although most of the physical damage had been repaired, there'd been lasting repercussions for her mental health.

'She's in fine fettle just now.'

'Fettle?' I asked, unfamiliar with the word.

Rosie laughed. 'It's your condition, health. *How's your fettle?* Or *How're you fettling?* Is like asking *How are you?*'

'I like it.'

'I'll tell you more about Mam when we're away from the cottage.'

She pushed open a solid wooden door and we stepped into a surprisingly large farmhouse-style kitchen with a wooden table and chairs in the middle.

'Mam? Autumn's here!'

A willowy woman entered the kitchen and, although she was shorter and slimmer than Rosie, the family resemblance was unmistakable. She had the same long dark hair, dark eyes and narrow cheekbones as Rosie, but without the dimples.

'This is my mam, Alice,' Rosie said.

'Thanks for letting me stay,' I said, smiling at her.

Her right hand fluttered to her hair, pushing it behind her ears while her left hand teased a button on her baggy cardigan. Rosie had warned me that she could appear jittery but not to take it as a sign that she was uncomfortable having me around because it absolutely wasn't that.

'It's so wonderful to finally meet you,' she said, her voice soft and gentle. 'Would it be too much if I hugged you?'

'A hug would be lovely,' I said, crossing the kitchen and embracing her. She felt so delicate in my arms.

'Thank you for being such a good friend to my Rosie,' she said when we parted.

'She's been a great friend to me too.' I smiled across at Rosie who was putting the kettle on. 'I'm not sure what I'd have done without her over the years.'

Toffee nudged against me, clearly wanting more attention.

'There's a treat jar over there.' Alice pointed to a cream canister on the windowsill. 'She'll be your friend forever if you give her a few of those.'

I gave my drink order to Rosie as I took a couple of treats from the jar. Toffee sat patiently by my feet with her paw out waiting for the first one. Under my instructions, she lay down for the second, and turned in a circle for the third.

'You've got her well trained,' I observed.

'Mam's brilliant with animals,' Rosie said, her voice full of warmth and admiration as they smiled at each other.

'And so are you,' Alice said, 'especially with the horses. Am I right in thinking you don't ride, Autumn?'

'I'm scared of horses,' I admitted, wrinkling my nose apologetically.

'But we're going to work on that,' Rosie said, passing me a mug with a horse on it. 'She'll be in the saddle and loving it before she leaves, although I have a feeling she'll never want to leave.'

Alice patted my arm. 'You're welcome to stay for as long as you want. I'm sorry we can't give you a bedroom of your own, but Rosie's very tidy so she's not a bad roommate to have. Why don't you show Autumn round the cottage while your drinks are cooling? I'll make a start on tea.'

Toffee followed us as we wandered round the cottage. There was a good-sized lounge with windows front and back. A pair of sofas flanked a real fire and there was a dresser, some bookshelves, and a beautiful writing bureau along the wall opposite the fire.

'That's where I write my letters to you,' Rosie pointed out. 'I love this room. It's so cosy.'

'It's gorgeous,' I agreed. None of the furniture matched but somehow everything worked perfectly together. Cushions, throws and pictures added splashes of colour to the otherwise neutral palette, and the whole room exuded warmth.

I followed Rosie down a corridor which ran alongside the kitchen.

'Mam's bedroom's at the end.' She opened the door to a pretty double bedroom in shades of pale blue, grey and white. A Peter Rabbit soft toy on the bedside drawers made me smile.

We backed along the corridor and she opened three more doors, pointing out a bathroom, a separate toilet, and a storage cupboard, before taking me upstairs.

'Oh, wow!' I said, as we reached the top. 'This is amazing.'

From the outside, I'd assumed the only light into the loft conversion came through the skylights but there was a Juliet balcony at the far end. I was drawn straight to it and gasped at the spectacular view.

'Derwent Water,' Rosie said, joining me by the window. 'I'll never tire of it.'

I didn't think I would either. The lake was a short distance away and I could see trees on this side and mountains on the other.

'It looks so calm and peaceful,' I said. 'It was a struggle to tear my eyes away when I was driving through the village.'

'It's my favourite of all the lakes, although I'm probably a bit biased.'

We stood there in silence for a moment, admiring the view, before Rosie turned back to the bedroom. 'It's a king-sized bed and I've got no problems sharing but we've got a blow-up mattress and spare bedding which we can squeeze into the lounge if you'd prefer that.'

It didn't bother me either way but I couldn't help thinking that having me in the lounge would be more disruptive for them both. Plus the bed looked inviting with a plain cream duvet and a teal-coloured tartan throw folded over the end, and there was that gorgeous view to wake up to each morning.

'I'm happy to share the bed if you're sure that's okay. I don't snore.'

She laughed. 'Neither do I. That's agreed then. We've got a couple of hours of light left so I'd suggest we grab your luggage, have our drinks, then I take you on a quick tour of the estate. Mam will have the tea ready by then.'

'She doesn't need a hand?'

Rosie shook her head. 'She loves cooking. The kitchen's her domain and she gets a bit agitated if I try to help so I leave her to it and usually do the clearing up.'

Half an hour later, I stood at the edge of Derwent Water, marvelling at the beauty all around me as Rosie pointed out various landmarks and Toffee splashed in the shallows, sending ripples across the calm lake.

'There are four main islands on the lake, all owned by the National Trust. The one to our left is Derwent Isle and it's the only one which still has a house on it, which they lease out. The next one is Lord's Island and, behind it, you can see Friar's Crag which is always heaving with visitors as you can get some gorgeous photos of the lake from up there. Well, you get gorgeous photos of the lake from pretty much anywhere but that's a particularly popular tourist hotspot. The island to our right – St Herbert's Island – is pretty much central in the lake and you'll love that one because it's the inspiration for "Owl Island" in Beatrix Potter's *The Tale of Squirrel Nutkin*. The fourth much smaller island between there and Lord's Island is Rampsholme Island, which is covered in wild garlic. The name literally translates as "wild garlic island". We've got stacks of the stuff on the estate too, so I hope you like the smell.'

'Can you visit the islands?' I asked.

'Derwent Isle is private, although the National Trust open the island and house to visitors on a handful of days each year. You can visit the others at any time but obviously you need a boat, canoe or paddleboard to get to any of them.'

'Could be fun.'

'Maybe one for the warmer weather,' she said, grinning at me. 'What else can I tell you? Ooh, facts! Derwent Water is the third largest lake in the national park. It's three miles long, one mile wide at the widest point and seventy-two feet at the deepest. You can walk right round it which I recommend we do while you're here. It's ten miles so it'll take a while, but it's mainly flat and it's stunning.'

She called to Toffee and we left the lake.

'The estate has seen better days,' she said, as we wandered along overgrown pathways. 'It's in a prime position and there's so much that could be done to make money to invest back into the upkeep, but his Lordship isn't interested. All he cares about is the horses and drinking.' She sighed heavily. 'The stables do well, but they don't generate enough income to support the rest of the estate.'

We arrived at Willowdale Hall. Seeing it close up and from a different angle to when I'd arrived, I could see how impressive it was, but I could also see that a lot of work was needed to bring it back up to scratch.

'We're fortunate that the building is sound. The roof's good and there aren't any damp issues – or no obvious ones – but it needs some preventative maintenance and his Lordship won't do it.' She shook her head. 'I need to stop calling him that. There aren't any titles in the family and, if there had been, they'd have been on his late wife Kathryn's side. It's Mam's fault. He stomps round the place barking orders like he's landed gentry and we're servants he can boss about so she started calling him "his Lordship" and it stuck. There'll be a day when I'm not concentrating and I'll call him it to his face.'

'He doesn't sound very nice.'

'His bark's worse than his bite. I feel sorry for him. Imagine living in there all on your own.'

'Did you say he has a son?'

'Yeah, Oliver, but we never see him. Oliver and Hubert – his Lordship – never got on. Kathryn was the peacekeeper and, after she died, they were at each other's throats constantly. Oliver finished college, left home to train as a doctor and never returned, although that's not necessarily a bad thing as I don't have much time for Oliver Cranleigh. Remember I wrote to you once about the school bullies? He was in their gang.'

'Then I don't have time for him either,' I said. 'Sounds like an idiot.'

'He was. Anyway, Hubert has been really good to Mam and me. After the accident, she couldn't work for ages and I was still at school so I couldn't completely take over but he let us stay in Horseshoe Cottage and promised me I could step up as the stables manager when I left school. He kept his word and we've had jobs and a home ever since when he could easily have kicked us out.'

'That's good of him.' I looked up at Willowdale Hall. 'It's a really beautiful house.'

'It is. Can you imagine Beatrix Potter being here on her holidays? I'd love to show you the bedroom she stayed in, but I don't think there's much chance of that, even if I catch his Lordship in fine fettle. He's really reclusive and nobody gets invited into the house these days. It's a shame.'

I'd have loved to see inside and particularly see where Beatrix Potter had stayed, but there was no point in Rosie ruffling any feathers with her boss.

We continued our walk with Toffee while Rosie told me more about the history of the estate and the Cranleigh family. Certain bits sounded familiar from her earlier letters, but it was still all fascinating. I'd have been impressed with the place anyway but to know that I was walking where my heroine had walked filled me with awe. How could I fail to find inspiration in the same place as Beatrix Potter?

12

Someone calling, 'Knock, knock!' stirred me from my slumber and I looked around the unfamiliar bedroom, momentarily disorientated.

'Are you awake?' Alice called.

I shuffled into a seated position and spotted her hovering near the top of the stairs. 'Yes, sorry. Come up.'

'I've brought you breakfast in bed,' she said, placing a laden tray on the blanket box at the end of the bed. 'Thought I'd treat you on your first morning.'

'That's so kind of you. Thank you. What time is it?'

'Quarter to ten.'

'Woah! I'm normally awake way before now.'

She smiled. 'It's not a problem. That long journey yesterday probably wore you out.' She tugged at the cuffs of her cardigan. 'I'm assuming Rosie told you she has lessons most of the weekend but she has Sunday afternoons and Mondays off.'

'Yes, she did. I thought I'd take a walk into the village. I drove past a lovely café yesterday so I might grab lunch there. You'd be welcome to join me.'

Her expression darkened and she tugged more vigorously on her cuffs. 'Erm, no, I'm good here, but thank you. I'll leave you to your breakfast. Shout if you need anything else.'

She scuttled down the stairs and I leaned back against the headboard, cursing myself. What an idiot! I already knew that Alice never left the estate unless she absolutely had to such as for a medical appointment, and that those rare occasions were extremely fraught. Trust me to casually invite her out to lunch as though it was no big deal. I'd have to ask Rosie later whether I should apologise or let it go and take more care in the future.

I ate my breakfast before going downstairs for a shower. Music was coming from the kitchen and Toffee bounded along the hall to bid me good morning. When I finished in the bathroom, the music had stopped and I sensed that the cottage was empty.

'Hello?' I called, creeping through to the kitchen wrapped in my towel.

There was a note on the worktop.

Walking Toffee
Enjoy exploring Willowdale
Spare key for you. A x

Leaving the key where it was, I was about to go upstairs when I spotted my breakfast tray – recognisable from the cute cartoon illustration of a horse and foal – on top of the microwave and tutted to myself. I'd considered taking it down when I went for a shower but had wanted to give Alice some space in case the invitation to lunch had caused her discomfort. How bad did I feel that she'd cleared up after me? I'd have to make sure I kept on top of things like that as the last thing I wanted was for my stay here to create any extra work for anyone.

It was shortly after 11 a.m. when I locked the door to Horseshoe Cottage and set off into the village. I usually took my sketchpad and pencils everywhere but decided to leave them behind today while I found my bearings. Without them, there was no need to bother with a bag. I placed my phone and EarPods in one pocket of my lightweight jacket and my purse in the other.

Rosie had warned me to expect frequent rain during my stay – the landscape wouldn't be so lush or the lakes so full without it – but there was good weather forecast for the next few days, so I wanted to take advantage of that and get out as much as possible.

Birds chirped and sunlight filtered through the gaps in the trees as I ambled along the estate pathways to the exit. Bluebells brightened the grassy verges, among which I spotted the early stages of crocuses and daffodils, and I breathed in the scent of wild garlic. The familiar smell transported me back to walks through Grandma's favourite park back home.

As I exited the estate, there was no pathway on either side of the road. There looked to be more sun on the left side so I crossed over to walk into Willowdale. I hadn't gone far when my phone rang with a FaceTime request from Madeline. Shoving my EarPods in, I connected the call.

'Hi, Madeline, how are you?'

She scowled. 'Still going stir crazy on gardening leave. I start at Glitter Box four weeks on Monday and it can't come soon enough. Anyway, sorry to disturb you on a Saturday, but have you got five minutes?'

'I do. What's up?'

'I have a potential job opportunity for you already. One of my new team members will be going on maternity leave in early July and she's taking two years. They're giving me full responsibility for replacing her and the obvious choice would be you, although

I will have to advertise the role. It's a more senior position and right up your street.'

'Oh, wow! I wasn't expecting anything so soon.'

'Neither was I. I appreciate you haven't seen the job description or the salary and benefits package – I'll email those to you shortly – and I know you weren't sure about a return to greetings cards when we met up for dinner, but that was hypothetical and this is real. So, do you think you might be interested?'

Moments ago, I'd felt relaxed, but now I felt tense.

'I'm sorry. I'd love to work with you again, but I don't think I can. I'd only be letting you down.'

She frowned at me. 'What makes you say that?'

'I haven't moved forward. We're not just talking a lack of sparkle in my drawings – we're talking complete inability to do anything other than sketch what's right in front of me.' My voice cracked as the enormity of being unable to create hit me.

'I thought you'd done loads of drawing in Paris.'

'I had, but none of it was from my imagination.'

'Aw, Autumn. I'm so sorry you're still struggling. That must be tough.'

'It's a nightmare,' I admitted. 'I'm scared it's never going to return.'

'Please don't get upset,' Madeline said, shaking her head. 'It'll come back, but you can't force it. You're obviously drained right now and is it any wonder after the tough start to the year you've had? Why don't you go on holiday – take some time to relax and recharge your batteries? I'm sure your creativity will return when you've had some me-time.'

'I'm actually on holiday now. My penpal Rosie invited me to visit her in the Lake District. I got here yesterday and I'm hoping the change of scenery and walking in the footsteps of Beatrix Potter will help me draw again.'

'It will. And do you know how I know that? Because drawing is part of who you are. Creativity runs through your veins. When the time is right, it'll come back.'

I wiped the tears that had escaped and sniffed. 'I hope so. I feel so lost without it.'

She gave me a weak smile. 'I'll email you the details about the job so you can mull it over. I can't advertise the post until I start at Glitter Box so you've got about seven weeks from now till I start shortlisting candidates. I'm sure your sparkle will be back by then. Will you be okay in the meantime?'

'I think so. Thanks for thinking of me for the job. I really appreciate that.'

She smiled widely. 'Purely selfish motives. You're the best so I want you on my team. No brainer. As I said to you before, I believe in you and you just need to believe in yourself. Take care, Autumn.'

'I will. Thank you.'

I disconnected the call and removed my EarPods. I felt strangely drained from that short conversation and needed a moment to sit down and gather myself. The marina was opposite me and there'd surely be a bench or wall to sit on there.

'Watch out!' a man cried as I stepped out to cross the road.

He swerved round me on his bike but didn't quite make it. I squealed as the handlebar clipped my right arm, knocking my phone flying from my hand.

The cyclist skidded to a halt. 'Are you okay?'

'My arm!' I held it with my left hand, wincing at the pain.

'Just a sec.' He cycled across the road and propped his bike up against the slate wall at the marina entrance then ran back to me.

'You'd better get off the road first,' he suggested.

I took a step forward but my legs felt like jelly.

'I've got you,' he said, putting his arm round my waist and guiding me to safety.

'Is that my phone?' I whimpered, looking down.

He picked it up off the road and grimaced. 'I think you're going to need a new screen.'

The screen protector had held everything in place but the screen was completely shattered. I doubted there'd be anywhere I could get it repaired in Willowdale but hopefully Keswick was a big enough town to have a phone doctor.

We made it to the other side of the road and, in the absence of any benches, I slumped against the wall beside his bike.

'I'm a first-aider,' the man said. 'Do you mind if I take a look?'

He gently moved my arm and asked questions about where the pain was.

'I'm pretty certain it's just bruised, but I'd recommend a trip to A&E to be sure.'

I sighed. 'Where's the nearest one, please?'

'Keswick.'

'Okay. I'll get an Uber.'

'Not round here you won't. There aren't any Ubers in the Lakes. I can call you a taxi or I can give you a lift.'

I wasn't about to jump into a car with a stranger. 'A taxi's fine. Do you know the number for one?'

'I don't, but I can look one up.'

I tried to get the keypad up on my phone but it remained in darkness. Completely dead.

'Or I can phone one for you,' he said, nodding towards my screen. 'It's no problem driving you, though. It was my bike that damaged you and I'm feeling pretty guilty about it.'

'It's fine, and please don't feel guilty. I stepped out without looking. If you could call me a taxi, I'd appreciate it.'

'What's your name?' he asked, scrolling through his phone.

I looked at him suspiciously.

'For the taxi,' he clarified and I felt stupid that I'd thought he wanted it to put me in his contacts.

'Autumn. Autumn Laine.'

'Cool name.' He unclipped his cycle helmet and shook out shoulder-length light brown hair. At a guess, he was mid-thirties, like me, or possibly a little older. He had what my grandma would have described as a 'kind face' – a wide smile, laughter lines, and sparkly eyes.

'It's ringing,' he said as he held the phone to his ear.

As he enquired about availability, I zoned out and prayed he was right that my throbbing arm wasn't broken because there was no way I'd be getting my mojo back any time soon if it was. Why did it have to be my right arm? Drawing with a plaster cast on would be pretty much impossible.

'Nothing for an hour,' he said, hanging up. 'I'll try another one.'

I watched him pacing up and down as he waited for the next call to connect. He was about six foot tall with broad shoulders. He was wearing petrol-blue cycling shorts – the baggier style with zips on them rather than tight Lycra – and a tight long-sleeved breathable T-shirt which clung to impressive biceps. The spatters of mud on his calves, clothes and bike suggested he'd been on a trail rather than the road. There were probably loads of challenging trails round here and the mere thought of even the simplest one terrified me. I'd never been mountain biking and hadn't been on a regular bike since I was about twelve.

Three calls later and the taxi options were exhausted.

'Please let me drive you,' he said. 'I promise I'm not some random serial killer about to chop you into little pieces and feed you to the ducks.'

I must have looked shocked because he laughed. 'Apologies

for too much detail. *Not* talking from experience. Big fan of crime books. Do you think you can walk?'

'To the hospital?'

'Just a short way into the village so I can dump my bike and get my car.'

I didn't feel like I had much choice. I was in pain and I couldn't risk not getting my arm checked out in case there was a break. There were no taxis, I couldn't drive myself, Rosie was working, and Alice wasn't an option.

'Okay. Thank you. You'd better tell me your name.'

'That might help. It's Dane "The Widow-Maker" Featherstone.'

I couldn't help smiling at the serial killer name.

'So, Dane, how far's your house?'

'Do you know the village?'

'No. I just arrived yesterday. I'm staying with a friend at Willowdale Hall. I was on my way to look around until...' I pointed to my arm.

There was a path on our side of the road now so we set off walking with Dane pushing his bike along the road to avoid bumping it into me.

'I'm staying with relatives at the moment,' he said. 'Did you see The White Willow when you arrived – the café in the village centre?'

'I did. I was planning to grab some lunch there after I'd looked around.'

'It's cracking scran. My aunt and uncle own it and they live a few houses before it so that's where we're heading.'

I'd never heard of 'scran' before but guessed that, given the context, it had to mean food.

'The café's open till four so you might manage to grab something afterwards if there's not too much of a wait at the hospital.'

'Do you think there will be?'

'Hard to say. We're not at the height of tourist season, but it's a Saturday so who knows?'

We walked in silence for a while as I cradled my arm.

'So how long are you staying here?' he asked.

'A couple of weeks. Maybe more.' I hoped he wouldn't ask further questions as I didn't really want to get into my complicated situation with a stranger – even a friendly and helpful one like Dane.

'Ever been here before?'

'No.'

'Then you're in for a treat, assuming you like the great outdoors.'

I hadn't really spent much time in 'the great outdoors' but Dane was clearly an outdoorsy type and I didn't want him to judge me, so I didn't respond. I could see The White Willow ahead so we couldn't be far from his aunt and uncle's place.

'This is me.' Dane stopped opposite an attractive whitewashed house, set back from the road with a gently sloping drive and garden. A slate plaque at the end of the drive gave the name 'Lake View' and I could imagine there was a fantastic view from the house's elevated position.

I followed him over the road and up the drive and, even though he invited me inside, I took one glance at the superb view across Derwent Water and said I'd wait on the wooden bench beneath the kitchen window.

There were a few sailing boats and some canoes or kayaks – I had no idea of the difference between the two – on the water. I'd never done anything like that either. If my arm wasn't broken, should I try to be courageous and adventurous by giving sailing or kayaking a go as well as horse riding? Even though Rosie had said I might want to wait for the warmer weather, I loved the idea of going across to one of the islands, especially the one she'd said was the inspiration for *The Tale of Squirrel Nutkin*. I could vividly picture Beatrix Potter's illustrations using the island.

'All set,' Dane declared, reappearing in jeans and a fresh T-shirt. 'It'll take less than ten minutes to drive to the hospital and there's usually a taxi or two waiting outside so you should be fine for getting back.'

'Thank you.'

'It's no bother.'

I was a little apprehensive about the car journey, worried that there'd either be an awkward silence or he'd bombard me with questions. Thankfully, it was neither. He gave me a running commentary on everything we passed – the difference between the two pubs, some of the activities in the village hall, the starting point for a couple of walks – and, before I knew it, we'd reached the hospital.

'Thanks for not chopping me up and feeding me to the ducks,' I said as I exited the car.

'You're lucky it's a Saturday,' he said, smiling at me. 'They get more than enough food from the tourists on a weekend. Had it been a Wednesday, you might not have been so fortunate.'

'I'll stay indoors on Wednesday, then,' I said, smiling back at him.

'A quick tip for you – if there's no path, try to walk facing the oncoming traffic so you can see what's coming.' He said it gently, not sounding like he was lecturing me. I'd never heard that, although I'd never been walking in the countryside before. It made a lot of sense.

A car pulled up behind us.

'That's my cue to move on,' he said. 'Hope your arm isn't broken and you're able to enjoy the rest of your holiday sling-free.'

With a wave, he pulled away and the car behind moved into his position. I looked for the signs for the accident and emergency department and, with a sigh, went inside to discover my fate.

* * *

Not broken – just badly bruised. I felt weak with relief as I left A&E sometime later. I had no idea how long I'd been there, so I reached into my jacket pocket for my phone to check the time and my stomach sank. It wasn't there and I knew exactly where it was – on Dane's dashboard. No chance of going into the town to get it repaired, then.

There was a taxi waiting outside the hospital, as Dane had predicted, so I asked the driver to take me back to Willowdale Hall, with a stop-off at Lake View on the way through Willowdale.

The driver slowed down as we passed The White Willow, ready to make a stop at the house, but there was no sign of Dane's car on the drive, so I asked the driver to keep going to Willowdale Hall. I'd have to collect my phone tomorrow. According to the taxi's dashboard clock, it was after 5 p.m. so the shops would be shut or closing soon – it wasn't like I could do anything to fix the phone now even if Dane had been home.

Rosie was walking towards Horseshoe Cottage from the direction of the stables with Toffee zig-zagging across the lane in front of her. She called Toffee to her side and waved as the taxi passed.

'Been anywhere exciting?' she asked, joining me after I'd settled the fare and the taxi pulled away.

'Hospital.' I held out my arm to show her the dark bruises.

'Ouch! What happened?'

'My fault. I crossed the road without looking and got hit by a cyclist. He suggested I get my arm checked in case it was broken.

It isn't, but my phone is because I dropped it so I need to get that fixed.'

'There's a phone doctor in Keswick but it'll be closed now. We can drop it off on Monday.'

'I need to get it back first. The cyclist, Dane, drove me to the hospital because there were no taxis free and I stupidly left it in his car.'

'Oh, no! Will you be able to get it back?'

'I know where he's staying, so I'll go back into the village tomorrow.'

Rosie gave me a sympathetic look and even Toffee looked up at me with big sad eyes. 'Sounds like you've had a shocker of a first full day here.'

'It's not been the best. And I haven't had any lunch, so I'm famished.'

'We can soon sort that out. Come on. Mam was baking cheese scones earlier. I'm sure she won't mind you having one before tea.'

I could smell them as soon as we entered the kitchen and my stomach growled in desperation.

'Mam?' Rosie called as Toffee lapped up water from her bowl. 'We're back.'

Alice appeared in the kitchen doorway and smiled at me. 'Have you enjoyed your—' Her eyes widened and her hands fluttered to her neck. 'Oh, my goodness! Your arm!'

'Oh, it's fine. It's just bruised.'

'She wasn't looking where she was going and walked into a lamppost,' Rosie said. 'But she needed to go to hospital to get it checked out and she missed lunch. Would you mind if she has a scone?'

'Of course not. As long as you're okay, Autumn. That looks nasty.'

'My fault for being too distracted by my phone, which I managed to drop and break.'

'Oh! Phone!' She grabbed a paper bag off the windowsill and handed it to me. 'A very nice man called round and asked me to give you this. He said it's all fixed now.'

I peeked into the bag and gasped. My phone was in there with a brand-new screen on it.

'Did he say anything else?' Rosie asked, looking over my shoulder into the bag.

'No – just that he'd fixed Autumn's phone. Anyway, help yourselves to scones. I'll time tea for eight so you can build up your appetite again. If you get the ones from the front cooling tray, they might still be warm. It's a nice evening so I'm going to have a walk down to the lake before I start on tea. Are you coming, Toffee?'

Despite having just been out with Rosie, Toffee didn't need asking twice and followed Alice to the door.

'Sorry about the lie,' Rosie said watching her mam disappear down the drive. 'She's in such good fettle at the minute and I know your fight with the bike wasn't a hit and run but it was still you being hit by a vehicle and it's the sort of thing that could be triggering for her.'

'Aw, bless her. I'd never have thought of that. And while we're on the subject, I did something stupid this morning. Your mam asked about my plans for today and I said she was welcome to join me in the village for lunch. She couldn't get away fast enough. I'm so sorry. I didn't think. Do you think I should apologise?'

Rosie grabbed a couple of plates from a cupboard and added two scones to each. 'Don't worry about it. She's obviously fine and you'll know for next time. I wouldn't mention it.'

We buttered our scones and took them through to the lounge

with mugs of tea. They were still warm and absolutely delicious. Alice, just like Grandma, had a gift in the kitchen.

'I can't believe your cyclist got your phone fixed,' Rosie said when we'd finished eating. 'That can't have been cheap.'

'Hopefully he's put an invoice in the bag.' I went through to the kitchen to retrieve it and returned to the lounge, pulling out a folded sheet of paper from underneath the phone. But it wasn't an invoice. It was a note folded round a copy of the lunch menu for The White Willow.

Hi Autumn,

Hope your arm's not broken. Realised you'd left your phone in my car so I got it fixed. I feel bad that you missed your lunch. Can I treat you one day next week to say sorry? Dane

'Nice handwriting,' Rosie said, when I passed her the note. Her eyebrows raised as she read it and she grinned at me. 'Ooh, someone's made an amazing first impression.'

'It's not a date.' I frowned. 'Is it? Do you think he's asking me on a date?'

'I don't know. Would you like it to be a date?'

'No! My head's a mess after what happened with Étienne.'

She frowned. 'But that was years ago.'

'It was, but then I saw him again last weekend and he kissed me and told me he still loves me.'

'What?' She grabbed my half-drunk mug of tea and dashed into the kitchen with it.

'What are you doing?' I asked, following her.

'I think we need something a little stronger than tea if you're going to drop bombshells like that on me. Glasses are in that cupboard.'

She took a bottle of wine out of the fridge while I lifted down a couple of wine glasses.

'Start from the beginning,' she instructed as we sat back down in the lounge with our wine. 'No edits. I need to know absolutely everything.'

I smiled appreciatively. I'd always planned to tell her but I hadn't wanted it to be the first thing I blurted out when I arrived. It was good that it was coming out sooner rather than later because keeping it inside was killing me.

13

Although I woke up on Sunday morning with a thumping head from a combination of too much wine and the pain in my arm, I felt so much lighter for telling Rosie what had happened with Étienne. She'd shown empathy and understanding which wasn't surprising as she'd written encouraging words during the unrequited love phase in my teens, excited ones when we got together, and comforting words when it all fell apart and he broke my heart.

I was honest with her about how much I'd enjoyed the kiss and how tempted I'd been to take things further, so why couldn't I be honest with her about *everything* that had happened when I was twenty-one? She was my best friend and she knew all there was to know about me – except that one thing – and I couldn't understand why I kept holding it back. Was it because I still hadn't come to terms with it myself? Was that why I'd been so anxious to keep my relationship with Étienne hidden from my parents?

She was incensed on my behalf that Étienne could even think that I'd forgive him and thought he was manipulative to go down the *it's always been you* route after all these years. If he'd been so in love with me, why had he chosen Chantal? And why had he stayed for so long when it wasn't working? He could have left at any time, but he hadn't until she'd gone back to her childhood sweetheart and told him to leave.

Rosie had riding lessons all morning while Alice prepared a Sunday roast. She refused my offer of help, so I wandered down to the stables to watch Rosie in action. I knew nothing about the equestrian world but even I could tell that a lot of money had been invested there while the rest of the estate went neglected. There was the capacity to stable twenty animals which Rosie had told me were a mixture of estate-owned and privately-owned horses and ponies. The focus was on teaching children and adults how to ride or to improve their riding skills and they did that in a large outdoor manège, a smaller indoor manège, or a grassy paddock, only progressing onto the paths and bridleways outside the estate when a certain level of competence had been reached.

I wasn't sure why I was so scared of horses. I'd never spent any time around them, but maybe that was the issue itself. To me, they seemed so big and intimidating and I couldn't imagine being able to mount one, never mind stay in the saddle when it started moving. Seeing Rosie and the class of young children tenderly stroking the ponies made me question my fears, until I reminded myself that ponies were smaller than horses and that there were some frighteningly enormous horses in the stables.

It was great watching her work. Her enthusiasm for riding and teaching shone brightly. So many people stumbled through life never finding a career that ignited their passion and we'd both been so fortunate to have found ours at an early age. I just hoped the passion for mine returned.

After a delicious Sunday roast, Rosie suggested we take Toffee for a long walk in the opposite direction to the village. The public footpath took us between Derwent Water and Cat Bells.

'It looks like quite a climb,' I said to Rosie, looking up at Cat Bells. 'Which peak is it?'

'The one on the left is Cat Bells and the one on the right is Skelgill Bank. It's quite a modest height for the national park – only 451 metres – but it's one of the most popular fells around here because the views are to die for.'

'It's not a mountain, then?'

She smiled. 'It *is* a mountain but Cumbrians use the term "fell" instead. It comes from Old Norse where a fell or fjall means mountain. If you're up for it, we can do the walk one day.'

'I think I'll need to build up to that. I'm used to walking for miles around Paris, but I've never conquered a mountain. I haven't got the kit either, although I do need a waterproof and I was thinking some walking boots might be a good idea as I don't think these are going to last.' I looked down at my trainers compared to Rosie's sturdy walking boots.

'There are loads of outdoor shops in Keswick so we can soon get you kitted out.'

We continued our walk.

'Any more texts from Dane?' Rosie asked.

'No. Just the one I showed you last night, so he's got the message, which was refreshing.'

I'd wanted to thank Dane for getting my phone fixed, but I still wasn't sure if he was being friendly or asking me on a date, so I decided that the easiest way was to ignore the lunch invite and focus only on the phone. It had taken me ages to compose an appropriate message.

TO DANE

My arm is bruised rather than broken – phew! Thanks for getting my phone fixed. That was so kind of you. How much do I owe you?

FROM DANE

Good news about your arm. No payment necessary. A mate of mine did it and he owed me a favour. Hope you enjoy the rest of your holiday. Don't forget to face the oncoming traffic in future

'Any regrets turning him down?' Rosie asked, a playful tone to her voice. 'Because you say *refreshing*, but I hear *disappointing*.'

'I'm not disappointed!' I insisted.

'Tell that to your face.'

'Why would I be disappointed? I barely know him.'

'But I think you liked him, didn't you?'

I did, and it was so unlike me. I was usually wary around strangers and had initially felt that way with Dane, but something had shifted when he'd removed his cycling helmet and I could properly see his twinkling eyes and warm smile.

'Maybe,' I conceded. 'Just as friends, though.'

'So why don't you text him back and take him up on the offer?'

'I can't do that now.'

'Why not? It's not like you actually said no to lunch – you just avoided mentioning it.'

Toffee dropped a stick by my feet and I tossed it for her to chase. Did I want to see Dane again? Surprisingly, my gut said yes and I wasn't sure why. I knew very little about him, but I liked that he'd made me feel safe and that he'd made me laugh despite being in pain. What if he wasn't just being friendly? What if it was a date?

'I'll leave it. I need some time and space to get Étienne out of my head and focus on drawing again. I don't need the added complication of a lunch date, not knowing whether there's more to it than food.'

'I wish I knew him so I could give you some background, but I've never come across him. I don't even know his aunt and uncle as they're fairly new to the village. The White Willow only opened at the start of last summer.'

She picked up Toffee's stick and threw it.

'You're probably right not to get in touch. If he's meant to be in your life, you'll come across each other again, probably when you least expect it.'

'And if we don't?'

'Then he's not meant to be in your life and he was just one of those random everyday encounters we have that don't mean anything.'

I pondered on that for a moment. 'You really think certain people are meant to be in your life?'

'Of course! I think they appear when you need them and we're the living proof of that. When Miss Saxon got all those letters from your class, she didn't read any of them or try to find good matches. She simply shuffled them up and randomly handed them out. Yours could have been given to any one of my classmates but it was given to me and I couldn't have asked for a better friend. I was lonely and you were too and you've been there for me for twenty-four years through some horrendous times and I honestly don't think I'd have made it through them without you. You were meant to be in my life and I was meant to be in yours, giving you a safe place to find yourself when you most needed it.'

Rosie sounded all choked up with emotion and I felt it too. Her letters and friendship had meant the world to me too.

'When you put it like that, I think your theory could be right. I don't know what I'd have done without your friendship.'

'You'll never have to find out,' she said as we hugged each other tightly.

14

Rosie and I went into Keswick with Toffee on Monday morning and I splurged on some hiking boots, several pairs of thick socks and a waterproof coat. After a pub lunch, I changed into my new walking kit and we set off along the east side of Derwent Water to give my boots a try.

What a gorgeous walk it was. The first stretch was right beside the lake and we visited Friar's Crag – the popular viewing point she'd told me about on my first evening – before continuing over boardwalks, across farmland, then back beside the lake. Toffee was in her element, especially when we paused on the pebbly beach at Calfclose Bay and Rosie tossed a stick into the lake for her.

'Half dog, half fish,' Rosie said as we watched Toffee swimming. 'She loves the water.'

There were a couple of large boulders protruding from the lake with squiggly carvings on the flat sides which faced each other.

'I like those stones,' I said.

'Me too. More fun facts for you. I know it looks like two stones but it's called the Centenary Stone – singular – because it's made from one glacial boulder from Borrowdale, which is beyond the southern end of the lake.' She pointed in the rough direction. 'It was put here in 1995 to celebrate a hundred years since the National Trust was founded, and if you ever hear anyone talking about the Millennium Stones, this is what they mean, except they're wrong about the name and the purpose.'

She paused to toss Toffee's stick again.

'Their appearance changes across the seasons,' she continued. 'When we've had lots of rainfall and the water's high, they're submerged. You might just see a tip but often it's nothing at all. When it's drier and the lake's lower, they're on the beach and you can walk round them. There are some stunning photos online so remind me to look when we get back home. Try crouching down and looking through them at the lake and fells.'

I did as she suggested and the change of perspective really did make a big difference. 'It's a stunning view.'

'In my opinion, seeing the stone as it is now with some water round the two parts is seeing it at its best. There's an almost magical quality about it. This might sound daft, but I can imagine fairies sitting on the top.'

The moment she said that, so could I, and it sent a thrill through me. For the first time this year, my fingers twitched to draw.

'Do you mind if I draw the stone with fairies on it?'

Rosie grinned at me. 'I'd love you to. Toffee says we're in no rush to get back and you can create for as long as you like while she continues her swim.'

There were some more boulders near the path but they weren't close enough to the stone for me to capture the detail. The pebbles looked dry, so I sat down cross-legged, dug the small sketchpad out of my backpack, and started sketching.

About half an hour later, Toffee flopped on the beach, panting, swimming over for today.

'I can't believe how quickly you can draw,' Rosie said, plonking down on the pebbles beside me and peering at my sketches. 'These are brilliant.'

'I haven't felt that urge in a long time and it's been even longer since I drew something straight from my imagination. That felt so good.'

She lightly nudged me. 'See! I told you you'd be inspired here.'

I looked across the lake and fells. 'I think this place is going to be good for me. I'm so glad you invited me.'

'I'm so glad you came. It's great to have someone to talk to. It can get lonely when it's just Toffee and me.'

We really were kindred spirits, neither of us willing to travel far from home because we had a loved one to look out for, and neither of us having a friend who we could pour our hearts out to in person. It was no wonder we'd become so close as penpals. There'd been nobody else to turn to.

I gazed back across the lake. This was only my fourth day here and I was already dreading leaving. I didn't want to go back to Sutton to an empty house. Or an empty life. And I didn't want to leave my best friend and her family either.

15

The following morning, Rosie returned to work and I got up early, excited by my plans for the day. Feeling motivated by how I'd felt drawing the fairies on the Centenary Stone, I'd booked a ticket to visit Beatrix Potter's farmhouse, Hill Top.

Hill Top is a working farm in a village called Near Sawrey a few miles from the largest and longest lake in the national park – Lake Windermere. Rosie had suggested I drive there via the west side of the lake but return on the east after catching the small car and passenger ferry. It would extend the journey back by about twenty minutes but she said it would be worth it to take in the different views.

It took me an hour to drive from Willowdale to Hill Top. The temperature had dropped and, with rain forecast from mid-afternoon, the sky was dull and grey, but there was still plenty to see. I drove past fields, many of them dotted with sheep, high and low fells, waterfalls, a reservoir and two lakes – Thirlmere, Grasmere and Rydal Water. Rosie had shown me the route on a map last night, pointing out the bodies of water and giving me facts about each. Pretty white and slate cottages sat sympathetically within the landscape and I wondered about the people living in the more remote homes and whether they ever felt isolated.

I turned off the main road at Ambleside and soon caught my first glimpse of Windermere. I kept wanting to pull over to snap a photo or gaze around me but I'd never reach my destination if I did that. I wondered if the locals ever took it for granted and stopped noticing their surroundings.

Pulling into the car park for Hill Top a little later, I had butterflies. I'd tried not to place too much hope on the impact this visit might have on kickstarting my imagination once more, but it was ever present. I understood now why I hadn't found inspiration in Paris – definitely looking in the wrong place – but surely I could find it in the home of my heroine.

There was a building in the corner of the car park for admissions, but visitors then had to walk a little way alongside the main road through the village to get to the entrance. A few minutes later, I was in the grounds, and I could immediately see Beatrix Potter's beloved Hill Top. My heart pounded as I headed along the path towards the house.

When her fiancé and publisher, Norman Warne, passed away from leukaemia shortly after proposing to her, a broken-hearted Beatrix Potter had escaped from London, a place she'd never liked, to the Lake District – a place she'd fallen in love with during family holidays. Buying Hill Top symbolised a fresh start, giving her a place to grieve, heal, and find her happy once more. How funny that I'd also escaped to the Lakes to avoid Étienne breaking my heart all over again and to rediscover myself. Like Potter, could I find my happy too?

Beatrix Potter later married local solicitor William Heelis and made Castle Cottage in the same village her marital home, but she still spent a significant amount of time at Hill Top. It was such a precious place to her that she left express wishes in her will that it remain as she'd left it and kept untenanted. What a gift to leave behind – effectively a museum of her treasured home which had provided so much inspiration for her stories and a sanctuary for her to write and paint.

A small group of visitors were blocking the doorway, talking to one of the guides, so I sat on an empty bench opposite the house. It was double-fronted and rendered in grey pebbledash, which could have looked dull if it wasn't for the climbing plants adding a splash of colour. I could imagine them looking stunning in the summer. Paned sash windows sat in green frames and I smiled, picturing a photo from the guide book Rosie had sent me showing an elderly Beatrix Potter standing in the porch, looking so proud of her home.

The crowd of visitors cleared and the guide – a petite grey-haired woman who was maybe in her sixties – smiled in my direction.

'You're welcome to come in now, if you're ready,' she said.

She asked me to avoid flash photography and told me that there were further guides in the house who'd happily answer any questions. Then I stepped inside and my body tingled with anticipation.

I knew from the guide book that the first room was what Lakeland farmers would call the firehouse or houseplace as it was where the stove was, but Beatrix Potter had referred to it as the entrance hall.

'It's a bit dark in here,' a nearby visitor remarked to her companion.

Admittedly there was limited light coming through the one window and a lot of the furniture was dark wood, but I thought the room was cosy.

The whole house was a delight and had been beautifully maintained. I recognised many pieces of furniture and parts of the house from Potter's illustrations and loved how there were books displayed in each room showing her animals within the setting. *The Tale of Samuel Whiskers* heavily featured Hill Top but many other books used the property too and I could see why. My fingers were twitching but I couldn't whip out my sketchpad and start drawing because I couldn't sit on any of the exhibits and, if I attempted to draw while standing, I'd be in the way of other visitors. I took stacks of photos instead and would see how they inspired me later.

The dolls' house was a particular delight. Many of the items inside had come from the London-based toy store Hamleys and been gifted by Norman Warne after Beatrix shared her idea for *The Tale of Two Bad Mice*, featuring the mischievous Hunca Munca and Tom Thumb, who stole various items from inside a dolls' house. Warne had wanted her to be able to accurately draw the pieces and it warmed my heart to see part of their short-lived love story.

I still had fairies on my mind after the drawing at the Centenary Stone and envisaged some naughty fairies flitting around the dolls' house, wreaking the same sort of havoc as Hunca Munca and Tom Thumb.

I loved every single room in Hill Top and every piece of furniture but there was one room upstairs that gave me such a thrill because it was where the magic had happened. Referred to as the library by Beatrix Potter, in an extension she'd had added, there was a large bureau bookcase in one corner where she wrote her letters and her books. I'd seen a photo of it in the guide book but nothing beat seeing it in real life. There were drawers at the bottom, a cupboard at the top, and a pull-out writing table between them with slots for letters. Grandma had a writing bureau much like this at home in Sutton, but without the top cupboard. It had been her favourite piece of furniture and I used to do my school homework and write to Rosie on it. I don't know why I'd stopped.

I longed to sit down and stroke the bureau, but touching the furniture was understandably not permitted to avoid damage. I stood by it and closed my eyes as I tried to picture Beatrix Potter sitting there, hoping to channel her creativity.

'It's an impressive piece of furniture.'

I opened my eyes and whipped round at the sound of the voice and did a doubletake when I saw who it was.

'Dane!'

'Autumn!'

He looked as surprised to see me as I was to see him. I noticed he was wearing the same T-shirt as the guide outside.

'You work here?' I asked.

'I'm a volunteer on Tuesdays and Wednesdays.'

'Oh! What a lovely place to volunteer. Thanks again for sorting my phone. Are you sure I can't pay you?'

'I'm sure. How's the arm?'

I slipped off my jacket to show him. The swelling had gone but a fair bit of bruising remained, the central parts still purple but the outskirts now brown and yellow.

'It looks worse than it feels. It's tender if I touch it but that's it. The good news is I can still draw.'

'You're an artist?' he asked.

I hadn't meant for that to slip out. 'Erm, yes. I'm actually an illustrator for a greetings cards company, or I was until they restructured and I lost my job. When I stepped out in front of your bike, I was distracted because my manager had just invited me to apply for a maternity cover role in the card company she's moving to and…' I tailed off, shaking my head, '…and that was a lot of boring information I'm sure you didn't want to know.'

'Not boring at all,' he said, smiling at me. 'And you can't keep me hanging with half a story. Are you going to apply for this job?'

He looked genuinely interested so I continued. 'Probably not. It's in London, which is where I was working before, but I don't know if I want to stay there, so that's something to consider, but the big issue is that I've lost my mojo recently which is why I'm here today. I thought – hoped – that being in the home of such a gifted illustrator might reignite my passion.'

He opened his mouth to say something but a couple of women had entered the room and were clearly angling for his attention with one loudly saying, 'Ask him! Go on!'

'Excuse me,' Dane said to me, turning to the visitors with a smile. 'Good morning! What would you like to ask me?'

'The paintings,' the other woman said, indicating the four enormous canvases of landscapes dominating the walls. 'Are these Beatrix's work?'

'No,' Dane said, 'but they are by a member of her family. These four are the work of Beatrix's younger brother, Bertram, but Beatrix did paint landscapes too, as did her parents. Take a look in the hallway.'

He led them to the door and pointed along the corridor. I'd noticed smaller paintings on the wall on my way in, but hadn't paid them much attention in my eagerness to see the library.

Dane pointed out to the women which family member had painted each one, but I couldn't see them from where I was standing so would look properly when I left the room.

'As you can see, Beatrix was part of an exceptionally talented family,' Dane concluded.

I thought about my own family and how art ran through at least three generations from my grandparents to me. Even though he didn't draw very often, Papa was also a really good artist.

'Sorry about that,' Dane said, returning to the library minus the two women. 'You were saying you'd lost your mojo and hope to find inspiration here.'

Hearing him say it back to me, I was surprised I'd shared so much as I wasn't one for opening up to strangers.

'It's a long story,' I said, shrugging my shoulders.

He studied my face for a moment and I wondered whether he would take advantage of that lead-in and tell me he was happy to hear it over lunch but, if that's what he was going to say, he evidently thought better of it.

'Well, I hope you find your mojo. Take as long as you want in here and I'll be on the landing if you have any questions.'

'Thank you.'

He left the library and I gave the writing bureau another once-over, took a few photos, then went to check out the paintings in the hall.

Dane was on the landing, deep in conversation with the same two women who'd interrupted earlier. He was showing them an illustration in *The Tale of Samuel Whiskers* of the mouse pushing a rolling pin across the carpet and pointing out which details from the drawing remained the same today.

If I'd been told that Dane volunteered and asked to guess where, the last thing I'd have thought of was being a guide at Hill Top. It didn't seem to fit with the long-haired mountain biker image and yet he was so animated as he spoke and clearly very knowledgeable. Perhaps I'd been a little hasty with my decision not to have lunch because, seeing him now, Dane Featherstone seemed like somebody I *did* have something in common with after all and who I'd like to get to know, especially if I extended my stay beyond a fortnight. With Rosie working, it would be nice to have another friend in the area, particularly one who was a fan of Beatrix Potter. But how did I make that happen after I'd already ignored his lunch invitation? And, if I did somehow pluck up the courage to ask him out, how could I make it clear that it was only friendship on offer?

As I stepped outside, I wondered if I was making a fuss over nothing. He'd asked me out for lunch because he felt bad about cycling into me. There was no reason to think there were any romantic inclinations. He could be in a relationship. He might even be married, although I'd taken a surreptitious glance at his hand in the library and there'd been no wedding ring. He'd said he was temporarily staying with his aunt and uncle in Willowdale. There could be hundreds of reasons behind that but one possibility was a relationship break-up. If that was the case, I'm sure dating someone else would be the last thing on his mind right now. Although he knew I was only here on holiday and a quick fling with a tourist could be a good way of moving forward without any drama or commitment. Argh! Why did I have to overthink everything?

16

I explored the grounds of Hill Top, taking more photos on my phone of the gardens and the house from all angles. Everything looked a little dull thanks to the overcast day, but I could picture it clearly in full colour in my mind and there were some sparks of something there. I wasn't sure what yet, but I could definitely feel some ideas brewing.

I wanted to see Castle Cottage before I left – the marital home of Beatrix Potter and William Heelis – and checked for directions with the guide by the entrance.

'It's just over there,' she said, pointing over the road. 'You see the large house on the end? That's Castle Cottage so Beatrix Potter didn't have far to walk to Hill Top – something she did pretty much every day. There's a great view from the layby but, if you want a closer look, there's a lane running past the garden but do be aware it's tenanted and not open to the public.'

I thanked her and crossed over to the car-filled layby. A dry-stone wall ran along the side of a lush green field and beyond that field was the cottage. I stood for a few minutes taking in the view, snapped a few photos, then ambled into the village and along the lane for a closer look.

Castle Cottage was beautiful. Pale cream in colour and L-shaped, it had green window frames, just like Hill Top. I could imagine Beatrix standing in the large upstairs bay window in what I assumed must be the master bedroom, looking over her first Lakes property, thinking about her next project, whether that be as an author, farmer or conservationist.

Beatrix Potter had been forty-seven when she married William Heelis and their marriage had lasted thirty years until she passed away in December 1943. It had been a good marriage, but it's believed she never got over the loss of her beloved Norman Warne. Right up until her death, she still wore on her wedding finger – alongside her wedding ring from William – the plain gold engagement ring Norman had given her.

I glanced down at the silver ring on my right hand and twisted it around my finger. I hadn't appreciated until now how much we had in common beyond our art. Except her heart had been broken by unexpected tragedy whereas mine had been broken by what? A weak man who'd failed to be courageous and adventurous and deprived us both of our happiness. So why was I still wearing his ring? Why had I kept it on for all this time?

I twisted the ring as far as my knuckle. A couple more twists and a quick tug and it would be free. *Go on! You can do it!* But I couldn't. I pushed the ring back into place and dropped my hand loosely by my side. Why was I still not ready to let Étienne go? If he hadn't returned to Paris and we hadn't kissed, would I have been able to find the strength to remove it today? I'd never know because those two things *had* happened and perhaps that was why I was still clinging on. I'd pushed him away in the park and told him it was over, but was there a part of me hoping he wouldn't accept that? He hadn't fought for me back then, but was he willing to fight for me now? I ran my hands through my hair and closed my eyes, breathing in the solitude. Did I want him to? I really wasn't sure.

As I made my way back down the lane, the sky darkened. There was a breeze now and I could feel some light rain in it. I'd timed that well, having seen what I wanted to in Near Sawrey.

Driving in the rain didn't bother me, but I'd have to take it slowly, being unfamiliar with the roads. I'd originally planned to stop for something to eat but maybe I'd head back to Willowdale Hall instead and get a late lunch there.

Thinking about lunch made me think about Dane again. I'd tell Rosie about my encounter with him this evening and ask her to help me compose a text. Maybe. I could already picture her reaction to me telling her I'd seen Dane at Hill Top. She'd see it as the universe making our paths cross and that he was meant to be in my life. Was she right? I couldn't help warming to that idea. Rosie had been right yesterday – despite barely knowing him, I liked Dane. As a potential friend.

I needed to cross the road and checked left and right to make sure there was no traffic. Who should be walking down the path to my left but Dane? I crossed just ahead of him.

'We meet again!' he called, quickening his pace as I waited for him.

'Looks like we're destined to keep bumping into each other,' I said. 'Thankfully not literally today.'

He laughed at that. 'I've just finished my shift. Are you done too?'

'Yes. I've just been to look at Castle Cottage and I'm heading off before the heavy rain.' This was my chance and I could make it really casual. 'I haven't had any lunch yet. Do you know any good cafés around here?'

'Which way are you planning to drive back?'

'Rosie – my friend who I'm staying with – suggested I mix things up and go back via the ferry so I can see more, but I'm not sure if it'll be worth it in the rain.'

He pondered for a moment. 'Up to you. You'll still see plenty, even through the rain. If you take the ferry, you could stop in Hawkshead first but if you go the other way, I think Ambleside's your best bet. Plenty of cafés in both but I've not been back in the area for long so I can't recommend any.'

'Fair enough. I might try Hawkshead then.'

There was an awkward pause. The words were in my mouth – *would you like to join me?* – but I couldn't seem to force them out.

The tiny droplets in the air turned into proper rain and I shuddered as they hit my head. Why hadn't I thought to wear my lovely new waterproof instead of my lightweight jacket?

'Time to run for it,' Dane said, breaking into a gentle jog and speeding up as I ran after him.

'Where are you parked?' he asked as we entered the car park.

I pointed to my hatchback. 'The red one over there.'

'I'm in the staff section. Enjoy your lunch and see you around.' With a smile, he raced off to the other side of the car park.

'That went well,' I muttered to myself as I settled into the driver's seat, slicking my wet hair back from my face.

I could only have been caught in the rain for a couple of minutes, but I felt disgustingly soggy, so I slipped my jacket off and tossed it onto the back seat. The car had already steamed up so I turned the ignition, put the heaters on full blast and took a few gulps from my water bottle while I waited for the windows to clear.

A knock on the window beside me made me jump. Dane was bending down holding a waterproof over his head. I wound the window down.

'I haven't eaten either,' he said. 'I don't suppose you fancy some company? I can bore you senseless with Beatrix Potter trivia if you want and you can tell me whether being in her home helped reignite your passion for drawing.'

I smiled at him. 'I'd love some company. I've no idea where I'm going, so should I follow you?'

'Yeah. We'll head to the car park in Hawkshead.'

A little later, we sat in Honeybee's, a cute café in Hawkshead – a village close to the ferry. Large murals dominated either side of the café – one of bees swarming round a honey pot and another of a colourful hive.

'Have you ever drawn a mural?' Dane asked, looking admiringly at the honey pot mural closest to us after we'd placed our order.

'Never, but whoever did this is very skilled. I tend to draw in small scale with doing greetings cards.'

'What sort of cards were they?'

'I specialised in woodland animals, mainly drawing badgers, foxes, hedgehogs, rabbits, squirrels and deer. Beatrix Potter is my heroine and the biggest inspiration for my art, although I'm also a massive fan of Cicely Mary Barker. Her Flower Fairy books are so beautifully illustrated.'

'Did you know she was best friends with Beatrix Potter? Potter was about thirty years older than her but they had so much in common.'

'Were they really? I've not heard that before.'

Dane nodded enthusiastically, then laughed and shook his head. 'Sorry. Couldn't resist. I'd have loved it if they had been, but there was no evidence that their paths ever crossed. They weren't with the same publisher and Beatrix Potter was more focused on farming and conservation by the time Barker's first book was published.'

'*Flower Fairies of the Spring*,' I said. 'It would have been amazing if they had been friends. I like to think of the two of them and Enid Blyton all having afternoon tea together and congratulating themselves on being trailblazing female authors.'

Dane had ordered a baguette and I'd gone for soup. Our food and drinks arrived so the conversation paused for a moment.

'Do you mind me asking what caused you to lose your mojo?' he asked while I buttered my bread roll. 'Was it losing your job?'

My initial reaction was to gloss over it but what was the point in having lunch with Dane if I wasn't going to let him know anything about me? We'd already bumped into each other three times now and I kept hearing Rosie's voice in my head. Maybe we really were meant to meet and I'd never find out if that was the case if I pushed him away. It wasn't like I needed to mention Étienne.

'It's not the redundancy, although that hasn't helped. I'm half French and my parents live in Paris. When I was eleven, I came to the UK to study and I lived with my grandparents in Surrey during term times. My grandma died when I was twenty-one but my granddad died this January. He'd been ill for quite a while and, when he needed additional care last November, he insisted on going into a hospice. It's hard to draw cute woodland creatures when someone you love is on their end-of-life pathway.'

Between spoonfuls of soup, I told him how I'd somehow knocked something new together for the pitch at work, but had known it wasn't good enough to keep my job.

'I went to Paris after Granddad's funeral and filled a sketchpad with Parisian scenes but that was just copying what I could see around me, which isn't what I do. It doesn't excite me. In the two months I was there, I didn't draw a single animal or anything else from my imagination until yesterday. Rosie took me to the Centenary Stone and said it had a magical feel and she could imagine fairies on it. It was like the fog cleared in my mind and I could see them too so out came the sketchpad and out came the fairies.'

'That must have felt good.'

'It felt amazing and I was buzzing when I got back to her cottage so I booked my ticket for Hill Top, hoping for more inspiration.'

'Did you find it?'

'Hard to say. Obviously the whole place was inspirational and I loved being there, but as for that translating into my illustrations... I have flickers of ideas but nothing solid. I might need a couple more visits, but I'm feeling positive about it.' I mopped up the last of my soup with my bread and sat back in my chair. 'I've completely dominated the conversation. Your turn. You said you were staying with your aunt and uncle, so are you on holiday too?'

His shoulders drooped and he shook his head slowly. 'A bit like you, I'm taking some time out to decide what the hell I want to do with my life because it all fell apart pretty spectacularly last year.'

'Happy to listen if you want to talk about it,' I said, getting the distinct sense that he did.

'Okay, but I need another coffee.'

One of the staff came over to clear our table so we ordered a couple more drinks.

'All my family are Cumbrian,' Dane said when she'd gone. 'I'm from Keswick originally, but I've been working in Manchester for seventeen years running the kitchen in my in-laws' restaurant.'

So he *was* married. I felt an unexpected flicker of disappointment.

'You're a chef?' I asked.

'Yes, but by default rather than plan. I'd been with Lynsey since we were twelve and her parents never liked me. I get why. I mucked about at school and didn't have any career ambitions – not exactly the dream boyfriend for your only daughter. Anyway, she discovered she was pregnant when we were both sixteen and they were fuming. They gave us an ultimatum – give the baby up for adoption and I clear off and leave Lynsey alone or keep the baby and they'd support us as long as we got married and I trained as a chef under her dad. He had a restaurant in town.'

He twiddled with the packets of sugar in a pot on the table, the memories of that clearly still raw and uncomfortable.

'I'm convinced he thought we'd go for adoption because of our age and because he thought I was flaky, but Lynsey and I loved each other so we agreed to get married at the start of the Easter holidays when she was four months gone. I moved in and our son, Ellis, was born at the start of September. It was difficult living with her parents but, to be fair to them, they gave us space to be a family and we couldn't have done without them helping with Ellis.

'Lynsey had deferred the second year of her A levels but she went back and finished them and wanted to go to university in Manchester. She was brilliant at sciences and hoped to go into medical research. Her parents decided we should all move to Manchester, so they sold their restaurant in Keswick and bought one there. Moving to Manchester wasn't my dream, but I went along with it because I didn't know what else to do.'

He paused as our drinks arrived and I felt so sorry for him. There was a definite weariness in his voice which was hardly surprising when his life and career had been under the control of his father-in-law.

'Lynsey got her dream research job, we moved into a place of our own in Oldham and the years passed by. It wasn't easy, but we made it work and I thought we had the sort of marriage that would last. Ellis joined the police and moved in with his girlfriend Georgia last September, shortly after he turned twenty.' He paused and shook his head. 'Still can't believe I'm the father of a twenty-year-old. Sometimes don't feel much older than twenty myself! Anyway, Lynsey and I helped them unpack a few boxes then left them to their first night together. We picked up a takeaway and a bottle of wine on the way home and I thought we were going to have a celebration that we'd done our bit, raised a good kid, and now he'd started the next stage of his life.' He paused and shrugged sadly. 'But that's not what happened.'

As he took a sip of his coffee, my stomach churned, dreading to know what was coming as clearly it didn't have a happy ending if his life had been in Oldham and Manchester and he was now living with relatives in Willowdale.

'I opened up a conversation about how strange it would be not having Ellis at home and our plans for the future and Lynsey went really quiet. She put her fork down, pushed her food away and told me that she'd didn't want a future just with me. Told me she'd felt that way for a long time but had wanted to make sure our son was happy and settled before she did anything about it. She packed a bag and went to stay with her parents that night, telling me I had a week to get myself sorted and move out.'

'Wow! That's harsh.'

'I didn't see it coming. I thought she was winding me up at first but her expression was so cold. When she started talking about no-fault divorces being finalised within six months, it was clear she'd done her research and was deadly serious.'

'I'm so sorry, Dane. That must have been such a shock.'

'It was. I'd just lost my son, my wife, my house and, of course, my job.'

'Her dad sacked you?'

'Not exactly, but it was made *very* clear that it would be difficult for me to continue and, should I wish to move on to another restaurant, they'd give me a glowing reference which might not be so glowing if I chose to stay for a while longer.'

'So in other words, get lost.'

Dane nodded. 'So I took the reference and walked away, but I was a bit stuck. Ellis and Georgia offered me their spare room, but they'd just moved in together and I wasn't going to cramp their style. I'd have come home, but my parents had relocated to Scotland where they run a holiday park in Loch Lomond and it wasn't an option to move there – way too far from Ellis. Fortunately, Aunt Kelly and Uncle Aled had just moved from Ambleside to Willowdale and opened The White Willow. They said I was welcome to stay with them for as long as I wanted and they even offered me a job. They're planning to open on evenings from May half term and I'll be the chef, although they understand that I don't want to do that long term. In the meantime, I've been working a few daytime shifts for them as well as volunteering at Hill Top and with the Keswick Mountain Rescue team.'

'You do Mountain Rescue too?' I asked, impressed.

'Yeah, I did it in Oldham. We worked across the northern end of the Peak District as well as parts of Greater Manchester. I love it. Keeps me fit and helps save lives.'

It was good to see a smile back on his face.

'And mountain biking must keep you fit too,' I suggested.

'When I'm not riding into pedestrians, it does.' He shrugged and sighed. 'So that's my sorry tale and, as I said, I'm looking to be inspired but I understand how hard it is to do that when there's lots of noise around you. There was no point me trying to contest the divorce – who'd want to stay with a wife who'd just told them she'd fallen out of love with them years ago? It's all been fairly straightforward and should be finalised within the next couple of weeks, but it's been tough on Ellis. He was disgusted with his mam and I'm not sure if their relationship will ever get back on track. That's up to Lynsey to sort out. I can't change what she did or how she did it.'

'Do you think you'll stay round here longer term?' I asked.

'If I can. Even though I've lived away for a long time, I've always thought of the Lakes as my home. I feel so much more relaxed here, but I can't live with my aunt and uncle forever. I've got money from my share of the Oldham house but I'd still need a mortgage to buy somewhere here – even somewhere small – and I can't secure or pay a mortgage unless I work a lot more hours. I could work full-time at The White Willow but I know I'd end up getting comfortable and staying in a job I'm not passionate about just because it's the easy option, when I really want to start over and do something different.'

'Do you have something in mind?'

There was a pause while Dane studied my face, presumably weighing up whether or not he should share.

'I can keep secrets,' I said, thinking the reassurance of confidentially might help. I was an expert at keeping secrets, having kept my own for years.

'There is something,' he said eventually, 'but I don't know if I can do it and, even if I can, the likelihood of making a living out of it is very remote.'

I leaned forward. 'I'm intrigued.'

He took another sip of his drink as colour flooded his cheeks, making me even more curious as to what his dream was.

'You don't have to tell me if you don't feel comfortable,' I said.

'No, it's okay. Nobody knows I want to do this except Ellis. Well, Lynsey does too, but she laughed and told me I was being ridiculous.' He straightened up and pushed back his shoulders. 'Here goes. You know I said I mucked about at school? I didn't leave with many GCSEs but there was one subject I loved – English. I had this teacher, Miss Eccles, and she was so passionate about reading and writing that I couldn't help getting hooked. When Ellis was little, Lynsey hated reading him bedtime stories but I loved it and would happily read several each night. We raced through books so quickly that I soon got bored of repeating the same stories so I started showing Ellis the illustrations but making my own stories up. Those stories have stuck with me and I've created new ones since, but I've never written anything down. When I moved here, I sat in front of my laptop thinking it was the perfect opportunity to capture them, but I had nothing.'

'You couldn't remember them?'

'I could, but I couldn't seem to get them from my brain onto the screen. So when I saw a shout-out for volunteers at Hill Top, I thought the same as you – where was better to get the creative juices flowing than the home of one of the greatest children's authors ever?'

'I'm sorry your ex-wife laughed. I think it's amazing that you want to write children's books.'

'Wanting to write them and being able to write them are two very different things and, given what you've told me about losing your mojo, I'm guessing you can relate to that.'

'Definitely. What a pair we are! What age appeals to you?'

'Picture books, so younger end – two to five years. I can't draw for toffee so I was worried that would scupper my chances, but I did some research and it looks like publishers prefer to provide their own illustrators anyway.' He rolled his eyes. 'No idea why I'm talking about publishers when I haven't written a sentence yet.'

'But you will, just like I'll find my mojo.' I felt my optimistic streak returning as I spoke the words, and with it, an idea. 'Why don't we help each other out? What if I draw you some illustrations and you write a story about them? It doesn't have to be perfect – just scribble down or type whatever comes to mind. And, for me, you could give me a plot or some scene ideas and I'll draw some illustrations. Trying to do something different could be exactly what we need to light the spark.'

His smile widened and his eyes sparkled. I hadn't paid much attention to the colour before – I'd just noticed the sparkle – but his eyes were a striking pale blue with a dark green rim, and I was struggling to look away.

'I like that idea,' he said. 'I like it a lot.'

'It's sorted then. We'll be creative buddies.'

Dane and I sat in Honeybee's for the next hour or so. The rain pelted against the window with increasing ferocity, but we were encased in a warm and fuzzy world of creativity. Rosie had been right about there being a reason for the pair of us to meet and I couldn't wait to get started on what we'd code-named 'Mission Sparkle'.

17

Honeybee's closed at 4.30 p.m. and, by quarter past, we were the only ones left.

'I think we'd better head off,' I whispered to Dane, conscious of the staff cleaning around us.

'You'll have to come back to Hawkshead,' he said as we waited for the bill. 'If you continue down this road, you'll come to the Beatrix Potter Gallery. It's another National Trust place, full of original drawings and watercolours.'

'Ooh, I'd like that.'

'It's also in the building where her husband, William Heelis, practised as a solicitor and they've kept the layout the same so, like Hill Top, you get a glimpse into how life was back then.'

We settled our bill – or rather Dane did, insisting on paying as an apology for my injury – and made a dash through the rain to the car park, laughing as we bashed into each other while trying to avoid the huge puddles on the road.

'This afternoon has been great,' Dane said as we stopped by the cars, parked side by side. 'When do you want to exchange tasks?'

'Does Friday give you long enough?'

'Friday sounds good. The White Willow at noon?'

I nodded. 'See you then and remember not to put too much pressure on yourself for perfection. This is just the starting point and it'll get easier after that.'

There was clear relief on his face as he smiled at me.

I followed him in my car to the ferry and we'd timed it perfectly, getting the last couple of spaces. There were three lanes and we were both directed into the outer spaces – Dane to the right and me to the left – with a car between us. I'd have loved to get out but it was bucketing it down so far better to stay in the car with the heater on.

I could make out the shapes of distant fells at the northern end of Lake Windermere. Trees lined each side of the lake and there were lots of boats, some moored and some braving the elements.

The journey across the lake only took ten minutes and there was quite a queue of vehicles on the other side waiting to cross.

Dane was going to visit a cousin in Bowness-on-Windermere so had warned me he'd be turning off just before we reached Bowness Bay, where the pleasure boats docked. Reaching the outskirts, he put his hazards on to signal to me that we were approaching his turning and lifted his hand in a wave. I waved back and sighed contentedly as I continued on my journey through Bowness, making a mental note to come back and explore another day.

On the road to Ambleside, I was treated to more delicious glimpses of Lake Windermere and pulled over in a couple of laybys to drink in the view. It was still raining, although not quite as heavily now, so I didn't get out to take photos. I'd return on a dry day.

Ideas about what I could draw for Dane swirled round my

mind. He'd told me that, because he'd used the illustrations in his son's books as the inspiration for his own stories, a wide variety of subjects had been covered – animals, vehicles, mythical creatures, food – so he didn't have a speciality as such. I'd challenged him on what he felt most drawn towards and he'd thought perhaps animals but had wondered if that was influenced by his volunteering at Hill Top, surrounded by Beatrix Potter's animals a couple of days a week. The only thing he was certain about was that he wanted to set his stories in the Lake District.

By the time I arrived back at Horseshoe Cottage, I'd decided on three illustrations to inspire Dane. I'd re-draw the fairies on the Centenary Stone and maybe add a dragon to cover mythical creatures and I'd create a scene from the estate with one of Rosie's ponies and a red squirrel to cover the animals. My final illustration would be of talking vehicles, focusing on the sort found on the lakes such as the ferry, canoes and paddleboards. I'd never drawn anything like that before and I relished the fresh challenge.

I was on a high when I pushed open the kitchen door, excited to tell Rosie about my day, but I stopped dead and the smile slipped from my face. Alice was sitting at the kitchen table, wringing her hands and rocking back and forth. Toffee was sitting up on the floor beside her with her head resting in Alice's lap while Rosie poured boiling water into a mug. There was a box of camomile tea on the worktop beside her.

'Hi, Autumn,' Rosie said brightly. 'How was Hill Top?'

I hesitated and glanced at Alice who was muttering something over and over, but I couldn't quite make out what. Rosie shook her head and did a cutting motion against her neck with her hand, conveying that I shouldn't ask.

'Hill Top was amazing,' I said, slipping off my boots and

adding them to the shoe rack. 'So much to tell you about. I got a bit wet so I might just grab a shower and get changed.'

Rosie gave me a thumbs up and mouthed 'thank you'. I walked past the table, willing myself not to stare at Alice but unable to stop giving her a quick concerned glance. Her eyes caught mine and she looked confused, as though struggling to place who I was.

'Have you seen the green man?' she asked me.

'Erm, no, I don't think so.'

'Your tea's ready, Mam,' Rosie said, placing a mug on the table beside Alice.

I slipped out of the room. Green man? What was that all about?

After I'd showered and changed, I stayed in the bedroom in case Rosie or Alice preferred I remain out of the way. Rosie had told me in her letters that Alice had occasional 'episodes' but had never expanded on that and I hadn't liked to ask. Was this one of those or something different?

I propped the pillows up on my side of the bed and dug out the small sketchpad containing the Centenary Stone drawing and a new large pad to use for Dane's Mission Sparkle pictures. I'd only made a few pencil strokes when my phone pinged. I thought it might be Rosie saying I was welcome downstairs, but it was Dane.

FROM DANE

Just got back and I'm buzzing with ideas. Thanks for today, creative buddy. See you on Friday

TO DANE

Me too! Already started on Mission Sparkle. Translation: I've managed 5 pencil strokes! See you then

I'd nearly finished Dane's picture when I heard footsteps on the stairs.

'How's your mam?' I asked Rosie.

'Bad fettle today. She's settled a bit now, and gone for a lie down.' She sounded exhausted as she wandered over to the doors by the Juliet balcony and peered outside. 'I'm taking Toffee for a walk while there's a break in the rain. Do you want to come?'

I interpreted that as a request to talk with no risk of Alice overhearing so I closed my sketchpads and said I'd love to join her. I'd been so engrossed in my work that I hadn't even noticed the rain stopping.

'It's the weather,' Rosie said when we were some way along the lane, well away from Horseshoe Cottage. 'It was raining heavily on the night of the hit and run. Light showers don't seem to affect her but when we get a torrential downpour, it's like she's back there.'

'Does she have PTSD?' I asked.

'I reckon so, but she won't talk to anyone about what happened. I've found counsellors who'd come to see her here so she doesn't have to leave the estate, but she won't entertain it. Toffee's great with her. When Mam gets upset, she steps up like a support dog, putting her head on Mam's lap and cuddling up to her, which helps calm her.'

'It must be worrying for you when you're working.'

'It is. I get anxious when I see heavy rain forecast and, as soon as it starts, I'm thinking about her, but there's not much I can do if she won't accept professional help. All I can do is check in on her when I can. Sometimes she goes on a wander round the estate, but more often she stays in the cottage. She might be distressed, but she's safe. She's never harmed herself, so it could be a lot worse.'

'That's so awful. I still can't believe that anyone would hit someone with their car and drive off like that.'

'Neither can I. You'd have to know you've hit something and, even if you think it might be an animal, you'd surely check.' She sighed deeply. 'We've long accepted it'll never be resolved and, even if they got a breakthrough and they found the driver, what difference would it make? The damage is already done and we have to live with it.'

Rosie's words were cheerful enough but the glistening of tears in her eyes gave a fuller picture. I put my arms out and hugged her, stroking her back as her body shook with sobs.

'Sorry about that,' she said when she pulled away. 'I usually just get on with it.'

'You don't have to. I'm here now. You can rant as much as you want to me and I'll have lots of hugs in return.'

'I'm so glad you're here.' She hugged me again.

Toffee was waiting impatiently ahead of us. She dropped her stick and stared at us, so I threw it for her and she chased after it as we continued our walk towards the lake.

'Your mam asked if I'd seen the green man,' I prompted. 'What's that all about?'

'Yeah, that's a weird one. She sometimes mentions the green man when she has one of her episodes and I have no idea what it means. In the early days, the police wondered if it might be a clue to the person who hit her – something to do with what he was wearing, perhaps – and hypnosis was suggested, but Mam refused. I've tried asking her about it during an episode but she never explains – just asks where he is or if I've seen him. I've tried asking her outside of an episode and it's like she has no idea what I'm talking about – looks at me like I've grown an extra head. So now I accept it as one of those things that'll never be explained like who hit her and why they left her on the road instead of helping her or reporting it.'

'That's a lot to accept.'

'It is, but we have to. We've got our lives to live and we can't spend them obsessed with something that happened a couple of decades ago. Mam's happy enough here and, thanks to her still working at the riding school, it's not like she's a complete recluse, cut off from everyone except me.'

We'd reached the lake edge where a large log provided the perfect place to sit, and pulled down our waterproofs over our bottoms to keep dry.

'Do you get out and about much?' I asked. 'And I don't mean walking Toffee or on one of the horses.'

'Of course! I go to the supermarket in Keswick at least once a week.'

We looked at each other and started laughing.

'Your life sounds so much like mine was,' I said. 'Working, caring, and very little else. Do you ever feel like you're a little trapped by it all?'

'Sometimes, but I'm not sure it bothers me. I can't go anywhere for any length of time, so I've never been on holiday, but I've never had a compulsion to travel. Who would I go with? And where could I go that's more beautiful than what's on my doorstep every day? Even if I wanted to go somewhere on my own, there'd be no point because I wouldn't be able to relax for worrying about Mam and I'd be counting down the days and hours till home time. I'm aware that I don't have a social life, but I've never had one. Before the hit and run, my life was centred round the horses and this place and I didn't have any friends who I saw outside of school. What about you? Did you feel trapped looking after your granddad?'

'Spookily similar. Never really had a social life and, even if I had, I'd have chosen to be there for Granddad because I wanted to be. I miss him so much. It'll be eleven weeks tomorrow since he died. How has so long passed already?' I shook my head in disbelief. 'So definitely not trapped. I wouldn't trade my time with my grandparents for all the friends in the world. And who needs a stack of friends when you have the best friend in the world just a letter or a card away?'

'Just like I said the other day. People come into your life for a reason and we both needed each other.'

We exchanged grateful smiles.

'Speaking of people coming into your life for a reason,' I said, 'you're going to love what happened today…'

Rosie's reaction was brilliant. Her eyes lit up when I mentioned Dane being a tour guide at Hill Top and she couldn't stop grinning when I told her about him knocking on my car window and asking if he could join me for lunch. She actually squealed with excitement when I got to the part about Mission Sparkle. Toffee stopped bouncing at the lake edge and rushed over to place her soggy head on Rosie's knee, as though worried about her.

'Aw, she really is a sensitive soul,' I said, watching Rosie stroke the spaniel and reassure her that she was all right.

'She's the best of the best. Yes, you are, aren't you, Toffee? Good girl. You go and play again.'

Evidently satisfied that Rosie was fine, Toffee returned to the water.

'I'm so chuffed for you both,' Rosie said. 'Sounds like you're going to be really good for each other and I'm glad you've found a friend so you won't be on your own the whole time I'm working.'

'Like you, I'm used to being on my own, but it'll be nice to have company for some of the time, especially if the creative buddies thing works.'

'And do you feel more comfortable now knowing he's going through a divorce and presumably only interested in friendship?'

'I do, although I feel really big-headed for imagining he might want more. As if he'd have been attracted to me!'

She widened her eyes. 'What? Why wouldn't he be? You're beautiful and you're a lovely person. Any man would be lucky to have you.'

'That's very kind.'

'It's very true!'

We sat for a few moments watching Toffee.

'You never talked about boyfriends in any of your letters,' I said. 'I remember a lad from school who you kissed at the leaving disco, but I don't remember you mentioning anyone after that.'

'Urgh! Liam McIntyre.' She gave a little shudder. 'I had a dream where we kissed and that kicked off a ridiculous crush on him. We had nothing in common and he wasn't even particularly good looking, but I was smitten. He kissed me after the school leaving disco and asked if he could meet me in the village a couple of nights later. I said yes and the stupid lad stood me up.'

'No! What a git!'

'I wasn't really bothered. The kiss hadn't been anything like the amazing one we'd shared in my dream. It was all slobbery, he had bad breath, and I'm fairly convinced it was for a dare. Since then, there've been a couple of moments with men who've had riding lessons but they were so insignificant and short-lived that they weren't worth immortalising in a letter. I've never been in love, although there was one man I could have seriously fallen for if the universe hadn't had other ideas.'

'Ooh, tell me more!'

The temperature had dropped so Rosie suggested we head back to the cottage and she'd tell me on the way.

'As you can tell, most of the estate has been left to grow wild but, each spring, his Lordship hires a gardening company to do a bit of tidying up and it's usually different gardeners each year.

Five years back, there was one called Tiago who came to the stables after his shift finished. He said he used to ride when he was younger, back in Portugal, but he'd had a bad fall and hadn't ridden since. He missed riding and wondered if there was anything I could do to help him overcome his fears of getting back in the saddle. I like a challenge, so I accepted and we grew closer.'

She grinned at me, making it clear what she meant by 'closer'.

'When the team finished their work here, Tiago didn't want to leave the horses or me, so he secured a longer-term contract landscaping a couple of gardens in the village. He was lovely and we had such a good time together, but it wasn't to be.'

Her voice was full of warmth and, even though she said she could have fallen for him, I couldn't help thinking she had.

'What happened?' I asked.

'The contract came to an end and there was no more gardening work. He still didn't want to leave and, even though gardening was what he loved, he took a bar job at the Lakeside Inn so he could stay here.'

'Just for you? That's so sweet.'

'I thought so. That was the point when I could feel myself really falling for him. And then he got a phone call from home and that was that. His sister had been in a moped accident and was fighting for her life. He said he'd call me and he did, but it was to say that things were really bad. His parents were distraught and he'd had to take on the running of the family business – a small hotel – and he couldn't imagine ever being able to return to the UK so, much as he didn't want to, it was only fair to both of us to say goodbye.'

'Aw, Rosie. That must have hurt.'

'There were tears on both sides, but what could he do? We had four amazing months together and I'll always be grateful for that. We helped each other. I was going through a low patch – my downer about hitting thirty – but he helped me get some perspective and see how fortunate I was to have a job I loved and to live where I did, and I helped him ride again. See! People come into your life for a reason, but sometimes they can't stick around, no matter how much they want to.'

'I remember you going through the low patch, but why didn't you tell me about Tiago?'

She sighed heavily. 'I wanted to but, at the time, I couldn't quite believe it was happening. I kept thinking I'd wake up and today would be the day he changed his mind about being with me because I'm not the sort of person things like this happen to. Men aren't drawn to me. They don't go out of their way to get jobs they don't want just so they can be near me. What if I wrote to you and you wrote back all excited but it had ended in the meantime? So I told myself that, if we survived the summer, I'd pour it all out. Only we didn't survive the summer.'

'I'm so sorry. He sounds like a great guy.'

'He was. I sometimes think about him, wonder what happened to his sister, whether he's still running the family hotel, whether he's settled down and married now. I wonder if he thinks about me. But it's not so often these days. Do you know that Katy Perry song, "The One That Got Away"? Tiago was my one that got away. I used to drive Mam mad playing it on a constant loop after he left.'

I smiled at her. 'That song makes me think of Étienne too. He's my one that got away.'

'Ah, but he's the one who wants you back.'

'He's the one who isn't having me back.' Even though I spoke the words with conviction, I imagined that kiss and my heart skipped. My fingers closed over my promise ring as I pictured his face. Would I ever be able to completely let go of that man?

18

It was raining again on Wednesday morning – slow and steady. I went downstairs to get some breakfast and Alice was in the kitchen, singing along to some music playing through the smart speaker.

'Morning!' she said, looking and sounding so much brighter than yesterday. 'Did you sleep well?'

'Great, thanks. You?'

'Like a log. Kettle's just boiled if you want to make yourself a coffee, but there's tea in the pot on the table.'

'Coffee for me.'

Alice sat at the table and tucked into a bowl of muesli and fruit while I made my drink and popped a couple of slices of bread into the toaster. She asked me if I'd enjoyed my visit to Hill Top so, as we ate, we chatted about what I'd seen.

'I probably shouldn't admit this,' she said, 'but I've never actually read any Beatrix Potter books. That's bad, isn't it, when she has a connection to this place? I love looking at the illustrations but I get so captivated by them that I never bother with the words.'

'I used to only look at the illustrations too, but I soon got hooked by the stories. Do you have a favourite character?'

'I'm going to be predictable and say Peter Rabbit. There are loads of rabbits on the estate and I can watch them for hours. There's something about rabbits in the wild that fills me with a sense of peace and happiness. I've got a soft toy Peter Rabbit in my bedroom, which Rosie gave me for Christmas years ago.'

She'd finished her breakfast so she loaded the dishwasher and asked me if I'd set it away when I finished eating.

'Almost forgot!' she said. 'A letter arrived for you yesterday from Paris. Where did I put it?'

'It'll be from Maman,' I said as Alice rummaged through some papers on the windowsill. 'She said she'd write.'

'Ah! There it is! Happy reading.'

She passed a cream envelope to me and wandered into the lounge. I glanced down at the envelope in my hand and my stomach lurched. That wasn't Maman's handwriting, or Papa's. It was Étienne's. He must have found out from my parents that I was staying with Rosie and had remembered the name of the estate.

My initial instinct was to toss the letter in the recycling crate, unopened, but I knew curiosity would get the better of me. Deep down, there was a flicker of hope that he'd learned from what happened between us and this was him fighting for me. Whether I wanted him to win that fight was an entirely different matter. With a sigh, I opened the envelope.

Reading the extremely personal salutation, my hackles rose. *À l'amour de ma vie.* To my one true love. He'd written the letter in French and butterflies flitted about my stomach as I scanned down the page.

I'd just reached the bottom when the kitchen door opened and Rosie entered. 'I've had a cancellation so I thought I'd check on Mam,' she said.

'She's on good form this morning – or should I say she's in fine fettle.'

Rosie laughed. 'We'll make a Cumbrian of you yet. What have you got there?'

I curled my lip up. 'A letter from Étienne.'

'No way! What does he say?'

'I'd let you read it but it's in French so do you want the translation?'

Rosie slid into the chair opposite me as I read out the letter in English in an overly dramatic tone, exaggerating his pleas. I didn't know what to make of it so it was either take the mickey, or break down in tears. I'd already shed way too many tears over that man.

To my one true love

As I sit down to write this letter, I realise that the last time I wrote a letter by hand, it was to you 14 years ago. I gave you my heart back then and you still have it.

I know how badly I hurt you and let you down, so I understand why you are still angry with me. It breaks my heart that I hurt you so much when that was the last thing I ever wanted to do.

I tried so hard to make our marriage work but Chantal knew that my heart really belonged to you. She said we'd proved her right that men and women could never just be friends and she refused to believe that we only got together after she and I split up. She threw my 'affair' at me every time we had a bad patch – which was often!

I regret not being with you but I cannot fully regret my marriage because of my beautiful girls, Elania and Delphine.

Chantal and I agreed on one thing – to do our best to raise our girls together. We pretended we were in a happy marriage for them, but we lived separate lives, barely speaking if the girls were not around.

At Christmas, we accepted that it was impossible to keep up the pretence any longer, especially as Chantal was with someone else – her childhood boyfriend – and had admitted he was the one who always held her heart like you held mine.

We have lived a life of lies for 14 years and it has been exhausting so I only tell the truth from now on. My truth is that it has always been you. I have loved you since I was a young boy and will love you still when I'm an old man. I know I let you down but I promise I will spend the rest of my life making it up to you if you will let me.

Yours forever, Étienne xx

I sighed when I reached the end. 'So, what do you make of that?'

'More importantly, what do you make of it?'

I dropped the letter on the table and ran my hands through my hair. 'I honestly don't know what to think. It sounds like he's had it rough.'

'So have you. He broke your heart.'

'I know, and for what? A loveless marriage where they stayed together for the sake of the children. That must be draining.' It struck me that the same thing had happened to Dane, although it had been one-sided rather than loveless in his situation.

I absentmindedly picked up a couple of toast crumbs off the table and dropped them onto my plate.

'You still love him, don't you?' Rosie said softly.

I looked down at my ring and twiddled it round my finger, releasing a huge sigh. 'Yes. It was always him – my one that got away.'

'What are you going to do?'

'Nothing rash, that's for sure. I need time to think.'

Rosie nodded slowly. 'I'd better check on Mam and get back for my next lesson, but you can walk me back to the stables if you want to talk some more. Although it's cold and wet out.'

'I think I'll stay here, but it would be good to talk it through tonight if that's all right with you.'

She went in search of Alice, leaving me to read Étienne's letter once more. With a further sigh, I stuffed it back into its envelope. I didn't want to give him any more of my time at the moment. My focus for this morning was another drawing for Dane – the animal one – and a wander into Willowdale this afternoon if the rain had stopped as I still hadn't explored. I was particularly keen to look at the marina to get some inspiration for my boats drawing.

* * *

After lunch, Alice took Toffee for a walk round the estate and I strolled into the village, facing the oncoming traffic this time. The rain had cleansed the sky, leaving it baby blue with fluffy white clouds. Through gaps in the trees, the sun warmed my face and I let the tension flow from me. There was no rush for me to respond to Étienne's letter. There was no need for me to respond at all if I chose not to. For now, I was going to relax and enjoy my afternoon.

As I passed Lake View, I glanced up at the drive but it was empty, as expected. Dane would be at Hill Top today. I wondered how he was getting along with Mission Sparkle and hoped he was feeling inspired like me rather than crumbling under pressure.

I was on the other side of the road from The White Willow – the lake side – so I couldn't make out the décor inside, but I could see that it was busy. I'd maybe treat myself to a cup of tea and a slice of cake on the way back.

Lakeside Inn was ahead of me, where Rosie said Tiago had worked. When we'd gone to bed last night, we'd talked more about him. I'd asked whether she'd considered reconnecting with him via social media. She'd thought about it, but had decided there was no point. She couldn't leave her mam and move to Portugal and he couldn't leave his family and return to England, so why torture herself by seeing photos of him online and holding out hope that somehow, some way, it could happen for them? It helped that she didn't have any social media profiles in her own name – only for the riding stables – so the temptation wasn't as ever present as it might otherwise have been.

I could relate to that. I'd closed down my accounts after Étienne chose Chantal so I couldn't obsessively search him out. It had meant I wasn't able to sustain friendships with my university friends, particularly my housemates because, scattered around the country, social media had been the logical and easiest way to stay in touch. But I was used to not having friends so I accepted that sacrifice.

I crossed over to the village green – a small area of neatly cut lush grass around the giant willow tree. A sturdy wooden bench just in front of the drooping branches was surrounded by golden, white and purple crocuses and a carpet of daffodils just coming into bloom. What a lovely spot to sit and enjoy the lake view. There was a postbox so I might sit there another day and sketch what I could see to send with a letter to Maman and Papa. They'd like that.

As I wandered round the village, several walkers passed me and each one smiled or said 'hello'. I had no way of knowing whether they were tourists or locals but I loved how friendly everyone was. It was as though there was an instant connection to each other simply by being in this beautiful place.

The village shop was open and a glance through the window showed it was a fairly standard shop carrying the basic supplies. There wasn't anything I needed and I didn't feel comfortable doing a lap just to look.

Willowdale Gifts next door was closed and a typed sign was taped to the glass panel on the door:

Thank you for your custom. Taking our winter break. Open again at Easter.

The bay window display was empty and there were shutters behind it preventing me from peeking into the shop to see what sort of gifts they sold.

Next door to that was a bakery which I hadn't spotted when I arrived, but that was closed too. A sign displayed in the window gave weekday opening hours of 7.30 a.m. to 12.30 p.m. so I'd have to be organised much earlier if I wanted to sample their produce. It could have just been my imagination, but I was sure the smell of fresh bread lingered in the air.

I continued past houses, nearly all white, slate or a combination of the two. Most had names and several had small key safes by the door so were presumably holiday lets.

Before long, I reached the end of the village. A moss-covered bridge wide enough for a couple of cyclists to ride side by side spanned the River Derwent. Beyond it, there were open fields with a backdrop of fells. I stayed on the Willowdale side of the bridge, leaning against a wooden fence, listening to the rush of water and admiring the view. Rosie had thrown a few names at me of the fells in this direction – Skiddaw, Latrigg and Blencathra if I remembered correctly – but I had no idea if I was looking at any of them.

A couple of women on mountain bikes cycled across the bridge and smiled at me as they continued towards the village. Rosie had said I could borrow her bike and helmet any time I wanted. Off-roading was out of the question, but I might be brave enough to cycle along the quieter roads. I'd ask Dane if he'd be willing to join me on one of his days off and give me some guidance. He struck me as the sort who'd be really patient, especially with a scared novice like me. He'd been so gentle when he'd held my arm after we collided, checking for injuries, and he hadn't had a go at me for stepping out without looking, which he could so easily have done. I pictured him removing his cycling helmet and shaking out his hair, his strong arms as he paced up and down trying to find me a taxi firm, the way his Lycra shirt clung to his toned body, and I flushed from head to toe.

'Where did that come from?' I muttered to myself, wafting my T-shirt in an attempt to cool down. How had I gone from innocently thinking about getting a few cycling tips from my new friend to focusing on his Lycra-clad body? Hopefully it was a momentary lapse in concentration and I'd be fine by the time I saw him again on Friday. If not, things might be about to get tricky.

Retracing my steps back into the village centre, I turned right by the corner shop and continued my exploration along the main road in the direction of the village hall and the other pub. The Hardy Herdwick – which had the cutest pub sign of a Herdwick sheep being buffeted by the wind – also served food, but their menu offered more traditional 'pub grub' such as pie and mash, scampi and chips, and lasagne, along with an extensive children's menu. It was less expensive than Lakeside Inn and likely more appealing to families.

Venturing down the street beside the pub took me to the village hall. The pebbledash was painted in a warm cream and it was much bigger than I'd appreciated from the road. What looked to be the main function room was in the middle with a one-storey room jutting out from the left and two storeys to the right. There was an encased noticeboard near the door which showed an active programme of events. There appeared to be something to suit a good mix of needs – a parent and toddler group, yoga, table tennis, flower arranging, a history society, and Spanish lessons – and there was also a programme of different activities in Pippinthwaite Village Hall in the next village. A colourful poster advertised various events planned for Easter weekend and another one wished a warm welcome to village newcomers with a couple of families named below it. How lovely was that? Just by reading the noticeboard, I could feel the sense of community. It was really quite touching and my throat tightened with emotion. I'd never experienced a proper community before. It must feel special to be part of one.

The door to the village hall opened and a woman with short white-blonde hair, flicked out at the sides, stepped out with a large bag hooked over each shoulder and an armful of folders. One of her bags snagged on the door handle and stopped her in her tracks, causing her to drop the folders, which skidded in all directions.

I rushed over to help her retrieve them.

'Thank you so much,' she said. 'Trust me to try it in one trip instead of two. Do you mind keeping hold of those while I lock up?'

'No problem.'

She used a key dangling from a lanyard round her neck. From a distance, I'd have put her in her early fifties but, up close, I could see the fine lines on her forehead and round her eyes which suggested she might even be in her sixties.

'Thanks for that,' she said, reaching for the folders, but one of the bags slipped off her shoulder and she grappled to reposition it, getting her lanyard tangled in it.

'Are you in a car because I can carry them to it if you want?' I said, fearing she'd drop them again if I handed them over.

'Oh, you darling. That would be a great help. It's the bright blue one over there.' She pointed to a small car parked beside the pub.

'I'm Trudy,' she said as we walked towards her car.

'Autumn.'

'That's a pretty name. I've never met an Autumn before.'

I smiled at her. 'Most people haven't.'

She opened her boot, which was nearly full already, but we managed to squeeze in the folders and bags.

'Were you looking for someone, by the way?' she asked.

I frowned then realised that was a friendly way of asking me why I was loitering outside the village hall. 'No, just exploring the village. I'm staying with a friend at Willowdale Hall.'

Her eyes widened. 'You're friends with Hubert Cranleigh? I'd heard he was practically a recluse these days.'

'Gosh, no! I don't know him. I'm friends with Rosie Jacobs who runs the riding school.'

'Ah, yes! That makes more sense. I used to teach Rosie when she was this high.' She put her hand out to indicate a small child, so I guessed she meant in primary school. 'Lovely girl but very quiet. Then I swapped for the older kids, teaching English in Keswick, and now I'm retired and giving a complete stranger my career history when she didn't even ask.'

I laughed, warming to how open and friendly she was.

'I might as well finish what I've started,' she said, her eyes twinkling as she smiled at me. 'I was born and raised in Willowdale but live in Pippinthwaite now and I'm the chair of the joint village halls committee. I run the book club in Pippinthwaite's hall and I'll be starting a creative writing class here after the Easter holidays, which reminds me…' She opened her boot and retrieved one of the folders. 'There it is! I printed off a poster for the noticeboard and I would have driven home with it if I hadn't met you.'

She waved a colourful poster at me.

'Is that for beginners?' I asked.

'Any level, any age, any genre,' she said. 'Are you interested?'

'I won't be here, but I…' I paused. I'd been about to say I knew a friend who might be interested but Dane had said I was the only person here he'd told about his dream to write children's books so I'd better not say anything. 'I was just being nosy,' I said, hoping I sounded convincing. 'It sounds great.'

'I don't know what level of interest we'll have, but the committee are such a wonderful group, open to trying new things.' She handed me a leaflet. 'I don't think we've ever seen Rosie at an event so can you pass this on to her and tell her she'd be very welcome?'

'I will do. Thank you.'

Trudy closed her boot and took her poster over to the noticeboard. There were only houses after this point, so I returned to the village centre. Time for some sustenance.

It was mid-afternoon mid-week but at least half the tables in The White Willow were occupied. Dane had told me that the café had been closed for a couple of years before his aunt and uncle took it on and it had been a sorry state inside. It was beautiful now. Dark grey quarry tiles on the floor were complemented by a warm cream high ceiling. The wall on the left was painted aubergine and included two feature panels of slices of logs stuck to the wall either side of a log burner. The wall opposite had a stunning mural of a willow tree with a bench under it and the lake in front, depicting the village green.

The tables and chairs were oak and there was an oak and glass serving counter in front of the kitchen, displaying delicious-looking sponge cakes, tray bakes and scones.

A young man who looked to be only in his late teens or early twenties showed me to a table by the window, handed me a menu and pointed out the specials boards. He returned shortly afterwards and took my order for a cappuccino and a slice of white chocolate and raspberry sponge.

I could see three other staff members and they were all women maybe in their forties and fifties. I had no idea how old Dane's Aunt Kelly was so I didn't like to hazard a guess as to which she was, if any of them. Just because she owned the café, it didn't necessarily mean she worked here.

As I tucked into the cake – which was to die for – I read through the leaflet that Trudy Eccles had given me for Rosie. It was amazing to think that there was so much going on in two small villages, although the activities might well attract people from other nearby villages, hamlets, farms and perhaps even from within Keswick itself.

What a coincidence that she'd taught Rosie when she was little. I gave a small gasp as the name registered with me. Dane had told me that the English teacher who'd inspired him so much had been called Miss Eccles. Trudy said she'd swapped primary teaching for secondary school English, so it had to be the same person. If Dane was hesitant about trying out the creative writing class, knowing that his former inspirational teacher was running it might convince him.

I swallowed the final forkful of cake and closed my eyes for a moment, savouring the delicious flavour. I'd have to come back again for another slice of that. Tomorrow night would be my seventh night in Willowdale, meaning I was already nearly halfway through the initial fortnight I'd agreed with Rosie. The days seemed to be passing so quickly and there was no way I could see myself being ready to leave the weekend after next. I felt so relaxed and at home here.

It was wonderful spending time with Rosie but I couldn't impose on her for longer than two weeks, especially when we were sharing a bed. If I was going to stay longer – which didn't feel like a question mark at the moment – I'd need to look into alternative accommodation. It wasn't like Willowdale had a shortage of holiday rentals, although Easter was fast approaching and it might be harder to secure something across the school holidays.

I settled my bill and left the café for my final stop – Willowdale Marina. As soon as I stepped outside, the wind whipped my hair across my face and crept up the sleeves of my jacket, making me shiver. The temperature had dropped significantly and the fluffy white clouds were now elongated and grey. I kicked myself for getting waylaid by coffee and cake and missing the decent weather. If it started raining, I'd get drenched. I needed to learn how to dress like a Cumbrian. Note to self: always carry a waterproof.

Rain was forecast for tomorrow so my best plan for now was to still go to the marina but only for a brief visit. I'd take a stack of photos rather than try to draw anything, and hope to make it home before the heavens opened. Home. I was already referring to Horseshoe Cottage as that! My task for tonight would be to search for somewhere to stay, preferably in the heart of the village.

After a quick stop at the marina, I set off back to Horseshoe Cottage and was almost there when light rain started, so I broke into a slow jog. Toffee greeted me at the door and rolled over onto her back so I could scratch her belly.

'Where's Alice?' I asked Toffee, realising as soon as I spoke that Alice was at the stables. Rosie had a large class on a Wednesday afternoon, so it was one of the days her mam helped out at the riding school. I'd have a little over an hour on my own before they got home.

I hung my damp jacket up to dry and went upstairs to look through my photos from the marina and start on my transport illustrations. As soon as I was in the bedroom, the butterflies in my stomach took flight because there it was, calling me from the bedside cabinet – Étienne's letter.

There'd been so much to take in during my wander round Willowdale that I'd managed to escape from thoughts of him, but I couldn't run forever. Sinking down onto the bed, I read his letter once more. Did I believe what he said? To be fair to him, Étienne had never intentionally lied to me. Yes, he'd broken his promise about us having a future together, but he'd let me know it was over when he could have left me hanging.

Reading between the lines, he sounded downright miserable. His relationship with Chantal had always been volatile and it was no surprise that she'd used our friendship and subsequent relationship as a weapon against him. How soon had the rot set in? How quickly had Chantal turned to her childhood boyfriend?

Étienne's words seemed so heartfelt and I had an urge to hug him and reassure him that it would be all right and we'd work something out because we loved each other. Could we have a second chance? I laid the letter beside me and gazed at my ring, moving my hand slightly so that the white topaz stone caught the light. I wasn't sure we could. He'd never lied to me, but I'd kept the truth from him – a truth that could have changed everything.

19

FOURTEEN YEARS AGO

Those weekends in Brighton with Étienne were the most amazing weekends of my life. At a time when I was grieving for Grandma and stressing about my finals, Étienne brought me happiness, serenity, and so much love. That final weekend, I couldn't stop gazing at my beautiful promise ring and thinking about our future together.

I returned to Sutton for the first weekend in April – the start of the Easter holidays – to spend some quality time with Granddad. He claimed he was doing well, but I wasn't fooled. I noticed the many times he reached out to take Grandma's hand or looked up from his puzzle book to ask for her help, a flicker of confusion across his face when she wasn't there, replaced by a deep sadness which engulfed his entire body that she never would be there again.

I'd only been home for a couple of hours when he first raised the subject of me going to Paris for a few days. I shut him down, telling him the only place I wanted to be was with him. Over the next few days, he kept mentioning it and it struck me that there might be more to his suggestion than I'd assumed. Perhaps it was less about encouraging me to spend time with my parents and more about giving him some space to grieve. He was a proud man and from the 'stiff upper lip' generation. It must be exhausting maintaining the *I'm fine, there's nothing to see here* persona in front of me when he had to be broken inside.

'It'll do you good to get away for a few days,' Granddad said, watching over me as I booked my flight online. Translation: *it'll do me some good to recharge.*

I'd just confirmed my flight when Mrs Slade from next door dropped in. I joined them for a coffee then told them I needed to nip into Sutton to get a few things for my trip. Really, I just wanted an excuse to let Étienne know I'd be able to see him next week.

I wasn't sure whether he could take personal calls at work so I sent him a text saying I had exciting news and, five minutes later, he called me back.

'Guess who's coming to Paris next week?' I said when he answered.

'Really? This is *fantastique*. But I thought you didn't want to leave your granddad.'

'I didn't, but I think he's finding it a bit claustrophobic having me around all the time and he needs a break. The flights across Easter weekend were crazy money, but I've booked one for first thing on Wednesday, flying back on Saturday evening.'

'I cannot wait to see you again. You can stay with me, you know.'

I hesitated. How would that look to my parents who didn't know that we had as close a friendship as we did, or that it had now gone way beyond that?

'You have no idea how much I want to say yes to that offer, but maybe next time. If you're okay with it, we could tell our parents about us. I'm assuming you haven't told yours already.'

'I haven't seen them since it happened – only talked – and they are still sad that it has ended with Chantal at Christmas so I wanted to give them time. I think they have had enough time now so perhaps we can fly to Bordeaux and tell them together.'

On the afternoon of Easter Monday, two days before my trip to Paris, Granddad asked if I'd accompany him to Grandma's favourite park – Beddington Park in nearby Wallington. With beautiful woodland walks, a lake, formal gardens and plenty of wildlife, it had been the setting for many of Grandma's watercolours.

Granddad and I sat on a bench, drinking tea from a flask. He asked if I was looking forward to Paris and, even though I didn't specifically mention Étienne, I could hear the excitement in my voice.

'You're more enthusiastic than usual,' he said, looking at me thoughtfully. 'Either I've bored you senseless in the time you've been home, or there's something you're not telling me.'

Nothing got past Granddad. 'You could never bore me. You know I love our time together.'

He smiled at me and kept his eyes fixed on mine, challenging me for an explanation.

'Okay, you've got me. There *is* a reason for the added enthusiasm. You know my friend Étienne in Paris...'

I gave him the edited highlights, explaining how our friendship had turned to something much deeper when he'd finally broken up with his on/off girlfriend. I missed out the part about my drunk letter as I didn't want him to worry that I'd got myself into a bit of a state after losing Grandma.

'We're going to tell both sets of parents while I'm in France,' I said. 'I think Maman and Papa will be pleased. I don't know about his. They're friends with Maman and Papa but they're really good friends with Chantal's parents, so it might be a bit awkward.'

'If it is, I'm sure they'll come round. All that any parent wants is for their child to be happy and if he cares as much about you as you clearly care about him, they'll know he's found happiness with you.'

I wanted to tell him that I was sure I'd found what he'd had with Grandma, but I thought it might be too soon to say something like that, so I slipped my arm through his and rested my head on his shoulder.

'How long have you been together?' Granddad asked.

'Exactly two months today.' As I said the words, I tensed.

'Everything all right?' Granddad asked.

'Erm, yes. Thought I was about to sneeze. It's gone now.' I stretched out. 'I'm feeling a bit chilly. Are you ready to head home?'

We tipped the last few sips of tea away, packed the flask and spare cup in my backpack and I slipped my arm through Granddad's as we walked back to the car. I tried to relax, but it wasn't easy with my head buzzing. Two months since Étienne came to Brighton, six weeks since we slept together, and no sign of my period since then. It didn't mean I was pregnant, though. My cycle could be erratic at times of stress and with Grandma's passing and my approaching finals, I'd had a particularly fraught start to the year. It was probably that, but I could find out for definite. Granddad and I had already discussed stopping off at the supermarket on the way home to pick up something for dinner so I drove via our nearest one. He hated food shopping and stayed in the car listening to the radio while I whizzed round with the trolley, making a sneaky pregnancy test purchase.

* * *

In the bathroom at home a little later, my stomach felt like it was on spin cycle and my heart was pounding so fast that I feared I might pass out. I sat down heavily on the toilet seat with my eyes closed, the testing stick tightly gripped in my right hand. I had no idea what I wanted the result to be. Étienne and I had talked about getting married and starting a family and wanting to do it sooner rather than later… but not quite this soon! Would a positive result be exciting or terrifying? And how would Étienne react?

I drew in a deep breath and slowly exhaled, counted to three and opened my eyes.

My heart leapt into my mouth and I inhaled deeply again. Pregnant. I reached for my phone on the side by the sink, but withdrew my hand. I didn't want to give that news over the phone. I'd be seeing Étienne on Wednesday and would deliver it in person and hope his reaction was as positive as the test. In the meantime, it would have to be my little secret.

Placing the test on the cabinet, I counted off the months on my fingers. The baby would be due somewhere between the end of November and the end of December. What a year this would be – front-ended with a death and back-ended with a birth.

I had so much to think about, but I couldn't stay in the bathroom much longer without Granddad getting concerned, so I gathered together all evidence of the pregnancy testing kit to be disposed of away from the house, and crossed the landing to my bedroom.

Closing my door, I stood in front of the full-length mirror on my wardrobe, raised my T-shirt and unfastened my jeans.

'Hello, in there,' I whispered, stroking my hand over my stomach. 'What a little surprise you are.'

It was too early for me to be showing, so I curved my back, pushed my stomach out and twisted and turned. Was this how I'd look in a couple of months' time? Shaking my head, I pulled my clothes back into place and lay on the bed, my hands clasped across my stomach.

Telling the parents about us was suddenly a much bigger thing. Would we tell them the baby news or wait until we'd had our first scan? I liked the idea of it just being the two of us for a while, lost in our own little bubble of impending parenthood.

I practised how I'd break the news to Étienne, but it felt too forced, so I took out my sketchpad instead, unable to resist drawing a stork carrying an adorable little baby.

The following day, I needed to focus on some university work so managed to keep my mind occupied but, as soon as I stopped to pack my suitcase late that afternoon, all I could think of was the baby.

Thoughts about the changes to my body developed into a happy little fantasy of Étienne holding my hand at our first baby scan, whether we'd have a boy or girl, and what we'd name them. I had a moment's panic about where we'd live, but Étienne had already mentioned how much he loved Brighton and could happily settle there. If he'd already been thinking along those lines when there was no baby, him moving to the UK surely wouldn't be an issue when there was a baby. The bigger issue was more likely to be our parents. My reason for staying here was to be close to Granddad – and because I preferred it – but I wasn't sure how well it would go down with either set of parents to have their first grandchild living in a different country. Also, I might appreciate the support if we lived in France. But what about Granddad?

I smiled to myself as I zipped my case closed. I was getting way too far ahead of myself. The first step was to tell Étienne when I saw him tomorrow and we'd take everything else from there.

20

PRESENT DAY

I put Étienne's letter back in its envelope. I needed to close down thoughts of him for now and focus on my Mission Sparkle work for Dane. The Centenary Stone drawing was complete and I'd drawn the outlines for the pony, but I wanted to make a start on the boats so, if time became too tight, I'd still have three drawings to present to Dane, even if a couple of them were incomplete.

I'd have preferred to sketch by the lake but, as it was still raining, the chair by the Juliet balcony with a view of the lake was the next best thing. I scrolled through the photos I'd taken at the marina, looking for a starting point, but nothing jumped out at me. There'd been a pretty sailing boat moored to the wooden jetty, so I drew a quick sketch of that before sitting back, chewing my lip. How did I turn it into a talking boat? I drew a mouth and eyes on the sail and quickly erased them as they looked terrifying and were more likely to induce nightmares than help children settle. I tried various points on the hull of the boat, and nothing worked.

I abandoned the sailing boat and tried a kayak which I'd now learned typically had a closed deck and was steered using a double-ended paddle. That didn't work either, so I moved on to a canoe but without success.

The finger of doubt prodded at me. Drawing the fairies on the Centenary Stone had been a fluke triggered by something Rosie said, and drawing a pony hadn't been difficult when I was staying near a riding stables so surrounded by ponies. The tricky part would be adding a personality to the pony and drawing the red squirrel to be different from any I'd drawn before.

Abandoning the boats, I returned to the pony drawing, but I wasn't feeling it anymore. I closed my sketchpad with a frustrated growl and dropped it on the floor beside me. I'd told Dane not to put any pressure on himself and I needed to listen to my own advice, but this was driving me mad. I'd thought the fairies were the start of my mojo returning, but I was back to blank once more.

Looking round the room in search of anything that could inspire me, my eyes rested on Étienne's letter. Could that be the problem? Was my mind so full of the past right now that I couldn't focus on the present or future? It was possible. After all, I'd kept what happened buried for so long.

21

FOURTEEN YEARS AGO

It was the day before I was due to fly to Paris and I was loading the dishwasher when I heard my phone ringing upstairs. I didn't get to it in time and was surprised to see two missed calls from Étienne. He must have phoned while Granddad and I were eating and I hadn't heard it. He hadn't left a voicemail but, if he'd tried twice in the space of twenty minutes, he was obviously keen to get hold of me.

A text pinged through.

FROM ÉTIENNE

> Need to speak to you urgently. Can you call me back as soon as you get this? X

My heart raced at the word 'urgently'. That couldn't be good. I perched on the edge of the bed and waited for my call to connect.

'Sorry I missed you,' I said when Étienne answered. 'I was having dinner with Granddad. Is everything all right?'

'No. I'm so sorry, Autumn, but I cannot see you anymore.'

My stomach did a backflip. 'What? Why?'

'Chantal is pregnant. We're getting married and moving to Dijon.'

'Is this a wind-up?' I have no idea why I said that. Of course it wasn't. He'd never joke about anything like that.

'I wish it was. I'm so sorry.'

'You can't marry her,' I cried. 'It's me you love.'

'I have to. I wish things were different. This is so hard for both of us. I'm sorry. I truly am.'

'Things *are* different!' My voice was so high, I didn't recognise it. I took a deep breath, ready to blurt out the news which I'd expected to tell him in person, but he'd already disconnected.

I stared numbly at my phone, struggling to take in what had just happened and Étienne's unwillingness to discuss it any further. That was so unlike him. Or had Chantal found out about us and been standing next to him while he delivered their happy news? Had she ended the call for him?

There was no way I was giving up that easily. Chantal was expecting Étienne's baby? Well, so was I, and he needed to know that.

Heart pounding, I phoned him back but it rang out. I paced up and down in front of my window as I tried again several times, but without success. I was going to have to text him instead.

TO ÉTIENNE

This isn't news I wanted to give in a text but you're not answering your phone so I have no choice. I'm pregnant too. Just found out and was going to tell you tomorrow. We need to talk urgently!!!

But my text wasn't delivered. I tried sending another and the same thing happened. He'd blocked me! A wave of nausea swept through me and the phone slipped from my hand onto the carpet as I wrapped my arms across my stomach. I rested my backside against the windowsill, wincing and regretting that second piece of cheesecake after dinner.

I glanced at my suitcase on my bed and swallowed down the lump blocking my throat. An hour ago, I'd been packing that case, imagining Étienne's face when I told him I was pregnant. How could it have gone from that to being over?

I grasped my stomach as it cramped, taking my breath away. Rushing across the landing to the bathroom, sweat prickling my forehead, I sank down on the toilet. My stomach hurt so much and, bizarrely, so did the top of my arm, near my shoulder. My heart was racing and I felt lightheaded. In need of a drink of water and a lie down, I bent forward to pull up my knickers and jeans and my breath caught. Blood. No!

Panic rose inside me and I fought hard to calm myself. It didn't have to mean anything. My limited knowledge of pregnancy included awareness that spotting could happen. Except that wasn't what I'd call spotting. That was a lot of blood and I needed to get it checked out quickly.

My stomach cramped again and spots swam in front of my eyes before everything went black.

* * *

I could hear sirens and they sounded really close. Was Granddad okay? My eyes flickered open.

'It's all right, Autumn,' Granddad said, his voice hoarse. 'I'm right here.'

Where was here? Darkness enveloped me once more.

The sirens had stopped but I could hear voices and had the sensation of moving.

'Granddad?'

He didn't answer and the voices faded away as the blackness took hold again.

'Autumn? Can you open your eyes for me?'

I didn't recognise the woman's voice but she sounded important, so I did as she asked, blinking several times in the bright light. I was in a bed, but it wasn't mine.

'Hi, Autumn, how are you feeling?' the same woman asked.

My eyes flicked round the room, trying to work out where I was. How was I feeling? Confused.

'My head hurts.' I wanted to put my arm up to rub it but it was trapped under a sheet and I didn't have the energy to move it.

'You hit your head on the toilet bowl when you fainted.'

Fainted? Yes, I'd been in the bathroom and I didn't feel well.

'There was blood,' I muttered.

'I'm really sorry, but you've had a miscarriage.'

Tears pricked my eyes and my lip started to wobble.

'Did you know you were pregnant?'

I nodded slowly, a tear trailing across my cheek and dripping onto the pillow.

'Found out yesterday.' It was an effort to form the words.

'You're in hospital,' she said, although I'd worked that out by now, 'and your miscarriage was a little more complicated…'

* * *

I hadn't been on the ward for long when Granddad appeared. The moment I saw him, I burst into tears. He gathered me in his arms, rocking me like a small child as the tears spilled out onto his jacket.

'It'll be all right,' he murmured in my ear, patting my back.

Would it?

'I thought I'd lost you today,' he said, settling into the chair beside the bed when my sobs eased. His eyes were red and his face pale.

'You don't get rid of me that easily,' I said in a feeble attempt at humour as I wiped my wet cheeks.

'How are you feeling?'

'I've had better days. I'm sorry if I scared you.'

'I heard a clatter and I called to you but there was no answer. Lucky the bathroom lock was so flimsy.'

'You broke down the door?'

'Had to.'

'What have they told you?' I asked.

'That you were pregnant but you lost the baby. I'm so sorry. Did you know?'

'Only just. I hadn't even suspected until you asked me how long I'd been seeing Étienne. I bought a test in the supermarket.'

'Did you get a chance to tell him before...'

My stomach lurched as he tailed off. I dreaded to think what had confronted Granddad when he burst through the bathroom door – something no grandparent should ever have to see.

'I wanted to do it in person,' I said, 'but that's not going to happen now.'

'You could delay your flight for a couple of days.'

'No point. He's gone back to his ex. She's pregnant and they're getting married. I can't compete with that. Not anymore.'

'It's not a competition,' he said gently.

No, it wasn't, because Chantal had already won the prize. They'd probably spent all weekend putting plans in place. They might even have set a wedding date. What could I possibly offer him? *Pick me! I've just lost your baby in an ectopic miscarriage, have had one fallopian tube removed, and there's a one to two in ten risk that the same thing will happen in a future pregnancy. Oh, and I want you to move away from your friends, family and your job so you can live in England with me.*

'Are you going to tell him what's happened?' Granddad asked when I didn't respond.

'I can't. He's blocked me.' I sighed. 'Can we change the subject, please? Do Maman and Papa know I'm here?'

'Not yet. I haven't been home and I didn't pick up my phone when the ambulance came.'

'Don't tell them. Please.'

'They'd want to know.'

'But I don't want them to know. I don't want anyone to know.'

'But Autumn...'

'I'm begging you, Granddad. Who would it benefit? Not me, that's for sure. Imagine if this had happened to you and Grandma at my age. Would Grandma have wanted her parents to know?' It was a low blow, but putting him in my shoes was the only defence I had.

He lowered his eyes. 'No, she wouldn't. But we have to say something. They're expecting you tomorrow.'

'Then tell them I wasn't feeling well today, that I fainted in the bathroom and knocked myself out, and I'm in A&E waiting to be patched up so I can't call them myself. Please, Granddad!'

He sighed heavily. 'Okay. I'll tell them that.'

'And tell them not to worry about me.'

'Okay.'

'And don't you worry about me either.'

He grasped my hand. 'I'll always worry about you. Grandparent's prerogative. I'd better get home and fetch you some things. What do you need?'

I ran through what to bring me for my overnight stay. Everything was in my suitcase on my bed, so he didn't need to hunt through my drawers.

With another hug, he left the ward. I glanced round me. There were another seven beds, all occupied by women of various ages. The patient in the bed opposite me glanced up from her book and smiled at me. I gave her a weak smile in return before turning onto my side and drawing my legs up towards my chest.

I'd been on such a high yesterday afternoon in the park with Granddad, telling him about Étienne. The positive pregnancy test had enhanced that and I'd been happily picturing my future with the man of my dreams and our baby. And in the space of a day, it had all been taken away from me.

22

PRESENT DAY

'Oh, Autumn!' Rosie said, her eyes sparkling with tears. 'I'm so sorry you had to go through all that.'

We'd come up to the bedroom after our evening meal to talk about what I was going to do about Étienne's letter. I hadn't specifically planned to share my pregnancy story but it seemed to make sense for Rosie to know the full story if she was going to help me make a decision about whether or not to respond.

'Thank you,' I said, brushing some imaginary fluff off the scatter cushion I was cuddling for comfort as we both sat cross-legged on the bed. 'I'm sorry I didn't tell you at the time.'

'Gosh, don't be. I never told you about Tiago, so I completely get it. Some things are just too painful to write in a letter. I'm assuming you didn't tell Étienne before you left Paris.'

'No. After that kiss, when he found me in the park, all I could think about was getting away from him before I did anything stupid again. Definite flight mode. I used to wonder what would have happened if I'd discovered I was pregnant a few days earlier, but I don't think I'd have done it differently. I'd have still wanted to tell him face to face so I was always going to be too late.'

'If you had found out earlier and you'd phoned him, do you think he'd have chosen you?'

'I've thought about that a lot too and I don't know.' I flashed my ring to her. 'He gave me this and told me he loved me the most, but Chantal had location on her side, a long history with him, parental pressure on both sides. I could have easily been brushed aside, out of sight, out of mind.'

'I'm not exactly his number one fan,' Rosie said, reaching for his letter, 'but from reading this, I don't think you've ever been out of sight, out of mind.'

'I do understand why he made the choice he did and I know it won't have been easy for him, but what I've always struggled with is how he handled it with me. I was so disappointed in him. I still am! I know it would have taken real guts to phone me with that news – and perhaps I should be thankful for small mercies that he gave me that dignity when he could easily have ghosted me – but I'd have thought so much more of him if he'd trusted me enough to discuss it instead of presenting it as a fait accompli. To cut me off then block me was cold. If he wasn't prepared to have a conversation, he might as well have blown me out by text.'

She waved the letter at me. 'What's your gut reaction about this?'

'To ignore it.'

'You know you won't be able to do that. You'll be obsessively watching out for the post every day, wondering if he'll write again. What's stopping you from writing to him and telling him it was over fourteen years ago and you never want to hear from him again?'

I tightened my hold on the cushion. 'Because, for me, I don't think it ever was truly over. There's always been this hope that one day he'd realise his mistake and come back to me. Pathetic, eh?'

'You loved him, but are you sure you still do now? Fourteen years is a heck of a long time.'

'I know it is, but the moment I saw him again, those feelings were there, and when he kissed me...'

'Nostalgia?' she suggested. 'I know it's not the same because I hadn't known him for long and I was only starting to fall for him but, if Tiago turned up on my doorstep right now and kissed me, I'd be having all the feels. Picking up where we left off after nearly five years apart would be another matter. You and Étienne have been apart for three times that and you might not think you have but you'll both have changed so much during that time. You were only twenty-one when the two of you got together. You were still at university. You can't tell me you're the same person you were back then after everything you've been through, and you can't tell me he is either. He's a dad now. His life went in a completely different direction to yours.'

I sank onto my back and covered my face with the cushion, releasing a frustrated 'Argh!' into it.

Rosie removed the cushion and looked down at me.

'You're right,' I said. 'Who's to say we have anything in common now except the past?'

'You know what I think you should do? Nothing for the moment. Finish your drawings, meet Dane for lunch on Friday and do your best to enjoy the rest of this week. This thing with Étienne isn't going to disappear. It's going to be niggling away in the back of your mind and that's probably a good thing because if that niggle is saying the same thing to you each day, then that's the outcome that's right for you. Whatever that is, you can write to him at the weekend with your decision.'

'That sounds very sensible. You're pretty good at this adulting stuff.'

Rosie pulled a face. 'Urgh! I wish I didn't have to be sometimes. It's so hard.' Her expression softened. 'How are you feeling about what happened with the baby?'

I rolled onto my side and propped myself up on my elbow. 'I've had my moments over the years. I worked out what my due date would have been. It fell on a Saturday which was just as well because I spent most of that day in tears so I'd have been a wreck if I'd had to go into work. Granddad was amazing, bringing me hot drinks, chocolates, a fresh box of tissues.' I smiled at the memory. 'After that, I chose not to get fixated by anniversaries. I hated the melancholy that accompanied them so it was easier not to think about them. Things could still blindside me, though. A colleague would announce she was pregnant or I'd be watching a TV programme and ectopic pregnancy would be mentioned and the emotions would be swirling. And even though I try not to obsess about anniversaries, I'm very aware of the passing of time. If things had been different, I'd have a teenager now. Imagine that! Life would have been so different.'

'I think life's full of *what ifs*. What if my dad was in my life? What if Mam hadn't been hit by that car? What if Tiago's sister hadn't had that accident?'

'What if we hadn't been given each other's letters?' I added, smiling at her.

'Exactly! And do you know what I tell myself? What's to say things would have been better if they'd gone differently? Obviously that doesn't apply to our letters because there could be nothing better than this, but what about all the other stuff? We'll never know. I find it easier to think that this is what the universe had planned for us all along, that we're exactly where we're meant to be, doing what we're meant to be doing.'

'I love your outlook on life. I need to be more Rosie.'

'Be more Rosie?' She shook her head. 'The only person you need to be is you because you're perfect as you are.'

23

The following day, I woke up feeling so much lighter and happier for having shared the full story with Rosie. It felt good to confide in her, but our conversation had also given me a fresh perspective on what a relationship with Étienne might look like if I let him back into my life. How had I not considered that we might be very different people and not at all compatible now? After all, we'd been apart nearly three times as long as we'd been friends. That was a long time.

It was a warm, clear day and I spent the morning in Rosie's bedroom with the doors to the Juliet balcony open. To my relief, the ideas came. I finished my horse and squirrel and was really pleased with them, but I decided to ditch the talking vehicles idea. It wasn't me at all and it didn't feel very Dane either. I couldn't imagine him feeling passionate about a talking kayak or the type of stories he'd write about them.

After lunch, I left the estate and took the track towards Cat Bells, heading down to the lakeside beneath the fell. I wandered along to the end of a wooden jetty – one of the stop-off points for the lake cruise boats – to drink in the view. There was nobody around so I opened my arms wide, tilted my head back, and breathed in the beauty surrounding me.

Feeling relaxed and at peace, I sat down cross legged on the jetty and sketched the view. I'd write to my parents later and send them the sketch. The one from the village green would have to go in a future letter.

When I'd finished drawing, I sauntered back up the beach and towards the track. I could see Cat Bells between the trees and thought about what Dane had said about being a volunteer with Mountain Rescue. What if I created an illustration where the Mountain Rescue team were all animals? It would be a different take on the familiar for me and it would hopefully trigger ideas for him. My pace quickened and I rushed back to Horseshoe Cottage, eager to start drawing it.

* * *

On Friday morning, I walked into Willowdale to meet Dane at The White Willow at 11 a.m. giving plenty of time to reflect on Mission Sparkle over coffee rather than only managing a quick look before being distracted by lunch arriving.

I tilted my head back to let the sunshine filtering between the trees kiss my cheeks. From despairing that I'd have nothing for Dane, I was now really pleased with my work and I couldn't wait to see which of the illustrations would trigger some story ideas for him.

We'd exchanged a few messages on WhatsApp to check progress, but hadn't spoken to each other since our trip to Honeybee's.

As well as discussing Mission Sparkle today, I was excited to talk to Dane about the creative writing class run by his former teacher. I hoped he'd consider attending.

I arrived at The White Willow ten minutes early but Dane was already there, sitting at one of the wooden tables outside, frowning and shaking his head at something on his phone.

'Morning,' I said, startling him as I approached.

'Autumn! Sorry, miles away.'

'Everything all right?' I asked, nodding towards the phone.

He sighed. 'Ongoing moan from Lynsey. Ellis usually makes a big fuss of her on Mother's Day but, this year, he didn't see her and she's still fuming about it nearly two weeks on. Now that he's living with Georgia, they understandably want to do things together. They took her mam out this year because they both took Lynsey out last year and were clear at the time that they'd be taking turns going forwards but, because of the divorce, Lynsey conveniently forgot that plan and it's somehow all my fault.'

'How does she work that out?'

'Apparently I've poisoned Ellis against her. As if he's not mature enough at twenty to make his own decisions. I don't think it helped that he only sent her a card – by post too – and no flowers or gifts. Lynsey's all about the gifts. She wants me to have a word with Ellis about his "childish behaviour" and isn't impressed that I've told her he's not being childish and I won't be having a word. She made her bed and now she has to lie in it.'

'Sounds exhausting.'

'It is. But Lynsey has already taken up enough of my morning and yours so should we go in and get a table?'

The young man who'd served me on Wednesday greeted us at the door and Dane introduced him as his cousin Felix, son of the aunt and uncle who owned the café.

'I'll introduce Aunt Kelly to you later,' Dane said as we settled into a double table to one side of the log burner, giving us extra room to spread out our work.

We ordered a couple of coffees from Felix and I took a moment to look around again.

'I love it in here,' I said to Dane. 'It's beautifully decorated and there's such a lovely atmosphere.'

'They've done a great job, haven't they? You should have seen it before – completely unrecognisable from what it is today. It's lucky they had the vision to see what it could become.'

'It's nice that they have their son working for them.'

'Yeah, Felix is a good lad. He's nearly a year younger than Ellis but they were in the same school year and they've always got on well, even though they don't see a lot of each other. Felix wants to be a chef so he studied that at college. The long-term plan is for him to run the kitchen on an evening – the job I'll be doing temporarily – but he needs a lot more experience before he's ready for that.'

While we were waiting for our drinks, Dane expanded on his family tree, telling me that Felix had an older sister called Maya who lived with her fiancé in Keswick where she was a teacher, and that his mam and Aunt Kelly were the oldest and youngest respectively of four children with ten years separating them. In the middle were two brothers who'd stayed in the area and whose grown-up families had also settled nearby. His dad was the middle of three boys so there were aunts, uncles and cousins on his side of the family locally too.

'It must be lovely having a big family,' I said. 'Neither of my parents had siblings and I'm an only child. Both sets of grandparents have passed away so it's just the three of us now.'

'You're close to your parents, though?'

'Yes. I know we don't live in the same country but distance doesn't have to be a barrier. We've always been really close.'

Felix delivered our drinks.

'Autumn would like to know what it's like being part of a big family,' Dane said.

'Noisy,' Felix said, laughing.

'I think that pretty much sums it up,' Dane said, smiling at me. 'It's absolute chaos when we all get together for a wedding or christening or our annual summer barbeque and I'm starting to lose track of all the names and ages of my cousins' kids, so I do a lot of blagging when we get together.'

'Sounds like you have a ready audience for your books,' I said.

'If I get any written.'

'You will. Which brings us nicely onto Mission Sparkle. How did you get on?'

He bit his lip and shrugged. 'Okay, I think. Do you mind if I see yours first?'

'If we do that, you promise you will show me yours? No backing out.'

'Yes, if you show me yours, I'll show you mine,' he said in a mischievous tone which had us both sniggering like naughty schoolchildren.

I removed the sketchpad from my bag and flipped to the first image of the Centenary Stone with the fairies and dragon.

Dane's mouth dropped open and he looked at me, wide-eyed. 'This is incredible. I knew your illustrations would be good, but I hadn't expected this level of talent. What a gift!'

'Thank you.' It was barely a whisper because I felt all choked up with emotion.

Until now, I hadn't realised how much losing my mojo and my job had chipped away at my self-belief. As Dane continued talking, pointing out all the things he loved about the illustration, I felt pieces of confidence being gently placed back where they belonged. I started to feel like me again. Rosie had reminded me in her last letter that I'd often told her I wasn't me when I wasn't drawing and that had absolutely been the case.

'Are you okay?' Dane asked, looking at me with concern. 'You look close to tears.'

'I am.' I swallowed and blinked a few times. 'You've just given me the most enormous confidence boost and it's got me all emotional.'

'I mean every single word. I'm in awe.'

'Is it working for you?' I asked, eager to shift the attention away from me before I did start crying. 'Is it sparking any ideas?' That was the important part to me. The compliments were very much welcomed and appreciated, but the whole purpose of this exercise was to spark Dane's creativity.

'Definitely.' He tapped his forehead. 'So much going on up here right now. Can I see the next one?'

'Sure. Turn over the page.'

There was a gasp as he turned to the red squirrel and pony.

'I love that pairing of the big and the small,' he said. 'I get the impression the squirrel's the pony's protector, despite it being the smaller of the two. Did you intentionally draw it that way?'

'I just drew them with no plan in place, although, when I'd finished, I have to admit that's what I saw too.'

I held my breath as he turned to the final Mountain Rescue drawing. A badger and a fox were carrying a stretcher down Cat Bells with a poorly boy rabbit on it, his long ears flopping over the sides, an anxious girl rabbit following behind with a hedgehog holding her hand as she stumbled.

Dane didn't speak and I wondered for a moment if he hated it, but then I saw his eyes glistening as he swallowed a lump in this throat. He pointed at it and nodded, clearly too choked up to speak.

'Are you okay?' I asked gently.

He cleared his throat and took a sip of his drink before speaking. 'I wasn't expecting to have a reaction like that. This is outstanding. I love every sketch and I want to create stories for them all, but this one right here has touched me deeply. That's what I need to write about – an animal Mountain Rescue team. Thank you. You, Autumn Laine, are an exceptionally gifted artist and don't let any job loss or moments of self-doubt ever let you believe otherwise.'

My cheeks flushed but I didn't feel tearful this time. I felt elated. I'd drawn three images from my imagination and they'd brought him to tears. There was no stronger reaction than that.

'Your turn now,' I said, smiling at him.

'What I've done is not a patch on what you've done here.'

'You can stop that right now,' I said, trying my hardest to sound all stern and serious. 'I've been doing this my whole life and you're just starting out on your journey. I also think I had the easier task than you. So what have you got for me?'

He reached into the inside pocket of his jacket, hanging on the back of his chair, and removed some papers.

'When I was doing this, my main focus was on helping you get your mojo back. Because you'd told me about being inspired at the Centenary Stone and how the first thing you've drawn from your imagination in months was fairies, everything I've done is set in a mythical world. The first is just a concept.'

I unfolded the piece of paper he'd handed me and read the typed concept in my head, not wanting to embarrass him by reading it out loud.

> The bad fairy has discovered the location of the valve to turn off the sunshine and the good fairy must stop them.

I could picture it instantly – a face in the sun looking terrified as the two fairies battled by the valve – and my fingers started to tingle.

'What do you think?' Dane asked, his voice anxious.

'I love it! Already excited about drawing it.'

'You're not just saying that?'

His vulnerability was endearing and I reassured him by explaining what I was picturing, which was rewarded with one of his gorgeous smiles.

'The second is a verse,' he said, handing me another piece of paper. 'Grace is a fairy and I'll tell you what inspired it after you've read it.'

The stars were high up in the sky, shining down on
Grace
Like sparkling diamonds from a mine, lighting up
her face
She wished so long, she wished so hard, she wished
with all her might
'I hate that I'm the smallest one. I wish to have some
height.'
The stars could not be listening because she didn't feel a
change
No tingles in her arms and legs, no feelings that were
strange
She sighed and curled up by the lake, and started
counting sheep
She'd dream of being taller while she was fast asleep
The stars winked at each other. This wish they'd make
come true
'Be tall, be long, be extra strong,' they whispered as
Grace grew

I looked up from the page, in awe of what I'd just read. 'That's brilliant, Dane! And, before you object, I'm not just saying that to be nice. I want to read more and I'm dying to draw it. I can completely picture this tiny little fairy waking up to find her legs are wet and she can't work out why and then she discovers she's a giant and her legs are in the lake.'

He grinned at me. 'I was hoping that's what you'd picture.'

'So tell me about this inspiration.'

'When Ellis was younger, he was the smallest kid in his class. It wasn't by a huge amount when he was at primary school but when he started at senior school, his mates shot up and left him behind. He got picked on for being small which he brushed off, but the thing that bothered him was that he'd always wanted to join the police. People kept unhelpfully telling him that you had to be tall to be a police officer and it didn't matter how many times Lynsey and I assured him that there were no height restrictions anymore, he was convinced his height would stand against him. He used to look at the stars and wish to grow bigger. Then, when he was fourteen, he went through this massive growth spurt and ended up shooting past everyone. He towers above me now. I'm six foot but he's six foot five. Him wishing on the stars popped into my head and I wondered what would happen if the smallest fairy did that and ended up being a giant.'

'What happens next in the story, after she realises she's a giant?'

'She goes back to the fairy village but she's so big that she stands on everything and destroys it. When she sneezes, she floods the village with her spit and snot.'

'Ew! Gross! But hilarious.'

'Thank you. I see it having a *be careful what you wish for* message and she's a much happier fairy when the stars turn her back to her original size.'

'You need to write the whole thing. It's brilliant.'

He looked genuinely touched. 'Thank you. And here's my final one which is a full story but it might take you a while to read so you're welcome to take it home and look later.'

I took the pages from him without opening them. 'I'm dying to read it – especially after what I've already seen – but my mind is exploding with ideas already and I think I'd like to scribble those down before I have a third one muddling them all up. Would you mind?'

'Mind? You've made my day – my year – by your reaction to the first two. I can't believe I've inspired you so much.'

'You say I have a gift, but so do you. These ideas are amazing. To me, the writing is brilliant, but I'm not the expert. I know someone who is, though. You'll never guess who I met on my wander round the village on Wednesday. Your old English teacher.'

'Miss Eccles? Seriously? How did that happen?'

'She was coming out of the village hall and dropped some folders. I helped her pick them up, we got talking, and she mentioned that she used to teach. I can't imagine there's another Miss Eccles who taught English in Keswick.'

'I'm surprised I haven't seen her around if she lives in the village.'

'She lives in Pippinthwaite, not here, but she's starting a creative writing class in Willowdale Village Hall after Easter and I thought you might be interested.'

'That would be full circle, being taught by Miss Eccles again. I might give that a try. Thank you.'

It was still a little early for lunch so we decided to order another drink and have some creative time together. Dane nipped back to Lake View to collect his laptop and we worked in companionable silence for the next hour. I'd selected the small fairy story to illustrate and Dane unsurprisingly chose the Mountain Rescue scene. Occasionally he'd ask me if I could think of an alternative word for something or I'd check what he thought of an aspect of my illustration, but otherwise we did our own thing. I'd always worked completely independently before and, even though Dane and I had our own tasks, I felt motivated knowing we'd be stopping and sharing progress.

'You two are looking very productive.'

I looked up at the woman who'd approached our table and recognised her as one of the staff members I'd seen here on Wednesday.

'We are,' Dane said, smiling at her. 'Aunt Kelly, this is my friend Autumn.'

'So lovely to meet you, Autumn, and thanks for giving my nephew a nudge with his writing.' An attractive woman with layered shoulder-length blonde hair, a wide smile and sparkly eyes, she exuded warmth, just like her nephew.

'He's told you?' I asked, surprised.

'We wondered why he was spending hours on his laptop and Felix kept winding him up about looking at naughty websites, so he fessed up and we're so proud. He showed us what he'd prepared for you and we were extremely impressed, but he says he couldn't have done it without you.'

'I couldn't,' Dane said. 'I might have to kidnap you and keep you here, Autumn. Aunt Kelly has a cellar.'

Kelly rolled her eyes at him. 'I thought you were meant to be writing children's stories, not creating horror ones. And, just so you know, Autumn, we *don't* have a cellar.'

She wandered away, laughing, but the conversation about me leaving reminded me I hadn't done anything about looking for somewhere to live.

'I want to stay longer,' I told Dane, 'but there isn't a spare bedroom at Rosie's cottage and I think we'll both be ready for our own space after two weeks. I noticed quite a few holiday cottages in the village but I don't suppose you know anyone who has a place they're trying to rent out for longer?'

'How long are you thinking?'

'A couple of months, perhaps?'

His eyes lit up. 'Two months is a lot of time to inspire each other.'

'I've got until mid-May to make a decision about that job, so it ties in with that.'

'Any more thoughts about taking the job?' he asked.

'I've barely given it a second thought, although that in itself might be indicative of how I'm feeling about it.'

'It probably does, although you've had some creative moments since then so you might feel differently after a few more of those.'

He made a good point, as the inability to draw had been the biggest reason for not biting Madeline's hand off, but the disinterest in leaving this place and returning to London was almost as strong a factor now.

'To answer your original question,' Dane continued, 'I don't know, but I can ask Aunt Kelly for you. She knows way more people than I do, so she might have heard something.'

We ordered some lunch and resumed our individual work until it arrived. Dane had ordered a burger with triple-cooked chips and I'd chosen smoked salmon linguine, which was mouth wateringly delicious.

'That was so amazing,' I said when I'd finished eating. 'Your aunt made this?'

'Either her or Felix.'

'You come from a very talented family.'

'They're so passionate about cooking and that was always the difference between us. I enjoy it, but it doesn't ignite that fire in my belly. I can't get excited about creating a new menu or trying out a new dish. It's all very much a process for me.'

'But writing ignites that fire?'

'It does.'

'Then that's what you're meant to be, just like I'm meant to be an artist.'

24

Even though I'd have happily spent the following day working on my Dane-inspired illustrations, I'd mentioned the possibility of a bike ride over lunch and Dane had jumped on it. He'd suggested a route through Willowdale, over the bridge, and along the bridleway to the outskirts of Keswick so it would have been logical for me to cycle Rosie's bike to his rather than him doubling back on himself, but I didn't feel at all confident about being on the road on my own and had asked him to collect me from Horseshoe Cottage instead. Rosie had adjusted the saddle for me last night and encouraged me to ride up and down the lane in front of the cottage and it hadn't gone well.

'Where did they coin that phrase *it's just like riding a bike*?' I asked her. 'Because I can tell you right now, this is *not* coming back to me at all.'

'It will,' she assured me. 'You just need to give it time and relax a bit more.'

'If I relax, I'll fall off!'

Dane's advice this morning was exactly the same as Rosie's. When I'd told him how much I'd struggled last night, he suggested getting me comfortable on the estate before introducing traffic.

'Try to relax a bit more,' he said. 'Untense your shoulders and soften your grip on the handlebars.'

'I can't! I daren't let go!'

He pulled up alongside me. 'Look at my hands in a soft grip and now look at them like yours.'

He tensed and his knuckles turned white. I glanced down at mine and laughed. That was *exactly* what I was doing.

'But if I loosen my grip, how will I stay on the bike?'

'You will because you'll still be holding on but you'll be more at one with the bike.' He placed his bike down and stood beside me, holding the middle of the handlebars. 'Sit on the saddle and hold on tightly. I've got the bike so you can't fall. Can you feel the tension through your wrists to your elbows to your shoulders and across your back?'

'Yes. My neck's even starting to hurt.'

'Which isn't what you want from a leisurely ride.'

He moved round to the front of the bike and placed one leg either side of the front wheel to hold it in place.

'Look at me rather than down,' he said.

I lifted my gaze to his eyes.

'I'm going to put my hands over yours and I want you to ease your grip and I'll tell you when it feels right. Keep looking at me.'

His hands were warm as he placed them over mine and I instantly felt more relaxed by his touch. My shoulders dropped and I felt the tension easing from my back, neck and shoulders as I slowly reduced my grip strength.

'Perfect,' he said, smiling. 'When I step away, I want you to keep that same grip and ride up and down the lane a few times.'

I did as instructed and was amazed by how different it felt. 'I'm not wobbling!'

'That's because you're not tense anymore.'

I still felt a little unsteady when we left the grounds of Willowdale Hall and joined the main road, but that was fear of traffic as much as anything. It wasn't a particularly busy road, but it wasn't a wide one either and I hoped no overtaking vehicles passed too close. Thankfully the journey went without hitch, although I much preferred it when we turned off the main road by the shops, after which we only encountered cyclists and pedestrians. I liked it even more over the bridge and on the tracks cars couldn't access.

'How far do you want to go?' Dane asked as we approached Keswick town centre. 'We haven't cycled far but I'm conscious you're not used to it. We can stop here and go back or we can continue to the lake.'

'I don't mind continuing to the lake but I'm not too keen on being on the main road.'

'We can't cycle through the town centre – it's market day and too busy – but we can skirt round it past the caravan parks and come out at the top of Crow Park if you like.'

I had no idea where he meant but I was happy to go along with the suggestion, so I followed him along the main road for a short distance before turning off down some quieter streets.

Crow Park was basically a wide expanse of lush grass leading down to the northern shore of Derwent Water. Dane and I stopped at the top and I marvelled at yet another stunning view, taking in the lake with the fells either side, although Willowdale and Willowdale Hall were hidden behind a peninsula.

There were lots of people and dogs walking across the trails or taking advantage of the green space. We cycled on the track running diagonally across the park, passing a couple of families playing football, and a group of teenagers tossing a frisbee.

'Coffee break?' Dane asked when we emerged from the park. 'There's a café over there.'

It was late morning so too early for lunch, but the cakes in Derwent View Café were too tempting so I chose a millionaire's shortbread and Dane picked a piece of chocolate tiffin to eat with our coffees. Our bikes were safely locked so we ambled down to the lake.

'I asked Aunt Kelly if she knew of anyone offering a short-term rental,' Dane said as we walked slowly along the gravelly beach, past the wooden jetties. 'She's going to keep her ears open. I also asked her if she knew Miss Eccles. Apparently she was born in Willowdale and her parents lived here all their lives.'

'They're not around anymore?'

'No. Her dad died a while back and her mam died last spring.'

'Aw, that's sad.' I took a sip of my latte. 'Did you tell your aunt about the creative writing course?'

'I did and she thinks I'd be daft not to give it a go. We both reckon you should do it too.'

'Me? Why?'

'Well, if you're going to stick around for a bit, it's a way of getting to know a few people, it might inspire you with some more things to draw, and I think there's a writer lurking inside you too.'

I stopped, eyebrows raised at him. 'What? Why would you think that?'

'Because when you draw, you're not just drawing a picture, you're creating characters with feelings and emotions and you're telling a snapshot of their story. I think you always have more story in your mind than you capture on that page. The illustration is your starting point for so much more.' He broke off a piece of tiffin, laughing. 'I'll just let you ponder on that shock concept.'

I stared at him, mouth agape. Was he right? When I'd drawn

the fairies on the Centenary Stone, an entire story had presented itself as to why they were there, transported to the lakeside by an evil sprite and they had to solve the puzzle on the stone to return to their land. When I'd created my flipbooks, I'd started with simple ones like a stickman completing an activity, but they'd become increasingly complex and I'd had such a thrill from that.

'You're like the new Beatrix Potter,' he said, before stuffing in another piece of tiffin.

'Oh, I don't think so.'

He nodded vigorously as he chewed. 'I do. So will you come to the class with me? I'm a bit scared of going back to school after all these years. I need someone to hold my hand.'

At the mention of holding hands, I pictured us in the lane outside Horseshoe Cottage with his eyes fixed on me, his warm hands over mine as he encouraged me to loosen my grip, and my heart did an unexpected skip. He was looking at me the same way now, his eyes so intense and mesmerising, and it skipped again. What was happening?

'So will you?' he asked. 'Pretty please.' He held his hands together as though praying and gave me a sad puppy-dog eyes expression which made me laugh.

'Okay, because you asked so nicely and because I can't resist those sad eyes. But you're the writer, not me.'

He dropped the puppy-dog look but kept his eyes fixed on mine. 'Can't we both be writers?'

It could have been posed as a tentative, hopeful question but it had the tone of a bold statement and, at that moment, I believed that it *was* possible and a huge part of it was self-belief. It was amazing to think that it was only four days ago that we'd had lunch together in Honeybee's and he'd shared his dreams with me. He'd been hesitant and embarrassed, bracing himself for laughter and a negative reaction like he'd had from Lynsey.

Met instead with enthusiasm, support and encouragement, he'd now shared his plans with his family and had written an inspired idea and a fantastic verse. I had no doubt that the full story would be equally fabulous and couldn't wait to read it when I'd completed my current illustrations. In a short space of time, he'd gone from secret aspiring writer to being an actual writer and, during the same week, I'd gone from months of drawing nothing from my imagination to creating several illustrations inspired by this beautiful setting and by Dane.

'What do you reckon?' he prompted. 'Are you with me?'

'I am,' I said. 'We *can* both be writers and we *will* be.'

'Yes! You won't regret it.'

As we hugged each other, another piece of my broken confidence slotted back into place. The one called self-belief.

25

I was buzzing when I returned to Horseshoe Cottage at lunchtime. Dane was covering an afternoon shift at The White Willow and, much as I was loving his company and would have happily spent the day with him, it was a good thing I couldn't. My leg muscles and my backside probably couldn't have coped with any more time in the saddle and I was eager to finish my illustrations so I could read Dane's story.

With Alice and Toffee at the riding stables with Rosie, the cottage would be empty for the afternoon and I could immerse myself in my art. I made a sandwich which I ate in Rosie's bedroom with the Juliet balcony doors open, drinking in the beautiful view.

By half three, I couldn't resist Dane's story any longer. I hadn't finished colouring my illustrations, but I'd made sufficient progress that pausing and returning to them later wouldn't hamper my creativity. I made a fresh coffee in a flask and took the story down to the lake edge and sat on the same log I'd sat on with Rosie earlier in the week. I poured myself a drink and took a moment to breathe in my surroundings – the gentle lapping of the water, the rustle of leaves in the light spring breeze, and the excited chatter of birds. Everything about this place made me feel so relaxed but also so alive. No wonder Rosie had no designs on travelling.

I unfolded the story, printed out on A4 paper, and smiled. *The Lost Gilderhopp*. I loved it already!

Although Dane had said it was a full-length story, it was written in verse too. It was the tale of a lilac and mint-green fluffy creature called a gilderhopp who got left behind in the forest on a family picnic. Scared and panicking, he came across another creature called a fizzbee and they made friends. She said her family would be able to help him find his. They took him in and, even though they were kind to him, he missed his family and wanted to get home. They kept saying they'd help him 'tomorrow' but tomorrow never came. The fizzbee who'd found him was upset for her new friend, especially when she discovered her family wanted to keep him because he was magical and they weren't. She helped him escape, although his journey home wasn't without further hurdles to overcome.

It was beautifully written, the verse structure was inspired, and it had me tearing up at several points. Dane was already a writer and I could definitely see published author in his future. How wonderful that I'd been able to play a small part in giving him that little nudge in the early stage of his journey and what an honour it would be to continue to support and encourage him and to have him do the same for me as I continued my own journey of discovery into my future career as an artist.

Gorgeous as it was by the lake, I had a clear picture in my mind of what the gilderhopp looked like – a cross between a sloth and a red panda, with the huge sad eyes of a slow loris – and I couldn't wait to capture him on paper. Just one week in the Lake District and I was bursting with creativity.

Rosie, Alice and Toffee were already back. Toffee rushed up to me for a fuss and Rosie and Alice greeted me warmly, asking about my day.

'I've read Dane's story,' I said after I'd told them about our bike ride this morning.

'At last!' Rosie said. 'Was it good?'

Although Dane wasn't planning on telling anyone outside his family that he had aspirations to write children's books, he'd said I was welcome to tell Rosie and Alice because they'd be curious as to what I was drawing and he didn't want me feeling I had to be secretive. They'd both loved the concept and the verse and had been full of compliments for my accompanying illustrations, but couldn't believe how restrained I'd been in not allowing myself to get side-tracked by reading the full story.

'It was something else,' I said. 'He has a gift and it actually makes me angry that his wife was so unsupportive of it and that her family pushed him into a career he didn't want. The people who love you should listen and nurture and…' I shook my head. 'I guess that's the point. She fell out of love with him somewhere along the way and her parents never liked him. I can't imagine how horrendous that must have been. It's a wonder he isn't all bitter and resentful.'

'He's probably relieved to be out of there and back in a place he loves, surrounded by family who care, and just wants to put it all behind him,' Alice said. 'So what's his story about?'

'You can read it for yourselves so I won't give any spoilers. All I'll say is it's beautiful and I think it might have been inspired by what you've just said about Dane wanting to get back to his family.' I was getting all choked up again, tears pricking my eyes. 'Honestly, it's sublime.'

Rosie rubbed my arm. 'I love how emotional you're getting

about it. I can't wait to read it, and I can't wait to meet Dane at some point.'

'You'll love him. I'll get something sorted.' I passed the story to Rosie and pushed my chair back. 'I won't sit and stare at you while you read it. I'm dying to start on the illustrations, so I'll head upstairs.'

'Did you get the card I put up there earlier?' Alice asked.

I shook my head.

She frowned. 'That's strange. I put it on your bedside... no, I didn't! Sorry. I was on my way to do that and got distracted. It's on the bureau in the lounge.'

'Thanks. I'll get it on my way through.'

I spotted the envelope immediately with a couple of other pieces of post. Butterflies stirred as I recognised Étienne's handwriting. What now? I glanced back towards the kitchen where Rosie and Alice were huddled over *The Lost Gilderhopp*, and took the card upstairs, away from that magical, inspiring story.

Perched on the edge of the chair by the Juliet balcony, I removed the contents. The hand-crafted card was beautiful in its simplicity – no words, but five raised hearts painted with a red watercolour with a black line curving from each to look as though they were a bunch of flowers. As soon as I opened the card, a photograph slipped out onto my lap and I picked it up. I recognised myself as a six-year-old, licking an ice cream in a park, with a blob of it on my nose and dribbles trickling down the sides and over my fingers. Almost off camera, with his eyes fixed on my face, was a young Étienne.

In the card, he'd written a short note in French:

Found this while helping sort some of Mum and Dad's boxes from the move. I told you I've loved you since I was a young boy and I mean it when I say I'll still love you when I'm an old man. I beg you to give me a chance to make things right.

Forever yours, Étienne xx

I looked back at the photo and couldn't help smiling. I suspected it might be the ice cream he was eyeing up rather than me, but the sentiment was sweet. Everything about Étienne had been sweet... until it turned sour. He'd been a lovely friend and an amazing boyfriend in our very short time together – kind, thoughtful, considerate – but that made what he did even harder to stomach because it made me question everything I thought I knew about him. The Étienne I knew and loved would have done right by Chantal and the baby and, even if he had chosen them, he would have talked it through with me first. Which begged the question: had I ever truly known him? Had having a holiday-based friendship given him the opportunity to present only his shiny side? I wasn't naïve enough to think that any relationship was perfect, but I wanted a partner who I could trust to be honest with me and be by my side to discuss issues – not someone who'd make decisions without me – and I wasn't convinced Étienne was that person.

As I slipped the card and photo back in their envelope, I caught the edge of my ring. When he gave me it, Étienne told me that it was the stone of courage and that's what had brought us together. What would be more courageous for me now? Taking a second chance on our relationship or walking away and daring to build a new life without him?

26

My thighs were aching on Sunday but I felt so good after getting some exercise on my bike ride with Dane that I agreed to walking up Latrigg with Rosie after lunch – a small fell north of Keswick which she assured me was an easier walk than scary-looking Cat Bells.

Toffee joined us and the first part of the walk across the park and a bridge over the A66 was fairly leisurely but, as we followed the trail between trees, I was soon puffing and panting, sweat trickling down my face.

'We'll stop for a drink,' Rosie said, stepping off the path so other walkers could easily pass us.

'I thought you said this wasn't a tough climb.'

'This is the steepest part, I promise. Obviously it continues uphill but at a much gentler gradient. There's no rush. I want you to enjoy this.'

Rosie was breathing normally and there wasn't a bead of sweat to be seen. To my shame, a group of people ran past us up the hill, including a man who had to be in his seventies.

'Fell runners,' Rosie said, smiling at my shocked expression.

'Can you do that?'

'No! I love riding and walking, but running doesn't do it for me.'

Taking another gulp of water, I declared myself ready to go again. This time, Rosie set a slower pace which made a big difference, although I still couldn't walk and talk and was happy for her to give me a running commentary of what we could see and what it had been like growing up in the area.

Every so often, I stopped to look back over Keswick and Derwent Water – a great excuse to take a moment to catch my breath and slow my heart rate.

'If we went straight on here, we could walk up Skiddaw,' Rosie said as we reached a fork in the path, 'but we're veering to the right towards Latrigg. Some fun facts about Skiddaw. It's the fourth highest in the Lake District at 931 metres and it's part of the Skiddaw family, with a circle of lower fells round it including the sweetly named Skiddaw Little Man. Even though it's high, it's actually an easy climb because there's such a well-used tourist path. Personally, it's not my favourite. The views are great, of course, but I find the climb a bit dull. Latrigg isn't as challenging, but I think it's a more interesting route.'

'Have you climbed all the fells round here?'

'I have, but it's years ago for some. Mam used to like hiking before the accident so we did loads of them together, including in other parts of the national park. Nowadays I mainly do Latrigg because it's quick and easy and Cat Bells because it's on the doorstep.'

The path to the summit of Latrigg curved back on itself and there was a steady flow of walkers in each direction, with the occasional runner. Some brave souls were taking the much steeper route up the hillside.

'I can see why people do that,' Rosie said, nodding towards a group scrambling up the grass, 'but I wish they wouldn't when there's a perfectly good path here. It damages the grasses and wildflowers.'

I'd found my stride now that the incline wasn't as steep and was beginning to enjoy my walk. Rounding a final corner, I couldn't deny that the view was worth the climb. It completely took my breath away – quite literally because it was extremely windy now that we were at the top and more exposed. We could see Keswick and the whole of the lake, surrounded by majestic fells. I was rather proud of myself for being able to recognise Cat Bells, name the islands in the lake, and spot Willowdale and Willowdale Hall.

'I'm impressed,' Rosie said. 'You'll be an expert on the local area in no time.'

A wooden bench was perfectly positioned to enjoy the view, but it was already taken. Several other walkers were sitting on the grassy slope taking it in, having a drink, eating a picnic.

'Is this the actual summit?' I asked, noticing that there was a pathway behind us up a further incline.

'There's a little bit further. The summit's just up there but you'd be forgiven for saying you've done Latrigg if you stop here.'

I shook my head. 'I'd feel like I was cheating. Let's conquer it properly before we sit down.'

It didn't take much longer to get right to the top. The view was still great but the perspective over the lake wasn't quite as impressive as it was by the bench, so we took a few photos and selfies at the summit then returned to the grassy slope to enjoy the best views over a drink and a banana.

'No wonder you come up here so often,' I said to Rosie as we sat side by side looking out over the town, lake and fells. 'It's spectacular.'

'I can't imagine ever tiring of it. It never looks the same, either.

The seasons, the time of day, and the different weather give this sense of seeing it for the first time whenever I make the ascent.'

'I'm glad you talked me into it. It was so worth the climb.'

'Cat Bells is too,' she said, nudging me playfully. 'I promise. Are you glad you've decided to stick around for a couple more months?'

I'd already shared my thoughts around finding somewhere to rent. Rosie hadn't been at all offended and completely understood that a long-term stay wasn't practical when we were sharing a bed, but she and Alice had both said I was welcome to stay as long as I needed, especially considering we were into the Easter holidays now which might make finding somewhere more challenging.

'Definitely. Thing is, I don't think I'm going to want to leave then either.'

'Then don't. You'd be making two women and one dog very happy if you settled here.'

'Aw, thank you. You and your mam have been so good to me.'

'You're a lovely person so it's not difficult. And scrap what I just said. It's three women you'd be making happy, not two. I should have included you in that. It's a bold statement but I think you've been happier here this past week than anywhere else.'

It *was* a bold statement, but it was an accurate one. I felt so different here.

'You and Paris clearly aren't meant to be and you've said yourself that there's nothing to pull you back to Sutton now that your granddad's gone. Considering how well you've settled in here and already gone from a ball of stress to someone who's starting to sparkle once more, it's obvious to me that this is where you *should* be.'

I swept my gaze around the view, taking in Rosie's smiling face and Toffee's wagging tail as I scratched behind her ears.

'I really think it is,' I agreed. 'And actually...' I twiddled with my promise ring, my mind racing with the decision I'd just made. I removed the ring and held it out in front of me, the lake framed by the silver band.

'It's over?' Rosie asked.

'Yes. This isn't my future.' I wiggled the ring. 'But this is.' I swept my arm across the landscape.

Rosie squealed and hugged me to her side. 'I'm so relieved to hear you say that because I don't think going back to Étienne would be right for you. What made your mind up?'

'This place. If Étienne and I were to get back together, how would it even work? I don't want to live in Paris. I never have. I don't want to live in London either, and Brighton was right at the time but it isn't now. It's only day ten but I've never felt more alive anywhere else. Willowdale feels like home, and you and your mam feel like family. And you too, Toffee,' I added when she cocked her head to one side, looking at me quizzically. 'I don't want to leave any of you, or Dane, so Étienne would have to fit into all this. How? He's a city boy and, even if he embraced countryside living, what's he going to do for a job? And that's before we even factor in his daughters. What sort of relationship would he be able to have with them if he was living here and they're still in Dijon? Which would mean he really needs to stay in France, meaning a distance relationship, and I'm not willing to do that.'

'This is all music to my ears but what if he said he was 100 per cent willing to move here if it meant being with you? How would you feel then?'

My stomach lurched as she said that, which told me everything. If I really wanted him, surely my heart would have leapt.

'It wouldn't change anything, which is a bit of a surprise to me, although it shouldn't be. If I still loved him as deeply as I thought, I should be running up and down this fell singing. Well, maybe not running – one thing at a time! But I should be delighted and at least thinking about inviting him over to hear him out, but I just can't see him here. This isn't his world. It's mine.'

'So what happens next?' Rosie asked.

'I'll write to him tonight. I might even send this back.' I secured the ring in a zipped pocket on my backpack.

Rosie put her arm round me and cuddled me to her side again. 'You're doing the right thing.'

We sat there in silence for several minutes but the wind was strong and we were soon a bit too cold and buffeted. We took some photos and began our descent.

'If this is home now, does that mean you're going to tell your old boss it's a no too?' Rosie asked.

'Yes. She's away on holiday this week, so I won't drop it on her yet, but I'll let her know when she's back.'

'What would you do if she said you could work for her but be based from home?'

I pondered for a moment. Home working was becoming so much more commonplace these days and it suited the type of work I did, but did I want to go back to corporate life?

'Still a no, I think. I've spent most of my career so far designing greetings cards and it feels like now's the time to step out of my comfort zone and find a new direction.'

'So many new starts!' Rosie said. 'Does it feel scary?'

'I thought it would, but it doesn't, which has to mean both decisions are right for me. I just have to hope my mojo fully returns because my redundancy pay isn't going to last indefinitely.'

'Hasn't it returned already? What you've produced this week has been phenomenal.'

I smiled gratefully. 'That's kind and I'm not denying they're good, but the inspiration isn't mine. I drew the first batch for Dane and the second from his ideas and I need to find me. Mission Sparkle has been great for getting back into it and restoring some lost confidence, but I need to find something fresh and I need a career. Dane reckons there's a closet writer in me.'

I told her about the conversation we'd had.

'I think he's onto something there.'

'You think I can write too?'

'I *know* you can write. You've been writing to me for twenty-four years and don't say they were just letters because some of your letters read like stories. You once sent me a flipbook. That was a story!'

'I'd completely forgotten I made you one of those. I went through a phase where I made loads of them.'

'See! You're a natural storyteller through your art. You just need to add the words.'

Arriving back at Rosie's jeep later, I felt such a sense of achievement. I'd summited my first-ever fell. It might not have been the highest or most demanding, but it had been a challenge for me and I'd done it. I'd also got back on a bike and it hadn't been as scary as anticipated. Discovering the sort of artist I'd be going forwards was going to be another challenge but I'd do that too. With friendship and encouragement from Rosie and Dane, I felt like I could conquer anything. I thought about what Grandma had said about being courageous, adventurous and happy. I was definitely being the first two and I certainly felt like I was in the right place to find the third. Right now, I felt like I was at the start of something wonderful.

27

We'd had glorious sunny weather for our walk up Latrigg yesterday, but today brought a temperature drop with an overcast sky and scattered showers expected. My leg muscles were aching so I wouldn't have been up for my next fell even if the weather had been nice. Being Rosie's full day off, she suggested a gentle walk into Willowdale as she didn't get into the village very often. As soon as she mentioned that she'd never been in The White Willow, I insisted on treating her to lunch there.

Dane's cousin Felix greeted us at the door. 'You've timed that well. Only one table left.'

I glanced past him and the café was indeed full, although it was 12.30 p.m., so bang on lunchtime.

Felix took our order a little later and I glanced across at the counter, surprised to see Dane there. I pointed him out to Rosie.

'He's a bit yummy,' she said, her voice low. 'Better looking than Étienne?'

I watched him for a moment, laughing at something his Aunt Kelly said. They were both very attractive men, but Étienne didn't have the natural warmth that Dane did. He didn't smile or laugh nearly as much either. I'd never thought about how serious he was before. We'd laughed together a lot, but in the short time I'd known Dane, I'd properly belly-laughed – something I didn't remember ever doing with Étienne.

'Yes. Better looking,' I said, still gazing at Dane.

'Somebody's getting a crush,' she whispered.

I snapped my head round to her. 'I am not!'

She giggled. 'Just saying what I see, and your strong protest and red cheeks don't do anything to convince me I'm wrong.'

'I like him. He's fun to be around and I'm in awe of his talent.'

'You keep telling yourself that's what it is.'

I rolled my eyes at her. 'Subject change. So, this is your first time in The White Willow, but did you come into the café before?'

'I did and it wasn't a patch on this...'

Rosie told me what she could remember about the previous café but I wasn't fully listening. Could she be right about me having a crush on Dane? No! That was ridiculous. I liked him and, yes, he was very attractive, but we were just friends. He was still married, albeit not for much longer and, even though I'd made my decision about Étienne and would be writing to him this week to tell him, I'd been in love with him for fourteen years and I couldn't just switch those feelings off. But if I stuck around and we both had some more time to heal, getting together with Dane wasn't an unappealing future possibility.

Dane brought our lunch over and my heart skipped, which I put down to Rosie putting notions of crushes into my head. I introduced them to each other.

'I didn't think you were working here today,' I said to him.

'I wasn't meant to be, but someone phoned in sick so I'm helping out.'

'Rosie and I are going to The Hardy Herdwick for a few drinks tonight. We wondered if you'd like to join us.'

'I'd love to. Cheers. What time?'

'We'll be walking past your house at about quarter past seven, so we'll knock for you then.'

He flashed me a gorgeous smile. 'See you tonight and enjoy your meals.'

'Someone's got a crush on you too,' Rosie murmured when he'd gone.

'Stop it!'

But I couldn't help liking that idea.

* * *

'Did you know that Beatrix Potter was an expert on Herdwicks?' Rosie asked as we set off into the village that evening for our visit to The Hardy Herdwick.

'I saw something about it in one of the guide books but I didn't read the detail.'

'She became a passionate farmer and environmentalist, as I'm sure you've picked up already. Herdies were under threat when she bought Hill Top. As well as buying up farms to preserve the countryside, she became a big supporter of preserving local animal breeds. She built up a celebrated flock with one of her farmers, regularly won at shows, and she wore suits made from Herdwick fleeces. Herdies are so much a part of our landscape now, particularly around Coniston, that it's hard to imagine the Lakes without them but, without Beatrix Potter, the landscape would have looked very different and the breed might not have survived if the farms had been sold off to developers.' She laughed lightly. 'I've just realised I sound like a guide book.'

'I love all your facts. They're really interesting. And Herdwicks look so adorable in the photos I've seen – like they're actually smiling. I'd love to see one up close.'

'I'm sure you will soon. Another fun fact for you. When Herdwick lambs are born, they're black all over. As they grow, their faces become white and their fleeces turn to light brown. After their first shearing, it grows back as steel grey and lightens with age.'

'It does not! You're winding me up!'

'I'm not. I promise you, that's exactly what happens.'

We'd reached Lake View so we called for Dane and the three of us continued on to The Hardy Herdwick. Inside, it was a traditional village pub with lots of dark wood, stone flags on the floor, and a real fireplace in the lounge and bar area. It could have been gloomy, but the walls had been painted a warm shade of cream which lightened the place. There were pictures of Herdwick sheep everywhere – a mixture of photographs and illustrations – and there were indeed black lambs and brown-fleeced sheep among them. I loved that fact.

A small soft toy sheep displayed with the drinks bottles behind the bar made me smile and the whole place felt warm, cosy and welcoming. I could see myself coming here often. The pub was busy with diners but we found an empty table in the bar and Dane got a round of drinks in.

'I can't remember the last time I came in here,' Rosie said, looking around. 'That's bad, isn't it?'

'It's difficult for you. You have a demanding job and your mam to watch out for.'

'Yeah, but Mam's fine unless it's pouring. I think I've been using her as an excuse to stay home and I should really stop doing that. You managed to make a good friend within days of getting here, so it shows it can be done.'

'That was a unique circumstance and I doubt our paths would

have crossed if I hadn't been so careless. But I hear what you're saying. Were there any classes on that village hall leaflet that appealed to you?'

'I quite like the idea of learning Spanish. I've no idea when I'd get to speak it, but I enjoyed German at school and picked up some Portuguese from Tiago. Might be good to have a weekly commitment and meet a few people not connected to the riding school.'

Dane returned with the drinks and plonked himself down on a bar stool.

'Rosie and I were just talking about the classes at the village hall,' I told him. 'She's thinking she might try the Spanish class.'

'Do you speak any other languages?' he asked her.

'I did a GCSE in German and it was one of my best subjects. Did you do languages, Dane?'

'No. We had to do a couple of years of French and I was hopeless at it – sorry, Autumn – so I dropped it as soon as I could.'

'How many secondary schools are there in Keswick?' I asked.

'One,' they both answered together.

'Then you must have both gone to the same one.'

It turned out they had, although Dane had been two school years ahead and they hadn't known each other. The conversation flowed seamlessly from Dane and Rosie reminiscing about some of the teachers and pupils at school to us talking about our childhoods in general. Dane was fascinated by us being penpals.

'I can't believe you've only just met for the first time,' he said. 'You act like you've been best friends forever.'

'Effectively we have,' I said. 'Just through letter rather than in person.'

'Which shows how important writing is,' Rosie added, 'and why you absolutely must write stories, Dane.'

'We've read *The Lost Gilderhopp*,' I said. 'It made us both cry.'

Dane winced. 'Is that good or bad?'

'Good!' Rosie and I cried together.

'Honestly, Dane, it was so moving,' I said.

Rosie pointed to my phone. 'Show him the picture.'

'I've drawn what I imagine the gilderhopp to look like but I might be way off the mark, so I won't be offended if it's not what you were thinking.'

I passed him my phone showing the photograph I'd taken earlier of my illustration of the gilderhopp. He was lilac and fluffy with patches of mint green on the insides of his ears, his belly and his paws. His long curled tail was lilac and mint striped with green fluff at the end, and he had a mint-green fluffy tuft between his ears.

'I can't believe it!' Dane exclaimed, his eyes wide. 'It's like you've reached into my head and scooped it out. If I could draw, this is *exactly* what I'd have created. You're a genius.'

'I haven't created the fizzbee yet. I've got an image in my head but I wanted to make sure I'd nailed the gilderhopp first.'

'He's perfect. I can't wait to see what you come up with for the fizzbee.'

The hours flew past and we were on our fifth round when the landlord called time and we realised we were the only ones left in the pub.

'I think that's our cue to leave,' Dane said, taking a final swig on his pint.

Rosie and I finished our drinks too, pulled on our coats, and the three of us stepped out of the lovely cosy pub into the cold.

I gave a shudder. 'Ooh, that's sobering!'

It was raining – that really light rain that seems insignificant but gets you drenched – and there were patches of fog.

'Power walk home, I think,' Rosie said as she zipped up her coat.

For once, I'd thought to put on my waterproof and was exceedingly grateful for it as we sped through the village, stopping when we reached Lake View.

'It's been such a good night,' Dane said. 'We'll have to do it again soon.'

He hugged me, which seemed the natural thing to do, but I was mindful of not lingering too long as Rosie was bound to see it as further evidence of my alleged crush. He hugged Rosie too and told her how great it had been to meet her.

'We haven't made plans for next week,' he said to me. 'I'm at Hill Top for the next two days but give me a shout if you fancy doing something on Thursday or Friday.'

He hugged me quickly again then ran across the road and disappeared up the drive.

I could feel Rosie's eyes on me. 'Don't say it!'

'Wasn't gonna,' she said in a sing-song voice before laughing. 'Sorry, I have to! You two are adorable together. I know you've both got exes to get out of your systems but, when you do, you're going to be magic together and I want it to be known that I'm the one who called it.'

'Come on, Cupid,' I said, linking my arm through hers. 'Let's get you home before you race up his drive and tell him the same thing.'

We continued along the road through the misty drizzle and patchy fog.

'Tonight was so good,' Rosie said, her words a little slurred. 'I love that pub. Everyone's friendly and it's all lovely and cosy. I've been missing out on so much.'

'Don't beat yourself up,' I said gently. 'I've been exactly the same in Sutton, drifting from one day to the next, knowing this can't be it, but never doing anything to change it.'

'Things *are* going to change. I *am* going to learn Spanish and maybe do some other stuff too. At least if you're sticking around for a while, I'll have a friend to do things with.'

As soon as she said that, it was clear to me that I didn't want to just stick around for a while. I wanted to make the move here permanently.

'How would you feel if I put the Sutton house on the market and moved here?'

She stopped walking and looked at me, eyes sparkling. 'Are you for real? You mean properly permanently relocate here?'

'Being in the pub tonight with you and Dane and getting smiles and hellos from the locals confirmed to me that this is where I want to be. I've finally found friends and a community and I don't want to let it go.'

Rosie squealed and flung her arms round me. 'That's the best news ever.'

We set off walking towards Horseshoe Cottage again, speculating on how much the house in Sutton might be worth, how quickly it would sell, and whether I'd be able to find somewhere to buy in Willowdale. I'd need to rent in the short term but, once the Sutton house sold, it would make more sense to buy if I could. I was so ready to make a fresh start in this place with the stunning inspiring views and the community and friends. For the first time ever, I felt like I was part of something.

28

I walked into Willowdale on Wednesday morning to meet Dane and get a lift to Hill Top. Yesterday had been overcast and drizzly again so I'd stayed indoors and worked on my imagining of the fizzbee, which completed everything I wanted to draw for Dane. I was bursting with ideas for illustrations for *The Lost Gilderhopp* and would have happily drawn a stack of them, but it didn't feel right to do that without Dane's input. It was his story, so I needed to understand what he wanted.

Scrabbling around for inspiration to draw for the 'new me', I decided another trip to Hill Top would be in order, so I'd messaged Dane and asked if we could travel together today.

Rosie's words about the pair of us being 'adorable' rang in my ears as I got closer to Lake View. Butterflies stirred in my stomach and, when I spotted Dane on the drive, they took flight. Was this Rosie's influence or was it genuinely the start of something? If it was the latter, I had no idea what to do with that. There'd only ever been Étienne and it had taken me five years and a lot of alcohol before I let him know how I felt, so I didn't exactly have a successful track record with men. If anything was reciprocated by

Dane, I wasn't sure I'd be able to tell. No man had ever flirted with me or given me signals before. Or had they and I just hadn't realised? They probably hadn't because I knew I'd been aloof and distant. It had become my armour.

'It's Willowdale's answer to Beatrix Potter,' Dane called as I stepped onto the drive. 'Good morning!'

'Good morning, Willowdale's answer to Arthur Ransome,' I quipped, referencing the Leeds-born author of one of my favourite childhood books, *Swallows and Amazons*, which was set around Coniston and written after Ransome made the Lake District his home.

Dane laughed. 'Arthur Ransome? I'm flattered.'

'Okay, so I know he didn't write for the same age group, but it was that or Wordsworth.' The poet William Wordsworth was one of the Lake District's most famous sons.

'"I wandered lonely as a cloud..."' Dane started, but he frowned, shaking his head. 'I've completely forgotten the rest of the words. We studied that poem at school and it's gone. Miss Eccles would be disgusted with me. Did you know that most people know it as "Daffodils" but the first line is actually the proper title?'

'I didn't know that. Every day's a school day. I learned on Monday that Herdwicks are black when they're born and now this! "Daffodils" – sorry, "I Wandered Lonely as a Cloud" – was one of my grandma's favourite poems and I could recite it all too but, other than that first line, all I can remember is the ending – "And then my heart with pleasure fills, and dances with the daffodils". I couldn't tell you what happens in between.'

'Some fluttering and head tossing, I think. Sounds like a shampoo advert. And on that note, shall we go?'

On the way to Near Sawrey, I shared my decision to relocate to the area.

'That's brilliant news!' Dane said, glancing at me with a big smile. 'As someone who has lived away and returned, I can't imagine anywhere better, although I suspect you've already worked that out if you're planning to relocate here after less than a fortnight.'

'It's not just the place. It's having friends and a community. I didn't have that before and I know how much I'll miss it if I leave.'

'Does this mean you'll be looking for somewhere to buy rather than rent?'

'Not at first. I still need a rental because, even if the Sutton house gets a speedy offer, it'll take a few months for the sale to go through. I don't suppose your aunt has heard about any rentals?'

'She's thought of something, but she says she needs to check it out before she says anything. Cryptic or what? No idea whether that'll come to anything, but I'll keep you posted.'

'Thanks. You said before that you can't afford to buy somewhere on your current income, but have you considered renting instead?'

'I have, but it's not cheap round here to rent somewhere on your own, as you'll soon discover. I might have to take the plunge and dip into the house sale proceeds because, if I'm going to give my writing a real chance, I need a proper writing space. Aunt Kelly is a star for letting me stay for so long, but I'm in a box room, sitting on a single bed with my laptop on my knee. I'd love to be able to put your drawings up on the wall but I don't want to damage the wallpaper. I did look into renting some office space in Keswick, but decided against it. What if I want to write on an evening? I can't imagine driving into town just so I can work from a proper desk.'

'I agree. You can't switch creativity on and off like that.'

'If a rental bargain came up, I'd be daft not to consider it, but I'm sure you've spotted that Willowdale has a fair share of holiday cottages. Landlords are usually more interested in the holiday let income rather than longer-term tenants, so I'm intrigued as to what Aunt Kelly has in mind for you. Ooh, I love this song.'

Dane turned the radio up and bobbed his head to Katy Perry's 'Roar'. His lips moved intermittently as though he wasn't quite sure of the lyrics but, when the chorus hit, he burst into song, bobbing his head more vigorously to the music, making me smile. He glanced at me as it reached the roaring part.

'Join in!'

We sang at the top of our voices with the windows down, sunglasses on, driving through stunning countryside on a beautiful day.

'Nice roaring,' Dane said when it finished.

'Right back at you.'

As we continued our journey towards Near Sawrey, I reflected on how different my life was now to how it had been just three weeks ago when I'd been in Paris, frustrated at my inability to draw, and dreading the invite to spend the evening with Étienne's parents for fear of being confronted by the past. The 'Roar' lyrics felt so appropriate and empowering. I'd had enough of living in the shadow of my past and now I was in charge. Now was my time to roar.

* * *

Hill Top was much busier than it had been last time I visited. I went into the house first but didn't like to linger too long with more people milling about. Plus I'd come with a plan to do some drawing and I wanted to be outside for that.

I walked across the orchard and looked back towards the house. It was a great view, but the gardens were walled and I couldn't see into them from here. I'd hoped to see both. There was a sloping field behind the orchard which would have a great view of both, but there didn't appear to be any access to it for visitors.

I didn't recall there being anywhere to sit in the garden from my last visit, but I went through the archway to double-check. In the far-right corner, I spotted a gap between the bushes and one of the farm's outbuildings which would be the ideal place to sit without getting in anyone's way. I placed the picnic blanket I'd brought with me, still folded, on the soil, and sat down. Perfect.

Removing my sketchpad, I looked across the gardens and imagined Peter Rabbit scampering through them, trying to escape from Mr McGregor, losing his little shoes in his haste. Hill Top and the vegetable garden hadn't actually been the setting for *The Tale of Peter Rabbit* – Beatrix Potter hadn't discovered Hill Top at the time she wrote and illustrated the story – but I could vividly imagine the action unfolding here.

Beatrix Potter's love for rabbits came across strongly in her stories, as did her disdain for foxes and badgers. *The Tale of Mr Tod* was a pretty dark one where Tommy Brock the badger kidnapped some baby rabbits – the offspring of Benjamin Bunny and Flopsy – and hid them in the oven of his arch-enemy Mr Tod the fox with the intention of eating them later. Although it had a happy ending for the rabbits, who were rescued, Tommy Brock and Mr Tod had a huge fight, smashing up most of Mr Tod's kitchen in the process, before taking the fight outside and tumbling down a hill. Whether they both survived the fight remained unanswered in the book, although Beatrix Potter later wrote a letter to a reader advising of the outcome – that Tommy Brock won and Mr Tod was badly beaten.

I loved all wildlife and, while I could understand that there would always be those who'd struggle with certain creatures for various legitimate reasons like damage and disease, I wondered whether Beatrix Potter would present badgers and foxes in such a negative light if she was starting out now. As a farmer, she maybe would, but I felt compelled to redress the balance, especially after Dane's reaction to my animal Mountain Rescue team.

Exactly as I'd done for that illustration, I pulled up some images of badgers on my phone to check for accuracy on proportions and markings and roughly sketched a badger husband and wife team. With *The Tale of Peter Rabbit* still in my mind, I imagined them coming out of their sett under the light of a full moon and rescuing Peter's blue jacket and shoes which Mr McGregor had made into a scarecrow.

I couldn't draw quickly enough and soon the words rather than the illustrations were tumbling out onto the paper as a friendship formed between Claude and Nancy Badger and the Rabbit family. Page after page I filled with words, adding a few scribbles as to what the accompanying illustration would be, before returning to the words.

Sometime later, I rolled my shoulders and stretched. I hadn't hunched over my sketchpad inspired like that for a very long time and I couldn't quite believe that I'd just written a story. It would likely be pants but, as I flicked back through what I'd written, a smile crept across my face. It wasn't pants at all. It had drama when Mr McGregor heard a noise and came out of his house to investigate, it had emotion, and it ended with a warm and fuzzy 'awww' moment.

Whether I could repeat that again remained to be seen, but I'd just written a story and it felt good. I couldn't wait to tell Dane. He was on the door to Hill Top today and I longed to run over to him right now, but he had a job to do and it wouldn't be fair or right to disturb him when there were paying customers needing his attention.

I watched Dane for a while. I wasn't close enough to hear

what he was saying but laughter intermittently drifted over to me. He was so engaging with people. I thought back to our first meeting and how wary I'd been, but he'd done everything possible to put me at ease as well as going out of his way to help. Anyone else might have shouted at me for being so stupid, but *he'd* apologised for *my* mistake. He volunteered here, he volunteered with Mountain Rescue, and he was going to help his relatives get the evening service up and running at The White Willow even though he didn't want to be a chef. He wrote the most beautiful stories and had such a positive outlook on life, despite how badly Lynsey had treated him. Her loss was my gain and I was very lucky to have him as my friend.

Turning my attention back to my sketchpad, I flicked over to a fresh page and sketched a couple more images to accompany the story I'd written. When I'd searched for badger images, a gorgeous photo had appeared of a badger cub and a fox cub snuggled together. It brought to mind the Disney film *The Fox and the Hound* with an unlikely friendship between a fox cub and a puppy whose friendship was tested when they grew older and the puppy became a hunting dog. What if the badger cub was abandoned and adopted by a fox family but tensions arose as it grew bigger than the foxes?

My pencil began working again, scribbling images and words. It was like there'd been a dam holding back all my creative thoughts and it had just burst, spilling them out onto the paper.

I completely lost track of time and hadn't realised Dane had reached the end of his shift until I spotted him jogging along the path towards me.

'What are you doing squashed in the corner like that?' he asked, looking bemused.

'It was the only place I could find where I'd be able to see the house and gardens without being in anyone's way.'

'Good day?' he asked, crouching down beside me.

'Yes, but unexpected.'

'Interesting choice of words.'

'I wrote a story. Two, actually.'

'Can I read them?'

I flicked the pages back to the start and handed him the pad. 'They're very rough and I'm sure they need a lot of work, but I've never written a story before. Well, I will have done in creative writing at school but I don't remember being good at it, and—'

Dane lightly pressed his finger to my lips. He only held it there for a matter of seconds but it made my stomach do the most enormous backflip.

'I'm sure they'll be brilliant,' he said, gazing down at the page.

I wanted to bury my head between my legs in case he hated them and I saw it on his face, but I made myself watch him to see the truth. The smiles had to be a good sign, but I wasn't so sure about what the occasional raise of his eyebrows conveyed.

He moved onto the badger and fox cubs story and, as he approached the end, I realised I was holding my breath, anxious to hear his verdict.

He closed the pad and handed it back to me. 'I was half-joking when I said it this morning but now I have the proof. You *are* Willowdale's answer to Beatrix Potter.'

'You liked them?'

'I loved them. If that's "rough", I can't wait to see and read the polished version. You *are* a writer. And a speedy one at that. You really came up with all that while I was doing my shift?'

'Yes and I have a numb bum now and can't feel my legs, so I might need you to help me up. I'll tell you what sparked it in the car.'

I put my pad and pencils in my backpack with my empty flask of water and held out both hands to Dane. He pulled me up but with a little more strength than either of us were expecting and we collided.

'Sorry!' he said. 'Did I hurt you?'

'No, I'm fine.'

Neither of us had stepped back. I could feel the warmth from him and smell his body spray. As I looked up into his eyes, I felt the air crackling between us and I had an overwhelming urge to kiss him. It would be easy to rise onto my tiptoes and brush my lips against his, which looked so soft and... What was I thinking? We were friends and we were both nursing broken hearts.

I stepped away but so did he and we did that awkward thing where we both repeatedly tried to speak at the same time then forgot what it was we wanted to say. Had he felt that same chemistry between us and not known what to do with it?

While Dane grabbed us both a takeaway coffee from the café, I nipped into the gift shop to buy a thank you gift for Alice. She'd told me how much she loved rabbits, so I thought she might like a Benjamin Bunny to keep her Peter Rabbit company.

Soon we were on our way home. I asked Dane about his day and he told me a couple of amusing anecdotes about the visitors, including one woman who couldn't seem to grasp that Beatrix Potter wasn't the author of *The Magic Faraway Tree* or *The Famous Five*.

'Do many people get Beatrix Potter and Enid Blyton mixed up?' I asked.

'Not often, but it does happen. I had a visitor once who thought Beatrix Potter was a man and another who thought that Hill Top was a purpose-built museum and the real Hill Top was in a completely different part of Cumbria, kept secret from the tourists. He got quite irate with me when I wouldn't tell him where it really was. It takes all sorts. So tell me about where your inspiration came from today.'

I explained my thought process behind the stories and then the conversation moved onto whether to meet up tomorrow or Friday and what to do.

'If we're going to go somewhere, I'm thinking tomorrow,' Dane said. 'Friday's Good Friday and the world and his wife will be out in force. The forecast's decent for tomorrow so are you ready for another bike ride?'

'I think I'm feeling brave enough. Actually, no. There's something else. I'd love to visit St Herbert's Island. Would you be up for hiring a boat?'

'I'm in! I haven't visited any of the islands since I was a kid. I presume your interest is because of Squirrel Nutkin?'

'You already know me so well. Rosie says there are red squirrels in the woods round Willowdale Hall but I haven't seen one yet.'

'Have you ever seen one?'

'Never. Have you?'

'A few times. They're sweet – smaller than greys, not so stocky, and they have cute tufts on their ears, a bit like the gilderhopp has on his head, although obviously not mint green.'

We talked about some of the wildlife around Willowdale. I sometimes heard owls hooting on the estate and Dane said he often saw them flying overhead. It wasn't unusual to see red and roe deer roaming wild, sometimes even wandering along the village streets in the early morning. He'd seen red kites and even a common lizard in the summer months, which surprised me.

'Do you fancy stopping for an ice cream?' he asked as we approached the outskirts of Ambleside.

'I'd love one.'

'We'll go to Waterhead. It's just outside Ambleside and doesn't take us far out of the way.'

The car park at Waterhead was heaving but Dane managed to

catch someone reversing out of a space and joked that I must be his lucky mascot because that never happened to him.

'This is lovely,' I said as we crossed the road to the lake.

'It's the northern tip of Windermere. If you get one of the pleasure boats from Bowness, this is the Ambleside stop but it's actually a mile into Ambleside, which takes some of the tourists by surprise.'

There was a boat moored at the large pier with passengers disembarking and a long queue waiting to board. Smaller motorboats were moored against shorter wooden piers closer to us, and there were several boats out in the bay too. Wooden rowing boats were pulled up onto the pebbly shore awaiting hire and there were a few rowers out on the lake.

We bought locally made ice creams from a café and sat on the edge of one of the wooden piers eating them, watching the visitors feeding the ducks, geese and swans. We'd nearly finished our ice creams when the pleasure boat pulled out. The passengers waved so we waved back and laughed at the compulsion to wave at a bunch of strangers from a boat or train and the pleasure it gave when those strangers waved back.

'Can I ask your take on something?' I said to Dane after we'd finished eating. 'I really enjoyed drawing and writing today. It gave me such a buzz and it was great to be working my imagination again, but I have a niggle. The Claude and Nancy Badger story wasn't really my work. All I did was take one of Beatrix Potter's tales and add an epilogue.'

'They were your characters.'

'True, but they were inspired by her story and they came alive in her setting.'

'The cubs story was yours.'

'Inspired by a Disney film.'

'I get what you're saying about the badger story. I guess that's an example of fan fiction, but I don't accept what you're saying about the cubs story. *The Fox and the Hound* might have inspired you to think about unlikely friendships, but that's where the similarity stops. That was *your* story, not Disney's. They say there are no original ideas left in literature and haven't been for a long time, so how come each book that's written is different? It's because of an author's voice, their characters, the execution of their plot, an unexpected twist on something familiar. And do you know what I heard when I read the badger story? *Your* voice. It might be an epilogue or fan fiction, but it wasn't written in Beatrix Potter's voice. I heard you.'

He spoke with such conviction that I knew he wasn't just trying to be nice. He genuinely believed what he was saying.

'You *really* think I can write?'

'I don't think it. I know it. And you can draw, which is a bit sickening. I need to find something you're rubbish at so I can feel better about myself.' He winked at me and the butterflies stirred once more.

'I'm rubbish at riding a bike,' I said.

'You say that, but you soon picked it up.'

'Erm, I'm not very good at cooking, so there's a skill you have which I don't.'

He studied my face for a moment and shook his head. 'I don't believe you. I think your definition of "not very good" means you're not Michelin star standard. Am I right?'

'Baking, then. I can't be bothered faffing about with pastry cutters and baking tins. I'd rather eat what someone else has made.'

'Ah-ah! Not convinced. You say you can't be bothered, but does that mean you're incapable?'

I laughed at him. 'Okay, you've got me there. There are plenty of things I'm rubbish at, but I can't think under pressure.'

'You have overnight to think about it and I invite you to present to me tomorrow one genuine thing you're not good at. And it can't be something random that most of us don't need to be able to do like juggling or riding a unicycle.'

'To be fair, *all* my circus skills are lacking. But I'll have a think and come back to you tomorrow.'

We stayed at Waterhead a little longer, watching the activity around us. A second pleasure boat had arrived and departed and, when a third one docked, Dane said it was time to move as the parking ticket would soon expire.

It had been such a lovely stop-off – somewhere I'd definitely visit again. Dane said we'd take a trip on one of the pleasure boats another day and I was already looking forward to that.

We chatted easily about nothing in particular all the way back to Willowdale Hall. Dane pulled up outside Horseshoe Cottage and I thanked him for a great day then got out. He wound the window down and confirmed the arrangements for our boat trip tomorrow when Toffee came bounding towards the car. I glanced across at the house, hoping it wasn't a bad sign that she was out on her own, but Alice waved at me from the lounge window, so she must have let Toffee out when I arrived.

'I love dogs!' Dane said, exiting the car to greet her.

'This is Toffee, Rosie and Alice's dog. Isn't she gorgeous?'

Toffee put a paw out for Dane to shake, then pressed against his leg while he rubbed her chest.

'I always wanted a dog, but Lynsey wasn't a fan and wouldn't even discuss it. Did you have pets?'

'No. I'd have loved a dog and a cat, but it wasn't practical when I was living between Sutton and Paris. When I started working and commuting into London each day, it wouldn't have worked either. If I buy somewhere here, I'd love a pet.'

'Same here.'

We smiled at each other and I loved how we had another thing in common. I'd never thought about it until now but Étienne hadn't been a cat or dog fan. If we had stayed together, would he have been like Lynsey, putting his foot down against pets?

Dane gave Toffee a kiss on the head and straightened up. 'I'd better let you get on with the rest of your day. It's been fun. See you tomorrow.'

He gave me a quick hug before driving off. I watched him disappear down the lane, smiling to myself. The more time we spent together, the more I liked Dane, and the closer I felt to him. I'd have sworn I had a great friendship with Étienne in the five years before we got together as a couple, but I was now questioning that. Something was different about my friendships with Rosie and Dane and I couldn't quite pinpoint what it was. Not that it mattered now. It was time to focus on Katy Perry's 'Roar' instead of 'The One That Got Away' and take back control of my life. I'd write to Étienne now and tell him our time had passed. I was making a new life in Willowdale without him in it.

29

The following morning, Dane messaged me to confirm that he'd booked a small motorboat from Willowdale Marina and asked me to meet him there at two. They didn't normally permit customers to take the motorboats near the islands for fear of grounding them, but the owner of the marina was a good friend of Dane's Uncle Aled and had given him special permission to moor up close to the island, telling him where was safest.

I set off slightly early so I could drop my letter to Étienne in the postbox on the village green, along with a Beatrix Potter postcard I'd picked up in Hill Top's gift shop and written for Maman and Papa this morning.

As I walked into the village, my feelings were all over the place. I was excited about visiting St Herbert's Island and very much looking forward to being with Dane again, but nervous about posting my letter.

I reached the postbox and dropped the postcard straight into it, but hung onto the letter, worried about whether I'd got the tone and message right. I'd kept it simple and to the point, but should I have written something longer? Should I have been completely honest and told him about the baby?

Étienne

I received your letter and card. I'm sorry that your marriage was difficult and that you're hurting.

Thank you for the offer. I appreciate it must have been difficult to put your feelings out there like that, but I can't accept. Too many years have passed and too much has happened in that time. I think it's better to leave the past in the past. Because of that, I feel it's only right to return the promise ring you gave me.

I once wrote these words to you: Be courageous, be adventurous, but most of all be happy. I still mean them. I hope you find your happiness.

Autumn

I chewed on my lip, debating. No, I'd send it as it was. Telling him about the baby wouldn't benefit me and might cause him unnecessary pain. I counted to three then pushed the letter through the slot, shut my eyes and dropped my head to my chest. That was it. Closed.

'Autumn?'

I flicked my eyes open and twisted round at the sound of Dane's voice. He was standing at the edge of the village green, clutching a couple of paper bags and frowning at me.

'Everything okay?' he asked, his voice full of concern.

'Yes. Just posting something. It's all good. What have you got there?'

He looked around shiftily as he came closer and opened one of the bags to reveal an enormous cream doughnut.

'Ooh, that looks delicious.'

'It is. There's one each, but don't tell Uncle Aled I've bought treats from the bakery instead of the café.'

'Your secret's safe with me. Are these for the boat trip or to eat now?'

'We'd best save them for the boat. Can't risk being spotted.'

From his cheeky grin, I suspected his Uncle Aled wouldn't be bothered at all, but Dane was milking the drama.

'Okay, and thank you. Very kind of you.'

'I had to get something to celebrate. I heard from my solicitor this morning. My divorce is now finalised.'

'Big news! How are you feeling?' Not that I needed to ask, as the big smile said it all.

'Happy and relieved. Is it bad that I don't feel sad?'

'Not at all. You were sad when it ended and I'm sure you were sad plenty of times after that.'

He nodded. 'Too many. I confess I wallowed for a couple of months, but then I realised there was no point. It wasn't going to change anything, so I needed to accept it and start afresh.'

'Good for you. Congratulations! If you'd rather go to the pub to celebrate, we can do that.'

'I promised you a boat trip so that's what we'll do, but if you're free tonight, a celebratory drink or two would be good. Rosie's welcome to join us too.'

'I'll ask her when I get home.'

'Ready to venture to "Owl Island" on a raft made of twigs?' he asked, making me laugh. In *The Tale of Squirrel Nutkin*, that was how Nutkin, his brother – the fabulously named Twinkleberry – and their cousins travelled over to the island with food offerings in exchange for nuts from the island's owner, an owl called Old Brown.

'If it was the height of summer, it would absolutely be a yes to the raft,' I said, as we set off. 'But seeing as it's only spring...'

'I'll remind you of this conversation when summer hits. The last time I went on a raft, I must have been twelve or thirteen. It was a school thing with teams competing to be the first to build a raft and sail it round a buoy on the lake. We thought we were so clever because we built ours first. Didn't think we were quite so clever when the ropes began loosening and the whole thing came apart before we even reached the buoy. We might have failed the task, but I remember laughing so much that day.'

'We never did anything like that at school. The only trips out I remember were to museums. I genuinely would like to have a go at raft building one day, although I think ending up in the water is an inevitability.'

'Too right! It's the objective. You're not doing it right if you don't capsize.'

'There are so many activities I haven't tried, so I think my time here is going to be full of firsts. Rosie's building me up to getting on a horse. I'm scared of them for no rational reason but I'm getting better. I can stroke them now without having palpitations. It's a work in progress – a slow one – but we'll get there.'

We arrived at the marina and, after instructions, a safety briefing, and confirmation of exactly where to gain access to the island, we strapped on our buoyancy aids, boarded the small motorboat and pulled away from the wooden pier.

Dane offered for me to steer and I did want to try, but I was keen that he take the first go so I could watch. The reluctance had been unnecessary as there really wasn't anything to it, so we soon swapped places. There were a few dozen other water users in various crafts, but it was easy to give them a wide berth as the boat slowly cut through the almost still water.

When I told Rosie we were visiting St Herbert's Island, she'd taken delight in presenting me with a few more facts – four to five acres in size and named after a seventh-century hermit who found sanctuary there and brought Christianity to the area. The viewpoint at Friar's Crag gained its name from monks sailing from there to visit St Herbert.

We travelled a circle round all the islands before approaching St Herbert's Island and looking for the approach point on the south side. As we'd had to be granted special permission, I suggested Dane take the wheel again.

'You've got this,' he said gently. 'What's the worst that could happen?'

'I capsize us or run us aground and wreck the boat.'

'You won't do that. I believe in you.'

With Dane's continued encouragement, I slowly guided the boat in.

'I did it!' I cried, relief flowing through me that I hadn't caused any damage.

'As if it was ever in doubt,' he said, smiling at me.

We removed our socks and trainers and rolled up our jeans to wade through the shallows onto the island, where Dane tied the boat off on an enormous log.

'I'm a little disappointed,' I said, hands on hips as I surveyed the immediate area. 'I thought Old Brown would be here to greet us.'

Dane smiled. 'I'm kind of glad he isn't after what he did to Nutkin.'

'Aw, but Nutkin was a lazy squirrel and repeatedly wound him up, tickled him with some nettles, and made a flying leap at his head. He's lucky he escaped only leaving his tail behind, considering Old Brown was about to skin him alive.'

We looked at each other and started laughing.

'There are some really gruesome parts to those tales,' I said, shaking my head. 'Peter Rabbit's dad getting cooked in a pie, Squirrel Nutkin nearly getting skinned...'

'Samuel Whiskers and his wife tying Tom Kitten up and making him into a roly-poly pudding,' Dane suggested. 'It was often the case with children's books. Have you ever read any of the original fairy tales? Some of them are dark enough to rival a Stephen King novel.'

We set off to explore the island. It was mainly woodland with several clearings. Dane told me that it was popular for wild camping and I could picture small tents or hammocks strung between the sturdier tree trunks. Logs provided seating and small stone circles with blackened centres showed evidence of campfires.

A couple of pheasants sauntered through the undergrowth, making me jump, which set Dane off laughing. We hadn't seen any other craft on the beaches when we'd circled the island and, after our walk, could confirm we were alone except for the pheasants, ducks and geese.

'Celebratory cream doughnut?' Dane suggested as we returned to the main clearing.

He handed me one of the paper bags from his backpack which had got a bit squashed on the journey.

'This is going to be messy,' he said, peering into his bag. 'I didn't think this through.'

'It's fine. We're surrounded by fresh water so we can soon rinse our hands.' I dabbed my squished doughnut against his. 'Happy divorce day!'

'Thank you very much.'

It was so peaceful sitting on the log, listening to the birds chirping, the occasional rustle in the grass, and the gentle lapping of the lake. Neither of us spoke, content to simply take it all in and enjoy the tranquillity.

As expected, we were both covered in cream and sugar when we'd finished eating and did need to rinse our hands in the lake.

'That sky's looking ominous,' Dane said, wiping his wet hands down his jeans. 'I thought it had got darker while we were eating.'

I looked up and took a sharp intake of breath. Ominous was an understatement. The whole sky was a deep petrol blue with angry grey clouds.

'It's raining over there,' I said, pointing to a clear cloud burst over the eastern fells.

'Let's hope it keeps travelling east.'

We hastened through the shallows back to the boat and set off, but we hadn't travelled far when the sky darkened further.

'Coats might be a good—' Dane started, but he didn't get to finish the sentence because the heavens opened.

'Too late!' I cried, squealing as I hunched my shoulders against the downpour.

It was coming down so heavily that I could barely see in front of me and I had to slow right down, fearing I might collide with a kayaker or paddleboarder. My long-sleeved T-shirt was plastered to my arms, my jeans were clinging and my feet were squelching in my trainers. We shook our heads at each other, laughing.

We were still some way from shore and I felt drained from concentrating. I pushed my wet hair back from my face as Dane took the wheel to give me a break, slowly guiding the boat forward.

The rain showed no let-up as we moored, unclipped our buoyancy aids, and grabbed our bags.

'Back to mine,' Dane said, grabbing my hand as we made a run for it.

There was a covered porch area at Lake View and I was grateful for the shelter it gave as Dane searched in his soggy backpack for his house keys. I squeezed my T-shirt sleeves to wring the water out and, grimacing at the sensation of the wet material against my skin, pushed them up. My arms were red from the cold, covered in goose bumps, and I couldn't stop shivering.

I kicked off my trainers as soon as we were inside and ran up the stairs, following Dane.

'Bathroom's in there,' he said, pushing open a door.

He opened an airing cupboard next to the bathroom and handed me a couple of large towels. 'Jump in the shower or have a bath if you prefer. Help yourself to shampoo and bubbles and stuff. I'll put you some dry clothes outside the door.'

'I'll be quick,' I said, worrying about him freezing while he was waiting for me.

'Take as long as you want. There's an en suite so I'll use that.'

Closing the bathroom door behind me, I groaned as I peeled off my cold, wet clothes and dumped them in a soggy heap on the wooden floor. A long, hot soak would be great but I was too cold to wait for the bath to fill so I turned the shower on and gratefully stepped under the hot flow. My first adventure on the lake had certainly been eventful, but it had still been fun, like everything I did with Dane.

I hoped he hadn't spent long looking for something for me to wear and was in the en suite shower right now. The thought sent my pulse racing. I already knew he was ripped from that tight Lycra top he'd been wearing the day we met. His wet T-shirt clinging to him earlier had emphasised all his muscles too, so it didn't take much imagination to picture him without a top on, soap running down his pecs to his abs and… I shook my head. These weren't the thoughts to be having about a friend on the day his divorce was finalised.

A little later, I curled up on the sofa wearing one of Dane's hoodies and some fleecy pyjama bottoms which he said were an unworn Christmas present, while my clothes were in the tumble drier. He'd apologised that everything was too big for me but said he'd felt uncomfortable about rooting through Aunt Kelly's drawers. I'd never worn anyone else's clothes before. I hadn't had close friends or a sister to swap clothes with and my housemates at university hadn't shared the same dress sense or size as me so it felt a little weird to be dressed in Dane's gear. Not as weird as wearing no underwear. I wondered if he'd thought about that. I'd hesitated in the bathroom after collecting the clothes from outside the door, wondering whether to put on my soggy underwear. I'd even got as far as slipping my arms into my bra but cringed when the cold material slapped against my body, so that was the decision made.

'You star,' I said as Dane handed me a mug of tea. 'I'm ready for this.'

'I'm so sorry about the weather,' he said, sitting on the other end of the sofa. 'It wasn't forecast for rain until much later.'

'Not your fault. I've never been caught out in rain like that. Have you?'

'Yes, but I'm usually way better prepared. I've done several rescues in bad downpours.'

'What's the hardest rescue you've done?' I asked.

'Recovering a body,' he said without missing a beat. 'It was in the Peak District. A woman slipped and fell a long way down a cliff. She was with her husband and two young kids. The death was bad enough but being with her family there, knowing they'd witnessed it all, will never leave me.'

'Oh, my God, Dane! That's so sad. How do you keep going after something like that?'

'By focusing on all the ones we *do* save and being part of an amazing team. Nothing beats that moment when you find the casualty, particularly if the details are sketchy and there's no phone tracking. The rescue dogs come into their own on those searches. There's no way we could do it without them. And then there's another buzz once they're back to safety and in an ambulance or with friends or relatives.'

I listened, fascinated, as Dane talked about some of his successful rescues. I'd been aware of the existence of Mountain Rescue but hadn't given much thought to the work they did as I'd never had reason to call them or known anyone who had. Among the more obvious rescues of lost or injured walkers, he talked about rescuing those who took ill, searches for missing children and vulnerable adults, rescues from floods and callouts to trapped or injured animals. He spoke with such passion that I couldn't help feeling a little inadequate. I didn't have the fitness level to consider anything like Mountain Rescue – I'd be a hindrance rather than a help – but, once I was properly settled, there had to be something I could do to help others.

'Have you been on any rescues since I got here?' I asked.

'The team have been out twice but both times were during the day when I was at Hill Top and too far away to respond.'

The buzzer on the tumble drier sounded so I retrieved my clothes and got changed, relieved to be wearing underwear again.

The rain had eased off but was still steady and my trainers were drenched, so Dane found me a pair of his aunt's flip flops and drove me back to Horseshoe Cottage.

'I've got a few errands to run for Aunt Kelly round the village tonight so it's probably easiest if I meet you and Rosie in the pub when I've done that,' he said as he drove through the gates at Willowdale Hall. 'Half seven?'

'Sounds good. Thanks again for the shower and clothes.'

I waved him away and ran up to the cottage. As soon as I stepped into the kitchen, my heart sank. Alice was pacing up and down, her head dipped, rubbing one hand across her forehead. I couldn't hear exactly what she was muttering but I caught the words 'green man'. Toffee was pacing up and down beside her, looking up at her.

Rosie appeared from the lounge. 'Found some!' she declared, waving a packet of paracetamol. 'Oh, hi, Autumn. How was the boat trip?'

'Brilliant, but we got caught in the rain, so I've been at Lake View warming up and drying off.'

'It was a heavy one all right.' Rosie filled a glass of water from the tap and squeezed out two tablets into her hand.

'Sit down, Mam,' she said gently. 'Take your tablets.'

Alice did as she was told and Toffee sat beside her, placing her head on Alice's lap like before. As soon as she'd taken the paracetamol, Alice rested her hand on Toffee's head and her body visibly relaxed.

'Hi, Alice,' I said.

She looked up and smiled weakly, but she didn't ask me about the green man this time.

'I'm going to make a cuppa,' Rosie said. 'Would you like one?'

'Thanks, but I had a couple of mugs at Dane's so I'm half human, half tea.'

It warmed me that I could bring a smile to her face. I went up to the bedroom and brushed my dishevelled hair. My decision would be winging its way to Étienne right now. I hoped he'd accept it and not write back to me. It might hurt him that I'd returned the ring, but he'd noticed me wearing it in the park and had been encouraged by that. I didn't want him to be encouraged. I wanted him to leave me alone now. *Our* time was then. *My* time was now.

30

Rosie was flattered to be asked to the pub, but understandably declined due to Alice's episode. I felt bad that I hadn't thought about it when the rain came down but Rosie assured me that, even if I'd been home, I couldn't have helped. It was therefore only me meeting Dane in The Hardy Herdwick, although I did feel a flutter of excitement at the thought of just the two of us huddled together over a drink or two in that cosy pub.

Dane was already inside, ordering a drink at the bar, so I'd timed it perfectly. We found a snug nook with a padded bench seat curved around a round table and toasted his divorce completion properly, with a drink rather than a doughnut.

He took a sip from his pint. 'I forgot to say earlier, I emailed Miss Eccles and asked her to put us both down for her creative writing class. Is that still okay?'

'It's fine.' I grinned at him. 'I'll hold your hand while we go back to school and we can pass each other notes in class. Has she replied?'

'Not yet. I mentioned that I'd been in her class and that

English had been my favourite subject because she was such a good teacher, but I'm wondering if that sounds cheesy now.'

'I think it's lovely and I bet she's flattered.'

'I hope so.'

Dane adjusted his position, which brought him slightly closer to me. I wondered if that had been by accident or deliberate intention. His leg wasn't quite touching mine, but it wasn't far away.

When we'd been out on Monday night, Rosie had told him about her mam's accident. Dane remembered reading about it in the local newspaper at the time and was sorry to hear that they'd never caught who did it and that there were lasting repercussions on Alice's mental health. I therefore wasn't breaching any confidences by explaining why Rosie hadn't joined us tonight.

'That must be so hard on them both,' he said.

'They just get on with it, but having me here has made Rosie realise she's become too insular, so she's keen to get out and about more. I'm sure she'll be up for our next night out.'

I was angled towards the door and smiled when I saw who'd just walked in.

'You'll never guess who's here,' I whispered to Dane, who couldn't see the door without twisting round. 'Trudy Eccles! And she's looking our way.'

In a few strides, she was at our table. 'Hello again, Autumn,' she said, smiling warmly at me. She turned to Dane and her smile widened. 'As I live and breathe, it's only one of my favourite-ever students, all grown up. How are you, Dane?'

'I'm great, thanks. Can I buy you a drink?'

'Ooh, yes, that would be wonderful, thank you. A lime and soda, please, no ice.'

Dane indicated that Trudy should take his seat so she sat beside me.

'I gave your leaflet to Rosie,' I said. 'She might be interested in learning Spanish.'

'Oh, how fabulous! We have a wonderful young woman who runs the class. She is Spanish, but settled in Willowdale with her English husband. She explores the history and culture as well as the language, so it's a really varied class. We've been running it for several years now and it's always popular.'

Dane returned with her drink and pulled up a stool.

'Cheers!' Trudy said, raising her drink to us and taking a sip. 'I got your email, Dane. You're both interested in my creative writing class? That's wonderful to hear. What sort of writing interests you?'

'Children's books for me – picture books with verses,' Dane said, 'although I'm an avid reader of crime and horror novels and might like to have a go writing something darker at some point in the future.'

Trudy clapped her hands together, laughing. 'I love that contrast – couldn't be much more different. What about you, Autumn?'

'It's a new thing for me. I'm an illustrator, but Dane has helped me see that my drawings are snapshots of stories, so I'd like to explore that.'

We told her about Mission Sparkle and I showed her some of my illustrations on my phone.

'My goodness, Autumn, what a talent you have,' she said, admiring the gilderhopp. 'And you have a fabulous imagination, Dane, for creating this creature. Although I always knew that about you. Got you into trouble with a few of your other teachers, I seem to recall, but it was always welcome in my class.'

Dane's cheeks coloured and I looked forward to hearing some more stories of his school antics later.

Trudy finished the last of her drink. 'I got completely

distracted. I didn't seek you out about the evening class – I came because I hear you're looking for somewhere to rent and I might have the solution for you. Do you have ten minutes to spare for me to show you it?'

I glanced at Dane, who nodded, and we both finished the last of our drinks before pulling on our coats and following Trudy out of the pub. She led us towards the village centre but we hadn't got far before she cut up a gravel side street. There was a row of four pretty whitewashed cottages with slate detailing around the windows and short front gardens enclosed by low fencing.

'It's the furthest one,' she said, pausing at the lane end. 'It was my mother's house. She passed away last spring, bless her soul. I thought I might like to move into it myself because I love the house and Willowdale, but I've spent years renovating my place in Pippinthwaite and I don't know if I have the time or inclination to start over with Mother's place. It doesn't feel right to leave it empty while I dither.'

We followed her to the wooden gate.

'Cotton-tail's Cottage,' I read on the sign.

'Ah, yes! Mother was a huge Beatrix Potter fan. Obsessed, some might say, as you'll see when we go inside. She claims my grandmother was friends with Potter, but I've never seen evidence of that. Father and I humoured her, though.'

Trudy unlocked the front door but didn't push it wide. 'I haven't done any clearing out of Mother's belongings so try to see beyond those. I'll need to rent it furnished as I don't have time to organise storage. Would that be okay with you?'

'It's fine,' I said.

'Good. So the furniture will stay but I'll clear away the mountain of Potter paraphernalia. Oh, and also bear in mind that nobody's lived here for a year so it has that peculiar smell houses get when they're empty, but I can assure you there's no damp. I kept the heating on throughout the winter and I get it checked regularly. You'll see why when we go upstairs.'

She pushed the door open into a wide hall with a staircase to the left. The Beatrix Potter love was instantly evident in pictures and plates covering the walls and in figurines on a dresser at the end of the hall.

'The hall used to lead through to the kitchen but we blocked it off,' Trudy said. 'There's a cloakroom and toilet under the stairs and storage for the vacuum cleaner and ironing board.'

She pushed open the door on the right and we stepped into a lounge – or perhaps more accurately a Beatrix Potter museum.

'I'm seeing this with your eyes,' Trudy said, laughing. 'It's full-on, isn't it? It's mine and Father's fault. Mother loved Potter and we could never think of anything to get her for birthdays and Christmases, so we kept adding to the collection. It made her happy, and that's the main thing.'

Alongside more plates and pictures, cross stitches, tapestries and even framed jigsaws covered the walls. Scatter cushions depicting scenes from the books adorned the sofa and chairs and there were hundreds of figurines on matching shelving units in the alcoves either side of a log burner. Stepping closer, I spied cup and saucer sets, snow globes, tins, candles. It seemed that, if it had a Beatrix Potter character on it, Trudy's mother had acquired it.

'I've never seen a collection like it,' I said, amazed that so many product variations existed. 'It's seriously impressive.'

'It's seriously something,' Trudy said, rolling her eyes. 'Come on. Let me show you the kitchen.'

She pushed back bi-fold wooden doors at the end of the lounge and we stepped into a spacious and surprisingly modern kitchen diner.

'It wasn't a bad size anyway,' Trudy said, 'but we had it

extended and a new kitchen fitted. You'll be able to spot a few items here and there like the clock and chopping board but, in the main, this is a Potter-free zone.'

The large dining table would be perfect for spreading out to work as the skylight above it would let in loads of natural light.

'There are three bedrooms,' Trudy said, leading us upstairs.

My stomach sank. From the outside, Cotton-tail's Cottage hadn't looked particularly big – more like a cosy two-bedroom cottage. The downstairs was bigger than expected although she'd said the kitchen had been extended, but it appeared that the whole property was deceptively large. There was no way I could afford a three-bedroom rental on my own, and what would I do with all that space anyway?

Trudy was such an enthusiastic guide so I smiled politely and let her continue the tour. Lesson learned – always find out the price first.

Upstairs, there was a modern family bathroom with a bath and separate shower, two large double bedrooms and a smaller one. Beatrix Potter had left her mark up there too, mainly in the form of soft furnishings and cuddly toys. Trudy told us that her mother had used the bedroom at the front of the house as the master and the one at the back had been her library.

There was a bed in the library, an armchair, a small coffee table, and several floor-to-ceiling bookshelves.

'Are these first editions?' I asked, bending down in front of some very old-looking volumes, worries about affordability temporarily floating away as I gazed in awe at the books.

'Yes. She's got quite a few.'

'That's why you keep the heating on and get the house checked,' Dane said. 'They must be worth a fortune.'

'They are. I really should box them up and take them to my

place, but I never seem to find the time. I don't want them, so it's all a faff I can't be bothered with.'

My heart thudded as I looked across the first edition titles. I wanted so badly to stroke them, to sniff them, but I didn't dare touch them.

I looked at what else she had. There were so many different versions of all Potter's books, singularly and in collections. The box sets went from the everyday mass-printed ones to the exclusive Folio Society editions in the same colours as the original publications. Dane bent down beside me and caught my eye, his expression telling me he was as astonished as me to see such an incredible collection and also perhaps a little mystified as to why someone with a passion for literature could be so blasé about them.

Trudy pointed towards the window. 'There's a garage out the back and parking for two cars which is handy for bringing the shopping straight into the kitchen – it's why we blocked the hall off.'

We followed her back downstairs and into the lounge. 'So, what do you think? Could you both see yourselves living here, after the place is cleared, of course?'

'Both?' Dane asked, glancing at me wide-eyed.

'That's what your aunt said – that you're both looking for somewhere to rent but on a short-term basis, which is perfect for me – tenants to give it the warmth and love it deserves and only a short-term commitment on my part, should I finally decide that I want to live here. Call me sentimental, but it's important to me that someone local lives here. I know you're not local, Autumn, but Dane is so I can rest easy that I've done my bit for the community.'

I smiled and nodded, not trusting myself to speak.

'How about I leave you to have a wander round and a chat

without me peering over your shoulder and I'll meet you back at the pub?' Trudy dropped the door keys into Dane's hand. 'See you shortly.'

I didn't dare look at Dane until the front door had closed.

'I'm so sorry,' he said. 'I didn't tell Aunt Kelly we were both looking to rent. I just said you were now and that I would be at some point, but—'

'It's fine,' I said, sinking down onto the sofa and giving him a weak smile. 'You should go for it and I'll keep looking. It's a great house.'

'But it was meant to be for you.' He sat down next to me.

'I know, but she only wants to let it out to someone local and I do understand that. I'm not local. It's too big for just me anyway. There's no way I'd be able to afford the rent and bills on my own.'

'Same here,' he said, resignation in his voice. 'Unless...'

My heart leapt at the positivity in that one word and I looked at him hopefully. 'Unless what?'

'What if we did what she thinks we want to do and rent this place together? It would give Miss Eccles what she wants with a local lodger, there's more than enough space for both of us, and it would be affordable if we split the costs. Hopefully. What do you think?'

It was the obvious solution and, as soon as he said it, I realised it had been simmering at the back of my mind since he'd voiced his thoughts earlier about moving out of his aunt and uncle's.

'It definitely makes sense financially,' I said, 'especially when I need to stretch my redundancy pay and you don't want to blow your half of your house sale, and I'd appreciate the company. I've never actually lived on my own before.'

'Neither have I. So you'd be up for it?'

His hand grazed against mine and my heart skipped. I imagined us snuggled up on the sofa with the log burner on, watching a film or reading. I pictured us at the dining table, writing together or me drawing while he wrote.

'I would. It's so perfect for us, right down to the cottage name.' I gave him a gentle nudge. 'But there's something serious we need to talk about before I commit – bad habits. I'm a bit of a toast fiend, but I somehow always manage to get crumbs in the butter and butter in the jam. One of my university housemates used to get so irate about it, as though I did it deliberately to wind her up. What about you?'

He grinned at me. 'I see your toast crumbs and I raise you mugs left everywhere. I always clear my dinner plates away but, if I'm having a cuppa, I never remember to return my mug. It's only when I can't find any fresh mugs that I realise I've got them scattered all around the house.'

'Do you leave milky dregs in them?'

'Yep.'

'Ooh, yummy! Mouldy, furry mugs.'

He adopted a mock serious tone. 'I do understand if that's a dealbreaker and you want to call the whole thing off. I know it's gross and I should really seek professional help for my habit.'

'Dirty boy!' I joked, giving him another gentle nudge with my elbow. 'I'm shocked! But if that's your worst habit, I think we'll be fine. If you can cope with my toast and butter mess.'

'I might be able to cope with that. Just.'

The thought of moving in with someone I'd only just met felt exciting rather than scary. It was unusually spontaneous for me, but everything about me being in Willowdale felt that way. It seemed to be how my new life was going to be and I was more than happy to embrace that change.

Dane pushed himself to his feet and took my hand, tugging me to mine. 'Let's go and talk money and keep our fingers crossed that it's affordable.'

We stood in front of the log burner, smiling at each other, and I could already hear Rosie drawing back her Cupid's arrow. She'd say that we might be friends for now but, if it was meant to be more, it would happen naturally and possibly more quickly than before if we were going to be living under the same roof. That didn't scare me either. If it wasn't meant to happen, we'd have done each other a big favour. And if it happened for me and not him, then it was only a temporary arrangement, so no harm done. Big tick to another courageous, adventurous thing which I also believed would make me very happy.

* * *

Back in The Hardy Herdwick at the same table as before with another round of drinks, I stared at Trudy Eccles, my mouth agape. Had I heard her right? She really wanted that amount?

'Can you just repeat that?' Dane asked, his surprised tone and frown confirming he was struggling too.

'Five hundred pounds a month,' she said.

'Each?' I asked.

'No. Between you. Plus bills, of course.'

'But that's so low,' I said.

'I thought it would be two or three times that amount,' Dane said.

'Well, it isn't. I'm not a greedy woman. I don't need the money, there's no mortgage to pay and, as I said earlier, you'd be doing me a favour by looking after it. My childhood home needs people in it and there's nobody I'd rather trust with it than one of my favourite former students and my lovely new friend who picks up folders for a stranger and who, from her reaction to the first editions, loves Beatrix Potter as much as Mother did.'

'She's my heroine,' I admitted. 'And Dane's a big fan too. He volunteers at Hill Top.'

Trudy's eyes widened. 'My goodness! Cotton-tail's Cottage could not be going to a more perfectly suited couple.'

My heart leapt at the use of 'couple' and continued to pound when Dane's hand found mine under the table and gently squeezed it. Neither of us corrected Trudy's assumption and I tried not to read anything into that from Dane's perspective. After the misunderstanding that we were looking to rent together, he might not have wanted to throw in further confusion. Or, like me, he might like the idea of us being a couple. And I liked that he was still holding my hand.

'I do, however, have a couple of provisos,' Trudy said, and I braced myself for something which might be a dealbreaker.

Dane released my hand and took a sip from his pint. 'We're listening.'

'The first one is that I said I'd clear the house but I'm not sure I have the time or energy to tackle that alone so I could use some help de-Pottering if one or both of you could spare some time. Or, even better, if you could do it all yourselves before you move in.'

We both nodded and confirmed we'd be happy to do that for her. I was excited by the prospect of examining all the items up close and we wouldn't be able to take that time if Trudy was with us.

'As for the other proviso, I should probably have asked this up front. Are either of you allergic to cats?'

'No,' we said together.

'Good. My mother's cat is very stubborn and has refused to make Pippinthwaite her home. I've taken her there several times and she has always made her way back here. I was scared she'd get hit by a car on the main road, so I left her here to fend for herself. That's not as cruel as it sounds! There's a cat flap so she comes and goes and I buy food for the neighbours to put out for her. Would you be happy for her to come and go and to feed her?'

Dane glanced at me and I nodded. What had we both been talking about earlier in the week? Wait until I told Rosie about all of this. She'd definitely say it was the universe hearing our conversations and providing for us.

'We'd love to look after the cat,' I said. 'What's her name?'

'Tom Kitten. What else would an obsessed Beatrix Potter fan call a cat, despite it being a girl?'

There wasn't much to say to that. I was sorry that Mrs Eccles had passed away because she sounded like somebody I'd have loved to meet.

'One more thing. I suspect that when you take the pictures down, you'll find the paint has faded. Would you be up for doing a spot of decorating or should I get someone in to do it? You'll be able to move in quicker if you want to paint it yourselves although you'll probably need ten tubes of filler on those nail holes first.'

We agreed to do the decorating ourselves, so Trudy handed over the keys, telling us she had another set at home. We provisionally agreed a moving-in date of a week on Saturday, giving us a little over a week to clear everything and decorate.

She swigged back the last of her drink and shook hands with both of us. 'Pleasure doing business with you. I bought a mountain of crates and bubble wrap months ago ready for the big clear-out so I'll drop them off first thing tomorrow, although you might find some original boxes in the attic for the figurines. Enjoy your evening, new tenants. You've got my number now so give me a ring if you have any questions or need anything.'

'Oh, my God!' I said when she'd gone. 'Did that really just happen?'

'I was going to say the same thing to you. Best divorce day ever!'

We stared at each other, grinning and shrugging, scarcely able to take it in.

'More celebratory drinks needed,' I said eventually, standing up. 'My round.'

As I stood by the bar, waiting to be served, I glanced across at Dane. He looked up from his phone and smiled at me, sending butterflies fluttering in my stomach. After I'd climbed Latrigg, I'd had this feeling that I was at the start of something wonderful. This was it. New home, new beginnings, and potentially a new relationship because, from the way Dane had held my hand under the table, I was pretty sure he felt something special too.

31

When I returned with the drinks, the stool Dane had borrowed was gone and he was sitting on the cushioned bench. He'd moved a little further round than before so we were much closer together.

'Cheers to a new cheap as chips home,' Dane said, clinking his glass against mine. 'I'm still reeling!'

'Cheers to being housemates,' I said. 'I can't believe we have the keys!'

We'd tried to insist on paying more but Trudy had said she'd refuse to rent it out to us if we paid even one pound over. She reluctantly agreed that we could pay for the paint and take over the purchase of Tom's cat food, but only after a considerable amount of persuading by Dane. Trudy Eccles was a strong-willed, feisty woman and I couldn't wait to see what she was like in teacher mode when the creative writing class started.

'I've thought of something I'm rubbish at,' I declared. 'I can't negotiate my way out of a paper bag.'

He shook his head and tutted. 'Even the King and Queen of Negotiation Land could not have swayed Miss Eccles, so I don't accept that as your rubbish thing. You'll have to think of something else.'

'Negotiation Land?' I said, rolling my eyes at him. 'Is that somewhere in your stories?'

'Not yet, but it should be!'

Over our drinks, we discussed paint colours and bedroom preferences and laughed when we realised neither of us had thought to look out of the front bedroom window to see if there was a lake view. We decided to make a bedroom decision once Trudy's mother's belongings were cleared and we could get a better feel for the rooms.

'I'll have to abandon you pretty much as soon as we've moved in,' I told Dane after he'd got another round of drinks in. 'I need to drive down to Sutton to pick up some more stuff and get the house on the market. I'm dreading that long drive again, but it has to be done.'

'Why don't I come with you? If you don't mind the company, that is.'

'You'd do that?'

'Sure. One of my cousins, Phil, has a vehicle hire business so he'd do us mates' rates on a Transit van if you need the space.'

'That would be amazing because I can't fit much in my car. It won't be an exciting trip, though. I'll need to clean and declutter for the estate agent's photos.'

'Much quicker if we do it together, and we'll already be in the rhythm of things from clearing Cotton-tail's Cottage.'

We were sitting so close together now that our legs were touching and neither of us moved away. Tucked away in that snug little alcove, it felt like we were in our own little bubble where good things happened and nothing bad could touch us. But if this friendship was going to work – and possibly develop into something more – it needed to be based on honesty from the start. I knew all about Lynsey, but I'd glossed over my relationship history. Much as I didn't want to bring the mood down, I wanted Dane to know it all and I had the perfect lead-in from his challenge.

'I've thought of something I am rubbish at,' I said.

He smiled at me and gave me a playful nudge. 'A real thing this time?'

'A very real thing.' I took a deep breath. 'It's relationships. I've only had one boyfriend. He said he loved me and wanted to marry me and have a family, and I couldn't hang onto him.'

Dane fixed sorrowful eyes on mine. 'What happened?' he asked gently.

'His name was Étienne and he lived in the same apartment building as my parents in Paris...'

As I told him our story, I realised that it had echoes of his relationship with Lynsey – first relationship, falling in love in our teens, and a partner who ended things with no warning and no discussion. He could easily have interrupted with those parallels, but he let me get the story out.

Except I didn't tell him the full story. I didn't tell him about my ectopic pregnancy. The words were there but I couldn't seem to force them out. Everything else, I shared with him, from trying to call Étienne back and discovering he'd blocked me right through to everything that had happened from the moment I bumped into Sylvie Toussaint in the apartment lobby. I even told him about the kiss, although I could feel my cheeks burning with a combination of embarrassment and shame that I'd let it happen and that I'd wanted Étienne so badly after all that time and all that hurt.

'When you found me by the postbox this morning, I'd been posting my reply to Étienne,' I said after I'd told him the final part.

'You looked like you were unsure about posting the letter.'

I needed to choose my words carefully to avoid mentioning the baby. 'I was, but not because I was regretting my decision. I wondered if I should have written more. I was trying to get into Étienne's head and whether he'd see a short letter as an invitation to write back with further declarations of love.'

'Do you still love him?'

I shrugged. 'There was obviously something still there because of how I felt when he kissed me, but when he found me in the park the next day, all I wanted to do was get away from him.'

'Do you think that might have been a self-protection thing, trying to stop him from hurting you again?'

I sipped my wine as I mulled that over. 'It could have been. When I was in Sutton getting organised for coming up here, I was constantly checking my phone. He didn't have my number, but my parents would have given him it if he'd asked because they thought we were friends. I kept going to the front door, thinking I could hear someone knocking and imagining it was Étienne begging me for a second chance. I bounced between longing for a grand gesture like that and feeling relieved that he'd listened when I said I wasn't interested.'

'But he didn't call and he didn't show up.'

'No. So I drove up here and I fell in love for the second time... with the Lake District. I stopped checking my phone, I stopped thinking about him all the time, and then that flippin' letter arrived and messed it all up again.'

'What does Rosie say about it?'

'She thinks I'm better off without him. She knows how broken I was when it ended and he's been the subject of so many of our letters over the years. Her take is that our time was then. I was only twenty-one and I'm thirty-five now and we'll both have changed so much that it's unlikely to work. She thinks the feelings I had when I saw him again were based on nostalgia and that's no basis for a future together.'

'I'm really sorry you were treated like that,' Dane said, briefly placing his hand over mine and giving it a light squeeze, sending a zip of electricity through me. I wished he'd kept his hand there.

'You deserve so much better,' he added, his voice low and so damn sexy.

'So did you with Lynsey.'

'We know how to pick 'em, eh?'

As his eyes searched mine, my heart pounded. He really did have the most mesmerising eyes and his lips looked so soft and kissable. His leg was still pressed close to mine. The air was crackling between us. *Do it! Kiss him. You only need to make it a soft peck and if he doesn't respond, you can act like it was a friendly thank you. Count to three. One... two...* But the sensible side of me kicked in. Dane's divorce had been finalised today and the last thing he would want or need was to jump straight into something else with the woman he'd just agreed to rent a house with.

I cleared my throat and pulled back a little. Dane did the same and there was an awkward silence, but only for the briefest of moments.

He took a swig from his pint and cleared his throat once more. 'That thing Rosie said about growing apart, there's definitely something in that. There are couples who meet and grow old together and are compatible the whole way through, but there are others who grow apart. That's how it was with Lynsey and me, although I didn't realise it at the time. I was aware that we were doing our own thing but thought we were okay, but clearly we were doing our own thing because we *weren't* still okay. We'd grown into two very different people with nothing in common except our son. I do understand why she ended it. The rub for me is the way she did it. Obviously went to the Étienne school of relationship endings.'

I smiled at that. 'I think she did. I'm sorry she hurt you.'

'Thanks, but she ultimately did me a favour. It was tough at the time, but I'd do it all a hundred times over knowing that what I have here was waiting for me. This place, my family, writing...'

He'd looked around the pub as he started his list, but his eyes met mine again as he added the final item. 'You.'

I'd never been good at reading signals but that one word was so loaded. He had feelings for me. I'd thought it earlier and now I was absolutely convinced of it and I suspected he was just as apprehensive as me about what that meant.

Last orders were called.

'I'm not sure I can manage another one,' Dane said. 'You?'

'No, I've had my fill. Home time.'

We finished the last few sips of our drinks, pulled our coats on, and stepped outside. The rain had stopped and the air was cool and fresh. Streetlights glistened in the puddles and an owl hooted overhead.

'I'll walk you home,' Dane said, offering me his arm.

I threaded my arm through it. 'Just think, in a little over a week, our home will be just round the corner. I can't wait.'

As we passed the lane end, we looked up towards Cotton-tail's Cottage. The Hardy Herdwick couldn't be much more local for us when we moved in there.

'It's going to be so good,' he said as we continued through the village. 'You know I said you were my lucky charm when we found that parking space in Waterhead? I genuinely think you are. From the moment we met, it's like everything has come together. We make a good team, don't we?'

'We do. The best.'

We walked in contented silence, laughing as we tried to

manoeuvre round puddles on the path without letting go of each other. He was so right about everything coming together – for both of us – but I'd learned from my mistakes. No secrets. If something was going to happen between us at some point – and it felt like it was – I wanted him to know everything.

'There's something I haven't told you about Étienne,' I said. 'Well, it's about me really, but it involves him...'

We'd almost reached the entrance to Willowdale Hall when I concluded the missing part of my story.

'When I said I was unsure whether I should have written more to Étienne, this is what I meant, but I didn't see what difference it would make or who it would help, so I posted the letter without telling him.'

We stopped walking and I released my arm from Dane's as we faced each other under the soft glow of a nearby streetlight.

'You've kept this secret all these years?' he asked gently. 'Only your granddad knew?'

'Yes, but Granddad and I never talked about it and I was grateful for that. Just before he died, I thanked him.' Tears rushed to my eyes as I pictured him on that final day. 'He wouldn't have heard me, but I had to tell him it meant a lot that he'd been there for me and had respected my wishes.'

A tear escaped and I swiped it away.

Dane reached out and gently tilted my head to look at him and my heart melted to see there were tears in his eyes.

'I'm so sorry you went through that,' he said, gently wiping away another of my tears with his thumb.

'I've had a lot of thinking time while I've been here and I like Rosie's outlook on life. Everything's as it's meant to be. I wonder what would have happened if I hadn't lost the baby. Would Étienne have chosen me? I'd like to think he would, but would we have made each other happy? I'll never know, but I can't help feeling that I wasn't meant to have that life because this is where I'm meant to be, in this magical place with my best friend Rosie, walking in Beatrix Potter's footsteps and…' I paused. *Be adventurous, be courageous, but most of all be happy.*

'And with you.'

Dane kept his eyes fixed on mine as he brushed his hands across my cheeks and into my hair then slowly lowered his lips to mine. I released a soft moan as I closed my eyes and melted into his gentle kiss. My arms slid round his waist and pulled him closer. As his kiss deepened, I sent up a little thank you to the universe for introducing Rosie into my life and for bringing me here. This was definitely where I was meant to be.

32

I woke up on the morning of Good Friday with a smile on my face and memories of last night's kiss on my lips.

Rosie had been in bed reading when I got home and could immediately tell from my enormous smile that something had happened. After I told her, she hugged me tightly and reminded me who'd called it right from the start. She squealed and hugged me again when I told her about Cotton-tail's Cottage, and said she'd be happy to help get it ready on her days off.

I'd arranged to call for Dane at 10 a.m. this morning ready for our first day of clearing Cotton-tail's Cottage, but I was ready by eight and itching to go.

'You look lovely this morning, Autumn,' Alice said when I joined her in the kitchen. 'There's a glow about you. Being here must suit you.'

'It really does, and I have some exciting news. Dane and I will be renting a cottage in the village until the end of summer, possibly longer.'

'Oh, how lovely! Which one?'

'It's Cotton-tail's Cottage near The Hardy Herdwick.'

'Beatrice Eccles's cottage,' she said, smiling at me. 'You'd have liked her. Massive fan of Beatrix Potter. She loved that they nearly shared the same first name. I remember her trying to convince her husband that they should change their surname to Potter, but he was having none of it, bless him. He indulged her passion, but even he had limits. You should have seen it inside. It was like a museum or a shop.'

'It still is. Her daughter hasn't cleared it. Dane and I are going to do it this week.'

She raised her eyebrows. 'Good luck with that. I think you might be quite some time.'

'So do I! We're moving in a week tomorrow. Is it all right if I stay here until then?'

'Aw, bless you for asking. Of course it is. It's been an absolute pleasure having you here and we'll miss you. You won't be a stranger, will you?'

'Definitely not. I'll come back and visit often. Rosie's still determined to make a rider out of me. She reckons that, once I'm in the saddle, I'll catch the riding bug.'

'I think you will too.' She finished her tea and loaded her mug into the dishwasher while I put the kettle on to make myself a drink.

'It's a beautiful morning,' she said, 'so I'm heading out for a walk round the estate with Toffee. I'm so pleased you're staying. I think it would break Rosie's heart to say goodbye to you. It's been so good for her having you here. I'm so pleased you two found each other.'

Her eyes sparkled with unshed tears and I felt emotional too as we hugged.

She called for Toffee, who bounded outside as soon as Alice opened the door.

'Saying goodbye to you would break my heart too,' she said, pausing by the door, and then she was gone, leaving me blinking back tears and swallowing down a big lump in my throat.

The kettle clicked off and I reached for a mug, but changed my mind. The cloudless sky held the promise of a beautiful day and, as I'd be spending most of it indoors, I'd take advantage of some fresh air now. I made a flask of coffee then ran upstairs to get my jacket and bag.

Walking past the lamppost at the lane end, my heart skipped as I relived that kiss in my mind. Butterflies fluttered in my stomach all the way into the village, thinking about seeing Dane again. I glanced up at Lake View but could see no signs of life, and The White Willow wasn't open yet.

My stomach was rumbling and I hoped that the bakery wouldn't be closed with it being a bank holiday. As I approached, the delicious aroma of fresh bread and pastries pulled me forward, reassuring me that there was food on offer.

I bought a bag of croissants and sat down with them on the bench by the giant willow on the village green. It was damp, but I didn't mind. Nothing could dampen my spirits this morning.

There were a few people milling around but the village was otherwise quiet and sleepy. This was such a beautiful spot. The willow tree was stunning, the lake view magnificent, and the bursts of daffodils everywhere were an absolute delight. How lucky was I to be making Willowdale my home?

I sighed contentedly as I took out my phone.

TO DANE

Morning! I'm on the village green with croissants and coffee if you want to join me x

FROM DANE

Any chance of the croissants and coffee being accompanied by a kiss from Willowdale's answer to Beatrix Potter? x

TO DANE

If that's Willowdale's answer to Arthur Ransome asking, then absolutely yes x

FROM DANE

Give me 10 x

That was followed immediately by another text which made me laugh.

FROM DANE

I meant 10 mins, but will happily take 10 kisses. Or more x

Floating among the happy thoughts this morning, there had been the tiniest dark cloud of fear that Dane might regret last night – emotional reaction after a few drinks on an unusual day – or that it had been a one-off, but that cloud had now floated away.

Less than ten minutes later, I spotted him. He smiled and broke into a run. I stood as he approached and he took my head in his hands and tenderly kissed me.

'That's one,' I whispered as we pulled apart.

He smiled. 'Going straight back in for number two.'

We kissed again and he held me close.

'I was worried you might not want me to do that today,' he said, taking my hand as we sat on the bench.

'Same here,' I admitted. 'I'm so relieved you did.'

'I've wanted to kiss you since I first saw you,' he said.

'When we collided on the road?'

'Before that. I've got a confession to make. When I cycled into you, it wasn't completely your fault. I saw you arrive the day before. I was on my bike on my way to Pippinthwaite and you were coming into the village, crawling along really slowly with your window down, looking around you. We see that a lot from lost tourists searching for their holiday cottage, but you didn't look as though you were trying to read cottage names. There was this look of wonder on your face and the most incredible smile and something clicked inside me. I had no idea who you were and I'd only seen you for a few seconds, but I desperately hoped our paths would cross again.'

'Aw, Dane! I remember that, but I had no idea it was you.'

'This is going to sound so corny but it was like the sunshine had just driven past me in a red hatchback.'

It wasn't corny at all – it was the loveliest thing anyone had ever said to me.

'When I was on my bike the next day,' he continued, 'I spotted someone with long dark blonde hair in front of me and wondered if it could be the same person. It was doubtful I'd be that lucky, but I had to find out, so I decided to speed up, thinking I'd race past you, turn round, and come back in the other direction, by which time I'd have hopefully thought of something smart and interesting to say to get your attention. But the moment I sped up, you stepped out into the road.'

I loved his vulnerability around wanting to find something to say to me the day we collided. My insides felt like melted chocolate as I drew him into another kiss.

'No wonder you didn't lecture me for stepping out in front of you,' I said when we came up for air. 'So when you asked me out for lunch, you were hoping for a date?'

'Yes, and I was gutted when you didn't accept.'

'I'm so sorry. I agonised over that. It was the Étienne thing. I didn't know where my head was and I didn't know whether you were wanting a date or friendship so I panicked and ignored it. I regretted it, though.'

'You did?'

'Of course! That's why I asked you if you wanted to join me for lunch after I saw you at Hill Top and then you blew me out.'

We both laughed at the near misses.

Dane rubbed his thumb over my hand, the gentle touch sending a thrill through me. 'We're about to move in together and I'm really conscious that's not something that would normally happen the week after a first kiss. So if you'd rather I didn't move in, I can stay at Lake View. I'm sure Miss Eccles will come round about you not being local and I'll still help you clear and paint and—'

I silenced him with a kiss. It would have been quick if we'd got together and then he'd asked me to move in with him but we'd made the decision to share a place before we kissed so it was a very different scenario. And it wasn't like we were young and immature – I was thirty-five and he was thirty-seven with a grown-up son. This felt right.

'That's number four,' I whispered when we drew apart. 'I really appreciate the offer, especially when I know you love Cotton-tail's Cottage as much as I do. I still 100 per cent want us to move in together as planned, but I don't want us to rush things just because we're under the same roof.'

'I understand and I agree. I've got no expectations about us sharing a bed the moment we move in. It's a big step for both of us.'

'I'm so glad you feel that way. I like what we have now and I'm excited to see where it goes.'

Dane smiled so tenderly at me. 'Me too. When the time's right to take it any further, I think we'll both know and it'll happen naturally. Is that okay?'

'I couldn't ask for more. Kiss number five coming right up...'

33

When Dane and I arrived at Cotton-tail's Cottage, Trudy had already dropped off the crates and bubble wrap as promised, along with packing tape, scissors and a huge pack of tissue paper for wrapping the ornaments. She'd also left some fresh tea- and coffee-making supplies in the kitchen along with a couple of packets of locally made biscuits, which was kind of her.

It made sense to see if Trudy was right about there being some original boxes in the attic, so Dane went up the ladder and found several cardboard boxes full of figurine boxes. Trying to match up the items with the boxes would take longer than wrapping each individual figurine, but it would protect them better.

We'd only been there an hour when Trudy called round to check we had everything we needed. We asked her what she was going to do with all the paraphernalia – or Potterphernalia, as Dane had christened it – once we'd boxed it up.

'It'll probably sit in my garage for years and I'll take it to the tip when I'm fed up of it being there.'

We'd both gasped and strongly objected. There'd be collectors who might be interested, charity shops, maybe even an auction house.

'I hear you, but I can't be bothered. All I know is that I don't want any of it – the books included. You can have them. Consider it a housewarming gift for two Potter fans. Sell them if you don't want them.'

We didn't want the Potterphernalia ourselves, although there were a couple of pieces I'd seen which I might like to keep, so we decided to try to sell them and give the money to Dane's Mountain Rescue team. Donations were invaluable for providing the volunteers with the right PPE and equipment, insuring and keeping the specialist vehicles on the road, and first aid supplies.

The books were another matter, especially the first and early editions and special collections which were worth a lot of money. We couldn't decide whether it was best to donate them to the National Trust or sell them and donate the proceeds to the National Trust and/or Mountain Rescue.

It was a painstaking task to organise the figurines into collections, photograph them individually and as collections, give each a gentle clean and pack it away in the correct box, but we'd managed to sort most of them by 5 p.m. and decided to call it a day and treat ourselves to dinner in the pub.

We were packing a batch of figurines into a crate when we heard a clatter and a plaintive mew.

'Is that Tom Kitten?' I asked Dane. We were both dying to meet her, but there'd been no sign so far.

We slowly approached the kitchen. A large and exceptionally beautiful cat was lapping from the water bowl. Trudy had said she was a Maine Coon cat, distinguishable by her big pointed ears. She was fairly fluffy with black, white and ginger stripes and, when she looked up at us, she had pale green eyes and the prettiest face – mainly ginger but with a white muzzle, and a couple of black stripes.

'Hi, Tom,' I said, my voice soft as I reached for a pouch of cat food. 'I'm Autumn and this is Dane and we've been looking forward to meeting you.'

'Hi, Tom,' Dane said. 'Aren't you beautiful?'

She surveyed us with the typical impatient expression of a cat wanting food, so I emptied the pouch into her bowl and she eagerly tucked in.

'I wonder how long it'll be before we can cuddle her,' I said.

Dane shrugged. 'No idea. Hope it's not too long. She looks so soft.'

We stayed in the kitchen while Tom finished her food. She had another drink and spent a few minutes grooming herself then trotted back across the tiles and out of the cat flap without another glance in our direction.

'Might be a while,' Dane said. 'Oh well, baby steps.'

* * *

We spent the whole of Saturday and most of Easter Sunday at Cotton-tail's Cottage. We finished with all the figurines and miscellaneous items and managed to organise the books too, photographing them and stacking them into crates based on age, taking tremendous care with the special ones.

Beatrice Eccles's collection included a first edition of my favourite book – *The Tailor of Gloucester* – which had been Potter's personal favourite. A beautiful, magical rags-to-riches story of an elderly tailor who fell ill while working on the coat and waistcoat for the Mayor of Gloucester's Christmas Day wedding, only to have his workshop mice sew it together for him and save the day, there was no way I could pack it away without looking through it. I felt like I needed those special white gloves archivists wear but we had nothing like that. My hands were shaking so much that I had to get Dane to turn the pages for me for fear I might damage them. I knew every illustration so well, but looking at them again in their first edition format gave me such a thrill.

'Keep it,' he said. 'Miss Eccles said we can have them.'

I gazed longingly at the cover, but shook my head. 'You have no idea how much I want to, but I can't. It's far too valuable.'

I kept the Folio Society sets and made a donation to Mountain Rescue for their value. I toyed with doing that for *The Tailor of Gloucester* but I couldn't justify it when I had no income coming in and no idea how long it would take to sell the Sutton house. A couple of hundred pounds for the Folio sets was one thing but thousands for the first edition was quite another.

Tom Kitten appeared late on Saturday afternoon and meowed for some food. She seemed happy to let me stroke her while Dane added a pouch to her bowl, but she didn't purr. She was as soft and fluffy as I'd imagined. We didn't see her on Sunday afternoon because we'd agreed to finish mid-afternoon and spend some time at our respective temporary homes before the residents forgot what we looked like. We left some food out for Tom, which had gone when we arrived on Monday morning.

Monday's task was to remove everything from the walls. Rosie joined us but Dane was called out after a couple of hours to rescue a walker who'd slipped and broken their ankle on Skiddaw, so we didn't get through the task any quicker.

Once the Potterphernalia was cleared, the cottage looked even bigger and we could properly see the furniture which mainly appeared to be fairly new. Trudy had been right about the state of the wall when the pictures came down – nail and hook holes everywhere and perfect squares and rectangles of darker paint beneath every item – so it was just as well we had permission to decorate, as it looked terrible.

Dane had his shifts at Hill Top on Tuesday and Wednesday. It was strange not having him around. I felt comfortable in the cottage on my own, but I missed his laughter, hugs and kisses so much.

Being on my own gave me a lot of time to think about my relationship with Étienne and how badly the ending had affected me. I'd completely retreated from the world, making my life all about Granddad and work. Granddad had needed me when he fell ill but I'd needed him more from way before that, and losing my mojo with my work had been all the more distressing because, without work (and without Granddad), I had nothing. That horrendous day fourteen years ago, I hadn't just lost Étienne and my baby. I'd lost myself too. But now I was back. I'd found somebody special, friendship, a community, a new home and I felt sure I'd find my new identity as an artist – or perhaps as an illustrator and writer – really soon. And I had a cat! Tom Kitten accepted more affection every day. She hadn't let either of us pick her up yet but she'd ventured into the lounge, had weaved round my legs on several occasions and had jumped onto Dane's knee at one point, pausing for a few seconds before jumping down again.

On the Thursday, with the holes in the walls filled and smoothed the day before, we started painting the lounge. My steady hand made me good at the cutting in, but Dane didn't have the patience for that and preferred the satisfaction of the immediate coverage the roller gave him, making us the perfect decorating team. He tried to wind me up that I'd missed a bit in the lounge, which earned him a paint splodge on the nose, so he chased me round the cottage trying to get his revenge, which had us laughing hysterically as we sank down onto the plastic-covered sofa, paint in our hair and all over our arms.

'I've never laughed so much in my life,' I said, cuddling up to him. 'Thank you for that.'

'Thank you too. For a while after Lynsey, I wondered if I'd laugh again.'

'Me too after Étienne. I lost myself for a very long time, but you and Rosie helped me find me again. All I need now is to find out who I am as an artist, and I'll finally be whole again.'

He kissed the tip of my nose. 'You'll get there. Once we've been down to Sutton and we're settled here properly, it'll come. I know it.'

All week, we'd skirted around the decision as to who'd have which bedroom. The front bedroom did have a lake view and it was so beautiful. I'd have loved that room, but it had only taken one glance at Dane's expression the first time we saw it to know that he was captivated. He acted like he didn't mind either way, but I could tell, and I wanted to make him happy.

'I'd like the back bedroom,' I said as we stood on the landing on Friday morning, ready to paint upstairs.

'No! You should have the lake view.'

'I want you to have it. I know we've removed the books, but I feel drawn to the back room because of the library connection. I'd prefer that one.'

Although, from the intensity of his kiss, I suspected I might not be in the back bedroom for very long. The chemistry between us was sizzling more every day.

We couldn't have timed the week better, finishing the final bit of painting late on Friday afternoon. We'd only done the lounge, kitchen and our two bedrooms and would tackle the rest of the house once we'd moved in.

I'd FaceTimed my parents last Friday evening to tell them all about Dane and our living arrangements. I'd emphasised separate bedrooms, but Maman had laughed and said it was my life and neither of them would ever judge me about any decisions I made. The following day, I called again and took them on a virtual tour of the house while most of the Potterphernalia was still in place, and then again last night after the lounge had been painted to show the difference. I wanted them to feel like they were part of my new life in the Lake District, and they seemed to really appreciate that.

* * *

On Friday evening, Alice wanted to cook a special farewell meal for me and had invited Dane too, saying that I was now family, which meant he was too.

'They're so beautiful. Thank you,' Alice said, giving Dane a hug when he arrived with a bouquet of flowers for her.

'Thanks for inviting me.'

'I had to meet the man who stole our beautiful Autumn's heart,' she said, smiling in my direction. 'You're very lucky to have her. She's been an absolute delight to live with.'

I swallowed the lump in my throat and suspected it wouldn't be the last time I did that tonight. It was ridiculous how sad I felt about saying goodbye, even though I'd only be living a fifteen-minute walk away.

'Mam and I have a surprise for you,' Rosie said, inviting us into the kitchen for dinner. 'We have a couple of extra guests.'

I looked round the kitchen, confused. Alice was the only other person in there, but I followed Rosie's gaze to the table, where a laptop was open with Maman and Papa's faces on the screen.

'No! They're on a live feed?'

'*Bonsoir*,' Maman called and they both waved.

'We hope you don't mind us crashing your dinner party,' Papa said.

'It's great to see you both.' I introduced them to Dane, feeling a little nervous. I'd never introduced a boyfriend before. What if they didn't like him? But then I quickly reasoned there was no possible reason for them not to.

Even though my parents were on the end of a video call, they'd prepared a meal and dined alongside us. It could have been awkward as it was Dane's first time 'meeting' them, but it couldn't have gone better. There was an instant warmth and connection between all the people I cared about most in the world, and the meal was filled with easy conversation and laughter.

We said goodbye to them after dessert, and I thanked Alice and Rosie profusely for organising that.

'I've got a little thank you gift for you, Alice,' I said. 'Back in a minute.'

I nipped upstairs and retrieved the Benjamin Bunny which I'd hidden in the wardrobe.

'Aw, he's adorable!' Alice cried, lifting the rabbit in his brown jacket out of his gift bag and cuddling him tightly, tears in her eyes. 'Now I have a rabbit to remind me of my wonderful Rosie and another to remind me of my gorgeous Autumn.'

The lump in my throat gave way to tears this time as I hugged her, and Rosie joined us for a group hug.

A little later, I walked Dane to the end of the lane.

'I'll see you tomorrow for moving-in day,' he said, kissing me. 'Are you excited?'

'I can't wait. I'll miss being here, but I'm ready for my fresh start with my own space. *Our* space.'

He kissed me once more and sighed softly as he reluctantly pulled away. 'See you tomorrow. Our new life in Cotton-tail's Cottage awaits.'

34

That first weekend together in Cotton-tail's Cottage was exactly how I'd hoped it would be. Dane had taken nothing from his marital home except his clothes and personal possessions, so he didn't have much to move in. I only had what I'd brought from Sutton for a fortnight's stay, so it didn't take me long to unpack either.

Although the kitchen was modern, the contents of the cupboards had seen better days, so we'd cleared out the mismatched crockery and worn pans and decided it would be easier to eat out for the first few days and buy some new kitchenware while we were in Sutton with more shops available. We had a light lunch in The White Willow and picked up a Chinese takeaway from Keswick for dinner and, on Sunday, we invited Rosie to the Lakeside Inn after she'd finished her riding lessons to thank her for her help with the cottage and her amazing hospitality.

It was my first time in the Lakeside Inn and it was clear that it was aiming for a different clientele to The Hardy Herdwick. The interior was light, airy, and modern with grey wooden tongue-

and-groove panelling round the bottom half of the walls, real wood flooring, oak tables and a mismatch of tartan and plain upholstery chairs in greys, greens and purples. It was beautiful and it still felt friendly, but The Hardy Herdwick had stolen my heart. A meal in the Lakeside Inn was definitely a special occasion treat.

The meal itself was amazing and I was glad we'd arranged it because it was important to me that Rosie didn't feel pushed out now that I was with Dane. She would forever remain my best friend and, without her, I'd never have found Dane. To show her that I wasn't going to suddenly ditch our Sunday afternoons and Mondays together, I asked if she thought I might be ready to get on a horse.

'Absolutely, yes. Do you want to try tomorrow?'

I met her at the riding stables mid-morning the following day, feeling better about giving it a try while the stables were closed to the public so there was nobody else around to see me. I wasn't confident I'd be able to get into the saddle without help, but Rosie said she never judged anyone for using a mounting block. The important thing was getting comfortable in the saddle, so what did it matter if a person climbed a few steps to get there?

'How does it feel?' she asked as I settled into the saddle and took hold of the reins like she'd shown me.

'Very high, but okay. I think.'

'Just stay there for a few minutes, getting used to it. Give Leaf a stroke.'

There'd been a couple of other small horses I could have chosen and I'd befriended them both, but a chestnut mare called Leaf felt right for me considering my name.

I stifled a scream when Leaf took her first steps but, with Rosie's guidance and repeated gentle encouragement to relax, we soon built up from a walk to a trot around the larger manège.

'Look at that smile!' she cried as my confidence built and I started to enjoy myself. 'I'm going to video this so you can see how much fun you're having.'

An hour was enough for me. My thighs were aching and I suspected other parts of me would follow as the day wore on, but I genuinely had enjoyed it.

'How did you get on?' Alice asked when I returned to Horseshoe Cottage with Rosie for lunch.

'You can see for yourself,' Rosie said, showing her the video.

We sat at the kitchen table with mugs of tea as I told Alice how it felt and confirmed that I would give it another go when I returned from Sutton, which delighted them both.

A clatter through the letterbox signalled the post arriving. Toffee padded into the kitchen and dropped a few envelopes onto Alice's lap.

'One for you, Autumn,' she said, passing an envelope to me.

'Exciting!' I said, but my smile slipped when I saw the handwriting.

'Surely not Étienne?' Rosie asked, her voice as weary as I felt.

I sighed as I slit open the envelope and scanned down the letter. I couldn't even be bothered to translate it for her.

'He's got my letter and is grateful to me for writing,' I paraphrased, 'but he can't believe I won't consider trying again. Then it's more of the same as last time, pouring his heart out about how much he's always loved me and believes we were meant to be together.' I folded it up and placed it back in the envelope. 'I do feel bad for him, but…' I shook my head. What more was there to say?

'He made his decision,' Rosie said, 'and it shouldn't be your problem that he now regrets it and wants you back. You've moved on. You're happy now and he has no right to keep pestering you like that.'

'No, he doesn't. You know what? I'm not even going to write back. If I do that, it's like inviting him to be my penpal again and I've got the only penpal I need right here.'

Rosie and I looked at each other and realisation dawned at the same time.

'It's going to be so strange not rushing to the door to see if I've got a letter from you,' I said.

'Same here. After twenty-four years of writing, we've just come to the end of an era. I think you'd better forget about the move and go back to Sutton just so we can keep writing.'

Rosie squeezed my hand and I saw the same emotion on her face that I felt. Yes, I was going to be a short walk away and able to see her in person regularly which was so much better than a letter, but those letters had been such an important part of the whole of our teens and our adult life. They'd been a lifeline. It would be hard to let it go.

35

When I returned to Cotton-tail's Cottage, there was a white Transit van parked in next door's parking space. The owners – a lovely couple in their late sixties who'd warmly welcomed us and had said how pleased they were to have the cottage occupied again – had gone on holiday and said we were welcome to park the van there.

'Do you think there'll be enough room for what you want to bring back?' Dane asked me, showing me the space.

'Should be. Other than Grandma's writing bureau, it's mainly clothes, books and art supplies. I'm not sure I want any other furniture, although I might change my mind when I'm there.'

We had a ready meal for our dinner before walking round to the village hall for our very first creative writing class.

'Are you nervous?' I asked Dane.

'I am a bit. I don't know what to expect. I've never done an evening class. Do you think it'll be like school?'

'I don't think so, but she *is* a former teacher. Only one way to find out.'

'It's my favourite tenants,' Trudy said, welcoming us into the room.

Tables were laid out in a horseshoe shape and there were eight chairs round them. Four were already occupied, so we gave our new classmates smiles as we sat side by side. The final two arrived just after. Trudy had a table at the front but was sitting beside it rather than behind it like a teacher. It held a container full of pens, a pile of lined paper, and a beautiful bunch of daffodils, which I thought was a lovely spring touch.

Trudy welcomed us all and moved straight into introductions. The oldest group members – two women in their seventies – were neighbours from Pippinthwaite and the youngest were seventeen- and nineteen-year-old sisters from Keswick who joked they were like the Brontës because there was a third older sister at home who'd be joining us next week. The ones who'd arrived last were a gay couple in their fifties who'd recently moved to Willowdale from Carlisle.

Trudy issued a few ground rules around confidentiality and respecting all genres and writing styles to ensure everyone got the most out of the class and nobody felt disrespected, which I thought was great for setting the tone. After that, she opened up a discussion about reading preferences, writing interests, experiences so far, and writing aspirations. Everyone was a little hesitant to share at first, but we soon warmed into it. I liked that there was so much diversity in the group, with novelists, poets, short story writers and one of the older women planning to write her memoirs.

'And now onto your homework for next week,' Trudy said as the meeting drew to a close. 'Some of you might have been admiring my beautiful bunch of daffodils. I won't be bringing flowers along every week because these are here for a purpose. When we see daffodils, who do we think of around these parts?'

'Wordsworth,' we all said in unison.

'My homework is a spark word or a sentence. I want you to write a piece which starts with the words, "I wandered lonely as a cloud" and/or is sparked by the word "daffodils". It can be a poem, short story, the start of a novel, or simply a piece of creative writing – whatever speaks to you. No word count and no pressure to share, although I do encourage the sharing so you can seek feedback and learn.'

After checking for any questions, we were dismissed until next week. Dane and I left the village hall on a high.

'I'm buzzing with ideas,' he said.

'So am I.' But I didn't tell him that it was for an illustration rather than a piece of creative writing. I couldn't wait to start working on it as soon as we returned from Sutton.

36

We set off on our long drive down to Sutton the following morning, timing our departure to avoid the worst of the commuter congestion on the M6. We spent the early part of the journey talking about our new classmates and the plans Trudy had shared for how she saw the class evolving.

'I've been thinking about you and Beatrix Potter,' Dane said when we set off again after a service station lunch. 'There are so many parallels between the two of you. Obviously you both have a talent for illustrations and writing, but had you realised there were loads of others?'

'Some, but I'm intrigued to see what you've come up with. She started off designing greetings cards and I love that we both have that in common. And she struggled with life in London and found solace in the Lakes after losing the man she loved, just like I did.'

'You both love animals and have made a career out of drawing them,' Dane continued.

'And we both stayed at the Willowdale Hall estate.'

'And now you're living in the cottage of the woman whose

mother was best friends with Potter,' he said, laughing. 'I think we'll take that one with a pinch of salt.'

'She was encouraged to draw by parents when she was young, and so was I – by my parents and grandparents, and art runs in both our families. That's all that I can think of. Did you think of any others?'

'Just one, but it's a really important one because it's linked to you discovering the type of artist you want to be. Beatrix Potter didn't like to just draw whatever it was she saw – she liked to take what was in front of her like her home and garden, then enhance it with her creatures. That's what you do. Every drawing I've seen of yours is brilliant but the ones that truly feel like they're you are the ones with recognisable settings like the fairies on the Centenary Stone, the giant in Derwent Water and the Mountain Rescue team on Cat Bells. I really think you both have that in common.'

'I agree, but how do I find something unique to me? It's not like Beatrix Potter restricted herself to her farms and gardens or even the countryside round Hill Top. She was all over the Lakes and even beyond that. In theory, Derwent Water could be my setting because I love it so much, but she used it too. So me drawing woodland creatures in the Lake District, even in a different style, even without the humanisation of wearing clothes, is still like me copying what she did.'

We continued in silence for a while.

'What if it was the Lakes but it wasn't woodland animals?' Dane suggested. 'What if it was fairies?'

'Fairies?'

'The ones you drew for me are so good and you said they were your first attempts. Imagine what you could draw once you've practised more and perfected your style.'

'Fairies,' I whispered, my heart racing. It was an interesting idea.

'And if you didn't want to ditch the woodland animals – and why would you when you're so good at them? – what if you put them in the same world with the fairies? Didn't you say that Cicely Mary Barker was another of your heroines? This would be your own unique creation with a nod to the two artists who inspired you.'

My mind raced with the possibility. Could I do that? It wouldn't be copying Beatrix Potter if I used the Lake District as my backdrop but included fairies in my illustrations. Could woodland animals and fairies in the Lakes be who I was?

* * *

We arrived at the Sutton house early that evening and hadn't got further than taking our shoes off when there was a knock on the door. I should have known that Mrs Slade wouldn't be able to resist coming straight round. It was probably killing her wondering who was with me.

'You're back, then,' she said when I opened the door.

'I am, but we've had a really long drive and I'm shattered. Would you mind if I popped round to say hello in the morning?'

'Of course, dear. And will it just be you or—'

She didn't even try to hide that she was peering past me into the hall, trying to catch a glimpse of Dane.

'I'll see you tomorrow,' I said with a bright smile, closing the door.

'Neighbourhood watch?' Dane asked, laughing.

'Something like that. She's a lovely woman and was a wonderful friend to Granddad but, if I invite her in and do the introductions, she won't leave. Up to you whether you want to say hello to her tomorrow or not.'

'Has she lived next door for long?'

'Forty years, I think.'

'In that case, yes, please.' He gave me a mischievous grin as he wrapped his arms round my waist. 'I'm sure she'll have loads of stories she can share with me about you as a little girl.'

'That's not fair!' I protested.

'Oh, and you're not going to pump all my relatives for embarrassing stories about me when we have our big summer barbeque?'

'The thought never crossed my mind.' I tried to sound innocent, but failed. It had been my plan as soon as Dane told me the date of his annual family get-together.

Dane drew me into a tender kiss and it struck me that I'd never kissed anyone in this house before. I felt like Granddad might appear at any moment with a bumbling apology for interrupting. Even though I'd been the official owner for all my adult life, this had never and would never properly feel like my home. It was my grandparents' home and I needed my own space. It was full of memories, but selling it wouldn't take them away. They were in my heart and my head and would remain with me wherever life took me. I didn't need to own their house to remember them.

I took Dane on a tour of the downstairs. It felt cold and echoey, so I flicked the thermostat to put the heating on while he was looking at Grandma's paintings.

'You were right about that Beatrix Potter parallel,' he said when I returned to the lounge. 'Talented artists throughout the family. I love how you all have your own individual style.'

We went upstairs and Dane picked up one of my sketchpads in my bedroom to flick through.

'I could spend hours looking at your work,' he said. 'But it's not going to help us get packed. You're bringing all this home with you?'

'Yes.'

'Then I'll spend some quality time looking at it all there, if that's okay.'

'I love that you're interested.'

'I'm interested in everything about you. Being here and seeing your work and that of your grandparents is giving me such a sense of who you are and what inspires you. It's going to help us find the new artist you.'

'She's come a long way already since Paris. She's nearly there. And I think that fairies suggestion of yours might be another big step forward.'

'What's in this box?' he asked, picking up a pretty cardboard box with the word 'Dream' on the lid.

'Flipbooks. Have a look.'

He took one out and flicked through it. I peered over his shoulder to see which he'd selected. It was one of my favourites – a rabbit with a lost tail finding a pot at the end of the rainbow and discovering a new tail inside it instead of gold.

'You are definitely a storyteller,' Dane said, putting the book down and picking up another. 'And here's your evidence.'

* * *

Our time in Sutton was intense. Despite being tired from the journey, we didn't have time to relax on the Tuesday night or we'd never have got everything done. I set Dane off boxing up my books and art supplies while I emptied the contents of my wardrobe and drawers into suitcases. We were up early the following morning to continue, allowing ourselves a one-hour break to visit Mrs Slade next door who did, indeed, delight in regaling Dane with stories of me as a little girl, although there was thankfully nothing too embarrassing.

Between organising and cleaning, we squeezed in a trip to the tip, a charity shop drop-off and a kitchenware purchasing session at a retail park. On Thursday afternoon, three estate agents came round one after the other to measure up, take photos and give their valuation. I'd kept the one with the best reputation to the end and I could see why they'd earned it because they were the most friendly and professional. I signed up with them and handed over a set of keys ready for viewings.

I was conscious that I still hadn't told Madeline that I didn't want to be considered for the job. The Easter holidays had ended a week ago, but I'd been so busy clearing and painting Cottontail's Cottage that I hadn't had the opportunity to make that call. At the back of my mind, I'd been thinking I could tell her in person while I was in the area but there was no way I could squeeze it in.

There was one thing I absolutely had to do, though, and I didn't care how late that meant I went to bed on my final night – I had to write one last letter to Rosie. Dane headed up to bed at about half past midnight and I sat at Grandma's bureau, leafing through my box of writing paper. I paused at some sheets with cartoon horses on them, but they didn't feel special enough. I flicked through a little further and found something much better. There was a raincloud in the top left corner with the start of a caption – *When the rain keeps on falling and the day makes you weary...* A bright yellow sunshine on the bottom right corner was accompanied by the rest of the caption – *...a best friend brings sunshine and helps you feel cheery.*

Dear Rosie

I'm about to go to bed for the final time in my grandparents' house and there was no way I could settle down to sleep without writing you one final letter.

If it was filled with news, it would be a short one because you know everything that's going on for me right now! So I'll make it a thank you letter instead.

THANK YOU for being there when the rain kept falling and for bringing sunshine into my life.

THANK YOU for 400+ letters full of news, hugs, laughter and encouragement.

THANK YOU for 24 years of incredible friendship and for helping me find my new home, new life, and myself again.

I'll miss writing to you and I'll miss that excitement each time I check the post, but I'm about to have something even better – my best friend just down the road with ready hugs.

For now, here's my final one by post for the most amazing, supportive, kind, funny, inspiring, beautiful woman I have ever had the pleasure to know.

Hugs and friendship forever, Autumn xx

* * *

On Friday morning, Dane and I were up early again to pack the van. I'd selected a few small pieces of furniture in addition to the writing bureau but there was plenty of space for everything. When we'd finished loading the van, I ran to the corner of the street to post my last letter to Rosie. I kissed the envelope before dropping it in the box and returning to Dane for a hug.

'Are you okay?' he asked, kissing the top of my head.

'It felt so strange posting that.'

'It's bound to. You've been writing to each other for more than two thirds of your lives. That's huge.'

We said a final goodbye to Mrs Slade and Dane sat in the van consulting a traffic app while I did one last check around the house to make sure I hadn't forgotten anything.

'Goodbye, Grandma and Granddad,' I whispered as I closed the lounge door, pushing down the lump in my throat and blinking back the tears. 'Thank you for everything.'

I really didn't want to cry but, as we pulled off the drive and the house disappeared from the wing mirror view, I released a shuddery sob. Dane placed a reassuring hand on my thigh and gave a squeeze as we stopped at a pedestrian crossing, and I felt stronger from his touch. It was just a house. As I'd already told myself, I had the memories in my head and heart.

About an hour into the journey, I rang Madeline.

'I thought I'd better let you know my decision about the job,' I said after we'd exchanged pleasantries.

'It's a no, isn't it?'

'Yes. I'm really sorry.'

'Please tell me it's not because you're still not drawing,' she said, her voice full of concern.

'No, it's not that. I've done quite a bit of drawing recently and have even done a bit of writing.'

'Writing! You know, that doesn't surprise me at all. Your illustrations were never just that – they were always stories. So are you taking some time out and writing a book?'

'It's a strong possibility. But that's not the only reason it's a no for the job. I'm relocating to the Lake District.'

'Really? Oh, my goodness, you have been busy with the life decisions.'

'It's not like me to be so spontaneous, but it feels right.'

'You sound really happy.'

'I am.'

'Then I'm happy for you. I'll miss working with you, but I'm glad you've found what you were looking for. I love the Lakes. Next time we're on holiday there, would you like to meet up for a drink?'

'I'd love to. Thank you for being so understanding.'

'Thank you for being a brilliant artist and a fabulous team member. Stay in touch and I'll hopefully see you in the summer.'

'Thanks, Madeline. And all the best at Glitter Box. They're very lucky to have you.'

'Indeed they are!' she joked. 'And I'll keep reminding them of that. You look after yourself, Autumn.'

'And you.'

Dane turned and smiled at me when the call ended. 'Sounded like that went well.'

'Really well. I thought she might try to talk me out of it, but she understood. It feels like another weight has lifted.'

Dane and I were both tired with aching muscles from lugging boxes and furniture so we took turns driving home, dozing while we were passengers. As soon as Dane, driving the final stretch, pulled off the M6 onto the A66, my energy levels and my heart lifted.

'Nearly home,' he whispered.

And it felt like it truly was.

37

I woke up on Saturday morning in Cotton-tail's Cottage to the sound of footsteps on the stairs. Moments later, there was a knock on my bedroom door.

'Only me,' Dane said, poking his head round the door and holding a tray. 'You mentioned that you missed hot chocolate and almond croissants for breakfast, so *voila*.'

'Aw, you've been to the bakery. You absolute sweetheart. And you've worked out how to use the drinks machine!'

In addition to new kitchenware, we'd treated ourselves to a drinks machine and a starter pack of capsules.

'Good to be back?' he asked, sitting beside me on the bed.

'So good. What do you fancy doing today because I don't think I can face unpacking?'

'I'm glad you said that because I was thinking the same. I was going to suggest we empty the van so Phil can collect it, and put everything in the spare bedroom for now. Maybe a walk this morning and creative writing homework this afternoon? Don't want to let teacher down by not doing our first assignment.'

'Sounds good to me.'

I thought I could hear someone on the stairs and Dane had obviously heard it too because he put his croissant down and called out, 'Hello?'

Next moment, Tom launched herself onto the bed, making us both laugh with relief.

'Good morning, Tom Kitten,' I said, stroking her belly and smiling at Dane as she purred. 'This is the first time she's come upstairs. Aw, do you think she's missed us?'

'I think she has.'

* * *

We were at the kitchen table doing our creative writing homework that afternoon when there was a knock on the front door.

'I'll get it,' Dane said, standing up and stretching. 'It's probably Phil coming for the van keys.'

'Bring him in so I can say hello.'

A couple of minutes later, Dane reappeared in the kitchen. There was someone behind him, but Dane was blocking my view of them and he didn't look happy.

'It's not Phil,' he said, his voice dark and his expression darker.

'Then who…?'

He stepped aside and my stomach plummeted to the floor.

'Étienne? What are you doing here?' He was casually dressed in jeans, a blue shirt and a blazer, his hair looked effortlessly messy and he was staring at me intently.

'I came for you.'

'Why?' I cried, standing up but not moving any closer to him. 'I wrote to you and said no.'

'Je ne te crois pas. Je t'aime. Je t'ai toujours aimé. Cela doit signifier quelque chose pour vous.'

I don't believe you. I love you. I've always loved you. It must mean something to you.

I glanced at Dane, but his head was bowed and I couldn't catch his eye. 'I'm not having a conversation in French in front of someone else.'

Étienne curled his lip up at Dane. '*Qui est-il*?' he demanded.

'My boyfriend,' I snapped.

'*Est-ce qu'il nous connaît*?'

'Yes, he does know about us,' I said, translating for Dane's understanding. 'English, please.'

'It doesn't matter,' Dane muttered. 'I'll give you some space.'

'Dane! No!'

But he was already out of the room. A flash of jubilation crossed Étienne's face, which was like a red rag to a bull.

'What the hell, Étienne? What are you playing at?'

'I want you back.'

'You can't have me back. I told you that in my letter and I don't care that you don't believe me. It's the truth and you've wasted your time coming here.'

He took a couple of steps closer and my heart started to pound. I didn't like being so close to him.

His voice softened and there was a vulnerability in his tone, mirrored in his eyes. 'I thought if you saw me and we talked…'

'I'm sorry, but it's not going to happen.'

'Please, Autumn. Will you listen to what I have to say?'

I scrunched my eyes tightly and ran my hands through my hair. 'Oh, for goodness' sake.' I opened my eyes and fixed them on Étienne. 'Okay. We'll go for a walk and I'll hear you out, but nothing's going to change. You'll say your piece and then you'll return to France. Without me.'

He didn't respond but there was obvious relief on his face.

'How did you know where to find me?' I asked.

'I went to the cottage where you were staying and spoke to the lady there. She said you moved out. I said I was an old school friend from Paris and she sent me here.'

I sighed. Alice. She wouldn't have registered that it was Étienne because, like me, she wouldn't have expected him to have the audacity to turn up here after I'd said no.

'Stay here. I need another layer.'

I ran upstairs, pulled on a fleecy top, and picked up my phone from my bedside drawers. There were six missed calls from Rosie and a text message.

FROM ROSIE

Your ex is on his way to yours! I'm so sorry. Mam realised too late. He left his car down the lane so he's on foot and I hoped to catch you before he arrived, but you're not answering xx

TO ROSIE

Phone was upstairs! It's OK. Going for a walk to let him say his piece then hopefully he'll leave me alone xx

I couldn't bear the thought of Dane being worried, so I quickly typed in a message before running back downstairs.

TO DANE

I'm so sorry. I never expected him to appear. I'm going for a walk with him to hear him out but then he's out of here. Please don't worry. It's over with him and there's nothing he could say or do to make me doubt that or my feelings for you xx

'You're in a car?' I asked as I locked the door behind us.

'I hired one from the airport.'

That made my decision for me as to which direction to go – back to Willowdale Hall and hopefully he'd have accepted my no by the time we got there and he could jump in his car and leave. I could kill two birds with one stone and reassure Alice that I wasn't upset with her for telling him where to find me.

'You wanted to talk, so talk,' I said after we'd reached the village shop in silence.

'I will if you stop being so angry with me.'

'Angry? What do you expect, Étienne? How many times do I have to say no? This isn't a game, you know. I'm not playing hard to get. I genuinely have moved on.'

'That kiss said not.'

I should have known he'd throw that back in my face. 'That kiss took me by surprise, but a lot has changed since then. I've got a new home and a boyfriend.'

'Him? Pah! He's not right for you.'

'Really? And you'd know that from a thirty-second conversation on our doorstep?'

He had no answer to that.

'Look, Étienne, I don't want to fight with you. You asked me to listen to you so I'm listening. The floor is yours.'

A cool wind wrapped itself round me, making me shiver. I wished I'd grabbed my waterproof too but hopefully this wouldn't take long. I'd borrow another layer from Rosie to walk home.

I expected Étienne to have nothing new to say and it certainly started off that way, with him declaring his endless love and being full of regrets for letting me go, but then came a shock revelation.

'Chantal wasn't pregnant. She lied to me.'

We'd reached the marina entrance and I stopped, staring at him. 'What? But you have two daughters.'

'From later.'

'I don't understand. Why did she lie to you and when did you find out?'

It was too cold to stand still, so I set off walking again.

'Chantal wanted me back,' Étienne said. 'She came to see me in Paris and asked if we could try again. I said no because I was with someone else. She guessed it was you. She told me there was a reason she wanted to try again – that she was having my baby and I needed to do the right thing and marry her or I'd never see my child. You know I've always wanted a family. I couldn't walk away from my child.'

'You wanted a family with me, remember? We sat on Brighton beach and you gave me a ring and told me you wanted to marry me and have babies together. A fortnight later, your ex claims she's pregnant and suddenly all that's forgotten. Why did you say all that crap to me when you didn't mean it?'

'I *did* mean it! But it all got so messy. You wouldn't leave England because of your granddad – which I understood and supported – but Chantal wouldn't leave Dijon. She told her parents and mine and there was so much pressure on me from everyone to be a family. What was I to do? Never see my child?'

I could understand the predicament he'd faced. Étienne had a strong relationship with Sylvie, but Jacques could be overbearing and demand a lot from his only son. Étienne was constantly trying to seek his approval and impress him. All of them shared strong values about the importance of family, so of course Étienne was going to 'do the right thing' by his pregnant ex-girlfriend.

'When did you find out she wasn't pregnant?' I said, trying not to sound as angry as I felt.

'After we married. I was still working in Paris, but I wanted to go to her medical appointments. She was vague about them and something didn't ring true, so I went to Dijon and confronted her.

She admitted there was no baby. I was so angry and demanded our marriage be over but then she found out she really was pregnant so I stayed, but it was never right. The trust was gone.'

I could hear the pain in his voice and my heart really did go out to him – what a horrendous situation to be in – but I had another question.

'Why didn't you get in touch with me when you found out there was no baby?'

'I wanted to so very much, but I was ashamed of being duped and of letting you go. I thought the only chance I'd have of winning you back was if Chantal and I were legally separated, but...'

'But that never happened because of the real baby,' I said when he tailed off. What a mess!

'Would you have taken me back?' he asked.

I sighed. 'I don't know. I still loved you, but you hurt me so much that I don't know if I would have risked it again.'

We walked in silence for several paces. 'How could you stay with someone who'd tricked you into marriage?' I asked eventually.

He looked at me with sorrowful eyes and I shook my head, cursing myself for asking something so stupid.

'Because you still loved her,' I answered for him. 'What was this hold she had over you?'

'She was the first woman who took any notice of me. Before I met her, women weren't interested. They thought I was a geek. They laughed at me and poked fun. Even you never spoke to me.'

'I never laughed at you or poked fun at you and what was I supposed to do? *You* refused to speak to me. There's only so much rejection a person can take before they give up.'

'I'm sorry. I wanted to speak to you when we were younger, but I could think of nothing to say. Chantal saw past the awkward teenager and found the man inside. She helped me to find me. I was grateful to her and I loved her for it.'

'So where did I come in?' I asked, a bitter edge to my tone. 'If she helped you find you and changed you into a man, what did I do?'

'Everything. You both gave me love, but you also gave me friendship. I didn't have that same bond with Chantal.'

I couldn't think of anything else to say, but it didn't matter because Étienne was on a roll. There was more detail about his disastrous loveless marriage, further declarations of love for me, endless regrets, and I found myself tuning out. I wondered where Dane had gone and what he was doing. I really hoped he'd picked up my message and it had given him any reassurance he might have craved. I didn't think of him as the jealous sort – he'd certainly never given that impression when we'd talked about Étienne – but it was one thing talking about an ex and quite another having them turn up on your doorstep trying to win your girlfriend back. My phone was in my pocket on silent and I longed to see if Dane had replied, but I needed to try to focus on what Étienne was saying.

I tuned back in and threw in the occasional question for clarification, but another thought struck me. This was all about him, what *he* wanted, the future *he* craved. I started to feel like a trophy that he wanted to win back and wave in front of Chantal to say, *Look! I won after all! You tried to destroy us, but Autumn waited for me and now she's mine.*

And I had waited. I'd waited for far too long, but I wasn't his. I didn't belong to anyone. That's not how relationships worked. Being with Dane these past couple of weeks had been a revelation. I had no idea that being in a relationship could feel like this and it made me wonder whether Étienne and I would have lasted. Our friendship had been sporadic around my visits to

Paris and our romantic relationship boiled down to four weekends together and a handful of letters. If we'd had quality time together, would cracks have appeared? With Dane, I had a strong friendship, chemistry, and something I realised now that I hadn't had with Étienne – a partnership where we were strong individually and even stronger together. With Étienne, he'd been the strong one, the decision-maker, the lead, and I'd followed, grateful that after five years of pining for him, he'd finally picked me. It was the thing about our relationship that had niggled me which I hadn't quite been able to place my finger on and now I could. Even though he'd claimed he'd move to Brighton to be with me, I doubted it would have happened because everything about our friendship and subsequent relationship had been on his terms and for his benefit instead of being a partnership.

We'd walked past Willowdale Hall and were now on the trail to the base of Cat Bells and Étienne was still talking. I really think he believed what he was saying and my heart did go out to him. If he was still deeply in love with me, he was going to be hurting and even though some would consider that karma, that wasn't how my mind worked. I didn't want to break his heart, but there was no happy ever after for the two of us and I was going to have to tell him the one thing I'd been determined not to say because I couldn't think of any other way of getting through to him.

When he finally paused for long enough for me to share my thoughts, I took a deep breath. *Here goes...*

'All these things you've said to me are things I longed to hear... a long time ago. I loved you so much and I wanted a future with you so badly, but that chance was taken away from both of us and we needed to rebuild our lives separately. I won't lie. It hasn't been easy for me. While you were with Chantal raising your family, I was nursing a broken heart. Even as recently as when I was in Paris, I thought it would never heal and I will admit that, when I saw you and we kissed, I did think about us having a future together. It excited me, but it scared me too and—'

'You don't have to be scared.'

I bit my lip to prevent me from snapping at him not to interrupt. He'd had his time and now it was mine. 'As I was saying, it excited me but it scared me and the reason I left Paris and came here was to get away from you because I couldn't risk you breaking my heart again. And not just breaking my heart, but breaking me.'

'I wouldn't have. Not again. I'd have spent our lifetime making it up to you. Please, Autumn, you know we're good together.'

'Were,' I corrected him.

He fished in his jeans pocket and my heart sank when he produced the promise ring. 'And we can be again.'

'No, we can't. It's over.'

'It doesn't have to be.'

Why wasn't he listening to me? What part of 'no' didn't he understand? I knew for certain now that there was no love left in my heart for Étienne. My heart wasn't broken anymore and, even if it still had been, he wasn't the one who could fix it. Nothing I said was getting through to him and there was only one thing I could think of trying. Maybe my own shock revelation would finally make him hear me.

I stopped walking and faced him. 'There's something I need to tell you. The day you phoned me and told me you'd chosen Chantal, I'd just found out that I was pregnant.'

His mouth dropped open. 'What?'

'I'd found out I was pregnant and I was going to tell you when I saw you the following day, but you ended it without giving me a chance to say anything. You made a decision, told me what it was, then cut me off. I tried to call you back, I even texted you with the news, but you'd blocked me. I had no way of letting you know about the baby.'

He grasped my arm, but I shook him off.

'You had my baby? Where is it?'

'I didn't have your baby. I said I was pregnant.'

'It wasn't mine?'

'Étienne! Of course it was yours! I didn't have the baby. Shortly after we spoke, I started cramping and bleeding and I passed out in the bathroom. Granddad had to break the door down and call an ambulance. It was an ectopic pregnancy which ruptured my fallopian tube. I lost the baby and I could have died.'

He was staring at me, eyes wide, mouth still open. Shock? Sympathy? I couldn't read him.

'You didn't tell me,' he murmured.

'How could I? You blocked me.'

'I had a right to know. It was my baby. You were pregnant with *my* baby and you didn't say.'

'Aren't you listening to me?'

I could read his expression now. His breathing was rapid, his eyes flashing, his jaw grinding.

'*Putain*!' he yelled. '*Salope*!'

I understood why he'd be shocked and perhaps angry but using the French equivalent of the f-word and calling me a bitch was uncalled for, especially when it was his actions that had prevented me from telling him what had happened. Had he not heard the part about the miscarriage? Or about me nearly dying? Of course not! Because this was all about him again and how he felt.

He gave me the filthiest look then stormed off down the trail.

'Étienne!' I called. 'Étienne!' Louder the second time, but he kept on striding, his long legs covering the ground quickly.

With a sigh, I walked after him, but he broke into a run.

'Étienne! You don't know where you're going!'

He sped up so I did too, my muscles burning from a fortnight of hard work, but I rounded a corner and couldn't see him anywhere. I was gasping for breath and had a painful stitch in my side.

'Well, now you know!' I shouted into the emptiness. 'This has been fun! Have a safe trip home.'

I rubbed my hands through my hair and set off after him once more but stopped. Why should I? I didn't know where he'd gone and it wasn't like I knew the area either. I'd only walked along here a couple of times, but I remembered there being pathway choices a little way ahead of us, so even if I did go after him, who was to say I'd pick the same path as him? He was a big boy and he could make his way back to his car when he'd had his sulk.

There was drizzle in the air now and the fog was rolling in, so he'd surely have the sense to turn back soon like I was going to because I was cold, tired and fed up. I was off to Horseshoe Cottage to warm up and reassure Alice she'd done nothing wrong. It was completely, fully, irrevocably over with Étienne and hopefully he finally understood why and would go home to lick his wounds. There was no future for us, but there was a person who I could see a very happy future with and I was going to ring him as soon as I got some network coverage.

* * *

Dane wasn't home when I returned to Cotton-tail's Cottage. He hadn't answered his phone. I sent him a text to say I was back and Étienne had gone, but it remained unread.

I tried to do my creative writing homework, but I couldn't concentrate on it. My ears pricked up at every tiny sound, hoping it was Dane. Tom coming through the cat flap scared the life out of me and my hands shook as I emptied a pouch of food into her bowl.

'I don't know where Dane is,' I told her. 'I'm so worried. Do you think I should see if he's at The White Willow or Lake View?'

Tom was no help, not even looking at me as she worked on her food. I went into the lounge and watched out the window, but there was still no sign of Dane. I put some music on to distract me and lit some scented candles to try to calm my nerves before returning to my vigil at the window.

A while later, Tom wandered through to the lounge and weaved round my ankles, purring. Instinctively, I bent down to pick her up and, for the first time ever, she let me. I buried my face in her fur. My attempts at holding back my tears were futile and I was soon sobbing. I sank down onto the sofa with Tom in my arms.

'I can't have lost him already,' I cried, my voice stumbling over the words. 'I just can't.'

My heart leapt as I heard the sound of a key in the front door. Tom shot off my knee and out into the hall.

I heard Dane greeting her and tried to wipe my tears but I wasn't quick enough.

'Are you okay?' he asked, rushing over and crouching down beside me, his eyes full of concern.

'I'm so sorry,' I cried. 'I can't believe Étienne turned up like that. He means nothing to me. You have to know that.'

He smiled weakly. 'It was a bit of a shock.'

'For me too. I'm so annoyed with him, but he's finally got the message.'

Dane sat down beside me. 'He's gone?'

'Presumably. He threw a strop and ran off, but I'm guessing he'll be at the airport now or on his way there.'

'It's definitely over? I know you'd written and told him that, but seeing him again…'

'Confirmed for me that I don't feel anything for him anymore,' I finished. 'Were you worried?'

'A bit. He's a good-looking bloke and you have history.'

'And from the photos I've seen, Lynsey's an attractive woman and you have history, but if she turned up now, would you feel anything?'

'Probably pissed off.'

'Which is how Étienne made me feel today. And just in case you have any doubts, the tears aren't over Étienne, they're over you. I was worried I'd lost you.'

Dane gathered me in his arms and rocked me. 'You'll never lose me. I was worried I'd lost you, though. What a pair we are.'

'You'll never lose me either.'

He lit the log burner and we lay together on the sofa as I told him about my confrontation with Étienne. Slow, steady rain pattered against the window, but we were warm and cosy inside. I felt closer to him than ever, lying against his chest as he stroked my hair. We must have been there for about an hour, talking and kissing, when a beeping noise interrupted us.

'That's Mountain Rescue,' Dane said as we untangled ourselves so he could get his phone. I went into the kitchen for a glass of water while he found out the details.

'I've got to go. Reports of a distressed man on Cat Bells refusing assistance. I might be gone some time.'

He kissed me then left to respond to the emergency. I returned to the lounge, instructed the smart speaker to stop the music, and put the TV on instead.

About twenty minutes later, Rosie rang.

'Have you seen Étienne since you left our place earlier?' she asked.

'No, why?'

'I was walking Toffee when I spotted his car still in the lane. I thought he might be sleeping in it, but it's empty.'

I gasped. 'Oh no! Dane's just responded to a callout to a distressed man on Cat Bells. Do you think it could be Étienne?'

'It's possible. You said he ran off in that direction. But surely he wouldn't be so stupid to attempt Cat Bells with the weather closing in.'

'He wouldn't have a clue about the weather. I bet it's him. If he's not in the car and he's not here, where else would he be?'

'In the pub? I'd suggest you check both pubs and see if he's there. If not, I'd call Dane to warn him and get yourself round here so you're not alone.'

38

I felt sick as I ran upstairs. I didn't have Étienne's number in my phone, but he'd put it in his letters and I still had them. Somewhere. I took a couple of calming breaths, trying to think where they were and remembered that I'd shoved them in a pocket on the suitcase I'd had at Rosie's, which was now under my bed. Unzipping the pocket with fumbling fingers, I tapped his number into my phone, my heart thumping as it rang out, but there was no answer. Not that I'd expected there to be.

Shoving my phone in my jeans pocket, I hurriedly pulled on a couple of warm layers, and raced back downstairs to put on my waterproof and walking boots. I remembered seeing a large torch in the garage and ran out to get it, praying it had working batteries. Thankfully it did and the beam was strong.

As I pushed open the door of The Hardy Herdwick, a wave of warmth and chatter hit me, along with the familiar aroma of beer blended with pub food. Tonight, none of that comforted me as I hastily did a round of the pub, making sure I missed no alcoves. No Étienne.

Stomach churning, I ran down to Lakeside Inn, but he wasn't

there either. I couldn't imagine he'd have ventured further into the village, so I headed in the direction of Willowdale Hall. I could have driven – quicker and warmer – but I wanted to check the route, just in case.

I crossed the road to the village green and shone the torch beam under the willow, but to no avail. Doing a half-walk, half-jog, I continued on to the marina. The metal barrier was down but I swerved round it and did a search of the grounds. A noise behind a trolley of kayaks filled me with hope and I swung the torch beam in that direction. A fox stared at me for a moment – a beautiful creature bringing a moment of calm – then scooted off in the other direction.

Returning to the road, I rang Dane. I hoped he'd answer, realising that I'd never ring him when he was on a callout unless it was urgent.

'Have you heard anything more about the walker?' I asked as soon as he answered.

'Just that he wasn't dressed for the fells.'

'I think it might be Étienne. His car's still at the hall and he's not in it.'

I heard Dane's sharp intake of breath. 'Where are you? You sound like you're running.'

'Walking fast. I'm on my way to Rosie's. His number was on those letters so I've tried ringing him and I've checked the pubs and marina, but he ran off in the direction of Cat Bells and he was angry. I'm convinced it's him.'

'We've got a clear last location, although there's no guarantee he'll stay there. Can you send me his mobile number?'

'Yes. Anything else you need?'

'Just for you to try to stay calm and stay at Rosie's. Don't come out looking for him or we might have another casualty to search for.'

'I promise I'll stay there.'

'It might not be him, but I think there's a strong possibility it is. Does he speak English?'

'Fluently. He was just being awkward earlier. I'm nearly at the estate so I'll send you his number. Keep me posted.'

We said our goodbyes and I pinged Étienne's number across, praying it would help them find him. The rain had eased but it was still foggy, which wouldn't make the search easy and was an extra level of danger for anyone lost on the fells. I knew from Dane that even experienced walkers with great local knowledge could get disorientated in weather like this.

I spotted a car in the lane, the advertising sticker on the back confirming it was a hire car and therefore had to be Étienne's, not that I'd ever doubted that. Vehicles couldn't get onto the estate without knowing the access code or being let in by any of the three residents.

Rosie must have been watching for me as she ran out with a hug as Toffee circled round me.

'No sign of him in the pubs?' she asked, leading me into the kitchen where Alice, sitting at the table nursing a mug of tea, gave me a weak smile.

'No, and I checked the marina too. I rang Dane and gave him Étienne's number. They have a last location so they're hopeful.'

'Do they think it's him?' Alice asked.

'It sounds like it from the description, but it might not be. Although if it isn't him, I dread to think where he might be.'

I removed my boots and shrugged off my coat while Rosie made me a drink, and I joined both of them at the table, gratefully wrapping my cold hands around the mug.

'I'm so sorry again about sending him to your place earlier,' Alice said, twiddling with a button on her cardigan. 'I should have realised it was Étienne.'

'Like I said earlier, it's not your fault. He lied to you about who he was. That's on him, not you.' I took a slurp of my tea. 'What if they don't find him?'

'If it's him on Cat Bells, they'll find him,' Rosie said.

'And if it isn't him?'

They both sighed and shrugged. If it wasn't him, presumably they'd organise a bigger search party. What a mess!

Nobody said anything for a while. All I could think about was Étienne all alone, shivering in the darkness on Cat Bells, and how guilty I'd feel if anything happened to him. A cotton shirt and a blazer weren't going to offer him any protection in this weather. It seemed hypothermia was inevitable, which could be fatal.

'You do know it's not your fault either,' Rosie said as I shuddered.

'It feels like it.'

'You're not responsible for his actions. He's a grown man, Autumn. He was the one who chose to come here against your wishes and he was the one who went rushing off when he didn't like hearing the truth. I hope they find him quickly and I hope he's okay but, whatever happens, you're not to blame.'

I appreciated the conviction behind her words and I knew she was right, but it didn't stop me feeling bad about it.

'How was Sutton?' Rosie asked, initiating a welcome change in subject.

I told them about our trip, the house going on the market and how I'd made a decision to get a company in to clear the rest of the furniture when it sold, meaning I wouldn't be going back again.

'You won't have managed to do any drawing while you were away,' Alice said.

'No. It was pretty full-on. I'm going to take a few days to get unpacked and settle in properly, and then I need to do some serious thinking about what I draw and how I earn a living.'

I was interested in their take on me drawing fairies, but now wasn't the right time – far too cheerful a subject to discuss under the circumstances. All I wanted was for my phone to ring with news that Étienne had been found and was safe. I might not love him anymore, but I still cared what happened to him. The thought of them not finding him or getting to him too late was unbearable.

39

It was nearly midnight when Dane finally FaceTimed with the news that they'd found Étienne. He was in hospital suffering from hypothermia and he'd sustained a broken ankle so was currently getting that set and bandaged. He'd moved from the last seen spot which had delayed them, but he hadn't got far with his ankle, so it didn't take too much longer to find him.

'Will he be okay?' I asked.

'His ankle will mend in time – it's not a bad break – and he hasn't been rushed into intensive care, which means the hypothermia isn't severe.' Dane's voice was so gentle and reassuring, calming my initial panic. 'He's had fluids and they'll keep him in overnight to keep him warm and monitor his heart rate.'

I sank back onto the sofa, although I couldn't fully relax. No matter what Alice and Rosie said, I still felt guilty that it was my words that had driven him to do something so stupid.

'Thank you for finding him,' I said.

'Hey, it's what we do. He's in the best place now and he's asking for you.'

I sat forward, raising my eyebrows. 'Is he?'

I'd have thought I'd be the last person he wanted to see, although I was the only person here he knew, so maybe he wanted to see a familiar face after his scary ordeal.

'Am I allowed to visit?' I asked.

Dane shrugged. 'I'm sure they'll make an exception, but it'll probably have to be brief.'

'That's fine by me. We've said everything we need to say.'

'I'll wait for you in the entrance.'

'Okay. My car's at home so I'll ask Rosie to drop me there and I'll be with you as soon as I can. Are you okay?' He was pale-faced and looked exhausted.

'I will be when I see you.'

'Me too. You know I'm only seeing him because he's alone and he's asking for me?'

Dane nodded. 'I know, and I'm not worried after our talk earlier. I'll see you soon.'

* * *

Dane was waiting for me outside the hospital as promised and we shared a much-needed hug.

'I'll show you where he is,' he said. 'I've already cleared it with the nurses, but they say you can only have five minutes with him, like I thought. It's just so he can see a friendly face with him being alone in a foreign country.'

When I approached Étienne's bed shortly after, he looked terrible. His face was pale, his hair was dishevelled, he had a bruise on one cheek and a couple of cuts on the other. I felt sympathy towards him, but I couldn't help feeling annoyed too. He shouldn't have stormed off into the fells in bad weather, putting his own life and that of others at risk.

'You look like you've done five rounds in a boxing ring,' I said to him in French as I sat beside his bed.

He smiled weakly. 'You should see the other guy.'

'What were you thinking?' I asked gently, shaking my head.

'I wasn't. Stupid, I know.'

I could have easily used up my five minutes and a whole pile more reprimanding him, but he'd undoubtedly already chastised himself severely.

'How are you feeling?' I asked instead.

'Cold and tired. Broken ankle.'

'So I hear. Have you let your parents know?'

'Will you tell them? I need sleep.' His eyes were flickering and it was clearly taking considerable effort to stay awake and talk to me.

'Okay.' I didn't have numbers for Jacques or Sylvie but I could ring Maman or Papa and ask them to pass on the news.

'I'm sorry,' he said, fixing sad eyes on mine.

'Lesson learned the hard way. Don't run off in bad weather in strange places.'

'Not that. The baby. I'm so very sorry.'

Tears pricked my eyes and I blinked them back. 'It was a long time ago.'

'I let you down. I let us down.'

A tear had escaped and I brushed it away and cleared my throat. 'It's in the past, but so are we. You do understand that now?'

'Yes. Another lesson learned the hard way. In your first letter, you said *be courageous, be adventurous, but most of all be happy*. I listened. It took courage to come here and I've had an adventure on the mountain. I hoped I would find the happy part with you, but I can see now that you've found it with someone else.'

He paused, as though hoping I'd correct him, but he was right. I had found my happy with Dane.

'One question,' he said. 'If you were not with Dane, would I have a chance?'

I didn't want to hurt him further, but I needed to be honest to avoid any false hope. 'It would still be a no.'

Tears pooled in his eyes. 'I need sleep now and the nurse is looking at us.'

I twisted round and caught the eye of the nurse, who gave an apologetic shrug and tapped her wrist, indicating that my time was up.

'I hope you find what makes you happy,' I said to Étienne as I slowly rose from the chair. 'I'm sure you will. But think about what that looks like before you rush into anything. Work out who you are. That's what I did when I came here.'

'It's good to see you happy,' he said. 'He's a good man. Saved my life. Make sure he treats you right.'

'He does. Goodbye, Étienne.'

'Goodbye, Autumn.'

Dane was waiting in the corridor for me and he put his arms out and held me while the tears rained down my face and my body shook. I wasn't crying for Étienne. I was sad for him and so relieved that he'd been found, but the tears were for me and the baby I'd lost. For fourteen long years, I'd told myself that the miscarriage had been for the best because Étienne had left me. I'd asked Granddad to keep it secret, knowing he'd never mention it to me again so I wouldn't have to confront it. But all that had happened was that I'd held back that grief and now it was real and raw and pouring out of me.

40

Tom was in the garden when we arrived home from the hospital and she weaved around our feet as we unlocked the back door, going inside as soon as it opened and heading straight for her empty food bowl.

'I'll put some food out,' Dane said gently. 'Why don't you go up and get ready for bed?'

I nodded gratefully. I'd phoned Maman via Bluetooth on the way back from the hospital and she'd assured me she'd pass on the message to Jacques and Sylvie but ask them to contact the hospital, not me, if they had any queries.

I'd just clambered under the duvet when Dane appeared with a fresh glass of water for me. Tom jumped onto the bed and curled up against me.

'Do you want to talk or do you want to go to sleep?' he asked.

'I'm shattered, but my mind's wide awake.'

'Want some company for a bit?'

I nodded.

'Give me two minutes.'

He returned a little later with another glass of water, wearing a short pyjamas set.

'My trousers were muddy,' he said. 'Do you mind?'

By way of an answer, I flipped the duvet back so he could slip into bed beside me. This wasn't what I'd imagined for the first time we shared a bed, but I wanted to explain why I'd been so upset, and I didn't want to be alone tonight.

We lay on our sides facing each other with Tom stretched out between us while I poured out everything that had been stirred up by telling Étienne about the baby – how keeping it secret had meant I never dealt with the grief but now it felt like it had caught up with me, how bad I felt that Granddad had found me and hadn't been able to talk to anyone about the trauma he'd experienced, and how I'd shut my parents out of such a big part of my life when there was no way they'd have been anything other than concerned and supportive. As I spoke, I realised something else.

'I steered clear of relationships after Étienne and I told myself that it was because I still loved him and held out hope that he'd come back to me one day, but I think there was more to it than that. I think it was the fear of meeting someone else and trying for a family and the same thing happening again, or me not even being able to have children and my partner abandoning me.'

'How likely is it that you can't have children?'

'Stats say there's a six in ten chance of a normal pregnancy in the future. I like to look on the bright side and it's good that the odds are in my favour, but it's not by much. And if I was pregnant, there's a one to two in ten chance of an ectopic pregnancy again.'

'Do you want children?' Dane asked.

'I did, but every year that passed with me staying single made it less and less likely. After I turned thirty, I looked into insemination, but I dismissed the idea quite quickly. I didn't want to do it on my own, so I accepted children weren't in my future. Well, I say accepted, but you saw the tears earlier. I think concluded would be a better word.'

He looked at me with such sadness that I thought I might start crying again. 'That's a tough conclusion to reach. I'm sorry.'

It was a deep conversation to be having with someone I'd only just started seeing and hadn't even slept with yet, but Dane showed no signs of discomfort – only empathy.

'Did you ever want a brother or sister for Ellis?' I asked.

'I did. I'd have loved another baby, maybe even two, but it was an emphatic no from Lynsey. She loves Ellis and was a good mam to him, despite current hostilities, but she struggled with having him so young. While her friends were out getting drunk and partying, she was at home with a husband and a baby and she felt like she missed out. Even though she went to university, she was a day student, so she got the degree without the university experience and felt like she missed out there too. She was careful around Ellis. He'd never have had an inkling that she regretted being a mam so young, but she made it clear to me that she was on the countdown to getting her life back and a sibling was out of the question forever.'

'That must have been hard on you when you wanted a bigger family.'

'It was, but our whole marriage was a compromise.' He gave me a wry smile. 'Always on my part.'

'Do you want another baby now?' I laughed lightly when I realised what I'd just said. 'I don't mean right this second, but at some point?'

He gently stroked my cheek and drew me into a tender kiss. 'I don't know. It's not something I've thought about. When Lynsey ended things, I wasn't interested in meeting anyone new, so a baby wasn't on my radar – just like it wasn't for you while you were single. Do you want a baby?'

'I don't know either. As I said, I didn't think it would happen because I was single, and then each birthday that arrived made it less and less likely. I don't want to completely rule out the possibility, but I am scared.'

'Of having another ectopic pregnancy?'

'Yes, but also of losing you. Let's just say that somewhere down the line, we make the decision that we *do* want a family and it doesn't happen, could it drive us apart?'

'Hey, if we can survive a ridiculously good-looking Frenchman turning up on the doorstep telling you how much he loves you, we can survive anything.'

Despite the seriousness of the conversation, that made me laugh.

'I want to be with you, Autumn, and somewhere down the line that might include children and it might not and that's fine as long as I have you. I stayed with Lynsey when I wanted another baby and she didn't. It's not a dealbreaker for me. Being with you is the most important thing.'

He kissed me again and Tom must have been uncomfortable with all the smooching because she leapt off the bed with a mewl and fled the room, making us both laugh.

I snuggled up against Dane's chest and he wrapped his arms round me. It was so relaxing lying there listening to his heart beating and feeling the gradual rise and fall of his breathing. What a relief to have that discussion. It was perhaps unusual to talk about a future together and having babies when we hadn't even said 'I love you' but we'd moved in together before that happened too. Who said there had to be an order of events?

* * *

Dane's phone ringing at half nine on Sunday morning woke us up – his Aunt Kelly apologising for the short notice and asking if there was any way he could cover the lunchtime and afternoon shift at The White Willow. He looked at me hesitantly but I gave him a thumbs up, so he showered and headed over there. I lazed in bed for a little longer until my stomach grumbled loudly, sending me in search of breakfast.

I checked my phone and was relieved to find no missed calls or messages from Étienne. He might not even have realised that he now had my number. I thought about sending him a text to check he was all right this morning, but I blocked and deleted his number instead. We'd said everything we needed to say yesterday and he wasn't my responsibility now. Maman had messaged to say that she'd spoken to Sylvie and Jacques who were booked on a flight this morning. They could take it from here.

After eating my toast, I took my coffee into the lounge. Rosie's Sunday lessons started at ten so I just had time to catch her and give her an update via FaceTime.

'Dane is a sweetheart,' she said, pressing her hand to her chest after I updated her on Étienne and the conversation I'd had with Dane in the early hours. 'I need to get me one of those. I don't suppose he has an equally fabulous brother?'

'No, but he's got lots of cousins.'

She screwed her nose up and laughed. 'Nah! I can't be bothered with all that malarkey. Happy with Mam and the horses. Speaking of which, I'd better crack on. Do you want to do something this afternoon or tomorrow?'

'I haven't finished my creative writing homework yet and I don't want to fall at the first hurdle, so can I say tomorrow?'

'Okay. Text me later and we'll sort something out. Good luck with your homework.' She blew me kisses then ended the call.

I took my coffee upstairs and wandered into Dane's bedroom

to look out over the view. The sight of Derwent Water made me feel so relaxed and soothed, which was just what I needed after a busy week and a nightmare Saturday.

My eyes drifted in the direction of the village green. I couldn't see it fully from here but I could see the top of the giant willow and that idea for a drawing that had popped into my mind after Trudy presented us with our homework nudged at me.

'Daffodils,' I muttered. '"I wandered lonely as a cloud..."'

Sod it! The writing part could wait. I absolutely had to start drawing this.

41

Dane was asked to work at The White Willow on Monday too, so I agreed with Rosie that I'd finish my creative writing homework during the morning then wander over to the estate for lunch with her and Alice, followed by my second riding lesson.

The post arrived when I was getting ready to leave the cottage and I laughed when I spotted an envelope addressed to me in Rosie's handwriting.

'Great minds,' I said, opening the envelope.

Dear Autumn

I'm in Willowdale and you're in Sutton for what may well be the very last time so there was no way I could let the opportunity to write one final letter pass me by – although I thought I'd better send it to your new home to ensure you receive it.

I'll keep it short and sweet. All I want to say is how lucky I am to have been the one who was handed your letter that day in school and how grateful I am for 24 years of letter-based friendship.

It's a new chapter now as you settle in Willowdale and I

look forward to the next 24 years of friendship. And the 24 after that, and…

I'll miss writing and receiving letters but seeing you in person every week is even better. Leaf's looking forward to more riding lessons and I'm looking forward to seeing your confidence grow.

Welcome home, my friend. This is where you were always meant to be. This is the place where you went from stressed to sparkling and I'm excited to be by your side as that sparkle gets even brighter. Nobody deserves this more.

Hugs, Rosie xx

That last paragraph broke me and it took me a good fifteen minutes or so before the tears stopped. Rosie always did know the right things to say.

* * *

'Look what just arrived!' Rosie exclaimed, waving a letter at me when I arrived at Horseshoe Cottage. 'It's so lovely, thank you. Made me cry.'

'I got yours too and it did the same to me.'

We hugged each other tightly, laughing, until Toffee jumped up, wanting attention.

'Did you manage to finish your homework?' Rosie asked as we sat down at the kitchen table with Alice for lunch a little later.

'Yes. It's not brilliant, but it's something.' I told her about the short story I'd written about a family of moles living beneath a carpet of daffodils who felt guilty about uprooting the flowers with their molehills and had a re-planting ritual every night. I admitted that I should have given it far more time and attention, but had been distracted with an idea for a drawing instead.

'Have you had any more thoughts about what you'll draw in the future?' Alice asked.

'I know I want to use the Lakes as my setting – why wouldn't I when it's so stunning? But I'm conscious of not copying Beatrix Potter. Dane came up with an idea to continue drawing my woodland animals but to include fairies too.'

They both looked at me for a moment and I held my breath, wondering if the silence meant they thought it was a terrible idea.

'Like the ones you drew on the Centenary Stone?' Rosie asked, her eyes shining. 'I love that idea!'

'I do too,' Alice said, nodding enthusiastically.

I released my breath, smiling gratefully at them for the positive reaction.

'I just can't quite get a handle on pulling it all together – the Lakes, animals, fairies. It's like there's an idea brewing right here...' I waved my hand around near my head, '...but I can't quite get it into here.' I tapped my temple with a finger. 'I feel like I'm at the start of something wonderful, but I can't quite reach it.'

'Frustrating,' Rosie said.

'It is! Dane keeps calling me Willowdale's answer to Beatrix Potter and I want to be her but not be her, which is possible if I incorporate fairies. Her illustrations have such a strong sense of place and I want that for mine, but I don't want to copy her. There's something in there about the Centenary Stone, but it's not a full setting. I need something else and I'm struggling to grasp what it is.'

Alice gasped and grabbed Rosie's arm. 'Oh, my goodness, do you remember when you were little and I used to tell you about the fairies of Derwentside Dell?'

Rosie knitted her eyebrows. 'Not ringing any bells.'

'You were probably too young. I'd forgotten about them myself until just now. Isn't it funny how something can suddenly come back to you? You know the avenue of willow trees on the side of the lake, near the abandoned boat house? I used to think it looked so magical – a tiny valley with beautiful willow trees either side – so I called it Derwentside Dell and told you that the fairies lived there.'

My heart and my mind started racing. An avenue of willow trees running alongside the lake? An abandoned boat house? How magical did that sound? And Derwentside Dell? What a beautiful name. I could already see it in my mind.

'Have I seen this place?' I asked Rosie.

She shook her head. 'It's out the back of the hall and his Lordship keeps that part of the estate private, which is fair enough. We've got loads of other space to explore.'

'It sounds amazing,' I said. 'Do you think he'd let me look if we asked him nicely?'

Rosie glanced questioningly at Alice, who shrugged. 'There's no harm in asking, but I can think of something that might help butter him up. I bet he'd love a drawing of Zeus.'

'His favourite stallion,' Rosie clarified when I shrugged.

'Of course! Okay. I can do that. I can draw horses.' I pictured the enormous black stallion and bit my lip. 'Even really big scary ones.'

Alice said she wished she could describe Derwentside Dell in more detail, but it had been so long ago and the memories were hazy. From what she could recall, it really did sound like the perfect setting for a magical fairy kingdom and the ideas were fizzing.

'We'd better finish eating and get down to the stables,' Rosie said, smiling at me. 'And I bet you'll want to draw Zeus before you even think about another lesson on Leaf.'

'You know me so well.'

42

Across the rest of the week, I found homes for everything I'd brought from Sutton. Grandma's writing bureau fit perfectly in the lounge and the room felt much cosier with books, photos, candles and ornaments on the shelves. I'd been conscious of not turning Cotton-tail's Cottage into a shrine to my grandparents, but Dane had picked out a few of their paintings that he loved so they were displayed in the hall and up the stairs, and Grandma's watercolour of me on the garden swing was on my bedroom wall. It made me smile every time I walked into the room.

We hadn't done anything about selling the Potterphernalia yet, so the crates were all piled up in the spare bedroom. I'd undertaken some tentative research with auction houses and book collectors, but I didn't want to rush into anything so it could wait for a couple of months. My priority for now was spending time with Dane, Rosie and Alice, giving attention to Tom Kitten, and to settling into my new life in Willowdale.

Maman and Papa were excited to see my new home and to meet Dane in person, so they'd booked some time off work in late May and were going to spend a fortnight in the area. I wanted to tell them about the miscarriage, but I'd wait until then so I could tell them in person. I had wondered if Étienne might have said something to Sylvie and Jacques which would have got back to my parents, but that didn't seem to be the case. Unless they were also waiting to see me in person before raising it.

Dane's son, Ellis, and his girlfriend, Georgia, also had plans to visit. I'd 'met' them both on a video chat and they seemed lovely, so I couldn't wait to meet them both in person. I'd been a little anxious about whether Ellis might be protective of his dad and think we'd rushed into things, but he'd told me he was relieved to see his dad with someone who clearly cared about him. It was obviously a dig at Lynsey and I hoped they'd find peace with each other as I knew the rift made Dane uncomfortable.

On the Sunday afternoon, after I'd been back in Willowdale for a week, I had exciting plans with Rosie.

'Promise me you won't be too disappointed if the willow tree avenue isn't as Mam remembers it,' she said as we stood outside Willowdale Hall.

'I promise. I haven't got my hopes up. Well, not too high.'

Rosie took me to the left-hand side of the hall and pushed open an elaborate wrought-iron gate. 'Here goes!'

I'd drawn an illustration of Zeus on Monday. When I'd overcome my initial fear of being so close to him, I'd been able to appreciate his beauty and, also, what a softie he was. I'd been very proud of the way I'd captured the shine of his coat and his strong personality.

Alice had thought it might be better if Rosie saw Hubert Cranleigh on her own to ask about access to the garden rather than have me accompany her in case he felt pressured by the presence of a stranger and less willing to grant our request. Rosie had told me that he was captivated by Zeus's illustration and could barely take his eyes off it while she enquired about visiting the gardens. He'd challenged her on exactly where we wanted to go and why and, after some thought, he'd agreed on the proviso that we didn't go anywhere else. That was fine. It was only the willow avenue – or Derwentside Dell, as Alice had named it – that we wanted to explore.

This afternoon, the weather was perfect – a bright sunny day with light filtering through the trees and the air full of birdsong and the chirp of insects which should show the avenue of willows at their best.

My heart pounded as we diagonally crossed a formal lawn and followed the curve of the lake. The lawn gave way to woods once more and the familiar smell of wild garlic which grew all over the estate. Hundreds of daffodils were now past their best, drooping listlessly, and I wished I'd seen them earlier in the month. They'd have been spectacular.

'There it is!' Rosie called, breaking into a run.

I followed her then stopped suddenly, my hand clasped to my heart. 'Oh, wow! Oh, Rosie!'

'That's special,' she said, her voice hushed. 'No wonder Mam imagined there being fairies here.'

Two rows of willow trees curved round the lake and up a slope. A gulley separated them, creating a walkway between the drooping branches. Butterflies flitted in the dappled sunlight and bees buzzed across a carpet of wildflowers.

'It's magical,' I whispered. 'This is it! I've found my place.'

My head was bursting with ideas, so vivid that I could almost see fairies flitting between the trees and flowers and the animals scampering about.

I felt a tug on my backpack.

'What are you doing?' I asked Rosie.

'Getting you these.' She placed my sketchpad and pencil case in my hand. 'Your hands are twitching. How about you give me your phone and I'll take photos while you do your thing?'

* * *

I ran up the lane by Cotton-tail's Cottage, bursting with excitement after several hours sketching at Derwentside Dell. Dane would have finished his shift about an hour ago and I found him at the kitchen table, tapping away on his laptop.

He looked up expectantly. 'Well?'

'I've found it! It was perfect. Look at it!' I whipped out my sketchpad and showed him what I'd captured. 'Rosie took photos and, oh my God, it's… my mind is blown!'

'You're shaking,' he said, pulling me into his arms and hugging me.

'It's the adrenaline. I'm so excited and very relieved.'

'I know what you'll be doing this week,' he said, smiling at me.

'What are you working on?' I asked.

'Week two's homework and finishing off something for you.'

He glanced at the table and it was only then that I realised that there was an enormous bunch of daffodils in a vase on the table and an envelope propped up against it with my name on.

'Aw, they're beautiful, Dane. Thank you. What's in the envelope?'

He shrugged innocently. 'No idea. You'll have to open it to find out.'

Intrigued, I lifted it up.

'Before you open it, I'd better give you the context. When Miss Eccles set us the Wordsworth homework, the start of this popped into my mind and I've been working on it ever since. I didn't want to read this out in class, which is why I did that short story, but I wanted you to have this.'

I removed a sheet of paper and unfolded it.

'You've written me a poem!'

'I was hoping to match Wordsworth's style, but it stumped me, so I went for the first and last line. The last was a bit shoe-horned in, but I hope you like the rest.'

'I'm sure I'll love it all.' I sat down and scanned down the page.

I wandered lonely as a cloud, drifting through the sky
The life I thought belonged to me had sadly been a lie
I felt that it was for the best to start my life anew
Back to the fells and to the lakes – a place I loved
and knew
Stories flew around my mind but struggled to come out
My dream of being an author was seriously in doubt
But just as I was losing hope, an angel met my gaze
Her smile was mesmerising, just like the sunshine's rays
Moments later she was gone, the light it seemed to fade
Would our paths cross once again? Not likely, but I
prayed
Then there she was ahead of me – a vision in the road
Not quite the meet-cute I'd have liked as into her I rode!
I took her to the hospital, she left her phone behind
Like Cinderella's lost slipper, had destiny been kind?
Her heart it had been broken, she didn't want a date
But there she was in Potter's house – this surely must
be fate
To sparkle was our mission, and to be each other's muse
It wasn't hard to do that – she took away my blues
Ideas started flowing, like from a dam that burst

In writing and in drawing, the two of us immersed
But words were not the only thing she helped me to
recover
To take a chance on love again, she helped me to
discover

Her talent shone so brightly, her kindness lit the way
Behind her eyes lay sadness, which I longed to
take away
I knew that she was hurting, that life had caused
her pain
But she had found a place to heal and find herself again
Her laughter filled my dark voids, her smile it healed
my soul
Her honesty lit up my world, her kiss made me feel
whole
I know that she is vulnerable, but she is also strong
My love for her will never die, she is where I belong
I'll be forever grateful for the self-doubt voice she stills
For her my heart with pleasure fills, and dances with
the daffodils

'That's so beautiful,' I whispered, scarcely able to speak for the emotions overwhelming me. Had he just told me he loved me?

'Just like the person it was written for,' he said, cupping my chin and gently kissing me. 'And I mean every word. I love you, Autumn. You've fixed a part of me that was broken.'

'I love you too,' I said. 'And you've done the same for me.' I gazed down at the poem again. 'Thank you for this. It's so special.'

I placed it down on the table, not wanting to crinkle the paper, and hugged him tightly.

'I've got something for you too,' I said, stepping back from him. 'Funnily enough, it was the thing that came into my head when Trudy gave us that first piece of homework. I've been secretly working on it in the garage. Wait here.'

I returned moments later with a large canvas and turned it round for Dane to see, keeping my eyes on his face for his reaction.

'You did this for me?' he asked, his eyes sparkling.

'For Willowdale's answer to Arthur Ransome from Willowdale's answer to Beatrix Potter, with love.'

He ran his hands into his hair, shaking his head. 'I don't know what to say. It's stunning.'

I'd drawn the Willowdale village green. Sitting on either end of the bench, looking like they were deep in conversation, were Arthur Ransome and Beatrix Potter, surrounded by their creations – a sailing boat, swallow flag and pirate flag for Ransome and Peter Rabbit, Squirrel Nutkin and Mrs Tiggy-Winkle for Beatrix Potter. They were painted with the palest of watercolours because, sitting between them, were Dane and me holding hands, looking adoringly at each other. My clothes were the same colours as Potter's and Dane's were the same colours as Ransome's but in deeper watercolour shades. Fairies flitted above, woodland animals drew close, and the gilderhopp and fizzbee were standing in front of us. Golden daffodils flanked either side of the bench and heart-shaped fluffy clouds floated in the sky.

I propped it up on the worktop, leaning against the kitchen cupboards and stood back with Dane. It had taken a lot of hours, but it might well be my best work so far.

'I've called it *No Longer Wandering Lonely as a Cloud*,' I said.

'That's so perfect.' Dane slipped his arm round my waist. 'I can't take it all in. Everywhere I look, there's some clever detail. Thank you so much. We'll have to hang it in the lounge.'

'I was thinking maybe in our bedroom.'

'But if it's in one of the bedrooms, you won't be able to...' He paused and looked at me, his smile widening. 'You said *our* bedroom.'

'You didn't think I was going to let you keep that gorgeous lake view all to yourself forever, did you?' I asked. 'Should we go and see how it looks?'

I took his hand and led him towards the lounge door.

'The picture?' he asked.

I gave him what I hoped was a seductive look. 'Maybe after.'

He knitted his eyebrows. 'Then what...? Oh! Yes! If you're sure.'

'I've never been more sure.'

As he took me in his arms in his – our – bedroom and kissed me passionately, I knew I'd truly found the sort of love my grandparents had shared. I thought I'd had it with Étienne but ours hadn't been a love that would last. Étienne had been the one who got away and I'd always be grateful that he'd been in my life because he'd shaped the person I was today – the person who'd fallen in love and was loved in return by the one who was here to stay.

When I'd talked to Rosie and Alice on Monday about trying to get a handle on my future as an illustrator, I'd told them it felt like I was at the start of something wonderful. I had been with regards to my art, but the moment I arrived in Willowdale, that had been the real start of something wonderful because I'd finally found the place I belonged and, with it, I'd found myself.

On the day he died, I told Granddad that he wasn't to worry about me anymore and that I would be fine. I was more than fine because I'd done what Grandma said I should always do. I'd been courageous in starting over in Willowdale, adventurous in my journey to become an author and illustrator like my heroine

Beatrix Potter and, in this beautiful place with Rosie, Alice, Dane, Tom Kitten, Toffee and all my other new friends and family, I'd achieved the thing she'd wanted for me most of all. I was happy. Beatrix Potter had escaped to the Lakes from her life in London and found her happy. I had too.

ACKNOWLEDGMENTS

I love the Lake District so very much and have been a regular visitor since childhood. As a kid, it was about skimming stones and splashing in the lakes in my wellies. As an adult, it's about the beauty of the place. The whole area is special to me, but Keswick and Derwent Water have become my family's happy place.

A couple of years ago, I had an idea for a story set in the Lakes and asked my fabulous publisher, Boldwood Books, if I could write a series set there. They gave me the go-ahead. I knew I wanted a neglected building but wasn't sure if this would be a farm, a manor house, or something else.

A year later, we holidayed in Keswick. We'd walked alongside Derwent Water on several occasions but always on the eastern shore and this time we decided to head west instead. This took us through a pretty village called Portinscale and on to a place called the Lingholm Estate. A board advertised a café, so we made our way along the enticing woodland pathway into the estate in search of sustenance and what a treat there was in store – and I don't just mean of the baked goods variety. The Lingholm Estate is absolutely beautiful and my heart leapt because, the moment I saw it, I knew I'd found the inspiration for my Lakes setting – a dilapidated variation of this wonderful place.

I must emphasise that Willowdale and Willowdale Hall are fictional, but they are inspired by Portinscale and the Lingholm Estate respectively. Those who know the area will recognise some familiar aspects but these are nestled alongside elements straight from my imagination. The lake and the fells are all real and I haven't repositioned any of them, but using a fictional place within a real setting means I can make it work for the stories I want to tell and the characters who'll tell them.

The Start of Something Wonderful is the first book in what we hope will be my longest series, as I'm bursting with ideas for building this new community. It's also a milestone one for me as it's my twentieth book. I can't quite believe I'm writing that! So my first thank you goes to you, the readers and listeners, who have loved and championed my books, enabling me to keep writing four a year. I am so very grateful for all the gorgeous reviews, comments on social media, and the recommendations to friends, family and social media communities.

I have Meena Kumari to thank for my hero's name. Meena won a ChildrenInRead auction in aid of BBC's Children in Need to name a secondary character. She suggested Dane, which I loved so much that I used it for the main character instead.

Beatrix Potter is a huge inspiration for this storyline, so I need to thank her for her gorgeous illustrations and stories. I've been reading a lot of them as well as biographies on the woman herself and, of course, watching the gorgeous film adaptation *Miss Potter* starring Renée Zellweger and Ewan McGregor. If you haven't seen it, do watch it, although it has been fascinating discovering which parts are true and which are Hollywood!

Thank you to the National Trust for maintaining Hill Top and making a visit there such a memorable experience. I've been several times and never grow tired of it. The websites of Visit Keswick and Visit Cumbria have been invaluable resources for my research into the area (although nothing beats being there in person) and thank you so much to The Gray Explorer on YouTube for his help on whether a motorboat could approach St Herbert's Island and where.

As a family, we've holidayed in or near Keswick four times over the past couple of years, so thank you to my husband, Mark, and our daughter, Ashleigh, for indulging me as we've combined family time with research. I know they don't mind really because, as I said in my dedication, the Lake District is our happy place.

There's a huge team involved in getting a book to readers so thank you to my copy-editor Cecily Blench, proofreader Clare Black, cover designer Lizzie Gardiner for the most sublime cover ever, and the amazing team at Boldwood Books, especially my editor. Nia Beynon, you are an absolute legend. Every time I think something isn't quite working but can't pinpoint what, you get to the crux of it and help make the story shine with all the bits in the right places.

I really hope you loved your first trip to Willowdale. The second book will be Rosie's story, but we have a stop-off at Castle Street in Whitsborough Bay first. If this is the first book of mine you've read, there's plenty in the backlist to dive into and I'd love to see you in my Facebook group, Redland's Readers, if you'd like to find out more about Willowdale, Whitsborough Bay, Hedgehog Hollow and Bumblebee Barn.

Big hugs

Jessica xx

MORE FROM JESSICA REDLAND

We hope you enjoyed reading ***The Start of Something Wonderful.*** If you did, please leave a review.

If you'd like to gift a copy, this book is also available as an ebook, hardback, large print, digital audio download and audiobook CD.

Sign up to Jessica Redland's mailing list for news, competitions and updates on future books.

http://bit.ly/JessicaRedlandNewsletter

Healing Hearts at Bumblebee Barn, another uplifting romantic read from Jessica Redland, is available to buy now...

Jessica Redland
HEALING
HEARTS
at
Bumblebee
Barn

ABOUT THE AUTHOR

Jessica Redland writes uplifting stories of love, friendship, family and community set mostly in Yorkshire where she lives. Her Whitsborough Bay books transport readers to the stunning North Yorkshire Coast and her Hedgehog Hollow series takes them into beautiful countryside of the Yorkshire Wolds.

Visit Jessica's website: https://www.jessicaredland.com/

Follow Jessica on social media:

facebook.com/JessicaRedlandAuthor
twitter.com/JessicaRedland
instagram.com/JessicaRedlandAuthor
bookbub.com/authors/jessica-redland

ALSO BY JESSICA REDLAND

Welcome to Whitsborough Bay Series

Making Wishes at Bay View

New Beginnings at Seaside Blooms

Finding Hope at Lighthouse Cove

Coming Home to Seashell Cottage

Other Whitsborough Bay Books

All You Need is Love

The Secret to Happiness

Christmas on Castle Street

Christmas Wishes at the Chocolate Shop

Christmas at Carly's Cupcakes

Starry Skies Over The Chocolate Pot Café

The Starfish Café Series

Snowflakes Over The Starfish Café

Spring Tides at The Starfish Café

Summer Nights at The Starfish Café

Hedgehog Hollow Series

Finding Love at Hedgehog Hollow

New Arrivals at Hedgehog Hollow

Family Secrets at Hedgehog Hollow

A Wedding at Hedgehog Hollow

Chasing Dreams at Hedgehog Hollow

Christmas Miracles at Hedgehog Hollow

Printed in Great Britain
by Amazon

30854668R00192